"[Robin D. Owens] provides a wonderful, gripping mix of passion, exotic futuristic settings, and edgy suspense."
—Jayne Castle, author of *Deception Cove*

"Will have readers on the edge of their seats . . . Another terrific tale from the brilliant mind of Robin D. Owens. Don't miss it."
—*Romance Reviews Today*

"[A] wonderful piece of fantasy, science fiction, romance, and a dash of mystery . . . A delight to read."
—*Night Owl Reviews*

"[This] emotionally rich tale blends paranormal abilities, family dynamics, and politics; adds a serious dash of violence; and dusts it all with humor and whimsy."
—*Library Journal*

"Maintaining the world building for science fiction and character-driven plot for romance is near impossible. Owens does it brilliantly." —*The Romance Readers Connection*

"Dazzling . . . Robin D. Owens paints a world filled with characters who sweep readers into an unforgettable adventure with every delicious word, every breath, every beat of their hearts. Brava!"
—Deb Stover, award-winning author of *The Gift*

"A taut mixture of suspense and action . . . that leaves you stunned." —*Smexy Books*

"A delight to my . . . heart . . . hits all my joy buttons."
—*Fresh Fiction*

"The author's creativity shines." —*Darque Reviews*

"I keep telling myself that [Robin D. Owens] just can't get much better, but with every book she amazes and surprises me!" —*The Best Reviews*

Titles by Robin D. Owens

HEARTMATE
HEART THIEF
HEART DUEL
HEART CHOICE
HEART QUEST
HEART DANCE
HEART FATE
HEART CHANGE
HEART JOURNEY
HEART SEARCH
HEART SECRET
HEART FORTUNE

GHOST SEER

Anthologies

WHAT DREAMS MAY COME
(with Sherrilyn Kenyon and Rebecca York)

HEARTS AND SWORD

GHOST SEER

ROBIN D. OWENS

BERKLEY SENSATION, NEW YORK

THE BERKLEY PUBLISHING GROUP
Published by the Penguin Group
Penguin Group (USA) LLC
375 Hudson Street, New York, New York 10014

USA • Canada • UK • Ireland • Australia • New Zealand • India • South Africa • China

penguin.com

A Penguin Random House Company

GHOST SEER

A Berkley Sensation Book / published by arrangement with the author

For information, address: The Berkley Publishing Group,
a division of Penguin Group (USA) LLC,
375 Hudson Street, New York, New York 10014.

ISBN: 978-0-425-26890-2

PUBLISHING HISTORY
Berkley Sensation mass-market edition / April 2014

PRINTED IN THE UNITED STATES OF AMERICA

10 9 8 7 6 5 4 3 2 1

Cover art by Tony Mauro.
Cover design by George Long.
Interior text design by Kelly Lipovich.

To all my readers who follow me into my different worlds;
To those who love the Old West;
And to those who love stories about ghosts;
this one is for YOU!

COUNTING CROWS RHYME:

One for sorrow,
Two for luck;
Three for a wedding,
Four for death;
Five for silver,
Six for gold;
Seven for a secret,
Not to be told;
Eight for heaven,
Nine for [hell]
And ten for the devil's own sell!

ONE

THE MINUTE HE walked through that door, Zach Slade's
career, the one he loved, was over.

Who was he kidding? His time as a cop—a deputy sheriff
here in Cottonwood County, Montana—was already over.
Due to a mistake on his part and a crippled foot and ankle.
His leg hurt less than the emotional ripping inside him. He
thought he could feel the weight of his badge in his jeans
pocket, but he couldn't. Only the weight of this last duty.

His gaze slid around the wide marble-floored corridor of
the old County Hall, which housed the Sheriff's Department.
No one around to see his hesitation, how his hand trembled as
he put it on the door handle. All the frosted glass and wooden
doors were closed.

He shifted his shoulders to release the tension. He was *not*
going to take a desk job, no matter what his boss thought.
With a tighter grip on the handle of his cane in his left hand—
the same side as his injured leg because he wanted to keep his

right hand free for his weapon—he pushed down the cool metal lever and moved from impressive marble to institutional carpet.

"Hey, Zach," the young, brunette, four-months-pregnant dispatcher said.

"Hey, Margo."

"Off the crutches!" she enthused.

"Just today. The boss in?"

She grimaced. "He's been waiting for you. You really leaving?"

Zach had already packed up the stuff he couldn't live without—precious little—and donated the rest to a thrift store. He'd sold his 'Vette as soon as the news came that he wouldn't be able to drive her since his ankle and foot wouldn't work the clutch. When he'd been stuck in a wheelchair. Another pang twisted his insides, and he kept it from showing on his face.

Margo looked at him with pity, as if his lapsing into silence were okay instead of answering her question. And Margo would gossip about everything except official police business, and soon he wouldn't be a cop, so he said, "Maybe I'm leaving."

Her forehead wrinkled. "I hope you stay. I like you, Zach."

He raised his brows. "Kind of you to say; plenty don't."

"They're just plain jealous and resentful 'cuz you did so well with the Billings city cops in Yellowstone County. You're one of us, no matter what else anyone says." She sniffed.

Zach would have liked to believe her, but he didn't. He pulled folded papers from his pocket and put them on her desk. "My recertification to carry a weapon."

"I'll process that for you right away."

"Thanks."

Her intercom buzzed, and Sheriff Walder said, "Send Zach in, Margo."

"Of course!" She beamed at Zach and he moved—slower than he'd wanted, but balancing with a cane was different than using crutches—to the thick oak door of the sheriff's office and entered.

His boss stood, came around the big, scarred desk, and offered his hand, scrutinizing Zach from under heavy, thrusting gray brows. "I was hoping I wouldn't be seeing you yet, that you'd give matters more thought."

Zach had already spent too many stretching-infinite months thinking. He shook his boss's hand.

"How's the ankle and foot?"

"As good as they'll ever be," Zach said, suppressing bitterness, lowering himself to the client chair as smoothly as possible. The bullet had struck his tibia just below the knee, shattering the bone and severing the peroneal nerve. Now he had foot drop and couldn't control the flexing of his left ankle. Couldn't control his own foot! His jaw clenched.

Sheriff Walder went back and sat in a chair that creaked under his big body as soft classical music played in the background. Walder liked that stuff. Atop his polished desk he had a line of manila files—four. "You do good work, Zach, and I want you to stay."

"Sorry, can't do that."

Walder tapped his forefinger on his desk, his thinking mode. The next gaze he leveled at Zach was intense. "I would have made the same mistake as Lauren and you, Zach."

Anger speared, sharp and brutal, setting off a trail of other little explosive feelings inside, messing with his head, screwing up his breathing. But he met the sheriff's eyes.

The sheriff continued in a measured manner, his gaze fixed to Zach. "If I'd been sitting shotgun with Lauren that night, not only would she have recognized the truck or the driver, I would have, too. And I'd have let her go up and talk to the drunk driver first, just like you did."

Images flashed through Zach's mind like the bar lights on top of their vehicle that night . . . the drunk driver weaving, Lauren telling him the name of the guy and that he was an ex-policeman on the town force, from a family of cops.

"Lauren didn't check him for guns, wanted to talk to him, maybe take him home," the sheriff said.

"I know," Zach said.

"And I'd have agreed with her." The sheriff sighed. "She didn't check him for weapons, and I wouldn't have corrected that mistake of hers. Just like you didn't."

Zach recalled walking up to the truck, the drunk turning

belligerent, reaching for a gun. Zach lunging, the gun going off, the god-awful pain of a shot to his leg. He blinked the vision away, but sweat dampened his back.

Hoarsely he said, "The jerk might not have pulled on you."

The sheriff shrugged. "No one knows. Thing is, Lauren made a mistake, you made a mistake, and it was one most of the people in this department would have made. Not one any of us will make again, but you paid the price for that reminder, and I'm sorry for it."

Zach nodded. The whole damn state knew of his situation because there'd been a television crew in from Billings, investigative reporters. They'd heard the shot and were nearly the first on the scene, and they hadn't let it rest.

And, of course, the investigative news folks had followed up. The ex-cop had often been pulled over by others, but not cited. Why not? Why had he been let go previously? Why hadn't his license been jerked? Why hadn't the former policeman been given help? Why hadn't Zach's rookie partner handled herself better? She must have needed more training, or the training the county was doing wasn't sufficient. All the myriad ways the situation could be spun bad, it was.

Bad enough for Zach.

The county commissioners had come through with a fat pension and disability for Zach due to public outcry, but the whole damn thing left a nasty taste in his mouth. Some of his colleagues saw *him* as the one who'd betrayed them, the outsider. Not the drunk ex-cop.

And in those circumstances, Zach's own feeling of betrayal cut all the more.

"Zach?" Sheriff Walder asked, but his eyes showed he knew the trail Zach had gone down.

"I'm sorry, too." Zach managed a sour lift of his mouth. "So is Lauren; she can't seem to apologize enough." But whatever respect he'd had for his partner had vanished.

"We're a sorry bunch. Me, the department, the county. The drunk driver's family, and him, rotting in a cell where he belongs," Walder said with more bitterness than Zach thought the man had felt.

"A bad man cost me a good one, and I've never liked that." His nostrils flared, then he tapped the first folder. "I can transfer you back up to the departmental station in the northern part of the county, this time put you in charge. You're closer to Billings there, and you have a good rep with that force since you helped break that multicounty meth ring."

"I can't stay."

Another sigh, out of Walder's nose this time. He set aside the first folder, moved to the second. "In fact, I reached out to the Billings police and they would be happy to welcome you to their force."

"Another desk job."

The sheriff's silence indicated that Zach had hit that nail on the head.

So, finally, the time had come. Zach ached inside and his fingers shook as he touched the star in his pocket. His hand closed between the points for an instant, and then he placed it carefully on the desk, not looking at it. He'd carried a badge as a police officer or deputy sheriff in one department or another for thirteen years, the star here for three. He'd wanted to live in the West. "I'm not staying in Montana." His voice was thick.

"Where are you going?"

"Out of Montana."

"The quickest way out of Montana is south, Wyoming and then Colorado. Your mother is in Colorado, right?"

In a gracious mental facility there. "Boulder," Zach said. He'd been born in Boulder, but the college town wasn't a good fit for a conservative military family.

Walder slid over another file and opened it, took out a card and a sheet of lined notebook paper with writing in his small blocky penmanship.

"Since you're out of the public sector," the man stated abruptly.

No, Zach would never qualify to be any kind of a cop again.

"I know a guy in Denver, a private investigator," the sheriff said.

Zach's lip lifted and his nostrils widened, a reflex as if he'd smelled a dead skunk. He was a public servant, damn it. One who didn't take money to look at a particular case with a particular slant. "I don't think—

"I gave him your name and number, vouched for you. He's a good guy, one who thinks like us. Tony Rickman of Rickman Security and Investigations." The sheriff bulldozed right over Zach, glaring until Zach took the card and the paper and put them in his wallet.

Chin stubborn, Sheriff Walder said, "I'll text you the info and e-mail your private account, so you have the data in both places, can't ignore it as easily. Could be good for you, Zach; don't blow it off." A long pause, and then the sheriff shook his head, stood, and came around the desk again, once more offering his hand. "Damn shame you're not with us anymore. Good luck to you."

"Thanks." Zach levered himself up and left, walking as slowly and precisely as he'd come, pausing a little after he opened the door. "Good working with you, sir."

"Same goes," Walder said.

And then Margo was right there, holding his recertification form, looking sad despite her brightly colored maternity clothes. He stuck the form in his wallet, pulled out a gift card envelope, and handed it to her. "For you and the baby."

She looked surprised and her eyes went all too wet. "Oh, Zach . . ." She hugged him awkwardly, hurried to her desk and tissues, and Zach picked up his pace and escaped.

Once outside the County Hall he had to watch every step on the stairs down to the street, cursing under his breath all the way, to the car he'd bought that morning. He should have bought a truck, but the price on this car was right, the owner was home so he could do the transaction immediately, and he could stand the newish sedan long enough to get him to Colorado. It was wheels.

An hour and a half later, Zach drove into the gray block of shade at the side of his favorite diner, close to the southern county line. Heat rose from the cracked asphalt of the parking lot, surrounded by scruffy yellow prairie grass. Low, bare brown hills looked equally hot.

He'd overestimated his stamina, this first day he'd graduated to a cane. No damn institutional-type metal cane, either, but a good one to fit his six-foot-four-inch height with a nice wooden Derby handle. With a rubber tip, dammit, to keep him walking silently and from slipping.

Still, he needed a couple of minutes before he went in for lunch. One last good-bye to his favorite cook and waitress, one last meal in the county, and he'd get out of Montana and on with his life.

He opened the car door to the heat, positioned his cane in his left hand, and pushed up. His bad leg was stiff, and despite an orthopedic shoe, his foot still drooped a little. He set his jaw and got out. Turned and saw the sheriff's vehicle, a Chevy Impala, that he used to drive. Inside were his ex-partner and another deputy. Both stared at him.

TWO

GREAT. A SOUR taste coated Zach's tongue as he glanced at his ex-partner and the other deputy. Leaning as little as he could on his cane, he pushed his vehicle door shut, then locked it with the fob.

His ex-partner, Lauren, stepped out of the passenger side of the vehicle, followed by another deputy, bigger and beefier and older—Larry—whom Zach had never gotten along with since Zach had taken the job three years ago: personality clash.

Zach straightened and stared unemotionally at the young woman who'd been his partner, who'd made a mistake that he hadn't corrected. An error that had gotten him wounded and nearly gotten him killed. Lauren was pretty, with blond hair and blue eyes and a round face.

She'd visited him in the hospital, when he was in a wheelchair, during physical therapy—where she didn't look at his leg. Always came with someone else and always apologized but never saying much of anything else, wanting him to give her benediction or something. The best he'd been able to do was, "We both made a mistake."

Apparently, she still needed more.

Guess word had gotten around that he was leaving.

Her breathing quickened as she walked up to him. Must have needed to bring along Larry to help her out. Might always need someone else to help her out. A really bad quality in a cop. "I'm sorry," she said.

"I'm sure you are," Zach said.

She looked aside. Larry had angled their vehicle near, like they'd be ready to chase if Zach gave them any reason. Acid burned in his gut. Nope, he'd never truly been considered one of them, only an outsider.

Not that he minded being an outsider, but the Montana job, his third as a deputy sheriff, had seemed like a good fit.

Only seemed. None of his previous departments would have treated him like this. He *had* been a valued colleague, friend, then.

Too bad, so sad, get over it.

"You're leaving?" Lauren asked.

"So?" he said.

She swallowed, and Larry took over the questioning. Cops were always nosy.

"Where are you going?" Larry asked.

"Look, ass—" Zach stopped himself. Larry was baiting him, would expect cursing, maybe even a swing. Better to mess with his head, to give him little reaction at all. Just that easily, Zach regained his calm. He rolled a shoulder in a contemptuous shrug. "You're not worth even talking to." He focused on his previous partner. "And I'm sorry it took you so long to get the guts to talk to me."

Lauren flushed red.

"You *asshole*," Larry said.

"Truthful guy, that's me," Zach said. He curled his lip.

Larry crowded him. "Where are you going?"

Zach smiled, with teeth. Because he knew it would make Lauren feel uncomfortable, he said, "None of your damn business, but since you don't have the fortitude to ignore an itch to know, I'm going to visit my mother in Boulder, Colorado." Even before he'd joined the department, the deputies he worked with knew his background. Everyone knew his mother was fragile.

Every cop Zach had ever worked with had seen how unsolved murders shattered families.

That had been true of Zach's. His older brother, Jim, had died in an unexplained drive-by shooting when Zach was twelve and Jim was sixteen.

Now his mother lived in an expensive mental health complex that Zach helped his father pay for, though Zach figured his father, the General, used the funds his mother had inherited.

His mother couldn't come to see him when he'd been in the hospital, and his father hadn't. Zach had heard that the General had inquired if the wound was life-threatening, and, later, in the one terse conversation Zach had had with his father, the General had laid out that Zach had done a damn stupid thing, as usual.

"Oh, going to see your mother," Lauren repeated, shifting her balance. Maybe the reporters were right, maybe she did need better training. Well, he didn't have to do it, and for that he was grateful.

Larry reached into his pocket and pulled out a toothpick, all the while meeting Zach's eyes. "Jackson Zachary Slade," he said, using Zach's full name before sticking the grungy bit of wood in his mouth where the toothpick attached to his lower lip.

Not again.

Ever since someone had told Larry about the Old West gunman called Jack Slade, Larry-the-asshole had poked Zach about that man, making "witty" comments at Zach's expense.

"Good that you're going. Montana isn't good for Jack Slades, *Jackson Zachary Slade*." Larry smirked.

Zach had never wanted to hit him more, but kept his temper reined in, his voice cool. He disliked those who compared him to the gunman. "I guess I learned that; a lot of jerks in Montana."

He stared at the couple. "At least I won't be lynched by vigilantes here like *that* Jack Slade." He paused a little. "I'm not a drunk, and I believe in justice."

Lauren paled. Larry's hands fisted. The whole nasty business that had led to Zach's wound had been because of a drunk ex-policeman who didn't want to be charged with a DUI.

But the two before him didn't matter anymore. What mattered was justice. He'd done his duty and what he thought was right. And a drunk driver who could have killed others, broken other families, was off the streets and sitting in a prison cell.

The August heat seemed to wrap around the three of them until Zach could almost believe he felt heat waves radiating from their bodies, see those waves as pale colors.

A crow cawed and he tensed, seeing four of them on the back fence.

Dread hit him. He didn't like crows. He'd never forgotten the crow-counting rhyme taught to him by his mother's mother, a wealthy and superstitious woman. *Four for death.*

He thought he caught a whiff of rotting. Damn crows.

Time to get Lauren and Larry gone so Zach could move on with his life. He nodded to his ex-partner. "You take care, now." His voice held an edge of bitterness that slipped out despite him.

"I *am* sorry," she said.

Once more he nodded, then watched as she tugged on the deputy's arm to make him break the stare with Zach. Larry shrugged and turned, adjusting his hat.

They got into their car and drove away.

Zach was glad to see them go, and he forced the black rancor aside once more as he limped into the diner. He ate and managed to be more than polite, sincere, as he said goodbye to the cook and waitress.

A half hour later, under stormy skies and sleeting rain, he'd left the county behind. He'd press on through bad weather and be out of Montana before nightfall.

No, Montana wasn't good for Jack—or Jackson Zachary—Slades, and he never intended to come back.

Denver, Colorado, the same morning

I like the way you smell. I'm staying, the figment of her imagination, a "ghost" dog, said. It—he?—sat on the end of her bed.

"No," Clare Cermak whispered as she slapped a palm down on her buzzing alarm clock. She stared at him in shock. Well, *through* him. He didn't have a touch of color.

"This can't be happening," she muttered. She was on her third day of denial of ghosts, but that still worked for her. A year might work for her. Forever.

She closed her eyes and scooted under the sheet.

Coldness touched her shoulder, and her eyelids sprang open.

The Labrador looked at her with big, dark gray eyes that had been chocolate brown when he was alive. He was too close up and far too personal.

She gulped. "You aren't—weren't—even *my* dog, Enzo." He'd been her weird great-aunt Sandra's. Sandra, who said she saw ghosts and helped them "transition." Who'd recently made her own transition, and had bypassed Clare's parents and brother and made Clare the sole heir of her estate, leaving Clare a fortune.

Yes, there was family money and trusts, but Sandra had added to it. Who knew pretending to talk to ghosts was so lucrative?

I'm your dog now. Enzo's tongue lolled as he gave her a too-perky doggie grin. *We should play, too.*

"I don't believe this." She sat up, hardening her heart against his large, dark eyes and wagging tail. Hardening her expression. "I don't believe in you. In any . . . ghosts." Though something was wrong with her vision, because she'd begun to "see" gray and white and shadowy and transparent images of people. She'd made a doctor's appointment for extensive testing.

Now a shadow was "talking" to her in her head.

That's all right. I believe in you! Enzo's imaginary tongue shot out and swiped at her face . . . and she felt a clammy touch on her cheek. Enough that she reared back and banged her head on the curved wood of her sleigh bed.

This invasion of the visions right here in her home and her own bedroom was new and unwelcome. Chicago, where her aunt had lived, was one thing. Right here . . . not at all good.

But you hear me, right? Huh, huh? I looove you, Clare. Always liked when you came. You brought treats. Do you have treats here? Enzo bounded off her bed, leaving no sign he'd been there, and whisked straight through her closed and solid bedroom door.

"I'm seeing things," she said weakly.

The spectral dog loped back into the room, drool dripping. Again Clare stared. The shiny droplets vanished before they hit her rug. Which was weird.

The whole thing was weird.

She'd turned weird.

You have no treats, Enzo said, giving her the big puppy eyes.

"I have no clue what you eat," she said, *talking* to an imaginary being—to herself. Despite living alone, she'd never done that. She grabbed a feather pillow and clutched it tight, as if it could be a shield to visions in her own mind.

Breathing fast, she glanced at the tablet computer propped on her bedside table. She was due in the doctor's office in two hours. Good. She'd try to determine if something was wrong physically, first.

Enzo *must* be a figment of her recently shattered, uneasy, and all-too-real-feeling dreams.

The imaginary dog hopped back up onto her bed, tilted his head, and wrinkled his forehead in mute begging.

Clare swallowed. She was an accountant, darn it. She loved a logical life . . . but she wasn't heartless. Even if the thing was only a memory, a figment of her imagination, she couldn't ignore the big doggie eyes any longer. And touching it would be more proof it didn't exist. Tentatively she reached out . . .

But as she slid her hands along the dog and into cold mistiness and shifted under the sheet to keep her legs warm, she recalled the other things she'd seen as the cab had driven her home from the airport the day before, and her heart thumped fast.

Outlaws and miners and cowboys had sauntered translucently down the streets. One had actually stopped and tipped his hat at her! She'd seen the arrogant strides of the rich founding businessmen, the swaying rolled-hip stroll of past madams. Not to mention horses.

Now this filmy dog whimpered in bliss, and Clare's hands

got colder and colder, as if she'd plunged them into an ice bath.

Stroke, stroke, stroke, along Enzo's side . . . He leaned into her. She should stop, but more than her hands were frozen. The thoughts in her head seemed nothing but icy crystals, she was so cold. He rolled over on his back so she could reach his belly. She felt no solid dog, of course, and energy seemed to drain right out of her.

Cold hands, cold crawling up her arms so that her teeth might soon chatter.

Enzo opened his eyes, and for an instant she thought she saw a glint of something *more* than dog, something older, wiser.

Again she pulled back and tucked her freezing hands into her armpits. "No. You're not here. You're definitely not real."

It is time for the gift to pass to you, and with the riches comes the gift. You must accept and learn. The echoey words weren't doglike, again held an edge of *something* else.

Clare shuddered.

Then Enzo blinked and rolled to sit and looked like a goofy pooch again. *I will help. It will be fun! I love you and you love me! Thank you for the petting!*

Cold, cold, cold, she scrunched down into the bed and pulled the sheet up, staring at the vaporous dog.

I'll be your sidekick! Enzo grinned and licked her cheek. She noted that his touch didn't seem as cold as when she'd initiated the contact. Rules. There might be rules in this madness. In seeing ghosts . . .

"No," she said, denying him. Denying that the thing was even there. Not logical. No and no and no.

THREE

~~~

A MOANING WOKE Clare and she sat up straight against the curving wood of her headboard.

The figure of a man stood at the end of her bed. In her *bedroom*! A shadow of shifting grays. From the size of her footboard beside him, she understood he was shorter than average even for the mid-1800s garb that her mind had clothed him in.

His suit and shirt and vest looked to be made of quality materials—good and expensive—and she saw the chain of a pocket watch across his front.

He had no beard or mustache, but his hair seemed darkish and reached his chin. He didn't appear like a gunslinger or a cowboy, but a businessman. His lowered brows and set mouth showed determination as the illusion stared at her.

I need your help. Each word dripped like cold, small droplets of icy water into her mind. The August night had finally turned tolerable, but she kept her window and ceiling fans rotating at top speed. Tomorrow would be another day in the high nineties.

And the ghost man brought a chill with him, much as Enzo had. Her gaze slid to the bottom of the bed, where the illusionary dog had been "sleeping." She saw nothing, but a tickle in her mind said Enzo was there.

Again the hallucination spoke, and this time she saw the slight darkness of his lips against his pale, pale skin as his mouth formed the words. *I. Need. Your. Help.*

"No." Whispery words spurted from her mouth. She made pushing motions with her hands. "No. Go away."

Events cycle. It must be soon that you help me. I am trapped. His mouth twisted. *Not where I died, but where I lost my sanity and sinned the most. Help me.*

Fear dried Clare's throat so she couldn't swallow, and she had to raise her voice past the rawness. "No!"

Enzo coalesced into whiteness even as the other faded. The dog lumbered up the bed and snuffled in her ear, whining.

She gave him two pats with trembling hands before she realized she was trying to pet a nonexistent mutt.

He licked her cheek again, and she felt the clamminess and she slid back down and pulled the sheet over her—all the way over her head—then turned on her side and curled up, hoping her quivering would soon still. Enzo poked his muzzle through the sheet and stared at her with wide, dark eyes.

Clare made a strangling sound.

I will protect you! he said mentally, and barked.

He couldn't protect her from her own mind . . . and, and, another whispering part of the back of her brain that accepted the illogic of night visitations told her that the ghost man wouldn't consider a dog much of a threat, neither in his current condition nor when he'd been alive.

As the steel bonds of fear loosened around her, she considered the apparition again, realizing that she'd seen a picture, or maybe a drawing, of him before. Her brain had picked an image to hang the illusion on. So he must be featured in one of her books on the history of the American West. She'd loved that time period. Once.

She wasn't going to look him up. In any way, shape, or form.

But since her physical exam had proved her vision and hearing okay, she'd have to set up an appointment with the top shrink in Denver.

By the time Clare left to pick up the last box of her things at her old job in downtown Denver the next morning, she'd begun muttering to Enzo as if he might really be there. Talking to herself. Another really bad symptom of the strangeness going on in her life . . . in her mind.

But the figment of Enzo was so damn cheerful, insistent in talking to her, interacting with her—getting those bone-chilling pats when she reached out and touched him—that she could hardly say no.

As she drove downtown, she began seeing shades and shadows of people again. Approaching LoDo, lower downtown, the visions of gray folk around her—in the street ahead of her, crowding around the car, striding on the sidewalks—distracted her so much she wasn't driving safely.

Especially since Enzo sat in the passenger seat. He commented about the city and *talked* to the shadows . . . thankfully only she "heard" Enzo. She circled around to the Capitol end of the Sixteenth Street Mall to approach the high-rise that held the accounting firm she'd worked for. Even there, filmy people crowded the area.

With sweat beading along her hairline and down her spine, she pulled into the first parking lot she saw—expensive!—near Civic Center and parked.

Enzo barked excitedly. *We are going out! We are walking with other ghosts! Hooray! Sandra stayed at home a lot and the ghosts came to her. She was a professional.*

Clare gritted her teeth. Sandra had been a professional crazy person. Then Clare found herself actually answering the dog before she knew it. "Enzo, I am *not* talking to you when we are out of this car." Even in the vehicle was iffy since people must have seen her mouth move—but maybe they'd thought she was singing along to music or on a hands-free phone call.

Enzo grumbled but didn't vanish as she was hoping he would when she stepped out of the car into the searing August heat. He kept a running commentary as she took the shuttle to her former place of business.

She'd given her notice as soon as she realized she didn't need the money from a job anymore, and someone else would. She'd spent time handing off her accounts, and today was just to pick up the last of her belongings.

Fear hopped along her nerves; her neck muscles had tightened into a rigid column, since she didn't turn her head, trying not to see Enzo and the other specters strolling along the sidewalk. Not ghosts. No. Ghosts simply weren't real.

Lately she'd spent too much time in Sandra's house, handling her great-aunt's New Age objects, glancing through her "business" papers. Yes, Sandra had made "seeing" ghosts pay very well . . . and embraced the whole psychic lifestyle along with burnt-velvet flowing caftans. With fringe.

Clare had packed those off to her sister-in-law, who might wear them for fun, or at a country club costume party.

As Clare left her old office with a medium-sized box of personal items, she fought back tears. She'd loved her job and liked the people she'd worked with.

The words that echoed in her head as she walked back to her car were from one of the partners. "We'll miss you. You made a real contribution to this firm."

That's what she always had wanted to do, always needed to do: to contribute to the community and to society. Not live off a trust fund like her parents, flitting around the world at whim, involved with no one but themselves.

She'd been happy being an accountant, really. So, maybe she'd gotten into a rut, but she'd liked that rut, even though now it seemed as if it had risen around her and blocked out all other possibilities in life.

But it had been secure. And growing up in a flaky family like hers, she'd needed secure.

Walking back to the car in her suit had her strained and dripping.

I like this city very much, Enzo said, sniffing lustily and wagging the whole lower half of his body as a ghostly businessman petted him. Clare cut her gaze away.

That ghost appeared vaguely familiar and wore expensive

clothes. Her mind no doubt summoned the image of a mover and shaker in early Denver, since she was near the Capitol.

She hesitated, eyeing his clothing—later in style, she thought, than the vision she'd seen the night before. The ghost man she didn't want to think about.

This one does not need your help, Enzo said, leaning against her a little. He brought cool relief.

The man smiled, shook his head, and said, *The timing is wrong for me.*

Clare jerked at the deep masculine voice resounding in her mind that ramped up her anxiety at the visions. She started walking again.

He raised a dark brow and fell into step with her. *You don't know much about us, do you?*

Juggling the box and her purse, Clare grabbed her cell from the outside pocket of her bag, checked a text. Yes! Her new psychologist had a free hour and was only a couple of blocks away.

It is not polite to ignore us, young lady, the imaginary guy said, then repeated, *You don't know much about us.*

Addressing the phone, ignoring the prickles on her skin that announced strange-stuff-happening, she muttered, "No. And I don't want to learn."

She could have sworn she saw amusement on the pale face.

I hope to see you later.

Not if she could help it. She disregarded the gray illusions, stuck her box in the car, and hurried away—not nearly as hot now. This had been a real mistake. She should have damn well hired a car and driver.

Enzo passed through her as he barked and greeted a transparent woman. Clare flinched. The ghost dog ran off to chase *real* squirrels in Civic Center Park. They squealed and skittered away from him, and Enzo's barks echoed eerily and triumphantly through the hot yellow summer sunshine.

She also ignored the huge and beautiful Denver Public Library, which had a special section on Western history. She was sure she'd find the guy who'd visited her in there, if she bothered.

And as she walked, nearly ran, filmy people gathered around her as if she were a magnet.

Terrible.

Panting, she entered the building where the psychologist's office was, and a few minutes later, the office itself, a pale, sterile place.

After her appointment, she stomped away. She didn't like the office. She didn't like Dr. Barclay. She really didn't like his questions and had crossed her arms and couldn't open up to him, even as he donned a soothing manner.

She'd paid an outrageous amount for nothing.

And despairingly made another appointment for a couple of days later.

When she and Enzo returned to her hot little starter house, she took one look at the pile of paper on the dining room table pertaining to Aunt Sandra's estate and walked right past it.

For the first time since she'd been an adult, she didn't buckle down and do her duty. Instead she collapsed on the bed with a headache. She hadn't gotten all the results in from her physical yet. Maybe she had a brain tumor. That would be easier to deal with.

Maybe the ghosts would leave her alone.

Enzo hopped onto her bed, settled at the end, and said, *We have to help the man who comes at night before those we met today. It's his time.*

Clare was afraid to ask what that meant. She pulled a pillow over her face and curled up, hoping everything would go away.

BOULDER, COLORADO

Zach rolled his shoulders to relieve the tension after visiting his mother in the way-too-serene mental health facility.

He couldn't get out of the place soon enough. The smells reminded him all too closely of the hospital he'd just been released from. Hell, all of his muscles were tense.

Before . . . before, he'd have hit the gym a few blocks away and worked out the anger and pity and guilt. But though the shooting had made news in Montana, he didn't think it would have traveled down here two states away. He wasn't in any sort of emotional shape to explain his disability to others who'd only pity *him*.

He'd spent an agonizing two hours with his mother, sitting with her, taking a small walk around the grounds. She'd retreated to a time before his brother Jim had died and didn't seem to know Zach.

A lovely, sparkling woman who broke his heart. At least he'd aged enough that she didn't call him "James" and ask him to take her away from the place. No, she didn't think he was his brother anymore. Thankfully, his features were a combination of hers and the General's, so she didn't believe he was his father. She'd come to accept he was her younger son.

The visit had been as wrenching as ever. None of them would get over Jim's senseless death.

Time to tuck that away again, get back on the road. His father's family home was here, but neither the General nor Zach could handle the New Age ambiance of Boulder, so the place was rented out to a prof who taught at the university. The Slades did better in the more conservative Colorado Springs.

And he wasn't going all the way into Denver, even though his mind played with the idea of giving that private investigator his former boss had mentioned a call. What kind of justice or closure could be found from someone you paid?

Zach's lip curled. And the thought chomped hard that he might not even be adequate for a PI job.

He left rubber on the street as he got out of Boulder.

DENVER, THAT AFTERNOON

Clare's teleconferencing program on her laptop rang with an insistent, asymmetrical buzzing beat that got her groggily out of bed. She staggered to the little back bedroom and opened the top of her computer, saw the icon of her brother, Tucker. He was taking care of closing up Aunt Sandra's house, dividing up the furniture and shipping it off to three places.

No way was she letting her handsome big brother see her

all pale and sleep-wrinkly. She zoomed to the bathroom sink and scrubbed her face with tepid water, letting it run over her hair well enough for him to think she'd just gotten out of the shower instead of having a midday nap.

Hurrying back to her small office, she hit the icon. "Hi, Tuck—"

"Hey, Auntie Clare!" Dora, nine years old, grinned out at Clare.

"Hi, Dora."

"Dad wants to talk to you. He's here somewhere." Dora glanced around.

"How's it going?" Clare asked.

"Good." Dora's expression turned serious. "It's an a-*mazing* house. We're sad and missing weird G.G. Aunt Sandra, but it's good to see the house one last time." For an instant Clare strained to look beyond Dora to the house itself.

The house was the one thing Tucker had asked to help out with the estate, and Clare had taken him up on the offer.

Dora hefted a sigh. "I'll miss it."

"Hey, pumpkin." Tucker swept his daughter up in his arms, hooked his ankle around a chair and slid it over, and sat. "Hey, Clare."

"Hi, Tucker."

Stroking Dora's head, Tucker said, "I know that the estate and house are yours since you didn't take any payout from G.G. Uncle Amos's trust, but is there any way we can keep it?"

Clare tried to keep her clenched jaw from showing. She'd sold the house, had a contract and a closing, and would take a substantial penalty for withdrawing. "Sure, we can keep it. I can deed it over to you."

Tucker's mouth turned down. "Not the folks?"

"Sure, if I knew they'd take care of it." They wouldn't. Tucker was ten times the father her own was, and Beth, Tucker's wife, was a great mother. Dora was growing up knowing she was the center of their lives, and very loved.

Smiling with a hint of teeth, Clare said, "You get Mom and Dad to give me a call today or tomorrow and I'll cancel the contract. Where are they now? I haven't heard from them in a year." They sure hadn't come to Great-Aunt Sandra's memorial, months ago. Too busy playing on the coast of Italy, or maybe France, or perhaps in the Greek islands.

Tucker's square face took on color. "I haven't heard from them, either."

"Where are you sending their portion of the furniture?"

A sigh from her brother, and then he said, "I've been dealing with Terrence, G.G. Uncle Amos's trust's attorney. He's found a storage unit in White Plains, New York, for the parents' share of the furniture, and his office will handle the transfer on their end."

"Has he heard from our parents?" Clare asked softly.

"No."

Dora looked at Clare with owlish eyes. "Jal and Viva are in the wind again. They sent me a present for my birthday, though."

She saw the lie of that in Tucker's eyes. He covered for the parents when Clare wouldn't.

"Tucker, if you want the house, it's yours," Clare said.

"I like the house," Dora said. "But I like our home in Williamsburg better!"

Tucker eased. "That's good, baby."

Clare said, "We sold it to a nice family, Tuck."

His smile curved. "Kids?"

"Four."

"They'll love this place," Dora enthused.

Enzo barked. *Yes, they will! Children always loved Sandra's and my home!*

Clare turned her head sharply to look at the ghost dog.

"Clare?" asked Tucker.

She blinked and rubbed her right ear. "I'm here."

His eyes narrowed. "You okay?"

"Maybe overdoing it a little working on the estate," she mumbled.

"Well, that's mostly done, and I'll handle the work here." He squeezed his daughter. "I feel better knowing there's a family moving in, don't you, kiddo?"

Dora nodded. "For sure."

Everything's good! Sandra would like them.

Clare hadn't thought that Enzo had even met them, and didn't want to ask.

"I love you, Auntie Clare." Dora puckered and made a loud smooching sound. At least it wasn't "weird Aunt Clare" . . . yet.

"I love you, too, Dora, and Tuck."

"Love ya, sis." Tucker winked. "Bye."

"Bye."

BYE! Enzo shouted. Dora frowned a little before Tuck closed the program.

Clare sagged in her seat.

Enzo barked in the middle of the night; a wave of chill air yanked Clare from sleep. She blinked, and her hand went out toward the dog, fingers turned frigid.

You must help me!

The apparition was back.

FOUR

ONCE AGAIN THE gray and black and white and transparent man stood at the end of her bed. *You've got to get it. YOU'VE GOT TO GET IT!*

Panting with cold and fear, Clare huddled against the headboard and drew up the comforter. She should add a blanket . . . in the hottest August on record. Yes, something was wrong. She should be grateful that this illusion didn't move close to her and try to interact with her the way the dog did.

He looked a little different, a little rougher. Was he fraying around the edges? What did that mean?

You must get it. The one I put in a box. Get it first. His lips twisted as he looked down at himself. *Then we will work to find the one I misplaced.*

Again his stubborn chin lifted and she felt the cold pressure of an intense gaze—or thought she did.

This is the right time. You are the right person. Things are falling into place. It's HERE, and finally the time is right and I may be able to go on, if you help me. She didn't like the desperate plea in the glittering rounds that might be eyes. Maybe this was a dream.

She stared hard, trying to catalog every detail of this vision, and she found darker spots in him. Without thought, she said, "What are those?"

He glanced down again. *Buckshot, a couple of bullets.*

"You died of gunshot wounds?"

His lips compressed into a line. *No. They were just still in me.* The words continued to come to her mind and she shuddered. *Please.* He stretched out a pale hand. *I did wrong, I admit it. I was a bad and mean drunk, I admit that, too. But I've been here more than a century and a half and don't deserve to stay so long!* His expression changed to despairing. *Away from my beautiful wife. She isn't with me. I can't find her. Help me, please.*

Enzo yipped and whined, turning large, pleading eyes on Clare.

She cracked . . . mind, heart, something. Sloughed off a piece of her that might deal with this insanity . . . just for now. The psychologist could help her put herself together, eventually, when she trusted him more . . . but for now . . . Wetting dry and cold lips, she whispered, "What do you need?"

I have found the box, a box my wife had that I used. Get it for me, please, I beg of you. That is the first step in freeing my tormented soul.

He should have sounded melodramatic, but the emotions she thought she felt rushing from him were so sad, too sad. She swallowed.

We can go now, the manlike vision . . . illusion . . . ghost? . . . said.

"Now? Right now?" Clare glanced frantically around the bedroom. It was tiny, hardly enough room for the bed, the transparent dog-thing, and the man-shadow. And if the city during the day spun out pale visions, what would night bring? "I don't think so."

The man-shape floated to the footboard of her bed and hitched a hip on it, balancing somehow, though she could see the curved wood through him. He crossed his arms.

"You're going to stay?" she asked, appalled.

He nodded, not speaking. Was that better or worse?

Maybe if she closed her eyes and tried to sleep, he would go away. Enzo hadn't. It looked like she had another imaginary friend she didn't want.

She sniffed in disdain and slid back into bed. She hadn't turned on the fans tonight. Though the heat wouldn't fall to the midsixties until four A.M., she was barely warm.

Three times that hour, she awoke, opened her eyes, and saw the ghost man staring at her.

Finally she sat up. "Where is this box?"

I can show it to you. Come.

Driving at night, when, if you were someone who believed in ghosts, undead spirits gathered. "No."

He sat on the far corner of the bed, staring at her with a black gaze that yet seemed to burn with determined fire. Enzo crept closer to her and thumped his cold tail on her thigh.

"Oh, all right. Let's get this over with."

She'd been right about the night. She drove slowly, creeping, really, through a fog of phantoms, ignoring shapes and wide mouths and pleading hands, shivering all the way. She turned on the heater.

Finally the specter who'd been leading her stopped, miles from her home. Mercifully there were fewer people here, probably because it had been outside city limits during the era that she was sensitive to.

The human mind can only comprehend ghosts from one slice of history, said the man, uncannily reading her thoughts.

Enzo barked. *Right, right, right!* He bolted through the car door and in front of a building.

Reluctantly, Clare got out of the car. The thunk of the door closing was muffled.

I am very lucky you are here to help me, the vision continued. He waved a hand that showed calluses in places that didn't look normal and modern to Clare. *The box is in there; you must get it.*

"Oh, no, I won't." But now she was close, she saw it was an auction house. She scanned the hours posted on the window and the flyer for the next auction.

It is in THERE!

Clare headed back to the car. "The next sale is tomorrow night. The place lists a website. We can look for your box there."

The ghost appeared confused.

"I'm heading back home. You can stay or go."

He walked into the building—as did Enzo—and Clare sighed with relief. She didn't admit that she missed the dog on the way back through weird white-shadowed Denver.

But both dog and man awaited her in her living room. Her shoulders slumped.

I saw the box! Enzo panted, drool as usual falling and not hitting her shabby rug.

I will see you tomorrow night. Lines grooved in the apparition's forehead. *This costs me much energy, but to be free, I will do anything. Promise me you will get the box!*

Enzo barked, *You need to do this Clare. For yourself and for him. HE is your first project! PROMISE HIM!* For the first time, that Other spirit she sensed also inhabited Enzo's body came to the fore, looked at her with dark, dark fog moving in the eye sockets, thundered in her mind.

Clare reeled back at the blast of cold, and hit the closed door.

PROMISE, they shouted together—or her own mind insisted.

"I promise," she said weakly, shivering.

The man vanished.

She went into the tiny second bedroom that held her ruthlessly organized home office, complete with a new computer. Enzo followed, circled and circled again, and when he looked up at her, his eyes were all innocent dog. Then he stared at the notebook.

I know that toy! It shows pictures and places. Let's look now!

Dragging up a chair, they found the auction house's website. There was a lot of antique furniture, some in excellent shape that made Clare's mouth water—but Aunt Sandra's house had just sold. Clare's brother was supervising closing it up and dividing the furniture. Clare could expect a truck with her share within the week. Other trucks would go to her brother in Williamsburg, Virginia, and a storage unit in New York.

Rubbing her eyes, which seemed to do nothing but move around grit, Clare zipped through the photos until Enzo barked. *I see it!*

Clare stared at it dubiously: a puzzle box made of plum wood of unknown origin and date. It didn't look like much.

Pretty battered. At least she might be able to get it cheap. She wrote down all the information, turned off the computer, and trudged to bed, accompanied by the imaginary dog. She should get a real one.

Maybe. When she was sanc again.

Enzo looked up at her sorrowfully. *You still don't believe in me.*

Clare opened her mouth and shut it, then said, "Not really."

He shook his head and for an instant he didn't look like the image of a dog, but a skeleton dog. . . . She wrapped her arms around herself.

Only a little bit of you believes in me. That is not enough, Clare.

The echo behind his voice scared her, as if he were once again more . . . or less . . . than a dog . . . spirit.

She got back into her nightgown, folded her comforter—doubling, then quartering the queen-sized cloth—turned off the lights and curled under the cover.

Enzo blinked down at her, head through the comforter and sheet. *You aren't doing good.*

What do you mean? Clare *thought* back at him, feeling drained of energy herself.

Enzo cocked his head as if listening, then drooped a little and said, *If you don't accept your gift that you can see ghosts, then you will die. And if you accept that you see them but don't help them, you can go crazy.*

Clare sobbed. Exactly what she'd always feared—madness.

The next morning, Clare couldn't throw off the night fears, or the fact that she'd made a really odd promise to something that might be an aspect of herself.

Her great-aunt's death had shaken her, for sure.

But a promise was a promise. Since her parents had casually made and broken so many, she made a habit of keeping all of hers. Even promises to herself—a hot fudge sundae if she said no to overwork, for instance.

Now she had no work, but *destiny* had rung in her mind and reverberated throughout her body.

And to remind herself of her promise, she took Aunt Sandra's perfume spritzer and sprayed scent on her neck and wrists . . . and sniffed. It wasn't too heavy. Tears welled in Clare's eyes at the fragrance of sandalwood, tuberose, wild berries . . . she'd looked up the mixture once. That dark and mysterious fragrance that meant "Aunt Sandra" to Clare, in all her weird kindness. The perfume that meant *Gypsy* to Aunt Sandra.

Clare gulped, shook the thought away, and moved on. She decided to buy a larger house, move to one of the more charming areas of Denver. She'd always liked the ambiance of Cheesman Park, but *nothing* would get her there now. She completely dismissed that idea. Everyone knew Cheesman Park had been a graveyard, and when they'd added the parking garage to the Botanic Gardens they'd found more graves.

Even if she didn't believe in ghosts, she didn't want to be in an area with a lot of dead people that was right in the time period now haunting her. . . . She did a quick check on her tablet computer. Yes, burials at Cheesman began in 1858. No way, nohow was she moving there.

Much of the Capitol area and LoDo had been built in that time period. Then there was the area around the Molly Brown house, but most residential homes around it had been demolished.

Looked like she'd be going to the Western floor of the Denver Public Library after all, just to find out what area might be . . . safe. And—she nerved herself at the thought— she might have to put in some hours driving around the city to find out where she could live. Even the suburbs and the plains might be touchy—Indians roved and camped on the plains.

Yes, she'd be doing some research.

With a huff of breath, she admitted she might as well research the vision of the man.

She needed to move fast since even at a high-end price, Sandra's house had been snapped up. Clare could put the items she wanted in her new house, instead of the storage area she'd planned. Finding a home would be a project to take her mind off her poor mental health.

She felt better after the decision. She'd always prided herself on her quick decision making—unlike the rambling conversations of her parents discussing all their options that had driven her crazy in her childhood.

Just one of those personality traits she didn't share.

She figured out exactly how much she wanted to spend on a house and had made a list of three columns: one of things she MUST have, like a landscaped yard; one with the features she'd prefer; and the last, "extras."

Before heading off to the library, she organized her briefcase with pen and paper, tablet computer, and her new top-of-the-line smart phone. This time she called a cab to drive her downtown. She wouldn't have to deal with traffic, parking, or apparitions who got in her way.

Or handle any imaginary figment other than Enzo, who ran through the house and the door of the cab, barking all the way.

Clare gritted her teeth. She would *not* talk to him, no matter what outrageous thing he said.

So, where are we going? Are we going to find the ghost man? We are going back into the city? I LIKED the city. Will the ghost man be there? Those remnants of ghost squirrel energy are YUMMY! Will you take me to the park again, huh, huh?

I AM GOING TO THE LIBRARY FOR THE REST OF THE MORNING. YOU CAN PLAY IN THE PARK! she "shouted" mentally.

Hurt doggie eyes. He turned and seemed to look out the window. She *wouldn't* feel guilty.

Once inside the clean and organized library with exceedingly helpful librarians, Clare felt more in control. Since the fifth floor housed the genealogical section as well as the Western collection, there were more people there on a weekday morning than she'd anticipated.

From the quiet conversations around her, she learned there were people researching their family trees, students, a writer or two, and a couple of research assistants of local professors.

She approved, smiling at the lovely environment. Imaginary Enzo had remained in the park.

She set up her tablet computer with Wi-Fi keyboard and accepted from the librarians the basic biographies on men who'd been in Colorado more than 150 years ago.

Instead of just flipping through the works for old photographs—or the drawing she half recalled—she sank into the stories.

And found Jules Beni, the founder of Julesburg, Colorado, who was not her guy.

But his killer was.

The infamous Jack Slade. The Jack Slade whom Mark Twain and Sir Richard Burton had written about. The first bad guy who defined all other American West bad guys. But not one most people knew.

Jack Slade, a man who could be considered a hero, with admirable qualities—setting up a whole division of the Pony Express and Overland Stage on time and on budget, ensuring the safety of the riders and drivers and stage passengers. But, as the vision had told her, he was definitely a bad and mean drunk.

Not the kind of guy she wanted anything to do with. Still, she ordered all the books the library had on him . . . some of which were reference only, not to be removed from the building. While she waited, she did a basic Internet search. There was a lot of information on Jack Slade, some that didn't sound right, too wild and fantastic—myth and legend.

She scowled. She preferred hard facts.

Most of the data was based on the stories Mark Twain told. Mark Twain, one of the greatest spinners of tall tales of all time.

Sighing, she began to make notes of what might actually be factual.

"I'll deliver those, Mary, while you help this customer." A loud voice broke into Clare's thoughts. She glanced up to see a tall, paunchy man, the research assistant. He appeared to be retired, but still middle-aged. Smiling, he gave her the books. "You know Slade was the mastermind behind the Overland Stage Company robbery at Virginia Dale in 1863. Sixty thousand in gold, never recovered. That would be millions today. Missing treasure, just like the Reynolds gang's bank robbery and the Lost Dutchman mine."

Clare frowned at her notes and the Slade timeline she'd found. "Wasn't he somewhere else in 1863?" And she was pretty sure that if he'd had a lot of money, or access to a lot of money, he wouldn't have been in financial straits when fired by the Overland Stage for shooting up a saloon.

The man chuckled, shaking his head. "Slade remains a shadowy figure, both larger than life and obscured by the stories and legends surrounding him. Nothing is solid about him, including his whereabouts at a particular time. And, like I said, he *masterminded*." The guy wiggled his own neatly curved brows. With another smile, he settled back at his own table.

An hour later, stomach rumbling, she put aside the materials she couldn't take home and picked up the books she'd check out. The library was great, but food sounded good.

As she walked out of the large entrance, she saw the research assistant and the other patrons pounce on her research books. She sniffed. There couldn't be anything more fruitless than treasure hunting.

"We're consultants," Tony Rickman, private investigator, a large man behind the equally large desk, said to Zach. His fingers were interlocked, a uniquely engraved wedding ring on his left hand. "We handle a variety of cases—security advice and audits, bodyguards, missing persons." A shrug of blocky shoulders. "Most of my operatives carry private investigator licenses. Not necessary in Colorado, but I prefer that."

Some undertone Zach caught in the man's voice, an edgy shadow in Tony Rickman's eyes, kept the *Not interested* lying on Zach's tongue from escaping his mouth. He shouldn't be interested in going private, serving for money instead of for the public good, working for an ex-military man. Instead, he questioned, "Most of your operatives?"

"There are . . . miscellaneous cases that don't need great physical abilities, but investigation, a good pair of eyes, and a sharp brain. You could use your skills. Be an asset."

Zach grunted. The man *hadn't* said legs. "No running?" Zach said sardonically.

Cool gray eyes met his. "No desk."

That was a point.

Rising smoothly with the help of his cane, Zach nodded. His lips didn't curl as they'd wanted to when he walked in. "I'll consider the info you gave me." The consulting fee Zach would earn was nearly obscene. Private paid well if he could swallow being in that area.

"You do that." Rickman unclasped his hands. "And consider this: Justice and honor matter to this firm and every one of my operatives."

Zach nodded again and left. A military man usually spouted stuff about justice and honor, in his experience, but the General's and most of his buddies' notions of those concepts had rarely lined up with Zach's.

For his father, justice and honor were for his friends and his class first, then others might be considered.

But . . . Zach had felt comfortable with Rickman, and Zach respected his old boss, the sheriff, and the sheriff's take on things. Maybe Rickman wasn't blowing smoke. Zach shrugged, still uncomfortable with the whole notion of going private. He'd figure it out later.

Right now he could use a beer. He smiled. For the first time he was glad to be back in Denver. Plenty of beer choices here: local microbrews, imports.

To his surprise, he liked being in the bustle of the city. A city with people with all different slants on life, much more so than the homogenized Plainsview and Cottonwood County, Montana. Taking the job there had seemed like a good move at the time. Tough luck everything went bad.

As soon as he came to the corner at the Sixteenth Street Mall and a restaurant with an open area, he moved in. For just after one P.M., the tables inside weren't crowded, though the ones behind the rail on the sidewalk were full.

A single woman just inside the restaurant sitting by the window caught his attention. Her conservative gray suit and the clean head-hugging cut of her thick brown hair with gleaming red strands showed that she considered herself a serious professional.

This impression was contradicted by the fact that she appeared to be talking to herself—or, perhaps, reading aloud from the book open in front of her.

He was a sucker for lovely contradictions.

"Jack Slade!" she announced.

Sounded like "Zach."

He walked in and gave her a slow smile, moved up to the square two-top. "Yeah? You called?"

FIVE

❦

THE WOMAN LOOKED up, flushed with embarrassment. "Sorry, I was reading about the, um, historical figure."

Zach stopped a grunt, held out his hand, and replied, "I got that. I'm Zach." She was attractive enough, and he was interested enough, to give her the rest. "Jackson Zachary Slade." He smiled. "No relation to the gunfighter."

She blinked, lifted her slim, elegantly shaped fingers, and put them in his own. "Clare Cermak." Then she glanced down at the open book. "Jack Slade wasn't all bad. He had posttraumatic stress disorder, you know."

Anger flared inside Zach, fiery and hot, and probably showed in his eyes, because she withdrew her cool hand and leaned back in her chair, away from him.

He said, "I'm tired of hearing about that. Anything bad happens and the perpetrator is excused because he has posttraumatic stress disorder." And the docs had stuck that label on Zach, too.

Her hazel gaze flicked down to neat handwritten notes, then back up to meet his and remained steady. "I'd say getting ambushed and shot with a six-shooter, then having a shotgun emptied into you, then being taken by wagon over rough trail for a hundred and sixty miles, operated on there, suffering for weeks, and then being sent by train to St. Louis for removal of more bullets, might cause post-traumatic stress syndrome. All this in 1860."

Zach winced. His one bullet had been bad. He didn't recall his time in the ambulance but knew the drive was only a few miles to the medical center. His stay in the modern hospital had been hideous. He didn't know what an old-time hospital might have been like, but it couldn't have been good. "Maybe you have a point. You sure know your stuff," Zach said, gestured to the chair opposite her. "May I sit?"

She nodded, her glance sliding to his cane, but she said nothing about that or his awkwardness. Another point in her favor.

She said, "You know about the original Slade?"

He shrugged. "Happens when your name is close to an infamous—or famous—guy. You've been studying Jack Slade?" He angled his head toward the book. It looked well worn.

"I'm reading about him. This is from the library; I'll be obtaining my own copy. The man was a very interesting character." She set a bookmark into the pages, closed the book, and put it in the outer pocket of a leather computer bag. The middle compartment showed four other books.

She tucked her cell into her bag, pulled out a portfolio and slipped her notes inside, returned it to the tote, and moved her coffee cup from his side of the table and sipped. Her eyes studied him over the rim.

The waitress sauntered up and Zach ordered a Tivoli beer.

Zach's telephone sounded the sheriff's classical notes. Had he spoken already with Rickman about Zach? Had Rickman double-checked Zach's references? The taste in his mouth went sour.

He glanced at Clare, who'd placed her cup in her saucer and watched him with a gaze that he suddenly noticed had shadows. She wasn't as simple as he'd thought. Again, interesting.

She nodded at his cell. "Go ahead."

Grimacing, he said, "Former boss."

She flinched; a smile formed on her pretty lips and vanished. "I have one of those, too."

The lady presented more puzzles.

Zach picked up his phone and thumbed it on, "Slade."

Clare's gaze flicked to her bag with all the books on the other Slade.

"Zach, did you talk with my deputies Lauren Aguirre and Larry Pickman lately?" the sheriff asked.

Warning bells went off in Zach's head, but he kept his voice easy. "Yeah. Lauren and Larry caught up with me the day before yesterday at the diner."

The sheriff grunted. "After I spoke with you?"

"That's right."

"They were both off duty then and yesterday." Zach's former boss cleared his throat. "Exactly when and where did you last see them?"

"On the twenty-third, approximately thirteen hundred hours at the Daisy Diner near the southern border of the county. Lauren wanted to say she was sorry for my trouble. They left first."

After the damn crows had cawed. Four crows. Death. Dread tightened the back of Zach's neck. A high-pitched whine came to his ears and he jerked his head to get rid of it.

Sighing heavily, the sheriff let silence hang. Didn't bother Zach. Finally his ex-boss said, "Looks like they had a single-car accident on the way back to Plainsview City. Ran off the road and down a bank. Rolled the vehicle. We had some nasty weather that afternoon."

Zach's gut tightened. "How bad is it?"

"The worst. They're dead."

"Christ. You don't need me to come back?" He shouldn't have to, but you never knew. So far the sheriff had treated him better than anyone else in the department.

"No. Just wanted to clear the timeline up. You spoke with Tony Rickman?"

"Yeah."

"So did I. He was impressed."

Zach snorted.

"Take the job, Zach," the sheriff said.

"Good-bye."

"Good-bye, and good luck."

Zach pushed away his half-empty glass of beer. The light clouds had drifted away and the day had begun to heat up in earnest. A trickle of sweat ran down his spine, sticking one of his good white shirts to his back and making him wish he'd taken off his jacket. He *hated* when he saw the crows. Hated even more when the stupid rhyme seemed to be right.

Otherwise, just emptiness at the thought of those deaths filtered through him. Not even anger, his usual response to senseless loss of life. Should he feel anything for them? The woman who'd made a mistake just as he had, one that screwed up his life? The man who'd liked to make jokes at his expense? He didn't know.

But they were colleagues, people he'd worked with, and now they were dead. An area of emptiness, of emotions more layered than the single, primal ones he still experienced, grew. He'd think about that later.

No one would expect him to come back for the funerals, and that was damn good. He didn't want to see anyone from that particular job again. The job he'd thought had been a career.

"Problems?" a soft voice across from him asked.

He blinked Clare Cermak's pretty face into focus. Not model-perfect, and with a gold-dust tan that seemed to be natural.

Clare's lips pursed, something he didn't care to see, and she leaned a bit toward her bag as if she were ready to pick it up and go . . . and Zach realized he didn't want her to leave. "Yeah, a couple of problems," he said.

Her brows lowered, then she said, "But not your problems, because you aren't at that job anymore?"

"You're right." He studied her, made a good guess. "You were an accountant."

Now her brown-red eyebrows lifted. "How did you know?"

He found a smile curving his own lips. She was easy to be around. "Your phone has a tax app and fancy calculator on the home screen."

"Oh."

"You're very neat and tidy," he said.

Her tongue came out and moistened her lips, and a flicker of lust flared in his groin. Very welcome, since nothing much had stirred down there for a while. He'd been told his wound had been severe enough, and he'd lost enough blood, that it might take him a while before his dick functioned. Now it seemed it was functioning just fine.

The truth was, no woman had attracted him in a while.

He stared at Clare Cermak and her steady hazel eyes, and couldn't help comparing her to Lauren. Yeah, he'd have bet his Corvette that Clare would always do her job. There'd be no slipups. Another fine trait.

She still frowned at him, vertical lines over her nose, bit her full lower lip. "You're a police officer?"

His smile faded. "How'd you guess?"

"You said 'perpetrator.' And your reaction to the idea of post-traumatic stress syndrome." Her eyes flickered at his cane, at him. "You seem in good shape."

He ignored the implied question about how he might have come to be crippled, leaned back, and crossed his good ankle over his knee. "Checking out my build, Clare?"

She laughed and her serious-mode expression faded, making her appear younger and more carefree. Pity she had those shadows in her eyes; she was beautiful when she laughed. Her long lashes swept down and up, flirting with him, and he relaxed even more. Maybe being here in Denver might turn out to be a good move.

"Absolutely I checked you out, Zach."

"Good to know." Zach smiled, then continued the conversation. "So you're an ex-accountant?"

She tilted up her chin. "There's no such thing as an ex-accountant. I am a CPA." She paused and the shadows darkened her eyes to brown. She sighed. "I just don't have a job anymore."

"Why'd you quit?"

That got her staring back into his eyes instead of looking at the suited men and women passing by.

"You think I quit?"

"Yep."

"You're good."

"I know, and more than just my observational skills."

Now her gaze was penetrating, intense. He knew that look, too. The lady was deciding whether to trust him. He didn't bother giving her a sincere smile; he wanted no prompts from him on her decision.

Because it mattered that she'd trust him and he didn't know why. Maybe just because he really liked the looks of her. He thought he heard a dog yip but didn't break the gaze.

Clare leaned forward, and his stare did slip a little to her newly revealed cleavage. The collar of her white blouse wasn't open that far, just enough to see the rise of nice breasts.

"I received an inheritance," she murmured.

His ear caught doubt in her voice. "Strings attached?"

"You might say that."

Something—someone—snuffled near them; Zach didn't turn to see but met her gaze again. "You don't have to work anymore?"

"No." Her lips flexed down. "And someone else could use my excellent job."

He dipped his head. "Good idea."

"Thank you." She slid his beer back toward him. "And I don't think you're an ex–police officer, either."

"Deputy sheriff," he said.

"Law enforcer." She nodded. "No such thing as an ex–policeman?"

He thought of the drunk ex-cop who'd shot him, now sitting in prison, convicted of assault with a deadly weapon on an officer of the law. "I wouldn't say that."

"Hmm," Clare said, once more considering him. He didn't mind that. "Maybe there are people . . ." She blinked. "There *are* people who live their job. I think you were—*are*—one of them."

Drinking to give him time enough to think about her insight, he realized that there were now four ex–law enforcers in his mind—himself, the guy who'd shot him, and Lauren and Larry. All done with such work forever. He clicked the empty glass down on the table, licked the last of the foam from his mouth—and when Clare's gaze flicked to his lips, his brooding eased.

Until she gestured to his cane. "Despite your circumstances, I think you'll always be a lawman *here*"—she touched fingertips to her breast over her heart.

A dog barked and Zach scanned the mall for one, didn't see it.

Clare said, "Not like the gunman Jack Slade, who was *the* law of the West at one time, then devolved into an alcoholic and was fired from his job."

Zach felt one side of his mouth kick up in a half smile. "He had PTSD." Could have happened that way.

Nodding soberly, Clare said, "You know, they didn't get all the lead out of him. That probably bothered him for the remaining four years of his life."

Zach lifted his hand. "I concede the point already." He paused. "I don't want to think or talk about bullet wounds." And he didn't know what possessed him to say that, either.

Clare's eyes rounded, pupils black against the hazel. "Is that how . . . ?"

"Yeah."

She swallowed, and her mouth must have been dry because she finished her coffee.

When she put her cup down, Zach reached out and grasped her fingers. Her hand remained cool, felt nice in the heating-up afternoon. He smiled at her. "I've remembered something else about Jack Slade. He had a vibrant, intelligent, loyal, and sexy wife."

"Maria Virginia," Clare said. Her smile turned teasing. "I'm sure that list of qualities isn't in the order you prefer."

Zach grinned, realized his face hadn't moved like that since he'd been shot. "Nope." Her hand was warming in his and he rubbed the back of it with his thumb, to keep that pretty smile going.

"So what would be the order?" she asked.

SIX

"I'M THINKIN' YOU'RE gettin' a little too personal." Zach put on a drawl that anyone who'd lived in Colorado for a while would have heard.

Her brows went up. "Native Coloradan?"

"Yep."

"I came during college. I was born in Chicago, raised here and there and everywhere. I have wandering parents."

His turn to blink. The more they talked, the more he understood they had a lot in common. He pointed his thumb at himself. "Military brat."

"Oh."

"But I was born in Boulder. Have a few generations of Coloradans behind me, I think, on my father's side, some Native American. Never looked into it."

His dad would never admit the Native American blood or discuss it, especially around his mom or her family, but from the slight tawny hue of their skin, they had to have had Native American blood in them not so many generations back. All the Slade men had hair so dark brown it looked black in most light. "My mother's family is from Massachusetts."

"My folks are mostly from Illinois, I think, though I may explore that."

Another *woof!* from the dog he still couldn't see on the sidewalk outside the window. But Zach followed the thought through. "Tracing your family background because of the inheritance." Her fingers had trembled in his, but she hadn't withdrawn them.

"Yes." Her eyes went distant, then she tossed her head, focused her attention back on him. Every time she did that, he liked it more.

"So," she said. "What would the order of that list be?" She frowned as if trying to recall the qualities he'd listed.

"Intelligent, loyal, sexy, vibrant," he replied promptly.

She chuckled. "Interesting order."

"Thanks."

"I'm not sure how vibrant I am."

"You'd look better out of that gray suit, that's for sure," he said.

"Ohh." Her appreciative glance went to his shoulders. He figured they were broad enough for her.

A melody played and her eyes sharpened.

"Your cell?" he asked.

"My real estate agent."

His brows rose. "Spending the inheritance?"

"My house is too small," she replied stiffly. "I've already sold my late aunt's house. Even as we speak, my brother is arranging for moving trucks to me, his place in Virginia, and a storage unit for the parents in White Plains, New York."

Professional interest prickled along Zach's nerves. "They don't have a problem with you inheriting a lot of money? Or did they get a big cut, too?" Just how wealthy was this woman? Her clothes and bag were modest, midlevel management.

"I got all the money and the house, but my brother took money out of a trust some time ago and I didn't. He and his family are comfortable and my parents live on trust fund money."

"Uh-huh." Zach didn't believe for an instant that her relatives wouldn't resent Clare's good luck. In his world, big money always caused problems between people.

Her cell rang again with the same sprightly, tinkly music. "Go ahead and get it," he said.

She leaned down and pulled the phone right out of her bag, no fishing around. Efficient. Nice.

"Hello, Arlene, this is Clare. Four listings already that match my requirements? Oh. Right now? I don't know . . ."

Clare's gaze cut to Zach, and he stopped himself from smirking. She didn't want to leave him and the conversation they were having to look at pretty houses. She'd rather stay. That boosted his confidence like nothing and nobody since the shooting. He leaned back in his chair, smiling, but waved that she should accept the appointment. He had no doubt they'd meet again.

Clare pursed her lips, tilted her head, staring at him.

"Go on," he said. High-pitched, quick burbling continued to come from the telephone. No doubt the agent knew she had a big fish on the line and wanted to sell to Clare as soon as possible. Still, he'd back Clare and her obviously careful ways against a high-energy and persuasive real estate agent.

A cool draft washed around his legs. The day remained sunny, with heat rising to sizzling. The restaurant must have turned the air-conditioning up.

"All right, Arlene." Clare turned her wrist to look at her watch. A person who still wore a watch so she could see the time faster than reaching for her cell or personal computer or tablet—which Zach also bet she carried.

Yep, one damn intriguing woman.

Under her tan skin, her cheeks pinkened as she flushed, her gaze darting to him. "Ah, Arlene, I don't have a car with me. I took a cab downtown."

That was interesting. She didn't strike him as the type who'd spend an extra penny on herself if there were other options, and it was impossible to get around the Denver metro area in a timely manner without a ride.

A lot of commonalities between them, and the shadows in her eyes, and something just *different* combined into a hell of an attraction for him. Intelligent, sexy, vibrant. He didn't know how loyal she might be. Trustworthy, though, he'd allow her that.

"I'll find a cab at one of the big hotels and meet you at the first house. Yes, I've memorized the address. I'll leave shortly."

"You haven't had lunch?" Zach asked. The more he looked at her, the more he thought he saw strain around her eyes, as if those shadows bedeviled her.

She frowned at him, lifted the cell from her mouth. "I'm not very hungry."

Once again the odd chill breezed through. Wonky air-conditioning.

And though he frowned, he understood when someone wanted to force food on you and you didn't want to eat.

"I'll leave as soon as you hang up, Arlene," Clare said, and the call ended.

She slipped the cell back into her bag, rubbed at her temples. "I didn't expect this to happen so fast."

"But you're ready for it," he pointed out. "And those moving trucks will be rolling."

Her hands lowered and she smiled again. "There is that. But I could find a good storage unit."

Zach shook his head. "Not nearly as efficient or tidy."

"That's right."

She stood slowly. "I'm sorry our conversation was cut short."

"Me, too. Do you have a card?" he asked.

Her hand went to her purse, then dropped away. "No. I only have business cards. I'll have to . . . think of something."

Woof! barked the dog Zach still couldn't see.

He shook his head as he reached for his cane, positioned it right, and stood. His leg had stiffened and hurt. He wasn't about to show that. "Another thing we have in common."

"Yes?"

"No jobs and money we're not sure about and needing new digs." He reached into his jacket pocket and took out one of his old cards, ignored the insignia and writing on the front, flipped it over and wrote his cell number on the back, and held it out.

She took it and put it carefully in an inner pocket of her purse, zipped that.

"We'll meet again, Clare Cermak."

"I'm sure we will." She, too, took a card from her purse, pale gray with black lettering, crossed out the engraved wording below her name, and wrote down two numbers. "That's my cell and my landline."

Of course she'd have backup communication in a landline. He stuck her card in his inner pocket, then took her hand and squeezed. "Good meeting you."

"Yes." She returned the pressure and slipped a ready ten from her purse. He intercepted her hand.

"I'll get it."

"Thank you, Jackson Zachary Slade."

The first time in a long time—maybe ever—that he'd liked hearing his full name. "Call me Zach."

She dipped her head. "Zach. Later."

"Later." He took his time pulling out a twenty and tossing it on the table, watching her nicely rounded hips sway in her slim skirt as she strode outside and to the busy sidewalk. He blinked, since there seemed to be a smudge to his sight now and again when he took in the full sight of her.

Crows cawed.

No! Zach tensed. Saw five birds rise from the iron railing separating the restaurant tables from the walkway. How had he missed them? But his breath released slowly. Five for silver. That could mean a lot of things, but not sorrow or death or secrets.

His phone sounded again, the anonymous buzz of an unknown caller. The readout showed *Rickman Security and Investigations*.

"Slade," he said.

"I've got a job for you. Interested?"

Silver—money, payment. "Yeah." He guessed so.

"If you're still in Denver, come on back to my offices and I'll brief you and introduce you to our client."

Zach's heart gave a bump of anticipation. He turned and walked from the restaurant, looked up at the skyscraper where Tony Rickman had his offices. "I'll be right there."

"See you soon." Rickman clicked off.

A deep breath brought city heat and smells, different than the Montana county he'd served for three years. He swallowed away the sadness at Lauren and Larry, found himself murmuring a little prayer his grandmother had taught him for their souls.

Change wasn't always good, but always happened.

SEVEN

THE REAL ESTATE agent opened the door of the cab and Clare slid out, nearly shivering with cold. Enzo had accompanied her and the driver had his air-conditioning running hard. She paid the fare and added an eighteen percent tip, and the cab zoomed off.

Arlene, young and Hispanic with a huge smile and incredible energy, chattered about the landscaping of the first house, the curb appeal. At first glance Clare liked the looks of the house, but she admitted to herself that she wanted more charm in a home. Especially since she now lived in a small rectangular structure. She and Enzo followed Arlene through the house. Despite everything, Clare wasn't about to make a quick decision. She intended to buy only one house in her lifetime—at least until she married and had children. Even then, if she loved the house and it was big enough for a family, she thought she could persuade a husband to live with her.

The image of an extremely sexy Zach Slade rose to her mind and made her whole body warm as she recalled the way he looked at her. Broad shoulders, tall and sleekly muscular, but with a lean look that made her think he'd recently lost weight. An ex–deputy sheriff, and shot. She had enough data to look him up online when she returned home.

In the meantime, she could keep him, and two prospective children, in mind as a "sample" family while she real estate shopped—think of two cars instead of one, or a minivan, and make sure the schools were good . . . not quite what she'd told Arlene already, so she'd do that after this first set of viewings.

Selling Aunt Sandra's home on the lake in Chicago gave Clare quite a budget. But what should have been fun became wearying. Enzo accompanied her and made comments, lifting his ghostly leg on trees, then walking *through* them. Did he truly mark his presence somehow? She hadn't noticed any doggie scent.

Anyway, he was distracting, and she had to watch herself from answering him.

She also felt the chill tingle of presences, knowing that there *were* ghosts in the house or on the land, but not from her "time period." She thought she could live with that, though.

How Sandra had lived in a house that had been built in the time period she was sensitive to, Clare didn't know; the very idea made her shudder.

"There are cases cops can't touch," Rickman said, eyes serious, as he stood leaning against the front of his desk.

Zach hadn't sat down this time, but moved to one of the office's windows, staring over the city at the interesting buildings and blocks interspersed with trees. "Yeah, a case the cops can't touch? Like what?"

"Like an old woman trying to track down her mother's heirlooms."

Zach snorted.

"Those pieces mean something to her, Zach," the PI said in a gentler voice than Zach would have expected from a military officer.

"She lost her mother when she was young, was sent to her father's relatives. Mrs. Flinton wants the pieces back. They remind her of her home before her mother died." There was a long pause. "She needs what the psych people call closure, Zach."

That socked him in the gut. Closure. Something none of his family had gotten.

There was no closing the cold case of the murder of his brother twenty-three years ago. The case of the drive-by shooting of James Slade remained open.

Yeah, Zach had heard a lot about closure in individual and family grief counseling. Knew how the lack of the *who* and *why* ate in the gut.

Destroyed a family.

Rickman said, "There's an auction tonight where Mrs. Flinton believes some of her mother's antiques might be, but I don't like the way she was contacted."

"Scam," Zach said.

"Yes. So far I haven't had any luck in finding out deep background on the seller. The auction house says he'll be there tonight. You're an observant man, Zach. A hard man, but someone I think Mrs. Flinton might trust just because you come off so straight."

Zach grunted.

"As I said earlier, I think you could be an asset to my firm."

Zach had done nothing to make the guy like him. Hardly cared if people liked him. Would rather have respect.

"And I respect you," Rickman said, like he'd figured out that aspect of Zach's character, too.

Zach knew he was being influenced by the compliment, but also believed the head of the private investigative firm was sincere.

"Tell me the details." Zach walked, cane sinking into thick gray carpet, from the window to hitch a hip on the arm of one of the client chairs, the cane helped him balance.

"We're talking about several pieces of expensive furniture and an antique silver plate service for six, complete with punch bowl and other fancy items. The thing is, when pressed, Mrs. Flinton doesn't have a strong recollection of the exact pieces."

"They could be new and made to look like antiques. If they were engraved—" Zach began.

"Yes, that could be forged. The con could be anything from just scamming her for the money she'd spend at the auction, to setting her up for more sales, to getting a foot inside her door to rob her. We did the security on her home, but she only has one full-time person in her place, a housekeeper nearly as elderly as she."

"Sounds like the seller who contacted her is a real confidence man," Zach said.

"That's right. All you have to do is attend the auction with her, keep your eyes open."

"I can look at the stuff, but I'm not an antiques expert by any means."

"Look at the seller and any accomplice he might have. The auction house is clean, but they allow consignment sellers. You're a people person, you can spot cons."

"Why me?" Zach asked. "You must have other . . . operatives."

"Actually I don't have one right for this job. Some of my guys like a lot of danger in their lives, a lot of action. A simple case like this wouldn't interest them—and most are ex-military more than ex-cop. Different mind-set. That matters."

"Yeah."

"You ready to meet Mrs. Flinton?"

"You're offering me the job?"

"That's right. And it looks like you're interested. Beats sitting around, doesn't it?"

"And you want to see how I work. Work with clients and with you. Handle myself."

Rickman just did a one-shoulder shrug at Zach's stating the obvious. "Now let's have you meet the client." He reached over and pushed a button on his desk.

The door opened. Too late now to give voice to second, third, hundredth thoughts about taking the job.

But if he didn't like the client—a client, not a victim . . . or was she?—he'd walk away.

Rickman straightened and Zach slid to his feet. She came in leaning on a walker. The tall woman, dressed in a quality but dated pantsuit, wore her thin silver hair in a wavy style. Her carefully made-up face showed a far-too-innocent expression for a woman of her years.

Her gaze went straight to Rickman as she took one careful step, then another. "Are you sure this is a scam?"

Tony inclined his head, gesturing to Zach. "May I introduce my associate, Zach Slade? He's an ex–deputy sheriff and policeman. Zach, what's your professional opinion of the setup?"

Angling toward her, Zach said, "I believe someone is playing on your sentiments to line his pockets."

Her lips quivered. She really should be less wide-eyed at this time in her life.

"With your permission," Rickman said, "I'd like Zach to accompany you to the auction tonight."

Now her blue eyes narrowed as her gaze fixed on Zach. She clumped toward him, chin stubborn, and held out a white hand with blue veins showing beneath. He took her fingers, felt a warm, strong clasp.

"Oh!" She grinned, and while her hand clamped around his, her glance went to Rickman. "I should have known you wouldn't have given me to one of your regular guys, Tony." She met Zach's eyes. "You have a touch of the *sight*, don't you?"

What the hell did that mean? The back of Zach's neck itched. He shot Rickman a narrow-eyed look and got a bland expression. Just what kind of place was the PI running, and just what had he and the sheriff discussed about Zach? "No, I don't have any sight," Zach said.

Mrs. Flinton removed her other hand from her walker and wrapped it around Zach's. "You're in denial, are you? You'll be fine with me. I promise." Her silver brows twisted a bit. "Hmm." Again she smiled at Rickman. "You said Zach just got in from Montana?"

"That's right," Rickman said.

She smelled of a light floral fragrance that Zach hadn't associated with old ladies until now. Clare Cermak had had a more exotic, spicy scent that had teased his nostrils.

"You can stay with me. I have a huge old house in Cherry Creek."

"Mrs. Flinton—" Rickman began.

"I don't think—" Zach started at the same time.

Her set chin lifted. "I insist. I have a housekeeper's suite that's been converted into a street-level walk-in apartment that would be fine for you. My own living area is in the main wing on the second floor. We can talk about a reasonable rent later, when you take me to tea."

Zach's stomach rumbled.

She appeared triumphant. "There! You're hungry, too."

Rickman pushed away from his desk, plucked Mrs. Flinton right out of the cage of her walker, and she let Zach's hand go. He let out a grateful breath.

"Come on, Aunt Barbara, let's take this a little slower, eh? Give the guy some room."

"I want to give him a whole apartment!" she said.

Zach retreated to the window overlooking the plains. His day was turning downright weird.

Rickman hauled giggling "Aunt Barbara" out of his inner office. A young Asian guy who moved like a martial artist, dressed professionally, came and picked up the walker, then nodded to Zach.

"I'll meet you at the Brown Palace in a half hour, Zach!" Mrs. Flinton called back, her fingers waving above Rickman's shoulder. "Mr. Yee, I have a new tenant for the ground floor."

"Sounds good. I will call the Brown Palace and make an appointment for tea," said Yee.

"Aunt Barbara, Yee—" Rickman began.

Zach had made a mistake in not closing the door. Mrs. Flinton, now solidly back on her walker, stared at him. "Zach Slade, you can't tell me that you aren't staying in a motel. Not even a hotel here in Denver, but"—her eyes became distant—"in the northern suburbs."

He wasn't going to admit she was right; good guessing on her part, though.

"Yee will escort you to the Brown Palace, Aunt Barbara. I'll see if Zach can make it."

"See that he does. He'll be good for you, Tony, and your business, and me. And we'll certainly be good for him." She jerked her head in a nod toward Zach, then at Rickman, glanced at the young blond woman manning the reception. "I'll see you later, Samantha; have a good day."

"You, too, Mrs. Flinton," Samantha piped.

"Maybe Samantha might like tea—"

A jolt went through Zach; was Mrs. Flinton setting him up

with a girl, too? A *girl*, not a woman. Clare Cermak was a woman.

"No," Rickman said. "The last time you took Samantha to 'tea' she got drunk on champagne and missed the rest of the day."

"Really, Tony, you are such a poor sport."

"Uh-huh."

Yee opened the outer door. "Come on, Mrs. Flinton. The Brown Palace is waiting for you." He smiled a charming smile that worked on the old lady. She turned and moved away with more grace and less sound than she'd shown before.

The outer office door closed, and Rickman came in and closed his inner door.

"Aunt Barbara?" Zach questioned.

Rickman took the chair behind his desk. "An honorary aunt, friend of my grandmother's."

"A very unique individual."

Rickman's eyes had gone a thoughtful deep gray, and something moved in his gaze that Zach couldn't put his finger on. "She likes you. Thought she would. And she's right much of the time. You going to tell me you aren't holed up in some motel in the northern 'burbs?" he shot back.

Zach gave him a flat stare that had no effect on the man. Zach needed to do that background search he hadn't bothered with before on Rickman. Zach had been so sure he wouldn't go private.

"And am I expected to pick up the tab for tea?"

Rickman stared. "Got under your skin, didn't she?"

Zach shrugged.

"Let her pick up the tab," Rickman said. His smile was crooked. "We'll be giving her the friends-and-family rate." A few heartbeats of silence. "Your consulting fee will be the one we discussed before."

Which meant Rickman himself would take the discount hit.

Zach didn't contradict him. He'd see whether he could work for the guy. Going private left a bad taste in his mouth.

Rickman grinned, showing his teeth. "Go have tea."

* * *

Clare and Arlene managed to finish looking at all four houses before rush hour traffic started at three P.M. and Arlene dropped Clare back off at her house. She and Arlene discussed each place on the way home, and more of what Clare was looking for. Clare ignored Enzo's comments from the backseat.

She dredged up a smile and a wave for Arlene but had to concentrate to pick up her feet instead of shuffle along the sidewalk. She actually considered a nap, especially since she'd have to attend an auction that evening. Of course she considered skipping it but didn't think Enzo would let her do it.

She plunked her leather bag that contained the books on Jack Slade next to a comfy old wing chair and sank into it, a little hungry but too weary to eat.

Enzo sat in front of her looking like an old black-and-white photograph. He scratched his ear with his hind leg. All right, an early silent movie.

I did not like any of those houses, Clare. The ghosts were not friendly.

Ignoring that she didn't believe in ghosts, she pulled the knitted afghan from over the chair and pulled it around her. Weird. The house should be hot.

Clare, are you listening to me?

Sleepy, she muttered, "You've been talking all darn day." Even when she'd been focused on Zach, Enzo's comments had buzzed in her mind, not that she recalled them much.

I LIKE Zach Slade. He smells right!

Oh, yeah, Enzo had said that, had danced around the table, had checked out the guy—well, she had, too.

Jackson Zachary Slade wasn't her usual sort, obviously more of a physical guy; just the way he moved showed that, even with the cane. She did like looking at his shoulders— hair a little longer and shaggier than she normally preferred, but it had looked good on him. His hair appeared silky, and black with tints of dark brown. He had strong features with prominent cheekbones and a skin tone that could indicate that trace of Native American blood he said he had. His eyes were a changeable blue-green, and the heat in those eyes as he looked at her had her own blood dancing a Gypsy beat.

A sexy, interesting guy who'd listened to her, and, even better, liked what he saw in her.

There'd been an enticing physical attraction, a hum in the air that promised heat.

Smiling, she wiggled a little and pulled the afghan over her shoulders, eyes nearly closed before she realized a pair of translucent gray trouser legs stood before her chair and she jolted awake, clutching the blanket close.

There he was again: Jack Slade, looking enough like the drawing to be identified by it. Which was rather interesting because the portrait hadn't been completely verified as the man.

"Jack Slade," she said.

He made a short bow.

"I met someone with a name like yours today."

The ghost bridled. *What?*

"His name is Jackson Slade." Now that she could compare them, the current Jackson Zachary Slade didn't look a bit like the vision her imagination painted before her.

My name, said the ghost, *is Joseph Albert Slade*, but his expression turned softer, sorrowful. *My lovely wife never bore a child; I never fathered one.* The shadows darkened in his eye sockets. *I don't believe much of the Slade line in Illinois persisted, either.* He waved a hand, as if that were unimportant, as if anything other than his own personal problems were unimportant.

"Did you kill Jules Beni?"

Jack's smile was fierce, showing a white gleam of teeth. He ran his fingers over his pocket-watch chain, then put his hand over one of the areas of his torso that showed the lead that had remained inside him. Jules Beni had been the one to ambush and shoot Jack.

"Did you kill Jules Beni?" Her voice was shriller than she liked, but her throat was colder.

EIGHT

◆─────◆

NO. THE APPARITION shrugged. *I put a reward, dead or alive, on Beni's head. The money was considerably more for him alive. My men killed him. He was dead when I got to the Cold Springs stage station.*

"Much of your life is nothing but legend," Clare murmured, flipping mentally through the facts, trying to figure out what next she'd ask him to satisfy her curiosity.

You promise you will get the box tonight? he insisted.

Her mind went to how much money she had. A fortune. She should easily obtain the box. "Yes."

Good. We will talk later, then. A brief smile from him had her nearly smiling in return. The gunman was not an incredibly handsome man, but not an ugly guy by any means. "There's no need to bother on my account," she said.

But he'd vanished and the cold diminished, and she tilted sideways in her chair. Surely she'd dreamed that visitation? Dreamed them all?

Maybe.

She hoped.

*　*　*

Zach could have stopped the gentle steamrolling of Barbara Flinton, but the old woman was as soothing as Clare Cermak had been exciting—as soon as he'd firmly stopped any talk about woo-woo stuff from Mrs. Flinton.

As he listened to her stories, her persuasion that she *needed* the antiques that were being offered that night at the auction house, his own past rose. No, he didn't think he'd ever find out what happened to his brother, Jim, and that would be a continuing ache.

But he could make sure that no one conned this old lady.

And he convinced her to listen to him that night at the auction, even as she pressed him to "just take a peek" at the apartment she had vacant. "Perfect for a young man like you, with a separate entrance so you can have private visitors." She winked at him.

He figured that Rickman had probably put a security cam over that entrance, especially if no one was using the apartment now.

When her driver texted that traffic was beginning to pick up and they should end their tea, Zach paid for the meal and helped Mrs. Flinton into the hired Mercedes, then gave in to her entreaties to go home with her. His car was safe in a parking garage, and he sure didn't want to fight rush hour—rush *three* hours—to head north out of the city, especially since he'd only have to turn right around and come back for the auction.

The car pulled into a quiet circular drive in Cherry Creek North and parked. Yee came around to help Mrs. Flinton out and hand her the walker, then told her when he'd return to pick her up for the auction.

Yee met Zach's eyes above the car when he exited the other side and gave him a brief nod. Apparently this guy, Mrs. Flinton's regular driver from the hired car company, approved of Zach, too.

Zach returned the nod, then stilled as he saw the house— the mansion. The rough-cut stone was gray with occasional flecks of silver winking in the sun, and the fence at the side of the house showed silver-tipped iron spears. Something inside him just surrendered and accepted he'd be living here.

Hunches were one thing—cops and deputies ran on those—but not many of them, including him, believed much in fate.

He scanned the whole area—the drive that wended between stone pillars, huge front yard, portico porch, front walk, and smooth pathway to a side door under a carriage light. No crows.

Keeping pace with a spry Mrs. Flinton, he followed her to the portico and they mounted the three steps of the stone porch at the same time and the wide wooden front door opened.

The woman who looked at Zach might have been as old as Mrs. Flinton, but appeared a lot more solid, muscle and fat. Her gray-shot-with-blond hair lay in a braid around her head; her pale blue gaze lingered on his cane. "Well, come on in, Barbara. Bet you're pleased with yourself; tea at the Brown Palace!" the woman said in a Minnesota-accented voice.

"I only had one glass of champagne, Bekka," said Mrs. Flinton in a virtuous tone.

It had been more like one and a half before Zach had taken the glass away when she'd confided she was on a limited alcohol regimen.

"And I've brought home a tenant." Mrs. Flinton stopped moving and gestured from herself to Zach to the housekeeper. "Mrs. Rebecca Magee, may I introduce Zachary Slade—"

Zach tensed a little to see if his last name meant anything to the new woman; it didn't seem to, nor had Mrs. Flinton commented on it, so only Clare had made a connection with the old gunfighter.

Mrs. Magee nodded and Zach nodded back.

"Mrs. Magee is a friend who takes care of the house and me." Mrs. Flinton beamed. "We're Barbara and Bekka."

Mrs. Magee snorted, narrowing her eyes at him as her gaze swept him up and down, then she switched her focus back to Mrs. Flinton. "Tony Rickman called and told me about him. I've freshened up his suite."

"Good, good." Mrs. Flinton picked up her walker and got

moving again, though she slid a glance at him. "Zach's going with me to the auction tonight."

A louder snort, and the housekeeper stepped back, holding the door wide open. "Finally, someone with sense."

"You told Tony on me." That sounded like an often-repeated line to Zach.

He followed Mrs. Flinton as she sailed into her huge mansion. Eyeing her walker, he figured she could give lessons in movement to him.

And it occurred to him that he might think of other lessons—like visiting a dojo and relearning some moves—and a whole range of attacks and defenses featuring a cane. He'd have to buy stronger orthopedic shoes, dammit.

He got a tour of the first floor of the house . . . a little echoey as only three sets of footsteps moved around in the big place.

Then Mrs. Magee showed him the apartment that was part of the original building but had been the housekeeper's. He glanced at her. "Where do you live?"

She smiled smugly. "In the old carriage house." She flicked a hand toward the back of the building. "Not on site." Her smile turned warmer when she looked at Mrs. Flinton. "Barbara is nice, but the late Mr. Flinton . . ." She shook her head.

Abuse? Zach's face hardened. Mrs. Flinton put her hand on his arm. "No, no, nothing like that. Just a demanding man who didn't sleep much."

Mrs. Magee drew herself to her full height, about five inches shorter than his six feet, four inches, fixed a stare on him, and crossed her arms. "I am not available for meals at two in the morning. Even if I work here."

Zach shrugged, gestured to the counter of the small Pullman kitchen. "I can cook."

The housekeeper sniffed. "We have breakfast at seven A.M., lunch at twelve thirty, and dinner at five thirty."

"You'll make enough for three, Bekka," Mrs. Flinton said firmly. "Just put the leftovers in the main kitchen fridge for Zach. He's a private investigator and will have unusual hours."

Not as bad as cop hours, Zach was sure. And since he wasn't starting a new job in the public sector—and, yeah, that still stung—he wouldn't be low man on the totem pole and have to take graveyard shift.

"Like this evening," Mrs. Magee said. She flapped her hands at Mrs. Flinton. "Shoo. Go take a rest, you were up at five this morning."

Mrs. Flinton pouted again and stumped out, her walker hitting the gleaming hardwood floors loudly with each step.

"Does she need help up the stairs?" Zach asked, before he realized *again* that he walked with a cane.

"Elevator down the hall," Mrs. Magee said, then gestured at the apartment. "Look around, it's furnished." Her slightly protuberant blue eyes considered him once more. "And though Mrs. Flinton might consider this a done deal, I know you have to agree, too." Her lips pursed, went in and out. "I think you'd be good for her, for us. We usually like to have a man in the house." She whisked from the doorway down the wide hallway.

"As long as he doesn't want meals at two A.M.," Zach said.

Mrs. Magee stopped and glanced over her shoulder, smiling. "Exactly."

As soon as she turned a corner into the back of the house, Zach closed the door that separated the apartment from the rest of the house. And realized his leg ached like fury.

Leaning on his cane, he scanned the large main room, getting the idea that a guy had lived in it not too long ago. The colors seemed too neutral for a woman. He wondered a little about Clare Cermak. She had that contradictory thing going . . . the bold Eastern European name . . . he wondered if he could do a little research on her . . . and the cool and tidy accountant manner. He could see her in red . . .

Picking his feet up carefully as he reached a faded but thick oriental rug—with fringe, for God's sake—Zach half fell onto the lushly cushioned leather couch. The audiovisual system was bad: small screen, only about twenty inches, old recording components. The place sounded quiet enough for him, no sense of a large and busy city, *that* was good . . . if he stayed . . .

His cell rang and he took it out of his jacket pocket, saw it was Rickman. "Slade."

"I've got a little information from the auction house on the con man. And he *is* a con man."

"Yeah?"

"Yeah. Name is Lawrence Whistler, or current alias. The guy told our local auction company, Compass, which has a good rep, that he is from Massachusetts and handed them an auctioneer's license and names of references. He just wanted to use their space on the way to the West Coast to set up his own place. Paid them a fee for storage of his stuff and asked to put his items on consignment in this auction."

Zach made a disgusted noise. "They believed all that?"

"The license was from one of the schools the local auctioneers went to. I followed up on that; no guy by the name of Lawrence Whistler ever attended. The phone numbers of the references checked out when the auctioneer called them a couple of weeks ago—they aren't so good right now."

"Huh. I can just tell Mrs. Flinton that Whistler didn't check out."

Stretching, Zach put the cell on the thick padded arm of the couch, leaned down and kneaded at his sore leg, clenching his teeth with pain as he massaged around his ankle.

"That won't work," Rickman said. Zach could visualize the man shaking his head. "Aunt Barbara will believe only what she wants to believe, and she really wants these antiques to be her family's. She'll insist on going to the auction, maybe even confronting the asshole. Your job isn't done."

Zach grunted, then decided that a phone call needed more than a sour expression, like words. "All right."

"Keep Aunt Barbara away from Whistler. We don't know who he is or whether he'll get violent if the deal goes bad."

"Right."

"And walk in with that cop arrogance, use that cop gaze on him."

"What?"

"You know what I mean. Your whole attitude is 'cop.' One of the reasons I hired you. Most of my men can really intimidate—you know they're bad dudes the minute they step into a room—but you have the cop style. Better for scaring the crap out of some people."

Zach laughed, and didn't hear much bitterness lacing it.

"You *are* a deputy sheriff, a peace officer, Zach. You always will be." A pause. "My business . . . and my guys need you."

Zach's mouth fell open. He had no doubt that Rickman had some ex–special forces men in his business. He respected those men—well, those not associated with his father, the Marine.

Silence hung, then he heard Rickman's huffed breath. "Different approaches to problems. Just take care of Aunt Barbara tonight, all right?"

"You got it," Zach said, and Rickman cut the call.

A hard ball of tangled emotions loosened a little in Zach's chest, unraveled a little more. The first thread had come undone when Clare Cermak had looked at him with appreciation in her eyes for a man she might like to have sex with.

Now Rickman had actually said Zach was *needed* at a business.

Just as he was, bum leg and all.

He leaned back on the couch, letting the cushions prop him up. A thin gray line of exhaustion edged his vision. He didn't want to nap, to fall asleep. To be lame.

Because if a healthy and well-functioning Jackson Zachary Slade could screw up his life so badly, what could a lame one do? Not only to himself, but others?

He let his eyes drift shut just for a few seconds.

And he was sucked back into the darkness of nightmares. Again.

Clare and Enzo were only a little early to the auction, about twenty minutes before the event took place, and more people than she expected milled around the room.

Enzo led her directly to the box and it looked even more scratched and battered than the picture on the website; not at all impressive.

This is Slade's box! Enzo sounded thrilled. He nosed at it, but the dampness on his muzzle didn't smear the light yellow-tinged wood. *Touch it, and you will be able to tell!*

"Yes?" she said doubtfully, then snuck a glance around to see if anyone had seen her talking to herself. So *hard* sometimes to not answer Enzo. Surely a box that had existed since before 1864—the year of Jack Slade's death—should have looked more valuable. In fact, someone should have recognized it as more valuable. Apparently not.

Touch it!

She picked up "box of unknown date and origin" and turned the finely grained wood in her hands. It was smooth except for the nicks and chips and occasional bad scratch, with several knots. No latch or other opening showed, and she realized it was a puzzle box. It could have been a block of wood from the heft of it. Frowning, she tried sliding each side of the box as she'd done with the few she'd seen before; nothing happened. But the longer she held it, the more it seemed to have a fizzy sensation on her skin.

You are touching a personal item of the primary ghost you are helping. You are progressing with your gift, Enzo said, radiating more cold than usual.

Clare stiffened. She'd begun to understand when he was simply a goofy dog, and when he was . . . more.

We had to find a gun for John Dillinger, once, Enzo said in a lighter tone, ear twitching a bit. *John Dillinger was one of Sandra's favorite ghosts.*

No, Clare was *not* going there, asking no questions, admitting to nothing.

Again she slid her fingers around the box. It wasn't inlaid with multiple pieces, had no confusing pattern.

One of the auctioneers strolled up and glanced at Clare apologetically. "It *is* a puzzle box," the woman confirmed. "But we weren't able to open it, at least without the force it would take to break it."

"Ah." Clare nodded, glad to put the thing back down.

The auctioneer sighed. "Not one of our better pieces. We have some lovely antiques tonight." She gestured at one wall.

Clare wished to appear casual in her interest in the box in case anyone was watching and might bid against her, so she strolled toward the wall of antiques.

It's Zach! Enzo barked. *Zach is here!* The spectral dog galloped away.

Now that he mentioned it, Clare's gaze immediately focused on the tall man leaning slightly on the cane. He held it as if he didn't need it at all, like it was a prop, though Clare knew better. A pang of pity went through her and she wiped any hint of it from her face.

An elderly woman standing next to Zach said something . . . and bent down to pet Enzo.

Zach's head angled. He looked down, shook his head, gazed at the woman, then turned and stared at Clare.

Her stomach tightened and she flushed. She didn't want to talk about Enzo to anyone, especially not Zach Slade.

NINE

❦

CLARE STROLLED TOWARD the old woman, and the ghost dog that should definitely be a hallucination.

The woman straightened from her walker, which held a light designer bag fastened to the inside front. She offered her hand with a beaming smile and a sly, sliding glance at Zach. "Hello, I hear you're a friend of Zach's!"

Clare wet her lips. Zach stood extremely straight, a closed expression on his face. She took the woman's hand, and the lady's gray brows zoomed upward. "My, your hands are cold. Only to be expected of one with your gift, though." She put her other hand over Clare's and patted it. "Zach, introduce this young lady to me!"

Zach whisked a gesture from Clare to the woman. "Clare Cermak, meet Mrs. Barbara Flinton."

"Pleased to meet you," Clare said and a little *ping* went off in her mind. She knew of the wealthy Flintons. She opened her lips to tell her new acquaintance that she was an associate at a prestigious Denver accounting firm and realized that was untrue. Her shoulders slumped a bit.

"I'm pleased to meet you, too. And who is this fine fellow?" Mrs. Flinton braced a hand on her walker and bent down again to stroke Enzo.

Zach's blue-green eyes darkened, with the green showing more. His brows dipped, though he kept the same expression.

"I don't know," Clare said, and caught a fleeting twitch of the lips from Zach.

I AM ENZO! the ghost dog shouted, jumping up and planting his paws on Zach. The man flinched and Clare stilled. Surely he couldn't—see? hear? *feel* that imaginary illusion.

"You're a very nice dog," said Mrs. Flinton.

Enzo stared accusingly at Clare. She lifted her chin and ignored his dark eyes that looked more like holes than she was comfortable with.

Zach cleared his throat and his gaze slid toward Clare. "We're here on business."

"Yes!" Mrs. Flinton straightened. "I'm looking for some family antiques. A few mid-nineteenth-century pieces my mother had."

"A con," Zach murmured. Mrs. Flinton didn't seem to have heard him. Clare noticed hearing aids in her ears.

Clare met Zach's eyes.

"We're here on business," he repeated, touching Mrs. Flinton's shoulder, then nodded at Clare again. "And you? I thought you had furnishings coming from your aunt's estate."

"I do." Again blood rose in her cheeks as she sent a swift look at the counter, which showed small, uninspired objects like the box.

Of course Zach noticed her glance. He frowned.

"I, uh, am acquiring a box for an, uh, out-of-town friend."

His gaze sharpened. He'd noted her hesitation, too, and that seemed to pique his curiosity. She wouldn't have minded except he might want an explanation that she had no intention of giving.

Drawing in a breath, Clare said, "I don't see any mid-nineteenth-century antiques." With Sandra's estate Clare had gotten pretty good at judging furniture. She gestured and continued, "I see some twentieth-century reproductions of mid-nineteenth-century pieces."

Mrs. Flinton stopped, turned her walker to look at Clare, eyes piercing. "Is that so?"

Clare shrugged. "So I believe."

The older woman plucked the catalog from her purse, unfolded it, and pointed with a gnarled finger. "It says 'nineteenth-century sideboard, wardrobe, and wash stand.'" She stared in the direction of one of the auctioneers and lifted a hand. The woman hustled over to Mrs. Flinton.

Indicating the furniture, Mrs. Flinton said, "Is that the mid-nineteenth-century furniture?"

The auction house woman looked at the furniture and frowned. "No. We don't have any mid-nineteenth-century furniture tonight."

Mrs. Flinton held out the catalog. "It says here—"

"What!" the woman exclaimed. "I don't know how that misprint occurred."

Clare's attention shifted from the women to Zach, who thrummed with tension. His gaze was focused on a smiling man in a dark blue suit striding toward them.

Everything about Zach's manner had changed, sharpened. He stood arrogantly, eyes narrowed, ready to take action. Clare stepped away, unsure of him in this mood.

"There's Mr. Whistler!" Mrs. Flinton said, smiling and gliding with her walker a step toward the man.

Zach took two strides and set himself in front of her.

But Whistler's toothy smile vanished and his rising hand dropped. He changed paths abruptly, and Clare thought he tried to make it seem as though he'd seen someone he wanted to speak with. He angled away from them, hesitating briefly now and then to drop a word in someone's ear, then sauntered to one of the exits and left.

Zach began to advance after him.

"Well!" Mrs. Flinton huffed. "Zach, please stay with me."

Zach hesitated, then stilled. He appeared predatory, nearly straining to follow Whistler. Then he muttered, "The client is always right. I *hate* this. I could've had him."

Mrs. Flinton tilted her head toward Zach, brow wrinkling as if she hadn't heard. Zach pivoted back toward them with a teeth-gritted smile of his own.

"Hmm," Mrs. Flinton continued, tapping Zach's muscle-clenched arm. "Shall we look at that silver I was prepared to bid on, with an expert?" She beamed at Clare.

Clare shook her head. "I'm no expert. You'll need one of the people who work here." Even with the crowd, she thought a staff member would be available for Mrs. Flinton. If Clare knew her name and status, so would the salespeople.

As Mrs. Flinton smoothly crossed the room to the silver, she gathered a middle-aged man who turned out to be one of the partners in the Compass auction house. They spoke a little about the silver; the man shook his head at the newly engraved initials on the pieces and pointed out that they were made to look old. Jaw flexing, he apologized to Mrs. Flinton for the quality of the work and stalked off to speak with his partner and brother.

Mrs. Flinton emitted a heavy sigh, moved to one side of her walker, and leaned against Zach. His arm came around her and he said, "I know you wanted these to be your family's antiques."

Her mouth turned down in a fierce scowl. "I wanted to hope. It's mean to prey on someone's hope. Zach, I want you to investigate where and when and how those pieces disappeared and what might have happened to them."

He winced. "The trail's long cold."

"You can start with Mama and Papa's last housekeeper, Mrs. Langford. She was young and came from a long-lived family. She might still be alive, or have relatives who might know." Mrs. Flinton stared up at him, her eyes a deeper blue than Clare had noticed before. "And you can work with computers, too, right?"

"Yeah," Zach said.

With a firm nod, the elderly lady said, "You're part of Tony's company. I'll let him know that I want you to work on this for me."

Zach had gotten a position already? What kind? A sliver of envy stabbed Clare. He had something interesting to do with his life. She . . . didn't. And where was Enzo? Not that she'd missed him. She scanned the room and saw him sitting next to the box, apparently guarding it.

"Now we can see what interests Clare, here," Mrs. Flinton said.

"No, really . . ." Clare began.

But Mrs. Flinton was off.

Zach reached down and clasped her fingers, causing her to glance up at him.

"Your hands *are* cool. Plenty of people here to generate warmth, but the air-conditioning is on, too." He grimaced. "Not much drop in the temperature in the nights nowadays."

"No." She liked the feel of his hand, callused in places she wasn't familiar with—from carrying a gun? Using it? Probably. She liked the tingles that went through her at his touch, too.

Most of all she liked the interest in his changeable blue-green eyes. They'd been hard when he stared at Whistler, but his gaze seemed softer now. He touched the thick strap of her sundress. "Pretty Clare."

"Thank you. I'm naturally tan."

"Beautiful," he murmured.

For the first time that evening her blood heated to warm her. She nearly closed her eyes, the sensation felt so sweet. Her lashes lowered and she smelled him . . . man, and a hint of leather and just Zach. Very, very nice.

"Thanks. I find you very, very nice, too."

Her head jerked up and her eyes popped open. She'd said that "very, very nice" aloud?

His lips had turned up in the first genuine good-humored smile she'd seen from him that evening.

Enzo yowled, and words formed in her mind. *The auction will be starting soon!*

With a sigh, Clare moved away from Zach's lips, so close that her own had tingled with anticipation. This was not the time or place to kiss him. And she didn't want to show him the box or lie to him about it.

Mrs. Flinton aimed a wide smile at them, and to Clare's pleasure, Zach tucked her hand between his side and elbow. He certainly was warm.

They crossed the room. She understood his slow pace and noted that he lifted his left knee more, only noticeable if you paid attention. His slow progress didn't bother her, and all the rest of his movements were executed with muscular grace. She wondered how much effort it cost him to try to walk normally—and how small her problems seemed when she considered his. Well, maybe losing your mind wasn't small, exactly, but she had hope that could be beaten . . . eventually. For right now she'd give in to the figments just to have her mind quiet so she and the psychologist could fix it.

Mrs. Flinton looked down at the box. "Interesting," she said.

"How did you know what Clare was looking at from across the room?" Zach asked.

"The dog told me."

Clare stiffened and attempted to school her face into the blandness that matched Zach's voice, even as Enzo had risen to his feet and was rubbing himself on her bare legs. She couldn't suppress a shiver.

"The dog?" Zach said. "You mentioned him before."

The silvery-gray illusion that was Enzo sat in front of Zach and lifted a paw, though he looked at Clare. *She can hear me if I shout. And he can hear me if I try hard, too. You should tell him about me.*

She wouldn't.

Mrs. Flinton lifted her chin and answered, "The ghost dog accompanying Clare."

Zach said nothing; he leaned on his cane and stared down at the box. "Junky box."

Clare's shoulders tensed, and she moved them to relax the muscles. "I know." She pressed her lips together, then said, "But I promised I'd buy it, and I keep my promises." Even to apparitions of her own mind. Maybe there was something in her that wanted this particular thing. Most of the events in her life lately had taken on a dreamlike quality. She hadn't ever been the sleepwalking sort, but that could be another, a *different*, problem she was suffering. Maybe there was something in the box that *she* had lost and needed. It might even have belonged to Sandra at one time.

Plenty of other options than Jack Slade, the gunfighter who was a "real" ghost.

One of the staff clanged a bell.

Zach stepped away from the table, and Clare realized a couple of her fingers had curved into his sports jacket and she let her hand fall. "Shall we leave?" he asked Mrs. Flinton.

TEN

CLARE SWALLOWED HER protest to ask them, especially Zach, to stay. Not to leave her with the dog, who seemed to also be visible to Mrs. Flinton, and who might also affect Zach.

"Leave since I won't be bidding on anything?" Mrs. Flinton's voice quivered. "Not . . . not yet. Whistler didn't come back?"

Clare examined the room, but apparently Zach didn't need to do that. He said, "No. Probably he's long gone and his name isn't Whistler anymore. I'll report that to Rickman and he'll decide how much to follow up."

"Whistler abandoned his items?" Mrs. Flinton asked.

"We don't know anything about those items. My best bet is that he stole them. Or he'll contact the auction house later."

Mrs. Flinton sniffled, then waved at the plum wood box. "The box is in the first lot to be auctioned. Let's stay for that." She stood straight and turned her walker to the rows of chairs.

"Thank you," Clare said. She looked up at Zach. "And thank you for staying. I know this is business for you."

He smiled down at her and her pulse sped up; her cheeks warmed as if she were blushing again. "Pleasure mixed with business," he said. Then he winked. "And what if I told you I was getting paid by the hour?" His free hand curved around her elbow. She hadn't realized that bone was cold, too. She should just keep him around as a personal heater. She felt warm all the way to her core . . . her body interested in his.

She struggled to recall what they'd been talking about, some topic that she, as an accountant, should have picked up on as they progressed smoothly toward where Mrs. Flinton sat . . . oh. "If you told me you worked by the hour, I'd be very surprised . . . unless you got a consulting job?"

The smile edging his lips flattened. "No. Trying my hand at private security and investigation."

Obviously he wasn't as pleased as she'd thought he was, and she didn't know why. "You'd be good at that," she replied matter-of-factly.

His brows came down. "You think?"

"Absolutely."

"What are you discussing?" asked Mrs. Flinton as Clare negotiated beyond the walker and Mrs. Flinton's end seat and took the second chair down, letting Zach sit next to the older woman—his client. He treated her very well, and that boosted him in Clare's estimation.

Clare raised her voice so Mrs. Flinton could hear. "I think Zach will be excellent in a private security and investigation job," Clare said into a sudden silence that fell when the auctioneer stepped onto the platform.

People turned to look at them, and Zach, who now appeared so coplike that even Clare, a very law-abiding citizen, noticed. Some people slid from their chairs and slipped out the nearest exit.

"Thank you," Zach said, setting his cane—which somehow now looked like a weapon. Interesting!—on the floor, then sitting down.

"Ladies and gentlemen . . ." the auctioneer projected, and everyone settled. "Lot one of unremarkable items to get you warmed up." He flashed a smile and there were a few sighs, some chuckles.

Mrs. Flinton snuffled, and Clare saw her watery gaze go to the large silver punch bowl as her chin wobbled.

Zach put a long arm around her shoulders, squeezed, then dropped it.

Clare leaned toward him and murmured, "You're kind."

His expression turned impassive, and she figured that masked his being uncomfortable.

Enzo wiggled into the space not quite large enough for a solid dog his size and collapsed on all of their feet. Mrs. Flinton smiled; Zach stretched out his legs so his feet were under the chair ahead of him, though his cane remained in Enzo's body. Clare felt the weight of Enzo's upper body, the chill of his drool hitting her even below her sandal strap, and she just suffered through, aware of his accusing eyes for ignoring him. Zach nudged her when the box came up.

She hadn't attended many auctions, but she knew the basics and lifted her paddle when she had to. Four bidders began, then diminished to three, then to two, and she got the thing for a hundred and fifty dollars.

"Paid too much," Zach murmured.

For a box that had been around in 1864? She didn't know. How special were old and scruffy items? The staff seemed pleased.

Mrs. Flinton led the way to the checkout table in an anteroom of the building.

"Thank you again for staying," Clare said. Zach's presence on her right side, his warmth and sheer solidity, balanced out the cold and mirage of Enzo walking along her left side.

Mrs. Flinton stopped. "You thanked me?"

"Yes."

"You're a good girl."

Clare paid and gingerly took the bag with the box in it, and then they ambled out into the night. In only a couple of minutes, a new-model luxury car drew up in front of them.

"Come to tea tomorrow at two P.M., Clare. Zach will give you the address when he accompanies you home," Mrs. Flinton said.

"What?" Clare and Zach asked at the same time.

"You two have a lot in common and should spend some time together," Mrs. Flinton insisted. "Inside, the dog distracted you from making more of a connection. Zach will accompany you home and make sure you're safe."

For an instant, sheer relief flooded Clare. Then she shook her head and said, "That's not necessary. You're his client."

Mrs. Flinton gestured to a stocky Asian driver who'd come around to open the door for her. "Mr. Yee is plenty of security for me."

"Mrs. Flinton—" Zach began.

"You told me where you parked today, and Tony Rickman has your car," Mrs. Flinton said. "He can have it sent around to Clare's address."

Anger fired in Zach. Yeah, he'd told Mrs. Flinton about the parking garage, but one of Rickman's operatives must have found his vehicle by the license number, which Zach hadn't given anyone. He hadn't done any paperwork to be hired by Rickman.

Zach shut down the irritation and loosened his grip on his cane, which he wanted to slam against the Mercedes. He had a job he wasn't sure of, though it had felt damn good to scare that son of a bitch Whistler with just a look. Zach had an apartment he wasn't quite sure of, either. Hell, he'd known Rickman had checked him out, would have gotten his license plate number.

With a sigh, he heard Clare give the location of her home to Mrs. Flinton, who arched her brows, nodded, and swept into the car. Yee closed the door on her, folded up her fancy walker, and put it in the trunk. He inclined his head to Zach. "Mrs. Flinton will be safe with me."

"Right," Zach said between his teeth, and watched as Yee drove away.

"I'm sorry you were forced to do this," Clare said.

He gazed at her, noting that she appeared pale under her natural tan. Man, how he liked to see the peachiness of color when she blushed. Staring, he narrowed his eyes. Might just be the lighting that made her pallid, but he didn't think so. "You okay?"

She jerked a shrug, opened the sack and took out the box, slipped the handle of the bag over her wrist. Her fingers worked on the wood as she turned it over, checking each side.

Zach studied the thing in her fingers and realized it didn't have an obvious opening. Okay, that made it interesting, and that the woman had bought such a box with no opening intrigued him, too. He didn't believe for a minute she'd bought it for a friend. Clare Cermak became more and more compelling. He certainly appreciated the sizzle between them.

"It isn't a solid block of wood, is it?" he asked.

"It's a puzzle box," she said in a stilted tone. "I haven't figured out how to open it."

"Will your friend know?" Zach kept his voice even. He didn't believe in her friend, and he thought she understood that.

She flushed, then went pale.

"What's in the box?" he demanded, a cop's tell-me order.

"I don't know." She looked up at him, angry.

He softened his tone. "Any idea?"

Slowly she shook her head, and it came to him that the contents *were* a mystery to her. "May I see it?"

"Sure." She handed it over to him quickly, another clue that it might not be something she'd wanted. Fascinating. She herself was a puzzle box a whole lot more appealing than the piece of wood he turned over in his hands. The box was smooth, but with an occasional sticky sort of residue like old grease covered with dirt and dust. He felt no moving pieces, either.

The bright outside lights had come on since the light blue-purple evening had become blue-black night.

"I guess I'll have to check the Net to open it up." Clare sighed.

"Why not let your friend do that?"

Again her flush seemed to warm away the slight tinge of gray under her skin. What was with this lady? She didn't strike him as overly emotional, and not nearly as out there as Mrs. Flinton, but Clare certainly reacted as if something were going on. Could she have been in on the scam with Whistler? But Zach had met her completely coincidentally. On the other hand, coincidences did happen. A bird called and he flinched. No, not a crow. Not.

And Clare frowned up at him, reminding him all too well that he had his own secrets and twitches.

She grimaced. "Yes, I can let my friend do that. He should know how."

"He?" Dammit, should Zach be interested in a woman this . . . with problems like he had? Maybe with demons like his?

Her lips moved into a half smile as she slid her glance toward him. "An acquaintance." He saw her stop another sigh;

her shoulders straightened. The guy was a burden, then, not a lover—at least not a current one, maybe a past mistake.

"May I have the box?" she asked.

Zach hefted it in his hand. "I don't think the cubbyhole inside could be very big; doesn't feel at all heavy."

Mouth twisting, she said, "I don't think it's ounces of gold."

A dog barked in the distance and Zach got a buzzing in his ears. He shook his head to make it go away and handed the light box back to her. When she reached out, her fingers trembled.

"Maybe I'd better drive." His voice was hoarser than he wanted because, damn, this quiet and tidy woman with the haunted eyes was appealing. But he didn't want to get mired in any of her problems.

Her full breasts rose under the top of her sundress as she breathed in. "All right."

"You've got an automatic transmission?" he asked, able to keep up with her slow pace across the parking lot. With concentration, he kept his left knee as low as possible and still kept his foot from dragging across the pavement. Grudgingly he understood that he needed to move on more than he had— he thought he'd been pushing himself physically, and he had, to get back into shape.

Now he needed to learn how to live as a cripple. Walk with stealthiness, use his cane as a weapon . . . maybe get the damn brace he'd been resisting.

When he saw Clare's car, he smiled at her very sensible choice, an older model that held its value. She handed him the key before he asked, and when he inserted it and turned, she went around to her side, a lady unused to having a gentle man open the door for her. If he'd been whole, he could have lengthened his stride, caught up, and surpassed her to open the door. His fist clenched around the cane. No more hitting things. Once had been enough.

He opened his door, stowed his cane in the backseat, sat in the driver's seat, leaned over and opened her door. Then he adjusted the seat and mirrors. The car was warm, but Clare looked like she shivered. "Are you all right?"

Another grimace. "Well enough. I'm waiting for some tests to come back."

"Doesn't sound good." Checking around them, he reversed and drove to the cut to the street.

Her chin lifted, her lower lip sticking out a little. For some reason he found that cute. "I'm fine. I *will be* fine."

Since he didn't care for comments on his own health, he said nothing more, but a chill tingle touched the back of his neck and sank into his shoulders—no sort of hunch or anything. If he'd been in a room, he'd have thought of drafts, but the summer night was warm. Too warm for the jacket he'd forgotten to take off before getting into the car. Clare had wrapped her arms around herself, so turning on the air-conditioning was out. He hit the switch to roll down the windows.

She tapped the detachable GPS and set it to "Go Home."

"I don't need voice directions; the map is good enough," Zach said. He *hated* the mechanical voices. He turned west.

They drove for a few minutes in comfortable silence. He couldn't recall the last time he'd felt easy being silent with someone close. Nice. "Clare," he said, liking her name on his tongue, a short and sturdy name. Another glance at her showed her pretty profile and the roundness of her breasts, the slight curve of her stomach. This woman wasn't a toned cop or athlete.

Her head turned and her hair swung, thick and shiny, smelling of some light citrus scent, clean and fresh. He recognized it . . . lemon and ginger, little bottles handed out by an upscale hotel. He drew in the scent of her, wanting that exotic note that had teased him earlier that day, even opened his mouth as if his tongue could taste her. Yeah, he caught that fragrance that tantalized—woodsy, spicy, some perfume mixed with her own Clare scent that indicated she was different than her appearance. Lust speared straight to his groin.

"Clare," he said, his voice thicker with desire. He made himself concentrate on the road, on driving, though his peripheral vision showed her breasts rising faster.

"Yes?" she asked, quiet, more vulnerable. That vulnerability called out to him now more than ever before . . . because he knew he was flawed so badly.

"I like you." Hell, that sounded dumb.

ELEVEN

BUT SHE CHUCKLED; more, she smiled so her cheeks turned full, and he wanted to kiss them, though not as much as he wanted to taste the nape of her neck, discover her flavor there. His dick thickened and he welcomed the sweet torment.

"I like you, too," she said.

"You're special," he said, and her expression closed down again.

"I don't want to be special. I want to be normal." Her voice turned crisp.

"Okay," he said mildly. "But you're rich."

Her body relaxed into the seat, and the curve to her lips returned, her arms uncrossed. "Yes, that I am."

"Feels good?"

"Yes, but . . ."

"But?" He took the last turn down her street, a dimly lit residential neighborhood. Now he was glad Mrs. Flinton had insisted he see Clare to her door. It looked safe, but a little shabby.

Nearby a dog growled.

"I want to be useful." Her jawline showed strong as he

pulled up to a small rectangular house with white siding. The porch light lit a tiny concrete stoop.

"I'm not the type to like just sitting on my rear," she said. "I want to *do* something."

He turned off the ignition, unbuckled the seat belt, and angled himself toward her. "I know what you mean." His own mouth flattened. "I've got enough disability and money to live on okay for the rest of my life." That came out bitter. He didn't care. If she hadn't researched him earlier, she'd do that soon, and better she see the whole shitty story online than his having to tell her. "I want to do something with my life, too."

She nodded, eyes serious. "But you've already found a job."

"I guess." More anger spilled out.

"Why aren't you satisfied with it?" She tilted her head.

"It's private work, being paid for, not serving the public, not helping folks who don't have the money to pay." That sounded too damn high-minded, but it was the way he felt. Emotions swirled around them. "If I'd been a police officer, I wouldn't have listened to Mrs. Flinton; I could have gone after Whistler and arrested him. Not as if he isn't going to try to con others. Better if he's off the street."

She blinked, then nodded slowly again. "I understand that." She glanced between the seats toward his cane. "But you can't work in the public sector anymore?"

"Not in the field."

"Oh. I'm so sorry."

They gazed at each other. He leaned down, closer, closer; she clicked off her seat belt and moved toward him, saying nothing. Barking started outside the car, and a cold stream of air from the mountains moved through his window. Clare frowned and Zach began to lean back, and then her eyes fired and she put her hands on his shoulders, tilted her head for his kiss, met him halfway.

He'd meant just a brush to test her and the kick they might have between them, learn the texture of her lips, but her tongue swept over his mouth and he opened it and welcomed her in. Here was the fire that he'd sensed below her buttoned-up accountant persona. Her tongue probed his mouth and he found himself groaning into her mouth with his breath.

She shuddered and pressed closer to him, her breasts against his chest. Pleasure roared through him, then stopped and built and spiked, wisping all thought from his mind.

Until he moved wrong and his leg shot pain through his nerves, killing all desire. Setting his hands on cold fingers, he lifted them from his shoulders, and when her eyelashes opened he saw loss and grief and abandonment in her eyes. What? What the hell was he thinking? He couldn't see that stuff in a person's eyes, not even a woman he was kissing. Could *not* sense that from her, emotions that resonated with his own.

Then her pupils focused and the shadows in her eyes became shades of emotions he couldn't fathom. She settled back into her seat, smiled, and it was an okay smile, not too bright, not sad.

"I think I told you that I like you, too," she said.

Released tension. This didn't have to be awkward.

"Yeah." He matched his stare with hers. "Completely mutual, Clare Cermak."

She nodded and opened the car door, slipped out with the smooth moves of a fit, healthy woman.

Zach snagged his cane, opened the door, and readied himself to get out. Clare awaited him on the sidewalk in front of the small path leading to the front stoop. Her fingers remained tight around the bag from the auction house. Zach definitely wanted to see what was in the box.

Slowly he exited, his bad leg stiff and aching from so much running around today. Real life, not like exercise at all. He'd have to change his program.

But he was facing real life, and that mattered.

He eyed the upper curves of her breasts, rising slightly over her sundress. He ached to get his hands on those.

Her breath remained fast. Her lips looked good, too. His favorite muscle hardened again. He grinned. Hell, having a sex life again, an interesting, pretty woman in his life was enough to think life was getting better. Even the job with Rickman, the apartment with Mrs. Flinton, both things that could be missteps, were first steps. His life progressed, and that soothed the anger within him.

He locked the car and held up the keys, pulling back to toss them at Clare.

Alarm crossed her face. "No, Zach! I'm bad at catch."

Zach kept his chuckle to himself. A woman who could admit to a weakness, a woman who couldn't match him in at least one physical thing, stroked his ego.

The dog barked and he heard it more clearly outside the vehicle, a bigger dog, a Lab, maybe. Moving around the car, his limp and the swing of his foot more pronounced than he cared for, he kept a smile on his face. She didn't even look at his awkward steps, seemed not to even notice.

More burden of feeling like a lesser man fizzled away from his heart into the hot air.

The concrete path to her door wasn't wide enough for two, so she walked in front of him. Light from the porch showed deep auburn highlights in her hair, her dress was thin enough to silhouette her shape, and he liked the sway of her hips and ass. Very nice.

His body agreed as his blood thickened in his groin, but his mind knew there was no chance of getting a woman like Clare into the sack on the day they met. She had great fire in her, sure, but she didn't let her emotions call the shots, Zach was convinced of that.

She opened the screen door, unlocked the too-flimsy main door and shoved it wide, then went into the living room. Zach followed her. Old furniture, some of it antique, was placed here and there, the pine floor polished and very clean. He approved of the long and wide man-sized couch that dominated the living room, angled toward the television, though her video system was pitiful.

The house was stifling; must be in the nineties, and it didn't look like she had so much as a window air-conditioner. The living room ceiling showed a light and fan. She turned on the light. Zach stared. She didn't seem to feel the heat at all. Sweat dampened his back.

And she didn't seem to think that she was in any danger from him. "You should be more careful who you invite into your house," he said.

She turned and still looked pale to him in the low light, maybe even worse. Raising her brows at his cane, she said, "I don't think you're a vampire."

That response took him off guard. "Vampire."

She shrugged her lovely shoulders. "Joke." Meeting his eyes, she said, "I can tell you were a cop. You've said you weren't happy only serving people who can't pay. To me, that means you're honorable. Mrs. Flinton, whom I know of, vouched for you and knows you're with me." She glanced out the wide open front door. "And someone will be delivering your car here any minute."

She dampened her lips. "I . . . I have defenses you don't know of, and"—she gestured to the half wall revealing the kitchen beyond—"I have pepper spray in the kitchen."

"Pepper spray in the kitchen," he said tonelessly.

"All right, all right!" She dropped the bag with the box on a coffee table that held a few large picture books on the Old West and hurried into the kitchen, coming back with the pepper spray, which she stuck on a bookcase shelf next to the door. He took it down and checked the expiration date. "You should have tossed this two years ago."

Crossing her arms, she lifted her chin. "All right. When . . . if . . . we, uh, spend some time together, I'll be more security conscious."

"Deal," he said.

"And, anyway, I'm sure the new-to-me house that I'm buying will have a security system."

He opened his mouth and she smiled, holding up a hand. "And I'll let your firm check it out."

"Did you find a house today?" he asked, remembering that she'd been meeting with a real estate agent.

"No." Her mouth turned down, and she looked around, sighing and shoulders slumping. "This house is a good starter house and it was the right price. But it's too small, and comparing it with Aunt Sandra's charming place in Chicago, where I've been staying . . ." She shook her head. "That house is gorgeous, by a noted architect."

"You're looking for something like that here?" he asked, hitching his hip on the round arm of the couch. He figured she'd find his family's Victorian home in Boulder full of charm.

Plastic crackled; Zach looked and saw the bag holding the box sagging. Clare had flinched and wrapped her arms around herself again.

Zach made a point of glancing at his watch. He'd like to

stay here with Clare, but the damn house was so hot! "Let's check out the box."

Clare went to the table, opened the sack, and took out the box. Frowning, she stood directly under the light and studied it, tilted her head, then pushed down near the end of one side. Nothing happened. "I think it's supposed to be like a teeter-totter," she said. "But it's stuck. Maybe I should get some wood oil or something."

"Maybe I could try?" Zach held out his hand.

She walked over and gave it to him. "That's the top, and the panel that should move. I had a puzzle box when I was a kid, and you slid a couple of pieces of wood to open it, so that's how I thought this one opened."

Something was a little off here that Zach couldn't put his finger on. "But now you think it needs to be pushed."

"Yes," she said in a stifled voice, rubbing goose bumps on her arms.

He reached out and put his arm around her waist, tugged her to stand beside him. With her came a nice trickle of cool air that seemed to swirl around his foot. Holding one end of the box, he pressed down with his thumb, felt a little give. He pushed harder, keeping the pressure steady. With an odd creak the box opened.

His breath whooshed out. Clare gave a strangled cry.

Inside was a mummified human ear.

TWELVE

"I SHOULD HAVE expected this," Clare said, her voice high to her own ears. Enzo sat next to Zach, tongue hanging out in a doggie grin. The shadow near her bedroom doorway was her imaginary friend, Jack Slade. Both Enzo and the apparition had told her how to open the box.

She shivered with cold and fear, glad she hadn't eaten anything for dinner since it might have spewed up.

Zach looked up from the box, face inscrutable, his pupils wide in the gloom, with only a faint rim of blue-green iris. "That ear looks damn old."

"The box is from about 1863, I think," she said.

"This has to do with Jack Slade, the gunman."

Clare twitched her lips up in a little smile at Zach's deduction and avoided looking at the secret cache in the box. "You know the story."

"Jack Slade cut off the ears of Jules Beni and wore one as a watch fob."

"Jules Beni was the man who ambushed Jack Slade and emptied a revolverful of bullets into him as well as a shotgun!" She didn't know why she defended the ghost.

Zach grunted. "They say Slade killed Beni."

Not true, said the slender ghost in shadows of black and white and gray, drifting closer.

"I . . . I like to think his men did it. Beni had stolen horses that were for the stagecoach and Pony Express. He'd returned to the area Slade had warned him out of. Slade put a reward out for Beni and told the military in Fort Laramie that he'd be hunting the man *before* his men found Beni," Clare said.

That is absolutely correct. The image of Jack Slade smiled at her.

"Not the sharpest knife in the drawer, Beni," Zach said. He actually touched the ear, lifted it out of the box, *sniffed* at it.

"Is it real?" Clare asked, though she had no doubt.

"Seems like." The grisly thing lay on his palm. Zach studied her again. "Where did all this happen again?"

Clare bent down and flipped open an atlas that she'd marked on the coffee table. She'd put small sticky notes on the places that kept showing up in her dream conversations: Julesburg, where Slade had been shot; the general area of Cold Springs Station where Beni had been killed—that was taking some time for Clare to pinpoint; and Virginia Dale, the station Slade had founded for his headquarters and lived in until his drinking and shooting up Sutler's store that had cost him his job. She pointed at the map. "In far northern Colorado and southeastern Wyoming."

Zach rubbed the ear with his thumb. Ewwww. "And when was Beni killed?"

Clare frowned, searching her memory. "Late August 1861."

"Seems to me an ear cut off in the August heat in southeastern Wyoming might mummify and still be around after more than a hundred and fifty years."

Gulping, Clare nodded.

A short honk came from the street. "I guess my car's here." Zach put the ear back in the box, then tilted the lid closed. Clare let out a little breath.

"I seem to recollect," Zach started in that Colorado ranch drawl Clare had noticed before, "that Jack Slade cut off both of Beni's ears."

"That's the legend," Clare whispered.

That is the truth, Jack Slade the specter said mournfully. *That's my great sin I need you to help me to rectify so I might pass on.*

Her inner shivers were getting stronger, and she might not be able to hide them from Zach. She wanted him gone before he noticed the tremors, and she wanted him to stay, just because he was Zach.

"And Jack Slade wore one of Beni's ears as a watch fob?" Zach said. "That's a story that sticks in the head."

Also true, the collection of shadows said. Involuntarily she looked at the vision. Yes, he wore a watch chain. No ghostly ear attached.

"So they say," Clare croaked, holding herself so she wouldn't shudder.

"No hole in this ear," Zach tapped the box as he leaned forward and put it on the coffee table. He stood, and when he smiled at Clare with masculine appreciation in his eyes, she forgot about her hallucinations. He stepped closer to her, lifted his hand as if to touch the vicinity of her chin, and she ran backward a step or two. "Don't you touch me with that hand!"

Zach blinked, then his head tilted back as he roared a laugh. When he was done he just shook his head and strode to the kitchen and washed his hands, Clare stood at the threshold and made sure he did so thoroughly.

When he came back she let him tilt up her chin and kiss her, more than just a press of lips; his tongue sought her own and she opened her mouth, gave in again to sweet desire. To blessed warmth.

Again he was the one to draw away and she was left aching, spinning in time and space and *needing* more, more heat and sizzle and release to this desire he stoked.

He walked to the doorway. "I like you, Clare Cermak. See you at tea at Mrs. Flinton's tomorrow."

The very idea cleared her mind a bit. "You? Tea?"

His smile flashed, easier than she'd seen before. The depressing fog of emotions that he'd seemed wrapped in earlier that day appeared diminished. If she'd had anything to do with that—well, probably just the notion of sex for him, she supposed—anyway, she was glad.

He said, "Mrs. Flinton offered me an apartment. I think I'll take her up on it. See you later."

The screen door slammed behind him when he left. She went to the front door and saw him wave to two men in a car that looked a lot like the one Mrs. Flinton had been driven away in. Clare wondered about the car service. Probably top of the line, and the one she was using was good enough and no doubt less expensive. Sounded like Zach had also signed on with a premier firm. Envy stabbed her; she'd been with the best accounting business in Denver. Zach got into a shiny newer-model car and drove off, giving her a wave, too.

She smiled reflexively at him, then shut the door to keep any cooler night air from getting into the house, which felt chilly enough. She touched the arm of the couch and thought she felt Zach's warmth, so she took the wool blanket she'd gotten out of the closet and folded over the couch, wrapped the throw around herself, and perched on the arm, not looking at the box. Enzo hopped onto the couch and stood staring at her with sad eyes.

You ignored me ALL NIGHT LONG!

"I didn't want to be taken for insane," she snapped.

Enzo slid her a sly glance. *Mrs. Flinton believes in me. We will have a fine tea tomorrow.*

Clare didn't have the energy to contradict him. Tomorrow morning she'd go to the library by hired car for more research, but she wanted to drive herself to Mrs. Flinton's, just to prove to herself that she could do it . . . even though she might have to map a way around town to avoid shades.

One particular shade bowed to her. *Thank you, Clare Cermak, for retrieving the box and the ear for me. The worst thing I did in my life was to cut the ears off Jules Beni, and now I must make amends before I am allowed to leave this place.*

No one really knew if Jack had cut off one or two of Beni's ears—until Clare had learned it straight from the ghost's mouth. Nor had anyone known for sure what had happened to the ears. The last report of one of them had been in a glass case in the Virginia Dale Station, but that information was hearsay, too.

Halfheartedly, she said, "You're welcome."

Enzo leapt from the couch and rubbed against the man, who petted him. *Clare is a very good woman*, the dog said.

Yes, she is.

I must return the ears to the place Jules Beni died and give them to him, as if I never cut them off, Jack Slade said.

Clare didn't know what that entailed and didn't want to ask. She sighed, then slipped from the chair arm to the corner of the couch, huddled in her blanket. "Where's the other ear?"

Lost near my headquarters, Virginia Dale stage station.

At least that building was still standing; Clare had a sneaking suspicion that the station at Cold Springs, where Slade had cut off Beni's ears, wasn't around since she hadn't been able to locate it on her computer. Which reminded her that she'd wanted to look up Zach's story on her tablet, but her bag in the tiny room she used as a home office was too far away to get right now, and she was too tired. She closed her eyes to sleep, though she suspected she'd already fallen into a nightmare.

When Zach stopped at Mrs. Flinton's house, he fished his old laptop out from under the driver's seat and limped to the side entrance to his apartment. Tomorrow he'd have to go back up to the motel in Northglenn and get the rest of his stuff. Man, his whole body ached. He set his jaw and hobbled to the side door. The guy who'd brought him his car had given him a set of keys for the apartment. Zach already had the alarm code.

He opened the fancy and heavy iron security door with a grunt, then the thick door of solid oak, which swung silently inward. As he closed the door behind him, his nose twitched. He smelled pie. So he set his laptop on the bar counter and took a tall stool. Yep, under a ceramic cover was a piece of pecan pie. His mouth watered. A note written in nice cursive said, *Milk is in the refrigerator—Bekka.*

Zach was so damn achy he didn't want to move off the round-cushioned stool; instead he fumbled at the silverware drawer just within reach, yanked it open enough to get a fork, and plunged it into the pie.

Homemade, oh *yeah*! Really rich on his tongue, a lot of calories, fattening. Eh, he could afford to put on some weight.

Still, he took each bite slowly, turning on his computer and checking his e-mail account in between bites. The first one he saw was an announcement of the date and time of a funeral for two deputy sheriffs. Tongue sour, he sent that message to archives, didn't quite delete it.

What would be his welcome if he showed up? Looks from the rest of his department as black as a crow's wing, and low voices muttering about him. Nah, he sure didn't need that. He was *done* with that; this very full day had proven so.

The next message was from Rickman, brief and to the point. *Aunt Barbara praised your actions tonight. Good job. Show up at 11:00 A.M. for consultation with T.R. in re: tracing Flinton antiques.* Zach made a mental note of that, figured now he was in a big city he'd have to break down and buy a smart phone. He was ready to click the e-mail closed when he saw an attachment labeled *Clare Cermak*.

He stared. Mrs. Flinton must have given Clare's name to Rickman. No doubt at all that the old lady had already burbled about the whole evening to the man . . . even regarding the invisible dog? Zach winced. But he hovered his cursor over the attachment . . . and opened it.

He skimmed the information. He already knew her address; he memorized her landline phone and cell numbers. Background of Gypsy extraction. He grinned at that. She *did* have fire under those prim clothes. Her parents were still living but world travelers, "employment unknown." Sounded like flakes. Might be why she'd been so focused on business. Zach could only agree with her need to contribute.

She had an older brother who was a golf pro in Williamsburg, Virginia; the guy was married with a nine-year-old daughter.

Seemed to be family money.

And Clare's Aunt Sandra Cermak had died a few months previously; Clare had been named the executor and sole heiress. *That* would bring problems, Zach figured. She'd inherited . . . millions, eight figures' worth of millions. Seriously wealthy.

Didn't stop his dick from rising as he looked at a gallery of photos. Beautiful woman.

A big paragraph in bolded type. Sandra Cermak had inherited the base of her fortune from her uncle, invested it well, but had made a lot more through her consulting services as a psychic.

A medium, a woman who saw and spoke with ghosts.

Bullshit, and no wonder Clare might be conflicted about her aunt and the woman's money. Clare didn't strike Zach as a woman who tolerated woo-woo. Just like him.

The memory of what Mrs. Flinton had said earlier at the auction house plucked at Zach's mind: *The ghost dog accompanying Clare.* Ghost. Dog.

But Clare hadn't said anything about a ghost dog.

Zach snorted, stood up from the stool, put the pie plate in the sink, and ran water in it to soak.

Just before he punched the button to turn off his machine, he saw the last paragraph, a comment by Rickman: *Aunt Barbara approves of Clare Cermak and says she can see and interact with ghosts.*

Zach winced.

Aunt Barbara also thinks that you have "the sight."

No, he damn well didn't.

But Aunt Barbara has informed me several times that she prefers to associate with people who have a touch of psi power.

Zach rolled his eyes and turned off his computer. His stomach squeezed and rumbled as if his juices didn't like what he'd read. As he limped to bed, he wondered what "Aunt Barbara" saw in Tony Rickman.

Didn't matter. None of them—Rickman, Zach, or Clare—believed in psychic gifts.

Zach slid into sheets softer than any he'd slept in since his grandmother had died. Luxurious sheets. The kind of quality of sheets that he believed Clare would have on her new bed. He couldn't wait to try them out with her.

And he would.

Clare gritted her teeth as she wrote another check to Dr. Barclay. She'd taken his first session the next morning to get the appointment over with.

He'd asked if she'd resolved her issues with her aunt before

Sandra had died. No. Clare hadn't told him there was no re-
solving clashing points of view on the reality of ghosts.

Then the doctor had led Clare to realize with a thunking in
her mind that not only hadn't she resolved her issues with
Aunt Sandra, but she'd been handling the full burden of that
estate, and the money from that estate had drastically changed
Clare's life. And Clare had quit her job. Not to mention that
she'd decided to move.

Death, job loss, and moving. Three huge stress factors in
her life.

Still . . . all she wanted to do was to talk about whether she
was going crazy because she was seeing ghosts; just fix that
one problem.

Dr. Barclay thought Enzo was a manifestation of a need
she had for friendship and fun. The gunfighter—for some reason she hadn't informed the psychologist that she'd discovered who he was—symbolized her rebellion against her
careless parents and their stupid lifestyle, or heavy unresolved
issues with Aunt Sandra herself, a psychic medium.

He was sure they could work through Clare's concerns and
eliminate her peculiar visions with biweekly sessions. Biweekly as in twice a week as opposed to once every two
weeks. It had been a good thing Clare had been sitting down
because she would have fallen off her chair at the thought of
paying so much to the psychologist. But if the sessions rid her
of seeing ghosts it was worth every penny. Probably.

She'd asked about the treatment schedule and he'd mentioned meds and an inpatient center as options if the visions
continued and she kept losing weight and having problems
sleeping. Those two options had tweaked her whole nervous system and she had to repress a shudder.

"Have a good day!" the receptionist chirped after Clare
had made an appointment for Monday.

Clare forced a smile, stuck warmth in her voice. "You,
too."

"Thank you."

Nodding, Clare crossed the elegant lobby to the outer
door. She'd worked with a couple of happy, optimistic people
and just didn't get them.

To Clare's surprise, Dr. Barclay came to stand at the

threshold of his office door, scrutinizing her. Checking to see if she'd made another appointment or examining her physical condition, which had not improved after a restless night? She nodded to him and left.

Enzo reappeared to whine at her. He didn't like the smell of the place and didn't even go into the reception room, let alone the inner sanctum that was costing Clare big bucks.

Walking down the gray and deeply carpeted corridor, she let her body sag. Dr. Barclay wasn't helping as quickly as she'd hoped. She'd be a thin and frozen skeleton before this thing was resolved, and from the looks he gave her, he was going to prescribe heavy-duty meds soon.

She didn't want drugs.

She did want this *over*.

She had some thinking to do.

Clare hit the library next for more information on Jack Slade and the headquarters he'd built at Virginia Dale. Though the Internet had good data on the current condition of the building that Slade had erected, and even mentioned the ear . . . most sites on the web reiterated what Clare considered a mass of legends and falsehoods about Joseph Albert Slade himself. She already had the books she considered definitive on the man.

After a couple of hours at the library, she nerved herself to once again leave the place and head for the restaurant she'd used yesterday. Walking in the sun didn't warm her as much as other people, nor did the sweaty folks in the under-air-conditioned mall bus Clare took to reach the restaurant.

She arranged the materials she'd copied from the library—noncirculating maps and reference items—and the books she'd checked out on the restaurant table. This time she sat outside in the warm sun.

It didn't take the brain of a private investigator or cop to follow the logic that if Zach had a new job with a security firm, the business was no doubt located in a downtown high-rise near the restaurant, since he'd come in the day before.

She wanted to see him again.

I do, too, said Enzo. *I like him a lot. He smells, really, really, REALLY good.* He sniffed lustily in demonstration.

She and her imaginary companion were rubbing along

fairly well today, probably since she'd tossed an occasional murmur to the dog.

So she'd ended up here in the sun at the restaurant to reward herself and hope for a much nicer session with a much more attractive man than Dr. Barclay, though that individual was sure of his sex appeal. Not that he'd done anything unacceptable. Not while she was giving him a steady income. Still, she got a sense that if—*when*—she beat these annoying illusions, the doctor might be interested in her. Nothing she could pinpoint, just a sense. And nothing that irritated or harassed.

She just preferred the rougher and more conflicted and incredibly more sexy Zach Slade.

"Hi, Clare."

THIRTEEN

꙳꙳꙳

SHE JUMPED AT the voice, the wrong voice, of the wrong man just outside the iron rail delineating the restaurant's space from the mall sidewalk. Frowning, she tried to recall his name. She'd seen him in the Western History room of the Denver Public Library more than once. He was the research assistant for a professor at a local college. Scrounging through her mind, she at least came up with his first name. "Hello, Ted." She smiled. "I'm sorry, I've forgotten your surname."

"Mather." He gave her a wide grin before he wiped a blue bandana across his brow. "Whew, it's hot today. How can you possibly stand it out here? Must be air-conditioned inside. You should go in there."

"I'm fine."

Enzo barked. *You should put on your hat.*

"I suppose I have a hat somewhere," Clare grumped. She leaned down toward her briefcase; dizziness had her stilling until she blinked and blinked again.

"Anything wrong?" Ted asked.

"No. Just looking for something," she said. Her mind cleared and she took out a visor. "There, that should be good enough." It would cut the glare of the light gray flagstones but still leave her head open to the sun.

You have not been eating well, Enzo scolded. *You are fighting me. Us. Your gift. Not eating well. Your health is deteriorating.*

"I'm still used to Aunt Sandra's place in Chicago near the lake. I haven't been home a full week yet." And it had been a cloudy summer in Chicago.

"I understand," Ted Mather said with a commiserating smile.

She'd actually forgotten he was there, a figure nearly too bright in a white polo shirt and beige pants. His hair was thinning and sandy and he had dark brown eyes. He was real, human, and alive, and he had color.

And her sanity was slipping. Her greatest fear.

She shoved that aside, forcing herself to deal with the man. "Can I help you?"

He chuckled. "No, I think I can help you. Can I join you?"

Help her? How?

Right now she began to think she should take any help she could get. From under her lashes, she glanced around the street. Her table was on the corner. No Zach Slade.

"Sure," she said.

He nodded and moved into the restaurant.

You need food! Enzo said. *Order some!*

"I'll be having tea later," she said.

Hours from now. You didn't eat dinner last night. You didn't eat breakfast this morning.

"I rarely eat breakfast."

"This is a good place for lunch," Ted Mather said.

"Yes," Clare agreed, though she hadn't had anything but coffee here the day before. She looked at the menu. A sandwich might be good. Soup might be better, though, warm her up, and she wouldn't worry about getting lettuce caught in her teeth if Zach showed up.

The waitress came and Clare ordered tomato soup. The woman gave her an odd glance but nodded and waited for Ted.

He smiled genially up at her. "Just decaf coffee, please."

"Sure," the server said, and left.

Ted scraped an iron chair against the flagstones. Clare gritted her teeth at the screech, bit her lip. She was obviously becoming too sensitized to . . . everything. Just when would the rest of those wretched physical tests come in?

"Clare?" Ted asked, now sitting across from her.

She forced a smile for him. "Yes, Ted?"

He beamed at her, reached down into his canvas messenger bag, and pulled out a fifteen-inch cardboard tube. "I got permission to copy this complete map for you. I saw you studying it this morning."

"Oh, thanks!" She'd used her tablet to take pics of several maps, in sections. Most of them had been the Pony Express trail with the stations marked. The map she liked most didn't have anything to do with Jack Slade, but it had excellent drawings and the dates that the route of the Mormon pioneers would have hit each stop. Pioneers often stayed at stations of the Overland Stage, including Virginia Dale, Slade's headquarters and where the other ear had been lost. She shivered.

With a big smile, Ted unrolled a copy of a southwest treasure map.

"Oh," Clare said. She'd liked the colors of the map, blue and beige, and had glanced at it.

Ted chuckled. "These are mostly shipwrecks and lost mines, not much about the 1863 Overland Stage robbery near Virginia Dale."

"What?"

He leaned forward confidentially. "I know that's what you're curious about."

It sounded to Clare that the robbery was what *Ted* was curious about.

"With all that research you're doing on Jack Slade," Ted said.

"Thank you for the map," she said politely. She shrugged. "But you're wrong about the robbery. It doesn't interest me."

"Of course not," he winked.

"There's no way such gold could be found today."

"New technology for locating treasure is coming up all the time," Ted said cheerfully. "And we're also discovering more about historical figures, able to trace them and their movements better."

Where did he come up with that faulty supposition? She began, "I don't think so . . ."

"For instance, after a hundred and thirty years, Australian bandit Ned Kelly's body was found in a mass grave. And after six hundred years, King Richard the Third's body was finally found in England." He waved a hand. "We'll know more about Jack Slade soon. It's only been a little over a century and a half."

"Slade's body is in Salt Lake City," Clare said; the man himself had been an enigma for decades. Most people had taken Mark Twain's description and stories at face value.

Ted huffed and waggled a finger at Clare. "It only takes time and effort and some money to trace anyone nowadays. Where Slade hid the gold is eminently discoverable."

She didn't think so; Ted obviously lived in his own dream world. He'd mentioned money, and Clare now had a great deal of that. Was this a scam? Like that guy who'd tried to con Mrs. Flinton? That sounded more reasonable. She said, "I'm not interested in that robbery, and Slade had nothing to do with it."

"Untrue!" Ted snapped. His easy smile had vanished. "Jack Slade masterminded the 1863 robbery."

Clare's temper wore thin. She pulled out her timeline and nearly slapped it on the table. "*When* was this gold stagecoach robbery in 1863?"

Ted goggled, licked his lips.

Tapping her timeline, Clare said, "In the winter of 1862 to early 1863 Jack Slade was in Illinois; then he headed to Montana."

"Plenty of room for error in 'the winter of 1862 to early 1863,' and 'heading to Montana' from Illinois," Ted insisted.

For sure, but Clare continued to press, "When in 1863 was the robbery?"

Ted's chin set. "I don't know."

Clare nodded. "Sounds to me that if anyone really wants to do some tracing, he'll have to do some nitty-gritty research. On more than the Internet." She took her paper and slipped it back in her briefcase. "Original source research." And if she believed in ghosts, she *had* the original source.

But she didn't . . . quite.

Ted rose. "I know how to do the research."

Con or deluded man? She didn't know, and as he frowned, she reined in her temper and said more softly. "There are a lot of legends out there."

"There was a gold robbery from an Overland Stage coach in 1863 and Jack Slade was behind it, and I'll prove that." His pale face with freckles turned red. He looked hot. She felt a little warm herself.

"I'm going to find that gold," Ted said.

Absolutely futile arguing with the man.

It's ZACH, Enzo said, wagging his tail. *I don't think I like this Ted. He doesn't smell right.*

Clare wanted to close her eyes at the idea of Enzo being able to smell, but not with a simmering man in front of her.

"Hey, Clare," Zach said. He stood just outside the iron fence. Though he smiled, his narrowed eyes stared at Ted in that cop look of detailed examination, Zach's stance dominant, authoritative.

Clare rose. "Hi, Zach."

With a short nod to her, Ted pivoted on his heel and stomped off, nearly bumping into the waitress with two glasses of water, the soup, and decaf coffee. Which Clare would end up paying for. She grimaced.

"What's wrong?" Zach asked. He didn't lean against the iron railing; probably too hot.

Clare waited until Ted strode to the street corner and hopped on the free shuttle that had just pulled up. "Not much." She gestured to the mug at the place where Ted had been. "How do you feel about decaf coffee, since I'll be paying for it?"

A corner of Zach's mouth twitched. "Cheapskate."

She gave him a stony stare. "I'm frugal."

"Uh-huh. I'll be right there."

And he was. He picked up the mug, snagged the waitress, and handed it to her, and asked for the luncheon special and the check by the time Clare had sat and taken a few spoonfuls of her soup. Rather bland, but that was probably her taste buds and not the food.

"So, Zach, tell me what you thought of Ted Mather."

I didn't like him. He has a nasty cloud around him, Enzo said. He'd moved outside the restaurant railing to lie down.

Clare tensed every time a person walked through him. No one reacted.

"Who's Ted Mather?" Zach took off his jacket and hung it over the chair back. The pale blue of his business shirt brought out the blue in his eyes, diminishing the green.

"The guy who was here just before you. He's the assistant of a local prof I've met in the Western History room of the library. Did he strike you more as a con man or delusional?"

Zach's gaze flickered as he considered, perhaps playing back whatever of the conversation he'd overheard. How much, Clare didn't know.

"Guy thinks he's going to find treasure?" Zach picked up the map and laughed. "Delusional. Pretty map."

"You want it?" Clare asked.

"You don't?"

"I don't believe the odds of finding lost treasure are worth the risk."

The waitress set a big toasted BLT sandwich in front of Zach. "Or ordering the lunch special without knowing what it is."

"How's your soup, ma'am?" asked the server.

Terrible. "Fine, thank you," Clare lied. It didn't even feel warm anymore.

Zach sat. "I don't mind a certain amount of risk," he said around a big bite of his sandwich. He nodded to the server. "Good food."

I bet it smells good in real life, Enzo said mournfully.

Smiling, the waitress left.

Of course Zach wouldn't mind risk; he'd been a police officer and probably enjoyed adrenaline rushes. The only adrenaline rushes Clare had experienced were those when she'd screwed up and had to fix a mistake immediately before someone else discovered it.

"When we were talking, I couldn't tell whether Ted was trying to get me to invest in his gold-finding scheme or not," Clare said.

"Didn't impress me as a slick guy," Zach said.

"No."

"A con would have had his whole scheme laid out, and answers to any questions you might ask."

"That's true." She sighed and swallowed another tasteless spoonful of soup. She could fall into brooding about her physical and mental health or focus on Zach.

Now that he concentrated on his sandwich, Clare noted the strain around his eyes easing. She hadn't spent a lot of time with him, but either the man himself or her new sensitivity to everything had her believing that she could tell when his leg pained him or something else bothered him.

"How has your morning gone?" she asked.

He snorted, finished chewing a bite, and said, "Well enough. I filled in the paperwork Rickman needed for my new job."

"Rickman?"

"Rickman Security and Investigations."

"Oh."

"I don't have a card yet, though I'm sure those are on the way."

She took a sip of water. "You're looking better."

His gaze met hers. "Thanks."

Dropping her eyes and carefully spooning another swallow of soup into her mouth, this one with a chunk of tomato, she said, "I think having a job agrees with you."

His lips flattened, and then he nodded and took a huge bite of his sandwich.

"Even if it isn't the sort of job you want."

Again he nodded, chewed, swallowed, then said, "Yeah, helping Mrs. Flinton last night felt good. How about you, Clare? We talked about contributing."

For an instant a whooshing wind blocked out her hearing, and her vision dimmed. Her accounting career seemed like ages ago.

Maybe like more than a hundred and fifty years ago. She *was* going crazy, but she wasn't going to tell Zach that, mention that she was holding on to the hope Dr. Barclay offered her or still waiting for her in-depth physical tests.

An image of Aunt Sandra rose before Clare's mind, wearing one of those cut-velvet scarf jackets, coming toward Clare with a big smile on her carefully made-up face that looked years younger than her true age, wafting the scent of the perfume Clare hadn't used that morning. That was a memory.

Sandra had sent a limo to pick up Clare the summer she'd visited when she was sixteen because Sandra had had a client for her psychic medium business that she couldn't refuse.

Clare shuddered. No. She would *not* be like that. No and no and no. She reached out for her water and it tipped.

Zach caught it and righted it.

He was staring at her. "Clare?"

Enzo was barking. He slipped through the rail and sat beside her with dark more-than-big doggie eyes.

Her mouth was dry. With focus, she got the water—why had they put ice in her drink?—and sipped. Then she summoned up enough calm to meet Zach's gaze. "I still have work on my aunt's estate."

She held on to that thought, hard, and took one steadying breath. "I'm hoping I don't have to go back to Chicago anymore, and I've been working nonstop on it for some time, but I think I only have a few last things to do."

Even as she spoke, her smart phone played music. She dipped her head. "And that's notification that a package has been delivered to my house, probably from Sandra's lawyer."

"I'm sorry for your loss." He reached out and took her hand.

The simple touch and connection staggered her. A spurt of tears stung behind her eyes as her phone continued its mathematical progression through a Bach concerto that she'd once liked.

Clare shifted her shoulders. "I didn't understand Aunt Sandra much, and she didn't understand me . . . but there was love." Once upon a time, before Clare had been embarrassed by her great-aunt. And Clare could admit to the love, now, aloud to a stranger who was getting under her skin.

"No one would expect you to be related to a psychic medium, Clare," Zach said gently.

She got what he wasn't saying. "You checked me out." All right, she'd been going to Google him, but Zach obviously had a lot more resources than she.

"Mrs. Flinton gave your name to Rickman. He was . . . concerned . . ."

"Since she invited me to tea today after meeting me in public for an hour last night." Clare nodded.

"Yeah. So Rickman checked you out and sent me his file." Zach's bluish gaze held hers. "And I was curious and didn't resist temptation." He squeezed her hand and his voice lowered. "I don't think I'll be able to resist much temptation when it comes to you, Clare Cermak of Gypsy extraction."

A fluttering low in her abdomen, *sexual* tingles, rushed through her. She was alive and had a fascinating man interested in her. Enough, for now, to focus on.

The music from her phone cut off.

"Go ahead and check," Zach said, releasing Clare's hand far too soon, picking up the second half of his sandwich, and munching some more. Clare could only envy his appetite.

She looked at the tracking app and noted it *was* from Aunt Sandra's attorney, then frowned at the note he'd attached, her stomach sloshing more with acid than the small amount of soup she'd had.

"What is it?"

For a moment she choked, glanced at him with a half smile. "We keep asking each other that."

His cheek creased in a long dimple as he smiled, too. "We're learning each other. What's up?"

"Aunt Sandra's attorney said that the package contained videos."

Zach put down his sandwich. "Was she the type who'd leave a personal video for you?"

FOURTEEN

YES, YES, YES! shouted Enzo, up on his feet and running around, barking. *Yes she made a talking picture for you, Clare. Yes she did!* He came over and laid his head on her thigh.

Clare hadn't needed his input to know. "Yes. And not only for me. He probably shipped one to my brother and his family, maybe individually for him, his wife, and my niece. I don't know . . ." Another grimace. "I probably have my parents'. They keep on the move." She looked at Zach. She'd like to stay with him, but . . .

Let's go see! Enzo said, then more quietly, *You need to watch yours.*

"Go." Zach echoed Enzo. "You and I will see each other in about three hours at tea, right?"

"Yes. Thank you for paying for my soup."

He stared at her half-empty bowl. "Doesn't look like you ate much of it."

"I'll do better at tea," she replied lightly.

He nodded. "And I'll tell Mrs. Magee to make something more substantial than cucumber sandwiches."

Clare blinked. "You know about cucumber sandwiches?"

"Mrs. Flinton reminds me a little of my maternal grand-mother." His expression closed down.

"Ah." Clare rose and lifted her bag to slide it over her shoulder. She'd already tucked her purse inside. The bag didn't contain as many books as the last time she'd visited the library.

Zach thrummed his fingers on the table, still looking at her. "Did you do an online search for me, Clare?"

"No."

His stare was sharp. "Do it."

She lifted her chin, kept her eyes matched with his. "I'd rather hear your story from you."

He scowled. "Not a story, facts."

"Of course." She softened her voice. "But I'd rather talk to you about whatever you went through. We're learning each other." She repeated his words.

Now his gaze pierced her. "Then you're going to have to open up more, too, Clare."

She pressed her lips together.

"Yeah, I thought so. See you later." He picked up the sand-wich.

"Later." But she didn't like ending on this note, so when she moved around the table, she came close to him and kissed him on his high cheekbone by his temple. "Thank you for the meal." She followed a racing Enzo out of the restaurant and around the corner, keeping her back straight, her stride smooth. She didn't look back at Zach, thinking he might have his cop-examination face on.

As she walked the few blocks to a hotel where she could catch a cab, she contemplated what she *hadn't* told Zach. The lawyer was sending Aunt Sandra's "journals." He called them "journals," but stated she'd called them "experiences and in-structions for Clare."

Like the video, "instructions for Clare on how to deal with her Gift."

She gave the cabbie a twenty percent tip, her pride stinging a bit from Zach's "cheapskate" comment and the fact that the taxi sure wouldn't pick up anyone in her neighborhood at this time of day when people were at work. Not like he would have if he'd driven someone to the airport.

The vehicle had been too cold, as usual.

On her stoop she found two stacked medium-sized boxes. Just how many journals did her aunt have? Blinking away tears, she recalled the loops of Aunt Sandra's overly elaborate cursive writing that Clare had trouble reading.

Another wearying challenge.

Oh, oh, OH! It smells like Sandra! Enzo said, and his eyes looked watery, too. As far as Clare knew, dogs didn't cry.

Grumbling, she picked up the heavy boxes using her legs, not her back, braced them against the house as she opened the screen door and unlocked the front door, then staggered in and set them down near the coffee table. When Enzo joined her, she said, "Maybe you should, ah, pass on, like Sandra."

No, he said.

She sank onto the couch, head drooping into her hands. This whole thing wasn't working well, trying not to talk to him and believe he didn't exist. But she didn't *want* him to exist. Didn't want Sandra's life.

It was easier to think she was going crazy, though that had her hyperventilating. Now tears did leak out of her eyes, dribbling warmth onto her fingers. After a minute she got up and started water for peppermint tea, then got a box cutter and opened the well-packed carton from the attorney.

The whiff of scent—more than just the perfume Clare had been finishing off—that consisted of Sandra's lotions, the incense she used during her sessions, wafted around Clare, and she sat down on the floor and wept.

It is sad we are left behind, Enzo said. For once he didn't come up and lick her or move into her body, making her even colder, and for that she was grateful.

"You can go on to be with her!" Clare assured him through sniffs, groping for tissues in her bag and blowing her nose.

No. You need me.

But she damn well didn't want him. Didn't want this. Even with all the money that came with this, this . . . stuff . . . that was tearing her apart. It had been only five days since she'd left Chicago and started seeing strange things. Not very long in general terms.

Long enough for her to doubt her sanity.

Anger warmed her, and she gulped back lingering tears and took out the inventory sheet. One line engendered dread: *Twelve journals with miscellaneous dates in each volume.* Hell!

Frowning, Clare pulled them out, one by one, all with colorful covers. She picked up one with a fairy dancing on the breeze that she remembered from a childhood visit. It fell open.

On the left hand of the page was a date ten years ago, on the right, about six and a half. Totally random entries, great, how was she supposed to research that! Then a sentence caught her eye:

I think Clare must be my heir. She doesn't think much of me, but that doesn't matter. Or perhaps it will be a child of hers or Tucker's.

God*dammit*! Clare dropped the book, opened the second box, and rooted around for hard copies of whatever Sandra had recorded. Lots of videos, one for each of her parents and them as a couple, one for her brother, her brother's wife, their little girl, and her brother and sister-in-law as a couple and them as a family. Finally one for her, at the bottom. Why hadn't the lawyer's office put it on top?

She readied the video, went back to the sofa, and sat down. Enzo came to her feet, looked up at her, and whined. With a huge sigh, she patted the sofa and he leapt up and settled next to her, not draping himself over her legs, thank goodness.

Clare pressed the play button on the remote.

Sandra, with her orange hair, blue eyelids, pink cheeks, and red lipstick, looked old and sick and scrawny, stabbing Clare with guilt that she'd avoided her great-aunt for so long . . . just saw her on holidays when Clare's parents were in the States, or when Clare went to her brother and his family's. Clare had actually been the one who visited Sandra the least once she was an adult—and had been all the more surprised that she'd been named as Sandra's heir.

Enzo wagged his tail and grinned. *She looks GOOD!*

Great-Aunt Sandra wore her favorite silk and cut-velvet scarf-jacket, deep blue with a sequined peacock and long tasseled fringe.

"Dearest Clare." Sandra smiled, showing perfect and natural teeth. "It's your weird great-aunt Sandra." She laughed. "Bet you didn't know that *I* knew you kids called me that." She raised her red-brown penciled-on brows, but her eyes remained merry. "All the kids." She paused and her old, soft face fell into folds. "As those of my generation spoke of my great-uncle Amos as 'eccentric.'" Shaking her head, she sighed, then looked directly into the camera, with the wealth of her home showing behind her. Clare was suddenly reminded just how fabulous it had been to play in that house. Hide-and-seek had been amazing, and Sandra had been absolutely marvelous in her childhood. Clare swallowed hard.

She wondered if Sandra had ever wanted children, or if her "gift" had prevented her. Was that why Sandra's house was so large? She'd expected to marry and have children?

Zach came to Clare's mind. She could see him as a loner, for sure, even though yearning for him, his touch, his lips, his body in bed with her bloomed inside her, made her ache.

Would it be an addition of crazy to complicate her life with an affair with him? Probably.

Could she get emotionally hurt? Oh, yes. But Clare began to think that grabbing whatever she could of life, living it to the fullest, was worth any pain.

"By now you've had your gift a while and know that ghosts aren't a figment of your imagination, and that they aren't going away."

Oh, no. No, no, *no*! Clare's thumb slid over the remote, but *Enzo knocked it from her hand*. A solid object. Her mouth dropped open and she stared, and though he appeared like the dog she'd kept seeing with her peripheral vision, he stood on the couch and his eyes were that otherworldly dark with knowledge that squeezed her lungs empty.

Sandra's voice jerked Clare's focus back to the video, where she saw the hazel eyes she'd inherited go steely and the red lips thin. "And, lovey, brace yourself, because I have more bad news and this will come as a real shock for someone as repressed as you are."

Clare tensed.

"There are great benefits to helping ghosts transition . . . both emotional and financial . . . the universe rewards you."

Ha, ha, ha. Clare would snort, but the woman had died wealthy . . . and Clare had found out how her parents could afford to globe-trot—from a trust Great-Great-Uncle Amos had set up for his nephews and nieces.

Would she be doomed to being a spinster aunt, too? She really didn't want to embrace the lifestyle of the eccentric or weird.

"Listen close, lovey. There are great rewards, satisfaction, and fulfillment that come with our gift."

Maybe for others, but Clare doubted that for herself.

"But there are also costs."

Oh, yes, the acid coating Clare's stomach was back.

"And the greatest threat, the greatest cost comes if you don't accept your destiny, if you ignore the ghosts."

Cold seeped into the room as the specter of Jack Slade, short and slender, solidified in the doorway to her bedroom, staring at her with an inscrutable gaze. Enzo settled next to her, looking nearly solid. *Listen!* he commanded in that low reverberating tone, glare fixated on her.

Dizziness had her tilting, her mind swimming, and she finally took another breath, drew it deeply.

Listen. It came like the rumble of the beginnings of a mountain avalanche that would destroy her life.

FIFTEEN

AUNT SANDRA'S LIGHTER voice spoke words that seemed to pierce Clare and coat her bones with ice. "If you don't accept your gift, you decline and die," Sandra said. "I watched it happen to Uncle Amos's brother, who inherited the gift first."

Clare's vision cleared to see Sandra's lips twitch into an unamused smile. "Though Amos's brother liked the money that came to him with the talent, fine. Just as, I believe, you do." Her voice softened. "Don't be hardheaded, lovey; accept the talent, our psychic gift."

Sandra's mouth drooped, and her shoulders slumped. She wheezed for a long minute, losing her upbeat appearance, fumbling for a handkerchief. Then she straightened slowly, drew a deep breath, coughed again. Now her expression was bleak, as if her natural optimism had faded. Her gaze fixed directly on the camera.

"I love you, Clare. Please accept the gift, learn to live with it. I know it will be hard for you, harder than it was for me, but please . . . try." Sandra blinked rapidly. She gulped. "I don't want to see you hurt . . . or follow after me so soon."

Clare gulped with her.

Sandra sat up even straighter. "You can do it." She put a clenched fist over her heart—that old and fading heart. "I know you can." Sandra lifted her droopy chin. "And I know you can be better than me. You have a good heart, lovey. Use it, let your heart rule your head for a little bit, please?"

Both Clare and her aunt Sandra inhaled at the same time. "Do this for me, first. If you think you really, truly can't, open the envelope my attorney is mailing you today. There *are* more consequences for the family, besides your death, if you refuse the gift."

Tremor after tremor rolled through Clare as she hugged herself.

Sandra cleared her throat. "Enough of that right now." She gestured to a low and sturdy prairie-style table where her journals were stacked. "I've written now and then about my experiences, telling you some stories. And sometimes wrote down what I think the rules to be about our gift, and whatever I recall Uncle Amos telling me."

"Rules," murmured Clare.

Sandra smiled wistfully. "I'm sure you're thinking about 'rules' now." Her fingers fiddled with the fringe of her jacket and her gaze shifted to the side . . . looking out the window, Clare knew. For an instant she grieved that she'd sold that beautiful house . . . but her parents would never settle and her brother lived in Williamsburg, Virginia.

Sighing, Sandra said, "I'm afraid you won't find my journals in good order, Clare." Another flex upward of Sandra's lips. "I'd have done better if I'd been a teacher." She stared directly at the camera again, "I wanted to be a teacher, did you know?" Shrugging, she went on. "But I made a very good life for myself." And Clare saw cheer bolster Sandra's body. She chuckled. "And the ghosts can be very entertaining."

One last intimate look. "I think that you are regretting not seeing me, feeling guilty. Don't do that, lovey. We both had lives to live." She looked to the side, "But John, John Dillinger here, says mine is coming to a close, and I'll pass in peace and have help all the way to whatever is next. You can do it, lovey. Be well. I love you." She blew a kiss and the video went dark.

Clare looked at the ghosts, Jack Slade and Enzo, thinking

of rules and consequences. "You'll hurt me if I don't . . . help you?"

Jack Slade scowled.

Enzo yipped and slurped her cheek with a cold tongue. *Of course not.*

The . . . universe . . . works in strange ways, Slade the ghost said.

Clare managed a nod.

Jack Slade said, *Gifts are given with strings attached.* He stared beyond her. *I had talents I used, and a sense of justice; sometimes they were great burdens, and I did well at first . . . but I didn't overcome my problems.* He switched back to looking at her. *Don't be like me.*

Licking dry lips, Clare asked, "If you . . . if ghosts don't hurt me . . . what happens to me?"

With a shrug, Slade said, *I don't know.* His strong chin jutted. *I haven't been near a ghost seer in a long time. It ain't a talent that comes around often . . . at least not around here.* He smiled, and there was humor and gentleness and compassion. *I'd be honored if you helped me out.*

"Out of where?" Clare muttered between cold lips.

His face hardened. *This hellish existence of no life, of memories and no reality, of impasse.* His eyes narrowed. *I listened to the old one speak of your family and your gift, and us.*

Enzo barked.

The old one, Great-Aunt Sandra. Clare stared at the ghost; he appeared a little more dissipated, but Slade-the-ghost had not made old bones, he'd lived to thirty-three.

She shivered again. Older than she if she died soon.

Clare lowered her head between her knees. Her heart raced at the threat to her life.

She thought of Zach Slade . . . the sexy man, and ignored Jack the demanding ghost—though both men were tough enough to handle life-and-death situations every day of their life. She was a sissy marshmallow.

And handling life-and-death situations on a regular basis had harmed both of them; she saw that, too, through the black spots floating before her eyes and as her torso went up and down from her pumping breath.

But nobody other than she could save herself. She had to do it.

Alone. Because who would believe her?

If you don't accept your gift that you can see ghosts, then you will die. And if you don't help them, you can go crazy, Enzo said.

Clare jerked in a shudder. Exactly what she'd always feared—madness. She was living in it now.

The video clicked off. End of the post-grave "instructions" from weird Aunt Sandra. Clare held on to that appellation as if it were a lifeline rope and she hung over a cliff after an avalanche, pebbles still pinging against her body.

What Sandra had babbled about was what *Sandra* had believed. This was not the truth. *Not reality.*

She spoke the truth, and you know it. Deep in your marrow, in the depths of your mind and your heart, you know this, Enzo said.

The alarm Clare had set for an hour before tea with Mrs. Flinton pinged. She stood on shaky legs and rubbed her arms under the long linen sleeves of her blouse. She'd dressed professionally again in a skirt suit but was suddenly sick of that, the past she held on to so strongly.

Heading toward the shower, she stood under it until she felt nearly hot and better, then dressed in a short-sleeved dress with a hem longer than she usually wore to keep her legs warmer. She picked up a sweater just in case Mrs. Flinton's mansion had air-conditioning.

Clare would be seeing Zach. That was a definite plus, though she still hadn't taken the time to do a search about him on her computer—later.

So many things she was putting off until later, a new and bad habit, since at work she usually tackled the most distasteful task first. All right, she definitely was fumbling with *stuff* in her life—but, again, as Dr. Barclay had pointed out, she'd had a lot of stress factors lately.

With a map in hand of the circuitous route she would be driving to Mrs. Flinton's, she headed out to her car. She'd like a new one but wouldn't buy until . . . until.

Enzo followed her with no goofy comments and hopped

through the door into the passenger seat, and her stomach clenched, feeling very empty. She grimaced. There'd be solid food to soak up the damn acid soon enough.

The drive went well; she must have kept her imagination under wraps because she saw very few apparitions. Five minutes away from reaching Mrs. Flinton's, she realized she was too early, so Clare drove around a few neighborhoods.

Large shady trees threw shadows over the streets, and she felt nearly warm in the ninety-seven-degree weather. She seesawed back to denial, refusing to consider that her body temperature indicated something was wrong with her. Or that a spectral dog was curled up asleep on her passenger seat.

Then she saw it. Her gaze caught on a bright green-and-white real estate sign first, and she slowed and pulled up in front of the house, holding her breath and hoping Enzo wouldn't wake.

Slowly, slowly, she hit the lever to move the seat back, hoping the wonky thing wouldn't stick and would be quiet. She opened the sunroof. Equally carefully, she stood and turned, staring at a Tudor-inspired house of brown brick and roof. It was framed by beautiful bushes and mature trees, with ivy along one side of the house. The exterior wall showed that distinctive plaster and half-timbered wood—surrounding a doorway that was a rectangle with a pointed top. The most charming features were the leaded glass windows, one bowing out round in the front.

The house stood two and a half stories, maybe three. More of a smallish mansion than a house.

She wanted it.

In this neighborhood, it wouldn't come cheap. No little plastic box with the info hanging on the low brick wall in the front, a wall that towered to twelve feet along the sides. Nope, no tacky plastic box revealing stats on a place like this.

She snapped pic after pic with her phone, found the location and address on her maps app and took a shot of that, then e-mailed it to Arlene with the text, *I want an appointment ASAP.*

Breath coming quick in excitement, she slipped back down into her seat.

Enzo opened his eyes, and for an instant she saw depthless holes and shuddered. Then he perked up and hopped to his feet, front paws on the top of the passenger seat and head out the sunroof.

Is that our new home? Oh, it IS. It IS! You found it! I will go check for ghosts of your time period. He slanted her a quick reproachful look. *I don't know why you don't want to live with ghosts.*

She ruthlessly shut the sunroof. He leapt out of the top of her car.

Hadn't she just decided *not* to purchase a new car? *Foolish* to consider a house now, with a new threat hanging over her head.

She didn't drive away. Rubbing her chilly goose-bumped arms, she jerked the seat forward again. The house would be more than a million, wouldn't it? Probably. More than two?

Her throat tightened at the thought of so much money being tied into real estate . . . even though something like this would hold its investment value.

She wouldn't pay two million dollars for this. Outrageous.

She lied. She'd pay almost anything for that house. It was *right*.

And Aunt Sandra's house, a few blocks from Lake Michigan, had sold for just under five million . . .

Enzo zoomed through the car door and hopped onto the seat, eyes gleaming. *It does not have any ghosts from your time period.* His tail wagged. *It is BEAUTIFUL.*

She wondered what the kitchen looked like.

Her phone alarm beeped, set for fifteen minutes until tea with Mrs. Flinton.

Settling back into her seat, she buckled up again and pulled out into the quiet street, pondering what the dog would think was beautiful.

Exactly on time, Clare parked her car in Mrs. Flinton's circular drive and got out, feeling a little relieved. *This* place looked even more expensive than the one she was thinking of buying . . . all right, the house she'd fallen in love with. She pushed her seat against the wheel and bent over to pick up the bouquet she'd picked up at a flower shop for Mrs. Flinton. Figment of her imagination or not, Enzo killed flowers. Better they look a little wilted with heat now than black from frosty cold.

When she straightened, she saw Zach Slade. Though he wore dark glasses, a smile edged his mouth and she figured he'd been staring at her butt. She couldn't stop returning that smile any more than she could quash the leap of her heart, the squeeze of it and the excitement that poured through her at the sight of him.

It's ZACH! Enzo shouted mentally.

Zach flinched.

Enzo ran up to the man, raced around him, but Zach gave him no more notice. Something she should be able to do. The man must have a steely mind.

She shut and locked her door, and when they walked toward each other she impulsively held out her hand, felt a glow around her heart when he caught it and squeezed. Since she had the flowers and he a cane, they circled in a little playful dance until they walked hand-in-hand to the door, where a woman in a flowered apron awaited them.

Zach closed his fingers over Clare's icy ones. Nearly flinched in shock at the cold. The temperature had to be in the midnineties! He slid his narrowed gaze toward her. She looked thinner, her cheeks holding a hollowness that hadn't been there before, as well as dark smudges under her eyes. Whatever shadows had shown in her eyes when he'd met her before seemed to have gotten the better of her, eating at her.

All his senses prickled in a hunch that those shadows and the decline in her appearance weren't from a physical sickness . . . and in their meetings before she'd been on the solid side of normal, emotionally. Not a physical problem. Not an emotional one.

A multitude of caws hit his ears, and he glanced to the telephone line to see a row of crows. He tried to ignore them. Tried not to count.

Seven. *Seven for a secret, Not to be told.*

Secrets. Usually he wanted to know secrets, especially ones that made a woman go from appealing to compelling.

Not now. No.

He heard the wings of birds as they flew away, but dread sifted through him.

Dropping her hand that he'd warmed with his own, he touched her lightly on her back—her cool back, not damp from sweat—as they took the few steps up the portico to the door.

He said, "Clare, this is Mrs. Magee. Mrs. Magee, this is Clare Cermak."

The housekeeper nodded. "Pleased to meet you."

Clare handed the bouquet to her. "A pleasure to meet you, too."

"Come in, come in!" called Mrs. Flinton from the dimness inside.

Mrs. Magee stepped back, and Zach and Clare walked into the wide entry hall.

Clare sighed. "You don't have air-conditioning on."

"No." Mrs. Flinton held out her hands. "The house was built to be cool enough in the summer, though my husband had the place retrofitted for air-conditioning, of course."

"Of course," Clare said.

Zach had discovered that both of the ladies he lived with, like most elderly, weren't fazed by the heat, so the house remained in the low eighties except for his apartment.

"I'll put these in water." Mrs. Magee bustled away with the flowers.

Clare was hesitating in taking Mrs. Flinton's hands, and Zach knew why. Finally courtesy demanded it, and Clare put her fingers in Mrs. Flinton's, squeezed briefly, and showed her a fake smile.

Mrs. Flinton's brows winged up. "My *dear*, you do need tea. Come along." She turned and whisked down the hallway into a parlor that was more feminine than the one she'd led Zach to the day before.

A sofa, a love seat, and two chairs upholstered in a pastel floral pattern formed the main sitting area, but a café table of iron curlicues in green with a glass top was set for three. Steam furled upward from the spout of a large teapot, in nearly the same pattern as the furniture.

Zach hesitated.

A dog barked and he frowned. Neither of the old ladies had pets.

"What was that?" he asked.

Clare looked over toward the table. "Enzo!"

"Enzo?"

Clare flushed. Her gaze flittered to his, then back. She bit her lips, now the plumpest thing on her face. Moist, pretty lips. She gave a crack of laughter, her shoulders slumped. "It's Enzo," she repeated.

"The ghost dog," Mrs. Flinton said firmly as she glided to the table. She sure handled the walker a lot more gracefully than he did his cane.

Now Zach repeated flatly, "The ghost dog." The one Mrs. Flinton believed followed Clare and she'd denied before.

She swallowed, then rubbed her hands. "Yes. The ghost dog." She sighed. "Oh, Zach."

He braced himself. He knew that tone. She was gonna unload on him.

SIXTEEN

HE SAID, "I don't believe in ghosts, Clare."

She stared him in the eyes, her own hazel eyes showing more brown than green. "Zach, neither do I. That's the big problem here."

And *thunk*, the atmosphere eased as the "secret not to be told" was revealed.

"Your seeing ghosts and not believing in them *is* a big problem. But I *do* believe and can help you." Mrs. Flinton nodded and waited by her chair.

Zach moved forward to seat her.

She smiled up at him and said, "Surely you've seen odd things in your life as a law enforcement officer."

He stared at her. What did she think she knew about him? Had she noticed when he saw the damn crows? The older woman remained serene under his glare. But he couldn't really disagree with her. He'd seen plenty of screwy things. Some explainable, some not. Even omitting all the damned crow sightings. "Maybe," he grumbled.

Mrs. Flinton nodded.

Clare pulled out her own chair and slipped in opposite the elderly lady, which left the final chair for Zach, his back to the door. He moved around the table, tapped Clare on the shoulder, and waved to the other place. "Please," he said.

She frowned.

Mrs. Flinton stood and placed the napkin she'd taken from her plate on the one opposite her. "I didn't think, Zach. You'll want to sit where I am, yes?"

Clare stood slowly, blinking at him.

The dog barked again and he tensed, then ignored it.

"Yes, Mrs. Flinton," he said, then met Clare's eyes. "I don't like sitting with my back to the door."

"Oh, I understand."

Mrs. Flinton smiled. "You don't watch a lot of crime shows, Clare?"

"No." Her gaze flicked to Zach, and she did that smile-and-glance-from-under-her-lashes thing that had lust zipping through him. Bad idea to act on the attraction.

"Bekka Magee and I do. Zach, you're right-handed, so you want your right hand to be toward the door and not the window. Are you armed, dear?"

"Not right now. This is mostly habit."

Mrs. Flinton stopped staring at his jacket as if she wanted to see his rig.

"Oh," Clare said softly, and moved to the center chair with her back to the door.

Zach's instincts didn't like that at all, that someone coming in could target her first. To his inner shock, he realized he'd prefer Mrs. Flinton in that chair.

He seated Mrs. Flinton, then Clare, then took his own place, ignoring a yip and a cold draft around his legs.

The scent of food teased his nose, and a couple of seconds later Mrs. Magee came in with a big tray. Zach started to rise, then stopped. He couldn't handle that tray as well as the older woman, couldn't help her. Bile burned in the back of his throat.

Mrs. Magee dished out the soup, laid halves of a big sandwich on each plate, and left after accepting thanks from them all. Mrs. Flinton poured the tea.

Even though the meal was much like his lunch, Zach didn't feel he could leave. He did manage to sidetrack Mrs. Flinton from ghosts to crime shows every time she brought up woo-woo stuff.

Clare picked at her food and occasionally said something that wasn't in reply to either Mrs. Flinton's or Zach's comments, and that weirded him out. But now and then he found himself staring at the curve of her cheek, the form of her lips, a discreet checkout of her breasts. Still extremely sexy to him, physically, and even though he knew what was behind the secrets in her eyes, he remained intrigued with her.

Teatime stretched until he could barely stand it, couldn't even glance outside the window because now and again he saw a black bird flying.

At last, Mrs. Flinton dabbed at her mouth and put her napkin down. "I think I will rest a little. Why don't you two walk in the gardens?" Mrs. Flinton asked with a big smile. "Enzo, why don't you stay with me awhile."

"I'd like that," Clare said, and she and Zach left the room. But by the time they'd reached the back door, she knew he'd put an emotional wall up between them. He didn't touch her, no matter how casually.

Her heart sank. She'd blown the relationship with him by acknowledging Enzo. Stupid!

When he opened the door and said, "I don't think this thing with us should go any further," she just swallowed and nodded. How could she blame him for thinking her crazy? She would have taken a huge step back from him if the circumstances had been switched.

"I understand," she said, her voice husky. Her smile was bright and false but the best she could do. "I'm glad you've found a good job and a good home, Jackson Zachary Slade."

"Thank you; sorry it happened this way." His voice held a little roughness she didn't bother to analyze.

She ducked her head to keep her tears from showing and walked through the back door into a lush and lovely garden, and strode down pretty red sandstone flagstones set in thyme . . . until she heard the screen door shut.

Glancing over her shoulder to make sure he hadn't followed her, she pulled a tissue from her purse and heaved a couple of sobs into it before she got hold of herself. After one last blowing of her nose, she glanced around and saw a grape arbor not too far away with a bench and a blue gazing ball on a stone pedestal. Something she'd like in her own yard . . .

No. She couldn't buy a house if she'd be dying soon; it would be the height of irresponsibility, to make her brother deal with such paperwork, even if she closed this week—have him sell *two* houses. And she had to face it, her health was bad. She wasn't eating, barely slept, was cold all the time. Because she didn't accept her psychic gift, a gift that had run through her family's Gypsy blood for generations—the gift of communicating with ghosts.

No. That wasn't real. Ghosts weren't real. How could she believe that? Not at all logical.

Was it more logical that she was simply going insane, that some humongous disorder she'd had all along was now wracking her when she'd come into a nice fortune? How sane was *that* belief?

The pressure bearing down on her all day began to crush her. To break her mind and spirit. Broken in two, one part her old logical self, another part Gypsy instincts and heritage shrieking for freedom.

This had to stop!

Zach left the house for an interview regarding Mrs. Flinton's antiques, his mood foul. He walked past Clare's car in the driveway. A very sensible car that an accountant would drive, just as he'd noted before. How had she gone off the rails so badly? Cold slipped along his spine. If that could happen to a solid woman like Clare, and in such a small amount of time, Zach's whole worldview might be sliding into another focus again, like a kaleidoscope.

He'd never liked kaleidoscopes . . . changing before you got a handle on the picture.

Realizing he'd hunched over, avoiding scanning the area because he'd see some damn crows, he stood tall, moved even slower, scrutinized the neighborhood. All fine.

He rolled his shoulders to ease the tension, but there remained an ache in his heart where he'd already put Clare and hopes for a connection with her. Since he'd recently been in her presence, his body had a low-level lust ache, too. Irritating that the first woman he'd been attracted to since he'd gotten shot was . . . too far gone into bizarre.

Which made him wonder if he'd be able to live with Mrs. Flinton after all, since she seemed to believe in the weird and illogical.

Opening his car door, getting in, and slamming it shut behind him, he figured he'd finish her case, then reexamine the living arrangements.

Clare scrubbed the last trace of tears from her face.

This insanity or ghost business or *whatever* had to stop! Now.

Forget Dr. Barclay and whatever time schedule he might have her on . . . that probably included heavy-duty medications or some inpatient treatment somewhere. She had to deal with this now. The sooner, the better.

Today.

She would have to commit herself to one path—fight the illogic of ghosts, the craziness of what was happening to her to her last ounce of strength, or give in to the illogical fact that there were ghosts. She could feel her mind crumbling, her body deteriorating.

How to do that? But just with the question, her mind clicked into planning.

She'd confront her fears, confront ghosts. There were plenty of ghosts in Denver, and time enough today to do that. She wouldn't wait for night. She'd need a good map. Would there be a map of persistent haunts in Denver? The library might have one.

When she did research in the library for a map of where known and active ghosts could be found, she'd pay special attention to anything downtown in easy walking distance. She didn't dare go in a car; too dangerous.

The sooner she did this, the better, and driving to the library could be iffy in terms of safety, too.

Anticipating the courtesy from Mrs. Magee and Mrs. Flinton that Clare could leave her car here, she called a cab to come pick her up, then walked back into the house, ready to get on with her life and face the future.

Enzo greeted her as soon as she went through the door. His tongue was dangling. For the first time since he'd shown up, she stared at him. Definitely Great-Aunt Sandra's Lab, with a little something extra in the eyes. "Hello, Enzo, I'm going to meet my fate."

He gamboled around her. *You believe in ME, in US, in ghosts. In your GIFT!*

Perhaps.

This is right, you will see. Mrs. Flinton can help you like I do, too. It's good we all met.

Clare thought of Zach and her heart twinged. There had been . . . more than a possibility for a good relationship with him. She stopped a sigh and straightened her back.

Mrs. Flinton entered the hallway, smiling, no doubt in response to Enzo's barks. Clare nodded to her.

"I am a logical person, Mrs. Flinton."

"I know that this is difficult for you, dear."

Almost, almost, she sounded like Great-Aunt Sandra, able to answer questions Aunt Sandra . . . no, nothing about the family gift, and that was very important. Perhaps Mrs. Flinton might know about "gifts" in general. But Clare wouldn't ask right now.

She forced a smile, though it twisted on her. "I've decided that I must decide on which flavor of craziness to embrace—the fact that I'm cold and dying and insane, or that I can see ghosts."

"Oh, my dear." Mrs. Flinton hurried to her and leaned over her walker to embrace Clare. "You aren't going crazy."

Enzo barked. *No you are not going crazy, you just have a gift!*

"I *am*. I can feel my mind—" Clare stopped and sucked in a sharp breath. When she got her voice under control, she said. "I've decided to confront my fears, to confront the ghosts. I'll find a map and figure out where the worst ones might be and go there to see them. Either they are real or I am beyond sanity and should admit myself to a mental health clinic, rest home, something, and wait for death."

Mrs. Flinton looked startled, held Clare tighter with her thin and fragile arms. Then she stepped back and shook her head. "No, dear, I don't think it's good to go on your own to confront ghosts. I don't think that's a good idea *at all*."

Clare lifted her chin. "Nevertheless, that's my plan."

"Let me get Zach to accompany you. You know, he has a gift, too. He has a touch of *the sight*."

Almost, that statement distracted Clare. "No. I should do this myself." No matter how quivery her insides were.

SHE WILL HAVE ME! Enzo yelled.

"I don't think that will be sufficient, dear doggie," Mrs. Flinton said.

"We'll be fine," Clare said. "I've called a cab to take me to the library. They must have books on ghosts of Denver."

"I daresay," Mrs. Flinton said, frowning.

"May I leave my car here? I'll pick it up tomorrow." She knew her smile now held a touch of wildness or craziness and didn't care. "If I can."

"Of course you can leave your car here," Mrs. Flinton said. "But I heartily advise against—"

Mrs. Magee appeared. "There is a taxi outside for Miss Cermak."

Clare said, "Thank you, Mrs. Magee. Thank you, Mrs. Flinton, for all you have done. I'll . . . I'll see you later."

"Wait! Clare, can you call me when you're leaving the library before you go to . . . on your mission?" Mrs. Flinton called. Clare pulled open the heavy door but looked over her shoulder at the two concerned women.

She swallowed. "All right." Then she exited, paying no attention to the irritated—worried?—conversation she left behind.

During the cab ride Clare organized her purse to make sure pen, pencil, and paper were at hand to whisk out when needed . . . and a quarter for a locker if she had to use a special room for research. But surely books on ghosts were more popular and less rare than the materials she'd looked through on her quest to learn about Jack Slade.

If she was efficient, and she prided herself on that, she could get in and out of the library quickly, before happy hour really got rolling, and be home before downtown locked in rush hour. That was the best timeline, best-case scenario, and now that she'd determined what to do and had a plan, optimism suffused her.

She logged on to the library's catalog with her phone and flicked through it, noting with a smile that several of the more than a dozen ghost/hauntings books were in the Western History room. She recalled that Aunt Sandra had mentioned a couple of books on ghosts and psychic medium gifts on her video while Clare had been in shock, but she didn't remember enough of their titles to look them up. Odd titles she'd cringe to be seen with.

When the taxi pulled up, she gave the cabbie a twenty and didn't ask for change. Enzo informed her that he would play in the park. He sounded optimistic, too.

But as she pulled open the library door, her spirits deflated a little. The place was so cold! Perhaps not to most people, but the air-conditioning reminded her all too vividly of how her health had been declining. How it would continue to decay unless something was done.

Well, she was doing it. Right. Now. She pulled her sweater around her and buttoned it up, wishing it were heavy wool, no matter how odd that would have looked.

She took the escalators up to the pretty reading room that soothed her, went straight to her usual table, filled out a couple of call slips for noncirculating reference books, and handed them to the usual librarian who helped her.

The woman greeted her, smiled, took the slips, and handed them off to a volunteer docent to retrieve the volumes. Clare headed to the stacks, gathered another two books, and took them to "her" table.

She passed Ted Mather, who seemed focused on his laptop, transcribing notes from a dusty book, though she'd seen how his shoulders had stiffened when he'd caught sight of her, his darting glance to her, and maybe even felt his irritation with her. So she didn't bother to greet him. Like Mrs. Flinton had said, Clare was on a mission.

Flipping through the books, she saw accounts of ghosts of Capitol Hill and Cheesman Park. The ones on Capitol Hill were on the far side of the governmental buildings, and not close in distance.

There were no good maps, and the circuit she traced quickly would take hours to walk, and the way things were, she still didn't want to drive.

The docent delivered her books and made a couple of

comments about Clare's area of study changing from legends of the West to ghosts of the West. Clare's reply felt strained.

Again she scanned the contents of the fattest book. No maps at all, more of a history of Denver than a lot of ghost stories. She made a note of it, then set it aside.

When she opened the second book to a flyleaf that had a map of LoDo, she whispered, "I've struck gold!"

She really should have anticipated that LoDo would have a lot of ghosts, since it was logical that Denver's earliest settlements—Auraria and Denver—would have the most ghosts or hauntings or supernatural activity or whatever in the city, just for being around so long.

Finally she pulled out a chair and sat. She grimaced as she made notes. Yes, most of the "confirmed sightings" were smack-dab in what she sensed was her primary time period for *feeling* them, 1850 to 1900.

If one believed in ghosts.

But walking LoDo was a definite place to start. She could put her plan into immediate action, take the free mall bus down to the terminus and walk. As soon as she had a list of several hideous places that should give her the most "evidence," she copied the map twice and annotated one copy, stuck it in the outside pocket of her purse, then rose and stepped back and took a pic of it in its entirety with her phone, then in sections.

Done! She glanced at her watch. And in good time, too!

She was down and stepping out of the building before she remembered to call Mrs. Flinton and tell her she'd be taking the bus from one end of the mall to the other—nearly slower than walking, but apparitions didn't inflict themselves on her nearly as much when on the bus.

Forcing herself to pat Enzo on the head, keeping her head up and shoulders straight, she strode away, hopefully not to her doom, but if it was, she didn't think she'd survive anyway, and that might just be a relief.

SEVENTEEN

❦

ZACH PULLED BACK into the drive and Clare's car was still there, which puzzled him. Maybe the old ladies had asked her to dinner.

Her and the ghost dog, Enzo. Crazy.

He'd avoid all of them.

The interview hadn't gone well. Mrs. Flinton had been right about the housekeeper living to a very ripe old age . . . but her memory hadn't been great, and the young woman relative—who'd flirted with him and irritated him more since she was blond, blue-eyed, perky, and obvious—hadn't had any leads for him, either. She stated she'd e-mail her middle-aged parents, who might be able to give him more information about people who might have worked in the household when it dissolved.

Meanwhile, thinking of Clare had gotten him thinking about money, whether Mrs. Flinton had any sort of financial records about her old home. Too bad Zach couldn't trust Clare to look at something like that. He hated messing with financial records himself, and if Rickman Security had a financial guy, Zach thought that person would be busy with more pressing cases.

This time he made little noise pulling up the circular drive close to his side door, opening his car door, nearly sneaking in. He changed into T-shirt and jeans, settled on the couch with the new laptop that was the property of Rickman Security, and began typing up his notes.

No more than a couple of minutes later, a hard rapping came at the door of his apartment to the rest of the house. Muttering a curse, Zach stood, took his cane, and walked slowly to the door. He opened it to see Mrs. Flinton staring at him with an expression that told him in no uncertain terms that he'd disappointed her.

"Clare Cermak has decided to face her fears and is going to walk in LoDo . . . where there are quite a massive number of unhappy ghosts," Mrs. Flinton stated. "Ghosts of the Chinese who lost their lives in the race riot of Hop Alley in 1880, ghosts of despairing and desperate women who were prostitutes in the red-light district, including three who were strangled by a serial killer in 1894."

Zach stared at her. "You know a lot," he muttered.

Her lips compressed into a thin line before she said, "I know the ghosts of Denver, Zach." A heavy silence. "Since I believe in them."

He raised his brows. "And you think I should."

"I think you have a gift—"

"No."

She inclined her head.

"Are you going to throw me out?" he asked, a pang zipping to his gut. He liked this place. He liked her and Mrs. Magee. He loved the food.

Her head tilted and expression softened. "Not right now. Especially not if you help Clare."

Zach rubbed his face. "What do you want me to do?"

"Whether you believe in ghosts or not," Mrs. Flinton said crisply, "you can see that Clare is unwell and should not be left alone to wander by herself."

"I guess."

Mrs. Flinton's phone trilled in her pocket. She pulled it out, glanced at the caller, and answered. "Clare, dear. Thank you for calling like I asked." The warmth that had been lacking in her voice as she'd talked with him infused her tones.

"You're still continuing with your plan?" Mrs. Flinton thumbed the volume up and held it out so Zach could listen.

"Yes, of course, Mrs. Flinton," Clare said.

Something tightened inside him—the ache of lost dreams, of a potential that would never be fulfilled.

"I still strongly advise against this, Clare," Mrs. Flinton said with that steel she'd used on Zach.

"I'm sorry you disagree with my plan, Mrs. Flinton, but I am determined to figure this all out. I'm either seeing ghosts or going crazy." An unamused chuckle. "Or both."

"My dear—"

"I'm leaving the library now. The only map I found was for ghosts of LoDo, so I'll be going there, taking the mall shuttle down to the LoDo terminal at Market."

"Market Street is a main thoroughfare of ghosts," Mrs. Flinton said.

"I know that, now." Another, higher chuckle from Clare roused Zach's cop instincts that something definitely wasn't right.

"I'm sending Zach after you. Why don't you find a place to wait for him?" Mrs. Flinton pointed to his outside door and made pushing motions.

Zach hesitated.

"That's completely unnecessary, Mrs. Flinton; please, don't," Clare said.

"Clare needs your help. Are you going to let her, and me, down?" Mrs. Flinton demanded of Zach in a low voice.

"What did you say?" Clare asked.

Mrs. Flinton glared and pointed to the door again. Stepping high with his left leg, with minimal use of his cane, Zach crossed to the door and opened it. Mrs. Flinton followed.

The old woman had stabbed him right in one of his most tender and sore spots. It hadn't been so very long ago that he'd sworn to serve and protect. He believed in that, and the alarm buzzing in the back of his brain told him Clare needed the protection . . . and Mrs. Flinton the service.

He marched to his car door, got in, and set his cane in the passenger seat footwell, listening to Mrs. Flinton soothe.

"The ghosts crowd around one on Market," Mrs. Flinton said. "It's better if you walk slowly." She rolled her hand for him to get a move on, but, hell, he didn't know where the damn bus terminal was, wait, Market and Sixteenth—but he didn't know the best, the fastest way to get there, so he had to jab at the GPS unit.

"Promise me you will walk *very* slowly and *listen to Enzo!*" Mrs. Flinton said.

"Oh, all right. I promise."

And Zach drove off, clenching his jaw and telling himself he was a damn fool. As he turned between the stone pillars of the drive he saw the shadows, and then the birds: nine. *Nine for hell.*

The hair rose all along his body, his neck, his arms. And, damn it, Zach had so rarely seen nine that he didn't know what that meant. Except Clare was in trouble.

Too many damn crows in Denver.

Mrs. Flinton was correct about the ghosts crowding. The instant Clare stepped off the bus under the Denver International Airport–like tent covering, specters pressed around her—visions?—but she *felt* the tension of them near.

They weren't the kind of images she'd become accustomed to—shadowy people in old-fashioned dress. No. Not at all.

Images of tattered, ragged, sometimes decomposing bodies. People charred with burns, with fatal wounds, crushed skulls and broken limbs . . . Some looked like decomposing bodies. She put her hand to her throat and swallowed hard.

Was fear, or something else, making them look the way they did? Had her mind really, truly, finally cracked?

CLARE! shouted Enzo. *COME WITH ME!* She could swear she could feel the pull of his teeth on her skirt drawing her . . . through the crowd of ghosts muttering that sounded like stormy ocean surf in her ears, rushing so loud she couldn't even hear the fast throb of her heart.

She wove in and out of real and imaginary people, managed to cross behind another bus, found herself panting on the other side of the street, walking a full block as she coped with the gruesome and fantastic. She thought she cried, felt wetness on her cheeks but it wasn't cloudy or raining.

Gasping, she stopped, fumbled her sweater buttons undone, tied the thing around her waist. Didn't care how she looked. Except she hoped she didn't seem like someone on drugs or mentally ill.

Even. If. She. Was. *Crazy.*

Clare, Clare, are you all right? Enzo demanded.

Her dried lips cracked. "No."

BREATHE. Count with me. Breathe in to seven and out to seven, the Peaceful Breath! ONE! Two!

And she did, and the too-bright glare outlining the shadow people disappeared a little, and the . . . the . . . images . . . turned more . . . normal. And she got a grip on herself and realized she'd gone straight in the opposite direction than what she'd anticipated.

Slowly, slowly, she looked around—with double vision. Old building faces replaced those more modern, brick with wooden porches and narrower fronts. The street sign didn't read Market, or the name before that, Holladay—a man who'd been a main person in Jack Slade's life—but the very first name, McGaa. She continued to steady her breathing.

Her first normal thought was it was a good thing she hadn't driven.

The second was to wonder if that was really Zach Slade coming toward her.

Sure it was. Mrs. Flinton had betrayed Clare.

Now she'd be seen to be completely bonkers by a man she admired and whom she'd wanted as a lover. No matter the fortune, this terrible "gift"—more like a curse—had already cost her more than she'd have been willing to pay for the damn money. Cost her her former life. Cost her a man she might have been able to have a relationship with.

"Clare!" He was there and had an arm around her waist, and she couldn't stop trembling. God*dammit.*

At least the people looking at her askance, a couple holding their cell phones like they were about to call 911, appeared steadied by Zach's presence, his handling of her. Obviously a man in charge.

"Okay, Clare, let's just move out of the pedestrian traffic, all right?"

She looked at him with those hazel eyes that now seemed to have little gold glints he hadn't noticed before. Once more she seemed too pale under the tan of her skin, but when he eased her away from the street, she followed docilely.

"Ghosts," she murmured, so low that he could barely hear, though he bent his head. "All around. Even the buildings look different." She continued to shiver within the circle of his arm.

They stopped in the cubbyhole doorway of a café, just outside the swing of the red door.

He stepped back, ready to drop his arm, but paused as he felt a tug on his pant leg. He glanced down . . . and saw a touch of see-through white *something*. If he squinted it might look like a dog. A Lab. A wave of cold crashed through him.

"Clare?" he asked.

She followed his gaze down. "That's Enzo."

Zach heard a bark. "I'm not believing this."

Clare shrugged despairingly. "Welcome to my world."

His eyes focused over her shoulder at the EZ Loan Check Cashing place across the street. A white haze hung around it. He noted the car with the motor running parked in a loading zone outside the tinted-glass storefront. A nervous guy sat in the driver's seat.

Zach's vision sharpened and all his instincts alarmed. He'd heard on the news that there'd been a series of robberies targeting check cashing services . . . and the vehicle looked right.

A white haze overshadowed the front window, appearing like an old-fashioned brick building with a LAND OFFICE sign. Zach blinked. The white figure of a cowboy coalesced and waved his hat in long swoops. *Robbery! Going on* now! The hollow words echoed in Zach's head.

Zach dropped his arm from Clare's waist. The phantom cowpoke vanished. So did the white mist in front of the building. The car and twitchy driver remained, all too vivid. Real.

He opened the café door and pushed Clare into the little place. "Go to the back of the building. Call 911. Tell them there's an incident at the EZ Loan."

Her gaze flew to his. She turned to look and he grabbed her. She blinked. "A cowboy," she said faintly. "He's yelling that there's a robbery in progress."

Zach's teeth gritted. "Maybe. Do as I say."

"All right." She fumbled at her purse, took out her cell, punched in a number. "Yes, the EZ Loan." She gave the address. Glancing at him, her eyes still wide, she said, "They're on their way." She stared across the street. "But robbers have been targeting check cashing stores in the suburbs," she whispered.

"Yeah, they've gotten away," Zach said, "but they're downtown today; their mistake." He opened the door and strode with what he hoped was casual, limping quickness . . . a man in a hurry . . . across the street to the EZ Loan.

Heart pounding, Clare continued to watch Zach through the full-length windows as she faded back past the tables to the doorway leading to the restroom.

No longer than a minute after Zach had gone into the EZ Loan did sirens wail, and then shots erupted along with screams. The car in front of the building gunned and jerked into traffic, the front end promptly hit by an SUV in a tearing crash of torn metal.

"Hey!" The driver of the SUV slammed out of his vehicle. But the other driver was out and running.

Café patrons pressed to the glass windows, but Clare hung back. More shots, and police cars coming down the one-way street both ways; officers poured out of the cars and proceeded carefully to the building.

Clare gasped and gasped.

Zach is all right, Enzo said, as he zoomed into the café through the red street door. She hadn't seen him leave. Dropping into an empty seat at a tiny table, she had to have confirmation. "He's all right?"

Enzo nodded. *Zach had already taken two down but the third got really scared, especially when he heard sirens, and shot, BANG. Then Zach got him, too. No one is hurt. Zach really uses his cane well.*

"Oh."

"Some cops are going in," reported one of the diners near the windows. "And the rest are handling traffic and stuff. Looks like whatever happened is over with."

Clare stood up and slipped from the café, though she dearly wanted some coffee, and she'd entered the establishment and stayed safe and had purchased nothing; that wasn't fair. Well, she'd come back some other time.

She moved among the crowd on the sidewalk just enough to get a good view. A few minutes later, policemen came out hauling the suspects, and Zach and another officer exited.

He looked . . . right. Where he should be, doing what he should do, his lean face interested and animated. Back at work at his old job.

And Clare felt separated from him by more than people and cars and the street. He was back in his element and for better or worse—no doubt worse—she'd stepped over into the crazy and illogical side of life.

A ghost from the past had warned of something going on in the present. In real life. She couldn't ignore that anymore.

Thinking of which, the ghost materialized right before her, right now! Then collapsed at her feet. She squatted down, forgetting and putting her hand on his icy chest.

He gave her a lopsided smile. *I didn't die here, not really. But I was bound here by Those Who Be, bound 'cuz of my bad nature.*

She shouldn't be looking at those eyes, eyes already dead, black eyes fading, fading to light brown as the whole world turned to sepia tones. The rest of him thinned; his chest went in with a sigh, then vanished as he said, *I'm glad to be going on along, now. Thankee.*

And he was gone, completely. She blinked and the browns and beiges vanished. Had she seen him well enough to lock him in her memory, maybe be able to discover who he might have been? No. She shook her head. Her hand dropped to the warm sidewalk, and slowly she stood, almost hearing her bones creak as she rose.

Waiting for you. Enzo's mind-voice sounded scary and deep and she didn't dare look at him, though she felt him beside her.

She didn't want to ask the question, but the words formed on her lips anyway, dropped quietly under the noise around her to ghost dog ears. "Waiting for me?"

There are always incidents to prod the reluctant. Not the robbery. That was not fated. But an energetic, perhaps vio-

lent incident that would trigger a bound and waiting ghost, yes.

A little too much weird-ghost-logic-rules for Clare to wrap her head around, though she strained to grasp at wispy concepts while Enzo paused.

You could do as your great-great-uncle Orun did: Ignore this incident. When Enzo "spoke" next, his tone sounded as clinical as one of the doctors she'd visited. *Though I don't know that you will last long enough for another incident or two. Your gift must be very strong for you to deteriorate so fast.*

Clare flattened herself against the building, one of the tall wooden beams that separated the windows. Wonderfully warm on her back.

Her ears rang and colors whirled about her in bright smears, and she knew that despite thinking she'd been *forced into* believing in ghosts and accepting her gift, this was truly the moment of truth. *She* had to *consciously* accept the logic-illogic of her psychic gift and ghosts. She had to give in, surrender to her new "reality."

She had to *decide* that she had a gift, turn her back on the past when she wasn't so cursed, and face the future as a . . . psychic. Or die.

Now her eyes were too dry to produce tears.

Choose, Clare. Enzo's words boomed in her mind as if a bell tolled, being amplified and funneled down all the streets of Denver to her.

EIGHTEEN

HER BREATH CAME raggedly and she thought her heart just might give out in the next minute.

Lips numb, she said, "I believe in ghosts. I have a psychic gift."

Would she have to clap her hands?

Enzo snorted as if he heard her, sat on her feet with a coolness like a breeze instead of like a melting ice cube, and looked up with a wrinkled doggie face. *We will be FINE.*

Clare hoped so.

Then the crowd parted again and she looked up to see Zach across the street, the man next to him gesturing to the open door of the back of a police car. Zach stared at her with an inscrutable expression.

Definitely on opposite sides of the reality line now.

He shook his head a little at her.

So he hadn't mixed her up in this, mentioned her name to the police. Such a good man. She dipped her chin in response and turned back to walk to the mall bus terminal. She'd take it to one of the stops close to a hotel with taxi service straight home. She didn't have the energy to deal with Mrs. Flinton.

She'd call and have someone pick up her car and drive it to her place.

She didn't look back but knew it was over between her and Zach.

The ghosts she met along the way—fully dressed and looking normal again—acknowledged her, murmuring in her mind.

She murmured back.

By the time Clare returned home, the news feeds had picked up the EZ Loan Check Cashing robbery "thwarted by an ex–deputy sheriff from Montana, currently on staff of Rickman Security and Investigations."

She listened to the television, but the sound bites didn't have any information she didn't know except the names of those apprehended, including the man who'd tried to escape on foot.

Her focus now was entirely on herself and her still-felt-problematic future.

One good thing—her real estate agent had called and set up a viewing of the house Clare wanted for the next morning. Just the thought of a new house, one with air-conditioning unlike this small rectangular hot box, had Clare sniffling. For the first time in a week she felt the temperature.

She opened both doors and windows for cross-ventilation and turned on the window and ceiling fans.

Maybe she could move on the other house rapidly, buy the thing.

She settled in her one comfortable chair and pulled out her tablet computer, looked again at the pics she'd taken just hours ago when she was . . . dying? . . . and yet trying to fi-nesse having the money without the gift? With a sigh she thought for the umpteenth time that if she'd been given a choice, she would have chosen no money and no gift.

Instead she got the option of money and gift or death. Craziness might still loom large; hadn't her great-aunt Sandra said something about that? Not that Clare wanted to contemplate the fact—facts! rules! with regard to this weird stuff? Ha, ha, ha—she didn't want to consider the fact that she might still be in danger of losing her mind. Much nicer to stare at photos of a two-point-five-million-dollar home.

Enzo came over and put his head on her thigh. The ghost dog was still cold, but tolerable. The chill didn't go straight to her bones and make them ache like just that morning.

His eyes were dark but didn't hold that more-than-dog otherworldliness that creeped her out. *I am glad you are staying here with me, Clare, and that you are not dying like your great-great-uncle Orun.*

That had her stirring a little, but did she dare attract the notice of the . . . spirit, the Scary Specter . . . that sometimes inhabited Enzo. Maybe. "What do you know about Orun? He must have been long gone before you were a live puppy."

Enzo rubbed his chin on her leg, rucking her dress up a little. *Sandra spoke about him, and she played with the box toy like you have*—he tried to swipe his phantom nose on her tablet and she jerked it aside—*that showed people's names and lines.* The dog trotted over to the box that held the video disks and nosed in it . . . and one levitated upward.

Clare yelped, shoved her tablet off her lap, and lunged toward the box, grabbing a disk. "Don't do that. No moving solid objects! How can you do that, anyway?"

You have a lot of psi power, Clare. I can borrow it when you aren't using it.

She stared, mouth down, panting breaths. "But . . . but you are a ghost, not material."

Power is power.

Clare raised her hands to run her fingers through her hair and maybe massage her scalp, since her poor head hurt inside and out, and clunked the disk against her face. When she looked at it, she saw it was a genealogical program.

Her heart bumped in her chest. Yes, of course, for research—both on her family and with the ghosts—the software could be invaluable, and something she could understand. *Facts.*

Abandoning her tablet, she went to the closet in her small office, where her secondary laptop sat with a thin layer of dust on a shelf. It was old and sturdy enough to have a video player.

There are papers, Enzo said, hopping up and down by one of the boxes.

She returned to the box and saw a brown paper portfolio nearly the same color as the cardboard. Opening it up, she saw two pockets; in one was handwritten notes, and the other had printouts.

A family tree!

Back at her desk, she looked at the family tree, all the way back to Bohemia and the generations there, then returned to the later generations, tracing the chart with her right index finger. Someone had emphasized certain names in deep purple: Orun, Amos, Sandra, *Clare*; at the next colorful name her breath just squeezed out in a whoosh.

"Ah, ah, ah." She tried, but breathing was hard. Darkness edged her vision; pinpricks of black floated before her eyes.

She felt a *thump* against her back, hissed out the last of her air as Enzo *leapt* through her, head and shoulders appearing above the desk, then sinking.

"Eeeee!" She sucked in a breath on a long, shocked squeak.

Her chair and desk began a slow room-spin as if she were drunk.

BREATHE! Enzo shouted. *Count with me to seven.*

She did. Her breathing and pulse steadied; her chair stopped midswoop, then righted.

"Dora," she squeaked when she had breath. "My niece Dora—" She couldn't say the words.

But Enzo was there nodding at her. *Yes, if you had not believed, the gift would have gone to her.*

"She's only nine!"

A ripple of a shrug went down Enzo's back. *It's a family gift, it stays in the family.* His head tilted. *I'm going in the backyard to play. You and Sandra are no fun when you are on the big toys. Not even anything to see but words, words, words.* His tail slapped against her arm and he took off for the back door and the enclosed yard.

Clare didn't call him back.

Now she *could* stab her fingers in her hair, and, of course, the more she did, the more she ruined the smooth sleekness, and it stood out from her head and the locks curled against her face and neck.

"Dora lives in Williamsburg, Virginia," Clare said aloud, not even pretending now that she was talking to anyone—Enzo, any ghost that might traipse through her house; she was talking to herself. She'd never approved of that—it showed a disordered mind—but she continued to whisper, "Dora likes living in Williamsburg, likes colonial history."

Clare had been tired but wired—body sagging with weariness, mind zipping around at a million miles a minute. Now she propped her elbows on the desk and sank her head in her hands, staring down.

Another reason she couldn't opt out. She loved energetic, optimistic, slightly nerdy little Dora. A girl who'd grow into a strong, vibrant woman.

If she didn't have some stupid family psychic gift thrust upon her at the tender age of nine.

Sweat coated Clare's body. Her light sundress stuck to her, the ceiling fan drying it with cool sweeps that she still didn't appreciate. She'd been so cold for this entire week that she'd fought her gift that she didn't think she'd ever like winter again—and Denver had cold winters; perhaps she should move . . . Hawaii?

Enzo growled. He was back. *You should stay here. Your gift is formed by your location. THIS CITY, this STATE is where you belong. We belong.*

More damned rules.

"Wha—what happens if I *don't* stay?"

His expression became disapproving. *You'll still encounter ghosts, but they will be easier to control if they are ghosts you understand.* He smiled and she thought it was genuine; she didn't like the often shifting from cute dog to Scary Specter. *Like cowboys, and gunfighters and miners and ranchers and railway men and pioneer women . . .*

"Uh." She rubbed her head, feeling as if each strand of her hair were bursting out of the coating of taming conditioner, turning into the uncontrolled curls she'd fought all her life. Again she felt tears rising under her eyes, prickling. Tears and pity for *herself.* Wah, wah, wah. Too much wallowing now, get over it.

Granted, she wasn't in the best physical or emotional

shape, so it was easy to cry self-pitying tears, but she would *not* give in again. She had more spine than that. She straightened said spine.

Enzo licked her hand. When she stared down at him, he had his own soulful doggie eyes. *I love you, Clare.*

Swallowing, she stroked him; it still seemed like plunging her hand into ice cubes. One scritch of the ears and she lifted her hand. "Yes, I love you, too. So, um, is Colorado my limit?" Maybe she *could* handle this . . . though . . . she frowned. "Didn't Aunt Sandra spend some time in New York City and other big cities back east?" Had to be mobsters from the twenties and the thirties everywhere; even Denver had its gangster factions. And what *had* been Aunt Sandra's time range? A grudging feeling coated Clare; did Aunt Sandra only have about three decades? And what were Clare's limits? She'd thought about 1850 to 1900. She glanced at the tower of journals.

But Enzo rubbed against her, answering the question she'd forgotten she'd asked. *You can go to Montana or Utah or Nebraska or Wyoming or California or Idaho or—*

"I get it. Ghosts of the Old West."

Another chill lick of her fingers. *You are SO smart, Clare.*

Smart enough to try to figure out the parameters of this weird infliction plaguing her. She stood and stalked to the box of disks, pulled out the ones for her brother and his family and her niece and turned them over in her hands. She had a sneaking suspicion that Aunt Sandra had a whole other set—and other instructions for her attorney—if Clare died fairly quickly, before probate was all tied up.

Which reminded her that she should make a will, should have done so before now. Thank heavens she was thinking clearly. It seemed as if her brain had de-iced.

She would *not* use the Chicago attorney; better to keep her business affairs local. She'd call her old boss for recommendations regarding a law firm and interview a few.

Setting the videos aside carefully, she understood she was also compassionate enough not to want Dora to have this terrible gift foisted upon her. Somehow Clare would have to try to prepare her niece . . . dimly she recalled Aunt Sandra talking to her about "special gifts" when she was a child . . .

but whatever help Aunt Sandra might have given her over Clare's youth had been lost since she'd lumped Aunt Sandra in with her feckless and partying and traveling parents.

Though she knew right now that Aunt Sandra must have worked hard and shown a knowledge and dedication to her work that Clare had never given her credit for.

More tears came and these she let flow unchecked, tears for Sandra, tears for Dora. Groping for the remote, she set Aunt Sandra's video to play once again from the start, then plucked a tissue from the box on the coffee table and blew her nose. She wandered into the kitchen wondering if she had any lemonade; she could really use some iced and tart lemonade.

And it was darn well time to rev up the swamp cooler in the living room again.

Zach's *self* expanded during the time he spent with the police. It was good being back in a cop shop, getting some respect from folks he also had respect for. The paperwork, as always, was crap.

Nice bullshitting, talking a little about the case, until he was done giving the report—that took hours he didn't grudge at all—and stood with the help of his cane. Then pity draped over him like a shroud, from the two who'd been talking with him. He thought he might have even seen a touch of fear in the one young man's eyes. Yeah, Zach wasn't *that* much older than the guy to have his career cut short.

And he walked stiffly away from the place, more because of his foot than any pride. A police car waited to drive him to his ride southwest of the main station, and he was dropped off at the paid parking lot with thanks that he returned.

He'd paid enough to take the time to sit and think a little, slump in the softer seat than the one he'd been in at the station. He let all the leftover tension drain from him, rolled it from between his shoulders, even left the door open to massage his foot, and that felt good enough that he knew he'd have to schedule a regular therapist to work on his ankle and foot.

His phone buzzed, a default sound he'd given Rickman until he knew the guy better. He'd had it set on vibrate. Now he pulled his cell from his pocket and saw that he'd missed another call from the man soon after everything had gone down, two calls from Mrs. Flinton . . . and nothing from Clare.

That last had a surge of melancholy yearning rushing through him. She'd be sympathetic; she'd know what he was going through, the longing for his old job.

He shook the emotion off, answered the phone, "Slade."

"You need anything from me or the business?" Rickman asked.

"No."

"Fine. Good publicity for the firm, so thanks for that."

"No problem," Zach said dryly.

Rickman barked a laugh. "You'll be getting a bonus in your check."

Zach just shrugged a shoulder, and strained muscles eased a little more.

"And I want to say that you're an asset to the firm. We've had a mutual wariness thing going on with the local cops."

Because most of Rickman's operatives were ex-military. Rickman and those guys might have federal contacts, but . . . they hadn't worked in the same places—police and sheriff departments—that Zach had.

"How'd they treat you?" Rickman asked.

Nearly like one of themselves. "Fine."

"You make some good contacts?" Rickman pressed.

"Yeah, sure." And Zach thought he had. He hadn't been flashy in taking the suspects down, hadn't used any more force than he'd had to, had known by the time the police had shown up that they'd have run his past. And the big City and County of Denver, Colorado, was *not* puny Plainsview City, Cottonwood County, Montana. Not to mention Zach was a third-fourth-fifth-or-something-generation Coloradan. He'd be given any benefit of the doubt about what took place in Montana. And he had been. Almost made him wish he'd stayed in Colorado.

Too late now.

"Contacts, Zach?" Rickman prompted.

Zach rubbed the back of his neck, feeling sweat flake away. The parking lot lights flashed on as night banished day. "Yes, boss. Like I said, I made some good contacts."

"That we—you—we can build on." A statement laden with satisfaction.

"Yup."

"Good. I'll let you go now," Rickman said.

"Later," Zach said. Weariness began to slide through him, along with relief that crows were difficult to see at night. He swung his leg into the car and drove away. By the time he made it to a major intersection, he knew he was going to Clare, though not sure why.

Mrs. Flinton and Mrs. Magee would have dinner for him . . . and questions . . . and, even, maybe, I-told-you-so's. He sure didn't want that.

Clare . . . it had been a big day for her, too.

He didn't know what the hell had happened. But he knew it was one of those "bonding" experiences the shrinks talked about. An event that included only the two of them that neither of them would ever forget.

Of *course* he hadn't told the police about whatever-the-hell he'd seen and heard when he'd touched Clare. He'd said he'd heard on the news of the check cashing hits, then observed the car, and so on. Just happened to be the first one to notice and call it in. He hadn't mentioned Clare at all.

The night wasn't cool, and he wasn't really looking forward to being at Clare's sweltering place, but maybe they could sit outside. He needed to be with her. Smell her scent, see her face . . . rest with her, no forced explanations necessary. Have a soft, womanly companion.

Maybe he could spend the night. Oh, yeah, his body, even more than his bruised feelings, liked that idea. Anticipation.

NINETEEN

WHEN HE PULLED up to her house, he saw the front door open, the ripple of drapes over the big window as the ceiling fan in the living room moved.

Walking up to the door, he heard an unknown woman's voice:

"By now you've had your gift a while and know that ghosts aren't a figment of your imagination, and that they aren't going away. And, lovey, brace yourself, because I have more bad news and this will come as a real shock for someone as repressed as you are."

Zach slowed, flipping through his memory of just that day's lunch . . . this must be the video from Clare's great-aunt Sandra.

Talking of ghosts. He slowed his progress.

"There are great benefits to helping ghosts transition . . . both emotional and financial . . . the universe rewards you."

So far Zach hadn't seen that. He was only a few steps from the concrete stoop and the open door, wondered whether he should go forward.

"Listen close, lovey. There are great rewards, satisfaction and fulfillment that come with our gift. But there are also costs. And the greatest threat, the greatest cost comes if you don't accept your destiny, if you ignore the ghosts."

A dog barked and Zach tensed. Sounded like it was coming from inside the house. But Clare didn't come to the door, and above Aunt Sandra's dire predictions, he heard a clatter of pans, smelled mouthwatering food—grilling beef, onions, potatoes. All he'd had since tea at Mrs. Flinton's was terrible coffee.

He took the last few limps to the door and rang the bell.

From the threshold he could see the television screen and a frail and elderly orange-haired woman who shared features with Clare.

"If you don't accept your gift, you decline and die," Sandra said.

Dire warnings that Zach couldn't tolerate. He banged on the door to drown out the video and Clare came into sight, walking through the kitchen door, wiping her hands on a dishcloth. She stopped and called out, "Who's there?"

She'd only see him as a dark shadow in the door. "It's Zach Slade."

Her body stilled with surprise. Then she crossed to the door and flicked the flimsy screen door lock open, and her smile shot through his heart and sizzled down to his groin. "Hey."

"Hey, yourself." He smiled back.

She looked easier, not nearly as nervy. Yeah, still haunted, but . . . settled, like she'd made a decision. That scanned for Zach. He always felt better after a decision himself.

He moved to the side on the stoop and she opened the door, held it as he took the one step up and into the house, brushing by her, catching her scent, this time the heavier, more exotic one. His whole damn body tingled; his dick began to harden. Yeah, he was glad to see her, all right. Wanted to be here, and not just because of the effect she had on his body.

With an unhurried step, she picked up the remote and clicked the video off. When she turned back toward him, she said nothing, and he realized then that she wasn't going to push. That if he wanted to deny the strangeness that had happened, that they'd both seen some damned old-fashioned-looking transparent cowboy yelling about a *real* and *current* robbery . . . Clare wouldn't force him into some admission of the truth. He could deny all he wanted.

But the knowledge had settled into his bones that this wasn't about him, and for that he was incredibly grateful. This was about Clare. *She'd* seen stuff, and because he'd had a hand on her and some sort of small emotional connection with her, *he'd* been able to see the dog and the cowpoke.

Clare would let him pretend. But when her gaze met his, instead of the interesting shadows he'd seen before, now he saw a terrible, tortured loneliness. She held herself stiffly, as if expecting rejection.

He understood then that he must make a clear-cut decision whether he was going to accept her or turn away. As she had made the decision whether to accept the ghosts or not.

And that view of his life in the kaleidoscope had shifted just enough for him to admit other people might have "a little something extra." Like Clare. Like Mrs. Flinton. Like his maternal grandmother.

Not him. Nope.

Her hazel eyes were wide. "I didn't think I'd see you again." She glanced away; her gaze went in the direction of the television, and she turned her head away to look him in the eyes. Shrugging and shaking her head, she said, "I was quite incoherent. A real mess."

With a wry smile she added, "You might as well know I've finally gone around the bend. I've accepted that I've inherited the family talent of seeing ghosts."

Zach waited a beat or two.

"You can leave if you want. I expect nothing from you."

That irritated him. She was giving up on him. Not fighting for him and the real sexual desire that flamed between them. Subtly he leaned forward into her personal space, his grip tightening on his cane. He could smell her better. Yeah, for sure, he wanted her.

"I think I'll stay, if it's all the same to you." His voice came out rougher than he thought, but he hoped she heard the sincerity.

She swallowed, and some of the shadows receded from her gaze. "Truly?" she whispered.

"Oh, yeah."

Then her chin lifted, her expression hardened, and determination replaced vulnerability. She drew in an audible breath. "I guess I should lay it all out then, bottom-line it."

"You accountants do like your spreadsheets and your bottom lines," Zach joshed.

"Apparently my relatives have passed down a . . . gift. An intuitive gift, the ability to see"—she swallowed—"to see ghosts."

"Uh-huh," Zach said. He could do this. He could listen reasonably. He *knew* Clare was a reasonable person. He could trust her to find and explain whatever odd logic applied to this situation.

"I saw a cowboy ghost waving his hat in front of the EZ Loan. Did . . . did you?"

Zach sucked in a breath through his nose, caught her scent again. He could do this. "Maybe," he mumbled. "When I was, ah, in contact with you."

Her turn to say, "Uh-huh."

Going over to the coffee table where research books were stacked, she chose a large picture book of historic Denver and flipped through the pages. She tapped the old photo of the street that now included the EZ Loan. "This is where we were."

He walked over, stared down, wouldn't admit to a tense gut. That was the white-gray, partly transparent building he'd seen. He recalled the sign LAND OFFICE.

A nervy smile twitched on and off her face. "I saw this building and a cowboy waving his hat, shouting that there was a robbery going on."

Another slow inhalation, an even slower dip of his head, as he couldn't deny her. "That's right."

She reached out, then curled her fingers before she touched him. He heard barking again, tensed. He'd heard a dog whenever he'd been with her, and he'd have to get used to that, hearing a ghost dog. Because the dog was attached somehow to Clare, not Zach; all about her, not him.

Clare glanced down; her fingers stroked an invisible head. She nodded and looked back up at Zach.

"You apprehended three dangerous thieves," she said with admiration.

"Suspects," he corrected. "Just doing my—" Zach stopped. Flinched. Felt like he'd been gut-stabbed as his past and present collided here and now with pretty Clare.

The jagged parts of his life hadn't appeared earlier in the familiar setting of the police station. No, that place had soothed him consciously and subconsciously.

But the now very real contrast of civilian life versus cop life slammed through him. He wasn't a deputy sheriff anymore, and like Clare and her damn ghosts, he remained in denial about that fact. Pretending that he'd accepted the issue when a huge anger raged inside him, at the unfairness of life, at destiny, at himself for being so goddamned stupid.

Easier to believe in seeing strange things than to know his old life was over. Like he'd told Mrs. Flinton that afternoon, he'd seen plenty of odd stuff in his career, damn near as unbelievable as Clare's wavery buildings and specters and dogs. Not to mention he'd seen other people react to experiences Zach couldn't sense. He knew of more than one cop, deputy, investigator whose hunches were solid gold. And that might include Rickman.

Yes, simpler to accept the inexplicable than to deal with his fury at his lost life.

Than to cope with the permanence of his nonfunctioning foot.

To have that out in the open between them. Here was Clare, looking as if she'd found her balance with whatever had plagued her, while he still teetered around between anger, despair, and unforgiveness. He couldn't forgive himself or even Lauren, who'd died before her time. And wasn't that a pisser of a thing—to hold a grudge against a dead woman?

But just telling himself to get over it didn't do one bit of good. His heart wasn't willing to let the ruin of his life go.

And he had to stop thinking that his life was ruined, too, another impossible matter. Nope, not open at all for much at all.

"Zach?" Clare asked softly.

Well, except maybe sex with a lovely woman.

"Yeah?"

"Are you hungry?"

Food he could appreciate, too, and talk about, too.

"Starving."

"I have shish kebobs and potato skins on the grill."

One side of his mouth kicked up even as his mouth watered. "Sounds great."

"Come on through."

"Smells good, too." He wound with her through a pristine kitchen and out to the backyard, which had a long slab of concrete running the length of the house and an old wooden picnic table. Just beyond the door stood a simple grill that most of Zach's male friends would sneer at. The odors were fabulous, easily making hunger his primary concern and emotion. Whew.

"Definitely done," Clare said. She glanced at him. "Do you grill?"

He grunted. "Some. Not for a while, though. I lived in an apartment complex for the last few years; didn't have one in the communal area and I lived on the second floor. Not much space on the balcony for a grill, and they didn't like when you did it, either."

"I would bet you anything that Mrs. Flinton has a grilling area," Clare tossed over her shoulder as she went into the kitchen.

"No bet," Zach said, though he hadn't looked around the estate much. He'd only been there a full day—or would be once he returned. One of those points in his life when situations and events stretched out time, felt like he'd known Clare for months.

Had wanted to make love with her for months.

She gestured him to sit at the table and when he did, she set a plate with half of a huge potato and three skewers with large chunks of steak sandwiched with onions, peppers, and mushrooms in front of him. Taking the remaining two skewers and potato half, she put her dish opposite his and asked, "Lemonade? It's good stuff."

"Absolutely," he replied.

A minute later she poured out two big glasses and also set out salads and joined him at the table.

They mostly concentrated on eating and talked about Mrs. Flinton and Mrs. Magee, and Clare became animated when she retrieved her tablet computer and showed him the photos she'd taken of the house she'd be looking at the next morning. She'd received a dozen pics from her real estate agent showing the interior.

Zach chewed his last bit of steak, a little too well done for him, then asked, "How much did you say this was?"

She puffed out a breath. "Two million, four hundred fifty-six thousand; two point five million rounding up."

"That's some rounding."

Her shoulders sagged and she glanced around the extremely modest backyard with a chain-link fence between her and all her neighbors. "I shouldn't buy . . ."

"You love the house," Zach said.

Her gaze flicked to his. "Yes, I do."

"It's in the country club district; no question it's an investment."

"That should hold its value." With a small laugh she swiped the tablet until the back terrace showed. "A built-in grill."

"I noticed. Six bedrooms and seven baths."

"And only one Clare."

"So, only one Clare, you gonna buy it?"

For an instant, her lips pressed together. "Yes. I am." Her head tilted to a defiant angle. "Just because Great-Aunt Sandra didn't have any children doesn't mean I can't plan for a family."

Zach froze.

Clare laughed and patted his hand. "Eventually. Not looking for anything near permanent until I understand my . . . circumstances." She left her soft fingers over his that were still curled around his knife. "Thank you for staying, Zach, I know this whole . . . all this *stuff* hasn't been easy."

He put the steak knife aside, turned his hand over, and clasped her fingers. "You're an interesting lady. Easy is overrated." He hesitated. "But I'm not looking for anything long term, either."

Maybe nothing so deep, either, though he thought he might already be in deeper waters with a woman than usual.

She squeezed his hand. "We're in the same column there."

"In the same column?"

"Rather like being on the same page. We'll keep things between us simple and comfortable."

"That works for me." Only a small pool of light from a weak bulb—bad choice security-wise—lit the area. But crickets chirped and a small breeze had picked up to rustle the leaves, all adding to the quiet depth of the night, the sensation of peace where he—they—could relax.

Zach studied the light and shadows of Clare's face, thinking that if they'd had a bigger fire in the grill it might have flickered like a campfire over her Gypsy ancestry, golden tan, and when he glanced down at their hands intertwined it was like golden tan and a tinge of copper from that dollop of Native American ancestry he had. Molten heat pulsed between them, a connection that wound through him, became a thread that spiraled around his heart then went south straight to his balls to make his dick heavy, needy.

With his blood slow and thick, his gaze focused on hers. He stood, still keeping her fingers in his, and moved down the table to the house.

"The dishes—"

"Forget 'em."

"But—"

"Tomorrow, Clare. You can leave worries until tomorrow, can't you?"

Her brows, pretty dark brown arches, rose, her eyes rounded. "Yes," she whispered.

He didn't think she'd ever done that, and a little thrill that he could affect her, make her forget something essential to herself, plucked that string between them, making it vibrate inside him. He pressed her fingers and felt them tremble as if she, too, felt that connecting cord. A new experience for him he wouldn't analyze. Go with the flow.

She opened the door and though the heat rose, it intensified the desire between them. Keeping her hand in his, he nudged her forward and their bodies touched, his groin to her ass, and he went from semi-erect to hard. He heard her breath catch in the stillness, her fingers fluttering in his. He didn't let them go but kept walking, the pulse in his temples louder than the click of his cane. She stepped forward and the slight rub of her bottom against his fly had him biting off a groan. Though they stood in a slight stream of air, he closed the back door, locked it.

"I'm not going to sleep with you . . . yet." Her voice was breathy.

"Just being with you is enough." An old and often-used phrase and he meant it here and now, but, man, he wanted her in bed and on top of him. He had to block that vision from his mind, and that took more effort than expected.

She led him to the living room and the couch, switching off the overhead light, and he felt the sweep of the air from the fan cool the sweat on his forehead. Only a small, fancy stained-glass lamp on a corner table sent colored glows throughout the room.

Clare's breathing had quickened and she sat in the middle of the couch, giving him the end. He propped his cane against the fatly curved arm and sank down next to her, his own arm curving around her, still holding her hand. His body throbbed with desire, and the explosion of sexual heat inside him, after so long a drought, had him barely hanging on to his control. So he sucked his need in, concentrated on enjoying the sweet, heavy sensuality between them.

"Talk to me, Clare."

"About what?" she said in two little pants.

"Anything." Anything that would distract him from the fragrance of her, the seductive brushing of skin against skin . . . their arms . . . as they sat, the soft length of her thigh against his, the softer weight of her breast against the side of his chest.

"I . . . I have a brother."

One word. Brother. Nearly, nearly broke the spell of desire weaving between them. He'd forgotten, but he wanted to keep her talking, so he asked the next easiest question. "Older or younger?" he croaked his words, but she didn't seem to notice.

"Older." A pause. "We get along but aren't very close."

Zach had loved his older brother, Jim, with all his heart, looked up to him, followed him.

"Do you have siblings?" she asked, her voice a little husky. Focus on that, not the past. The present. The future that would include making love to this woman.

"What about your parents?" he asked quietly, knowing she'd ask in return, but he could handle that; it wouldn't break the tantalizing feelings between them. He released her fingers and began stroking her arm from hand to shoulder, loving the smooth slide over her skin, the tingle on his own palm, calming his emotional pain, charging the air between them with desire. When he reached her fingers again, he turned her hand over and caressed her palm with his thumb. Her body sagged against his side.

"Parents?" she whispered. Looking at her in the multicolored glow, he saw her blink slowly, then stare at her upturned palm that he circled with his fingertip. A breath soughed from her. "My parents are . . . not responsible . . . living off money they didn't earn." Her voice sharpened a little, and he drew his hand up her arm and pulled her closer in a squeeze. His erection throbbed. But this was not only about sex.

"My father is a general in the Marines," he said, a little too harshly.

She turned to him then, her thigh sliding away, but her eyes focused on his, and he stared at her pretty face, pointed chin, cheeks flushed from the heat . . . and maybe lust. Her mouth curved, looking flushed and fuller, too. He leaned toward her, slowly, but nothing shadowed her eyes and her lips parted.

He didn't see her tongue, wanted her to lick her lips. Wanted to taste that mouth, those lips, tangle his tongue with hers. And when he kissed her, she closed her half-lidded eyes and he followed, enjoying the tenderness between them, the rising desire that kept him hard, on the edge of need, riding that edge, reveling in it, relishing the sensations too much to move fast.

TWENTY

SWEEPING HIS TONGUE along her mouth, his whole being clenched when he first tasted her. Perfection, a dark chocolate kind of taste, not at all sweet like he'd expected. Dark chocolate. Oh, yeah.

He probed with his tongue and she opened her mouth, rubbed her tongue against his, then she wound her arms around his neck and she felt so good against him that he moved to lie with her on the couch, pulling her atop him. She straightened her torso, her legs—longer than he'd noticed; why hadn't he noticed those?

Hard and burning up, flames licked inside him as she settled on him, her body soft and tantalizing. He sucked on her tongue and her whimpers mixed with his moan as he ran his hands down her back, over the curve of her fine ass, found the edge of her dress, slipped his hand under it, touched the smoothness of her thigh, feathered his fingers up till he felt the edge of her panties. *Want the heat of the woman. Want the softness of the woman. Want the woman's moistness.*

Want.

"Zach!" She lifted herself, pressing them center to center, rubbing his erection. Not so low a groan now, especially when he saw her breasts so close to his face. Nice and full. Like her mouth, fuller from passion now?

"Zach." Low and whispery. A choked sob.

What the hell?

"I can't do this now."

"Do what?" he croaked, and he focused on her face just in time to see a tear run down her cheek and drip onto him.

Crying! Sexual hunger! Emotions clashed inside him.

"It's just too soon. And I'm not a tease, I swear. I'm sorry." She arched backward again, causing him to grunt, set his teeth, and hang on to control so he wouldn't embarrass himself, as she began to leave him.

Leave. Him.

No. And not just because he wanted sex. This was the first time in too many months that someone had actually held him close, touched him more than just for medical reasons, or for a few seconds, or with more than affection. He needed that. He needed more of Clare.

"My fault," he said, his own gritty words surprising him. He rarely apologized, but he needed her touch, her emotions spilling out onto him, her genuineness. So she saw ghosts; she also had given him something he needed every time they met. Respect? Tenderness? Acceptance without questions? He'd bet she still hadn't run a search on him. He tightened his arms around her waist. "Stay, please." Then he loosened his grip so she could go if she insisted.

"You're aroused."

A laugh, a little painful. "Oh, yeah, but this isn't just about sex." That truth actually came out of his mouth. Geez.

Right thing to say, though; she gave one more of those long sighs and subsided back on top of him, her head turning to lie against his shoulder. Back where she belonged. For now. Zach stuck the burning of unsatisfied lust into a corner of his mind as his brain came more online. "Tough day." He stroked her back.

She sniffled and he snagged a tissue from the coffee table, dabbing at the silver tear trails on her cheek. "Epic day," she said, her body trembled a bit.

After a moment's silence, probably as she went over the day as Zach tried to relax, she said, "But, all in all, we did good."

He grunted. "That's right. Bottom line"—he resisted cupping her ass—"we did good."

"Yes." She took the tissue from him. Her breathing had slowed, her own body becoming more lax. She stroked his face and his dick surged and his heart squeezed. He listened to his heart.

"You got the bad guys."

"We got the bad guys."

Long breaths from her now, and he knew that she must not have been sleeping well. Disturbing dreams had hit him the night before, too.

Minute by minute, her trembling went away.

She cleared her throat. "Why did you become a police officer?"

His mind had been drifting and that yanked it back, focused him, thrust him into a choice. Leave now and break whatever moment they shared. She'd feel rejected.

He discovered that would hurt them both.

The quiet summer night wafted peace around them.

"Zach?"

So he tried to relax, petted her, as he dredged up words of the old story he rarely told. "We'd just moved to a new base and Jim and I had unpacked, done all the regular things that Mom and the lieutenant colonel insisted on, and I wanted to explore. We were finally . . . in the D.C. area."

"Jim?"

"My older brother." He couldn't believe he was talking about Jim, about this. About that epic day. But her serenity was sinking into him. Her breathing had slowed.

Their heartbeats had slowed, too. He could feel hers now. And after a few beats, she said, "Go on."

"I wanted to explore. Go off base this time. I was twelve—old enough, I thought—and had been told the next time we moved I'd get the privilege of being able to go off base." The smell of her was twining around him again, becoming more important than the events of the past. Really good.

"But my father got an unexpected promotion and we moved sooner than our parents had anticipated." He'd have shrugged, but that took too much energy.

Now he let out a long breath, and much of the tension of the day went with it.

"My father didn't want me to go. I argued with him. With Jim." He paused, didn't know how much she was paying attention, but now that he'd started the story, he wanted to end it. "A lot of times it was just me and Jim against everyone else," he murmured. The moving, the many new schools, the expectations of them by everyone, from their parents to other kids on the base.

"Mmm-hmm."

"I waited, sneaked out, and wandered, but didn't actually go off base." Now the inevitable climax of the story had come, had jerked him into wakefulness. The tension was back, and he had to force the next words from his throat. He hadn't talked about this since his time with the last family therapist, years ago.

Clare touched his cheek. Yeah, he wanted her on his chest and more than just tonight, so he'd better suck it up and get the other thing off his chest. "I didn't sneak off base." He'd respected his brother enough that he just walked around the perimeter. Unfortunately, Jim had believed Zach's resentful threats. "But everyone thought I might have, and Jim went off to look for me. He headed into the city where he and I had discussed we'd go first. Was in the wrong place at the wrong time."

One. Deep. Breath. "And got shot. Died. He was sixteen."

The first shot that had wrecked Zach's life. Ruined his family.

Worse than the one that had crippled him and ended his career.

"Gang stuff. His killer was never found. So I became a cop."

"Oh, oh!" Sounded like she wept again. For him. Too emotional a day for her, he guessed. He felt the swish of the tissue as she wiped tears away, heard a delicate blowing of the nose. Ladylike.

"Jim was the . . . glue . . . of the family, the one we all loved best. When he was gone, we were gone." Zach's throat went scratchy, achy. No, he would not think of those terrible days after Jim's death. Because they stung, he closed his eyes. Definitely hadn't gotten enough sleep last night, and strained his eyes.

"I'm sorry," Clare whispered, sifting her fingers through his hair, rubbing his scalp. Simple tenderness and caretaking. From a woman who could become more than lover, a friend.

She *hadn't* left him, and now she put her face against his neck, skin to skin with animal comfort, her breath flowing gently, deepening as she slid into sleep.

Zach didn't move. The story was done; the past was past. Even today's images tagged with jumbled emotions were past, over. Along with Clare's breathing, he noticed the continuing song of the crickets. A coolness wrapped around his feet, eased the heated ache of his bad foot. The front door remained open, the breeze freshened into cool gusts. Too tired to move, letting peace sink into him, his muscles loosen, he put his arms around Clare. Yeah, very nice that he had someone near, to sleep with, that simple animal comfort again. He let the night take him.

He woke to a howl and opened his eyes to see an apparition, a man of shadows dressed in an old-fashioned suit drifting toward him—them. Zach's arms tightened reflexively around Clare.

Blinking, he studied the whites and grays and blacks, scouring his memory for why this . . . being . . . looked familiar.

Clare gasped, and he knew she'd wakened. She gripped Zach's shoulders, lifted her head.

"Jack Slade," she said.

TWENTY-ONE

ZACH JUST STARED. He'd only seen the profile drawing of the guy, but as the specter turned, he knew she was right.

And she was unsurprised.

A dog appeared near his face, his tongue coming out in a swiping lick that only brought cool air.

Puzzle pieces . . . like the puzzle box . . . clicked in Zach's mind. He kept his eyes on the ghost and his arms around Clare. "You've seen him before."

"Yes," Clare said. She sat up, moving off his body to the edge of the couch . . . aware of his injury, then, making sure she didn't hurt him. A big rush of feeling settled near his heart. Yeah, good call in not heading out.

When she'd changed position, the dog and man had blinked out of Zach's vision. Since he wasn't in contact with her.

He should let this be. But he felt good. And this was about Clare and not him, and she was an interesting woman, and it was *Jack Slade* of all people—ghosts—and a puzzle, and he liked puzzles . . . So he sat up, his muscles protesting a little at sleeping on the couch with a weight on him, but more because he'd taken out three bad guys in a short, brutal, very strategic fight. Zach stretched, set his arm around Clare's waist.

The dog, Enzo, sat an inch from his feet, eyes big and dark. The man hovered at the threshold of a tiny hallway that went to the bathroom, Clare's bedroom, and a little home office. Zach stared at the famous man, five feet, six inches, maybe. Zach wasn't used to taking into account floating inches off the floor. Thin, maybe a hundred and thirty. The ghost's light-and-shadow expression wasn't good enough for Zach to read.

"Jack Slade," Zach murmured.

Clare watched him from the corner of her eyes, as if she were waiting for him to get up and leave.

Zach faced the famous gunman. "So, did you kill Beni?"

Brows down, a flash of light in the dark eyes. *No. My men did, and got the lesser reward for doing so.* He turned back to Clare, giving Zach the cold shoulder, literally; Zach felt a chill wave from the guy, even as Zach's insides felt a little icing from within. He thought he could hear the gunfighter's words in his head. Eerie, bordering on scary.

He waited, breath hitching, for what the phantom would say next.

Clare wet her lips; Zach's attention went straight to her mouth and sex, and his dick twitched. *The* best reason for staying with her as far as he was concerned. "That's why you've been studying him," he said. "He's been haunting you."

"Oh, yes."

I regret my intrusion, the ghost Slade said in a snide tone that made the courtesy a lie. He even gave them a sarcastic half bow. *But I insist that we deal with my business now that you have accepted your ability, ghost seer, ghost layer. We do have a time limit.*

"A time limit for what?" Zach asked. Wariness began to replace fascination.

The ghost's jaw flexed as if he had real muscles.

I must return to the place where I did my darkest deed and redress it.

"Returning to the scene of the crime. Which crime was this?" Zach ladened his tone with distaste.

More flashing, real flashing, from the specter's eyes. His spine straightened. Though he was a small man—maybe medium-sized for his era, Zach didn't know—the stagecoach chief certainly had presence. Most likely in life, too. The details of the man's life were hazy in Zach's mind.

"Cutting off Jules Beni's ears," Clare said crisply.

Of course Clare would know all the details, have them on the tip of her tongue. She, too, had straightened ramrod stiff in the circle of Zach's arm.

Now Jack Slade appeared sad. He nodded, fingered his watch fob—where he'd kept one of those ears? Zach's belly squeezed at the thought.

The anniversary of the date comes soon, the ghost said, his face twisting into something Zach wasn't sure he wanted to see, maybe even thinning to a shredded-flesh-over-skull deal.

"How soon?" Zach demanded.

September first.

"That's only six days from now!" Clare sounded appalled.

Zach got the feeling she was one of those people who had a schedule and paced herself to it, moving faster when necessary, but liking the steadiness of the everyday. He could help her overcome that.

Jack Slade's face set, no flashing eyes this time, more like hollowness. *If I am to move on. I must return the ears to the place where I cut the ears off.* He moved his shoulders as if under a huge weight. *That event still resonates in that place. It will continue to do so until I make amends and return the ears.*

Not quite easy for Zach to wrap his mind around that sentence and whatever crappy woo-woo rules the damned spirit had to live under, but he felt tension run through Clare's body.

"Return the ears?" Clare's voice rose to a high squeak.

Zach glanced to where he'd put the puzzle box on the coffee table just last night. Yep, still in the exact same place.

The ghost drifted more purposely toward them. His face fleshed out a little, turned into a pleading expression, he held out a hand. *Please. Please help me leave this horror of a half life.*

Clare began to tremble. Zach could almost hear the fight between reality and this weirdness in her mind.

Breathe! The dog hopped around as if it were a small terrier. And that word sounded in Zach's mind. Oh, yeah, mind-speak continued to be strange, and maybe scary if Zach gave in to that sort of thing. Zach pulled Clare closer. Her skin felt cool to the touch. He reached to where an afghan lay crumpled on the floor, picked it up, and wrapped it around her. For himself, he'd begun to sweat, and the ceiling fan swept it away. The night must still be in the seventies because there was no relief coming from the open front door.

Think! Work the case. An unusual case, but still a damn problem. He gestured widely to attract the phantom's attention and pointed to the puzzle box with the ear. "That's one of the ears, right?" The whole auction thing made sense now.

Yesss, the ghost hissed.

"Where's the other?" Zach asked.

Somewhere near Virginia Dale, Jack Slade said. Meant nothing to Zach. But Clare nodded.

"You gave tips to Clare about the ear in the box, right?" Zach asked. "You should be able to find that other ear."

The shadow man grinned, appearing almost real and like someone Zach might actually be interested in having as an . . . acquaintance.

Yes! His gaze latched on to Clare again. *Now that there is a conduit to help me leave, I can sense the other ear!*

"Great," Clare said grudgingly.

I will go now. Thank you! He nodded gratitude and flickered out.

Breath whooshed from Clare. She leaned on Zach. "Thank you for being here." Facing him fully, she narrowed her eyes as she examined him.

"An interesting puzzle. I'm in." He kept it light, stood and drew her up; his foot dropped and he flopped it around and discreetly leaned against the arm of the couch.

Yay! the dog said in his mind, and probably in Clare's, again jumping around, rubbing himself like a cool breeze on Zach's legs. When Enzo did that to Clare, she flinched, pulled the afghan around her, and stepped closer to Zach, her breasts just slightly away from his chest and her stomach close to his renewed erection.

"What's Virginia Dale? A what or a who?" he asked, frowning because he thought he'd heard and now had forgotten.

"Ah," Clare said. "Jack Slade's headquarters he built when the Overland Stage line moved south because of Indian attacks."

Nope, Zach hadn't known any of that, but he knew Slade had lived in Colorado and Wyoming before ending up in Montana. "The trail moved south. What state are we talking about? Where's Virginia Dale?"

"Here in Colorado. Northern Colorado about forty minutes northwest of Fort Collins. And Virginia Dale, Colorado, is not to be confused with Virginia City, Montana, where Jack died."

Zach nodded. "Easily within driving distance." He gestured to the puzzle box with the car inside that rested on the coffee table. "Sounds like he expects you to return the ears to where he cut them off."

Clare grimaced. "Yes."

"And that would be?"

A line formed between her brows. "Um, one of the Pony Express and stage stations." She shook her head. "Cold Springs, I think." She sagged against him, and he wrapped his arms around her, shifting to brace himself a little more against the couch. But he smiled. Clare had forgotten about his disability, had been the first person he'd met in nearly a year who had treated him normally, and he would always treasure that.

She felt damn good in his arms. "Factoring everything in, and leaving a bit of room, one week, max, and this should be over," she said.

His arms tightened even though he knew she wasn't speaking of their . . . friendship.

Sighing, she said, "What time is it?"

Zach glanced at the large living room wall clock. He'd noticed the woman had a clock, sometimes more than one, in every room. "Five forty A.M. Dawn's coming," he said matter-of-factly. With the continuing nightmares he'd become all too aware of the time of daybreak.

"Oh. Hardly worth going back to bed," she said. "Would you like an omelette or cereal?"

He grunted. He'd rather head to the bedroom with her. "Coffee would be good," he said.

She stepped away, took off the afghan and folded it, draped it over the back of the sofa, and smoothed the throw so it looked nice. Then she crossed to the kitchen and Zach turned his head so the light coming on didn't blind him. Reaching for his cane, he limped back and forth through the living room to get the blood running in his foot.

Definitely time to find a good therapeutic masseur. The sound of beans grinding came from the kitchen; he walked to the threshold to ask Clare for a recommendation, saw her still-tense back, and figured she wouldn't have spent the money on something she'd think was an indulgence.

Zach hunched and released his shoulders. Maybe Rickman would have names—for a massage therapist and a dojo that specialized in cane work. Zach had been lucky to take down the three idiots and knew it.

He watched Clare move around the kitchen, and the ache to have sex with her intensified . . . more like he wanted the intimacy with her than the actual physical climax, and wasn't that an annoying realization?

He clumped over to the front door. It faced west, so he saw some lightening of the sky and the stars fading away, but no colorful sunrise. He wondered how hot the day would get, but not enough to turn on the local morning news.

Stooping, he opened his duffel that he'd left there and fished out his tablet, settled himself back on the couch, and was looking at some maps of the Overland trail, the Overland Stage line, and the Pony Express when Clare walked out with a couple of good-sized mugs of steaming coffee.

He set the tablet aside, stretched his arms and torso before he took the cup, and had to suppress a grin when her stare focused on his chest when his muscles flexed. "Thank you," he said.

She smiled and sat down beside him. "So how did your day go yesterday?"

He nearly spit out coffee as he laughed. He angled his head. "Pretty damn well."

Barking. But he heard nothing in his mind and didn't see any ghostly Labrador.

Clare sipped her coffee. "Yes, mine was . . . notable, too."

She cleared her throat, looked at the open front door. "When do Mrs. Flinton and Mrs. Magee expect you?"

He wasn't sure when the old ladies got up. "Breakfast is at seven thirty, even on Saturday, I guess. But they'd better not expect anything," he said.

Clare looked surprised, then her expression smoothed. "Ah, you don't want people . . . concerned about your well-being?"

"I don't want them checking up on me."

"Deal," she said shortly.

"Didn't really mean you," he muttered. The morning peace had been broken, and he'd done it.

Her pupils were dilated in the dimness; she'd turned off the kitchen light. "I promise you I won't check up on you. But that's a mutual thing. You don't check up on me. Like you did yesterday."

"You needed it," he said, remembering how terrible she'd looked when he'd met up with her in LoDo, trying to shrug off the recollection that he'd had to be chivvied into it by Mrs. Flinton. He felt guilty now that he'd had to be forced to help Clare. For the first time he wondered what she would have done about the robbery if he hadn't been there.

He sized her up, let a quiet breath out of his nose. She wasn't the type to have walked in and tried to handle the suspects herself—unlike many of the women he'd dated before. Not reckless, this woman.

But she frowned and looked pointedly at his cane. "This . . . relationship . . . will be based upon rules that apply to us mutually. If you get to 'check up' on me, I get to do the same to you." She paused. "For instance."

His teeth clicked together and he ground out, "You have a point." The excellent coffee was gone and he stood looking down at her, hearing and ignoring more barking. Bending, he lifted her chin for a hard kiss, liked the heat that zipped along his veins. Then he straightened and stared at her. "I'll be in touch, and you keep in touch, too." He snagged his tablet and his gaze swept over the books. "Count me in on this whole situation."

"Uh," she said. Her eyes appeared a little unfocused, and

that made a side of his mouth lift in smugness at her reaction to the kiss.

He flipped a hand at her and picked up his bag. "Later."

Clare showered and dressed, then perused the most comprehensive biography on Jack Slade. The killing and mutilation of Jules Beni took place at Cold Springs Station, now in Wyoming. She spent a couple of hours researching the place and couldn't find it . . . which made her more determined to discover the exact place, though the ghost of Jack Slade would know easily enough.

So she'd trundle once more back to the Western History room after touring the house she was interested in. Maybe she wouldn't like the feel of it, or Enzo would be wrong about ethereal inhabitants.

But she loved it. Absolutely loved the place. As she walked through the small mansion it *felt* right.

We resonate well with the residence's vibrations, Enzo yipped. *This will be good for us. We will live here and be happy together!*

Well, Clare hoped that sometime Enzo would move out, on, whatever. And was it foolish of her to eye the exercise room and the tiny elevator with an eye out for Zach? Not that she could see him bending his pride enough to use the thing.

Enough bedrooms for two personal offices . . . and, down the road in *her* life at least, a couple of children.

Enzo's nails clicked up the back stairs; Arlene had seen Clare's interest and knew her well enough to let Clare wander around without any prompting.

The master suite upstairs had a fine view of the country club, not that they'd let an assistant-accountant-cum-ghost-seer in: smooth green lawn, lovely old trees, golf course. Clare disliked the modern master bath with granite in gray and gray painted cabinets. Her least favorite color was now gray.

Look, look at the BIG tub! Big enough for two or three of me! Enzo thrashed around in the spa bath as if water filled the thing. Great, now there was ghost water?

No, the bathroom furnishings would eventually have to go, but since they appeared to be new she'd live with them a few years until she couldn't stand it anymore, much like her current house.

One small room off the master suite on the second floor contained a massage table. That might be interesting. She stretched her arms and shoulders, felt tension in her neck.

She'd lingered in the master suite, then descended the stairs again, hand sliding along the original carved wooden railing . . . and through a cool area.

Enzo yipped. *That is the ghost! Sandra could have seen her, but you can't!*

"Thank heavens." Clare still heard Arlene's voice coming from the opposite end of the house, wheeling another deal on her phone, so Clare could answer Enzo aloud. "Will you ask her if she'll be a bother? I love the house." She rubbed the newel post carved in the form of a large stylized pine cone.

She approves of you! You haven't looked outside yet! Come here, come here, so I can show you something!

No, she'd concentrated on the inside, didn't care for the staged furnishings. But she had a few family antiques at her old place and a truckload of Sandra's coming shortly.

Clare went out the back door off the kitchen, glanced at the built-in grill setup, and thought again of Zach. Following Enzo, she crossed the fancily patterned brick patio to what must have been an early garage. Opening the door, she found a very nice room, a tiny kitchen, and doors that might be to a closet and half bath.

Enzo raced in circles around the room. *Look, look! A perfect consulting area!*

TWENTY-TWO

SHE STIFFENED AND shuddered. "No!"

He stopped and sat in front of her with a shocked expression, the fur over his brow ridges wiggling. *But you must consult.*

"Must I?" she snapped. "And I *will not* talk about this right now. Not at all in the near future. Give me a little time, can't you!"

The doggieness began to be replaced in his eyes, and she turned and walked away, striding across the patio and back into the house.

Arlene came toward her with a huge smile on her face, a smile that faded when she saw Clare's expression. She swallowed and disappointment flitted across her features. "Ah, then, I'm sorry this didn't work out—"

Clare guessed she was berating herself for not staying with the client and letting the sale go sour.

"No," Clare said gently, yanking her emotions back on track, ignoring the silent presence of the dog when he strolled in. "I like this house very much, but the price is too high."

"Let's see what we can do," Arlene said.

Clare and her real estate agent drove to a nearby restaurant and talked numbers. Since Clare wished to move in immediately, she finally decided to pay cash for the house. A huge amount of cash at a figure that caused a lump in her throat but wasn't what the sellers were asking, so she thought she got a little deal at least. Arlene danced out of the café to push everyone around and get the closing done in three days counting today, which she thought would work. Clare figured she could get her old house ready for sale in a month.

The end of this month approached rapidly and she'd be making a trip to southern Wyoming. Maybe. Deep in the back of Clare's mind was the niggling thought that maybe the specter of Jack Slade might not be able to find her if she moved. Particularly if it were to a place that was nothing but vacant plain when he'd lived.

On the other hand, the man had managed to set up stations across five hundred miles of open plains, so he was accustomed to the emptiness of the West.

She ate the last bit of croissant, leaving a fifteen percent tip because the place was mostly self-serve, and waited for the cab outside the restaurant. She'd like living in the area, though it would be faster to get around by bicycle than walking. They said you never forgot how to ride a bike, and maybe she would learn that firsthand. She'd like one with a good-sized basket.

As she waited, she realized she wasn't as cold, and Enzo seemed to feel like he didn't have to stay as close to her as he had. He hadn't brought up the idea of consulting again.

Still, if she tried, she could feel his location in her mind, like a chill spot in a certain direction.

She'd accepted that she could see ghosts. Other people had that same gift. It had been described throughout history; she wasn't alone.

The cab drove up and she got in. Enzo caught up and galloped into the backseat with her, grinning and panting. *See, see! You are better now.*

Clare *had* noticed that there seemed to be a lot fewer phantoms on the streets heading back into downtown.

Mostly you will see people you can help at this time, Enzo said.

Is a time element always involved? Clare asked, glad she'd also slipped one of Aunt Sandra's journals into her briefcase so she could come up to speed on the rules of this new life of hers.

The dog nodded with no hint of that huge *Otherness* that sometimes spoke through him. The huge, weird, strange, awesome *Otherness*. She wasn't quite sure what to call it, but did want to avoid whatever *it* was if at all possible.

When she left the cab at Civic Center Park, she enjoyed the simple green and yellow of the day—green trees and grass and yellow sun. All right, there was blue sky with huge white cumulus towering-castle clouds, and the gray of the flagstones, the multicolored library and the odd angles of the art museum. None of which she'd been able to appreciate much since she'd gotten onto this roller coaster of strange.

This time when she walked through the park to the library, no ghosts pressed around her. Nobody curtseyed or tipped a hat, sauntered or strolled with her. Except Enzo. He heeled like a real dog.

The ghost must also want to pass over, he said. *Some are afraid*. He sighed gustily, spraying droplets of vanishing, ectoplasmic goo all over. See, she was accepting this with so much grace she could make jokes. Ha. Ha.

Enzo accompanied her into the library for once, and for an instant she thought he'd abandoned his doggie ways, but he ran back and forth along the long entrance hallway barking his head off. It was interesting seeing who reacted to him. The security guard in the entryway had given him a squinty-eyed look.

Clare took the elevator to the Western History room accompanied by Enzo and nodded to the faces becoming familiar. Ted Mather smiled at her, and a bit of relief released from her. It was hard to work in a tense environment, so she was glad he'd agreed to disagree with her.

She zeroed in on finding Cold Springs, but despite her newfound skill with the materials, she couldn't locate the place. When Arlene called to give her the appointment for closing on her new house, Clare decided to quit and went to a salad place near the library and art museum for lunch.

She was finishing up her sparkling water in the courtyard when she was approached by the ghost of a little girl. Clare choked. Feeling good for a few hours had lulled her mind into forgetting her new circumstances.

When the child, surely under ten years old, looked at Clare, her eyes were like silver fog, glints in mist.

All right. Clare could do this. She could help the little girl . . . move on. Pass over. Walk into the light, whatever.

You can DO this, enthused Enzo.

Clare sat straight and smiled at the apparition, hoping she didn't look scary.

But the little girl bounced over to her. Not like any kind of walking. Clare swallowed. "Can I help you?" she asked softly, not moving her lips much. A lot of people had taken a break in the courtyard.

Nodding, dark curls bobbing, the girl said, *Have you seen my hoop? I need my hoop before I can go.*

Clare cleared her throat and thought of the one "rule" she knew about this whole strange mess. "Did you . . . um . . . die late in the summer one year?"

The girl's eyes slid in Clare's direction. Wasn't she supposed to ask about death? Did that bother them? She didn't recall that it had bothered Jack Slade, though it been a while back that she'd mentioned it.

"I'll look for your hoop," Clare said. She blinked and blinked again, trying to slip into that other "sight." The girl was much more defined than anything else . . . buildings rose, wavered, vanished . . . and what happened when there was more than one set? Clare didn't know what had been here *when* the girl had been here.

I lost my hoop and my life when the moon was nearly dark, the girl said suddenly and from right beside Clare's knee. Clare started.

"Oh." There was timekeeping and timekeeping. A monthly ghost? Who knew? And Clare suddenly wanted this *over*. With another big breath, keeping her own eyes narrowed to focus that other world, she scanned the area. Yes, a hoop! A wooden hoop, about half the size of the girl, who, Clare saw, held a small stick. All right. She could do this.

You can do this! Enzo cheered.

Getting up, focused on the light gray hoop, Clare scuttled through real people and ghostly shades. Those who weren't ready for her help? Weren't at a time when she could help? Later, she'd think about all that stuff *later*. She had a job to do right now.

The wooden hoop lay on the ground. Could she touch it? Clare didn't know, but she curved a hand around it. . . . like closing her fingers around a searing dry icicle. She clenched her teeth and straightened, feeling like she was ripping the object away from sticky ground.

A loud squeal came: *I can see it! I can see my hoop!*

There came little pattering footsteps and the girl grabbed the hoop. More ripping, this time like a layer of flesh from Clare's palm as she released it. Tears stung her eyes at the pain. Setting her hands on the top, the girl jumped through the hoop, feet first. And disappeared.

Hoop and girl rippled in a shocking burst of color in what had become a sepia beige-and-brown world, then vanished.

Clare stood panting, her mind spinning. "Enzo?" she croaked.

Yes, Clare?

Clare settled her mind to pluck words from the chaos. *Are there other, um, beings than ghosts?* She wasn't sure where that idea came from. But she was trembling now.

Yes, Clare, Enzo said in that deeper-than-doggie voice he used sometimes.

"O-kay." *Like you, for instance?*

Perhaps. And like the one your great-aunt Sandra called John Dillinger.

"Clare, are you all right?"

It was Ted Mather who'd put his arm around her shoulders . . . and that was when she realized she was swaying. Darn it!

He didn't smell or feel right, so she made sure her feet were under her and drew away. Her right hand still curled against pain, she took the couple of paces back to the bench she'd been sitting on that still held her bag. No one else had taken the spot and it didn't look as if anyone had stolen anything. How much time had passed? To her it seemed like just a few minutes, but it could have been any amount of time. Any at all.

Her heart thundered, pulse rushing in her ears.

Ted followed. "You haven't been looking good lately."

For sure a clammy sweat covered her, too. Would that always happen? She used a controlled fall to hit the bench, swung her body around more as if she were a puppeteer than by control from her brainpan. She put her feet on the ground, straightened her spine, made her face pleasant, and looked up at Ted.

Not for long, since he dropped down beside her on the bench and she bit the inside of her cheek not to protest.

"I think I might have a summer cold." She tried a cough, and it came out far too easily, and racking.

He frowned. "You should be home."

"I'm in the midst of moving." To her delight, her offer had been accepted and Arlene had set up the closing rapidly . . . three days. Clare had checked in with her brother, who'd been packing up the moving trucks from Aunt Sandra's house—had Clare only left there a week ago? And he would have the truck bring everything to the new place on the same day.

She *should* be working on the move. She should be sorting stuff in her old home—the sentimental and valuable to keep, everything else to go to one of the thrift stores. She hadn't packed her house with items . . .

"Clare!" Ted demanded her attention.

She twitched up a smile. "Yes, you're probably right. I should go home." She stood, and even though it wasn't ladylike or professional, she needed a good stretch. Since she was a weird ghost-seeing person with no job, she had little image left and really worked her muscles, reaching her arms toward the sky.

Maybe she'd take up yoga. Great-Aunt Sandra had loved yoga.

After shifting her shoulders and shaking out her feet, she *did* feel more like herself—her changing self. Still, she managed a sincere smile at Ted. "Thanks for your concern, Ted."

He offered her a bottle of unopened mandarin orange fizzy water. "Here, I got you this."

"Thank you." She twisted the top off, and drank deeply. "Very good, thank you."

Shrugging, he said, "I didn't want you to think I was a

loon about that stage robbery. You're right, I have to check better sources."

She was the loon. The taste of the water went flat and her eyes went beyond Civic Center to focus on the skyscraper that had held her old office. Right now she *yearned* for some nice books to balance. "Everyone makes mistakes," she said. Quitting her job hadn't been one. She feared she wouldn't be able to function in an office environment anymore, and someone else had needed her job to survive. She didn't.

She wasn't quite sure what all she needed to survive, but money wasn't an issue anymore.

"You're quite welcome for the water," Ted said, but he looked disgruntled, as if he didn't like her daydreaming.

"I feel much better. I think I must have made a turn in this sickness." Not a sickness, not a craziness, just an affliction for the rest of her life. And she'd break up the time packing boxes with genealogical research. Aunt Sandra had lived into her nineties; what of the others who accepted the gift?

Ted's deepening scowl impinged on her. "Thanks again. Take care," she said.

"Yeah. Will we see you in the Western History reading room soon?"

He was *not* hitting on her. No such vibes, and even the thought . . . ewwww.

She'd have given him another cough if she hadn't just said she thought she was getting better, and all too easy to start coughing and not quit. Instead she shook her head. "No, I think I'll rest at home. I left the desk in the Western History room tidy enough." The librarians and docents preferred to reshelve books themselves.

"You always leave your space tidy," Ted said mildly.

"I like tidy," Clare said. "Good luck on your studies and with your job for the prof." She couldn't recall the prof's name, though Ted had told her twice. Her brain now had holes in it for sure.

Sweeping up the detritus of her lunch, she hurried back into the restaurant and deposited her recyclables into one of their bins, then headed back out. Ted was entering the library doors, and that banished a little tingle along her spine—not a good tingle as if she were with Zach.

She hadn't called him. No reason to.

Forty minutes later she was picking up boxes at a liquor store at a small strip mall close to her current neighborhood and stacking them in her car. Driving around her area of town was much easier. Though she did see the tall figure of a Native American standing on a rise, wrapped in a blanket and staring west toward the mountains.

Clare would have to learn more about the tribes here.

"Enzo?"

The dog appeared around another car in the parking lot, though he hadn't accompanied her earlier. Clare puffed out a breath.

He sat in front of her and scratched his ear with his hind leg, grinning. *Hello, Clare. Hello! Long time I haven't seen you!* Hopping to his feet, he ran toward her, through her with a chill, licking her hand along the way.

Whoops! Right THROUGH Clare! Hey, Clare!

"Hi, Enzo. I, uh, saw a Native American ghost. Can I . . . uh . . . help him?" Why hadn't she researched the rules yet? "What about religion and stuff?" She flapped a hand.

All religions have spiritual people who help the dead move on, said Enzo, switching to that deeper voice of his.

"I guess that's a yes."

No answer. She shut the door, accepting the presence of Enzo on the passenger seat. "I'll help him . . . soon." Another thing to do: to continue to read her great-aunt's journals, glean the rules from them. So far she hadn't found much that she hadn't discovered on her own.

Time to buckle down.

Zach lounged in one of Rickman's client chairs. The man had called him in to talk about the robbery the day before. Apparently he was working on a "hot" case this Saturday morning. That he didn't keep banker's hours pleased Zach.

Behind his desk, Rickman leaned forward, hands clasped before him. "You aren't telling me everything about the incident yesterday."

Raising his brows, Zach gave a slight nod. "You mean that when I touched Clare Cermak, I could see the ghost of a cowboy waving his hat and yelling, 'Bank robbery'? That what you want to hear?"

Rickman winced, spun his chair around so he could stare out the window. He looked like a brood had fallen right over him like a painter's dropcloth. "No. I *don't* want to hear that." He cut the air with his right hand. "Absolutely not. Why do I get all the characters?"

Zach didn't know whether that meant guys with attitude or people who interacted with those who—were touched by *strangeness* like Mrs. Flinton or Clare Cermak. "I could introduce you to Clare, if you want." He offered just to bug the guy.

His boss glanced at him over his shoulder. "Not right now. Maybe later."

All right, that surprised Zach. "That's all I have for you." He'd given the guy a written report on his lack of progress on Mrs. Flinton's case, and his idea regarding tracing the financials.

"Fine. Here." Rickman swung back to his desk, pulled out a drawer, and flipped a couple of cards onto his desk. One was a magnetic key to Rickman Security and Investigations' workout rooms in the building. They were just a bulletproof door away from a fitness club that shared some of the facilities, though from what Rickman had said, some of his staff didn't consider the arrangement very secure. Didn't bother Zach. He also had a recommendation for a masseur who worked in the club next door.

The other white card had a dark blue drawing of two men in suits and flat hats fighting with canes and read, *Bartitsu for You.*

"Bartitsu?" Zach asked.

"Cane fighting." Rickman's mouth twitched. "I hear the studio caters to the steampunk crowd."

"Steampunk," Zach said flatly.

"Not much steampunk in Montana, huh? Some in Boulder."

Zach grunted. "Some of everything in Boulder."

"And our local Denver science fiction readers and writers community has a thriving steampunk group."

"Right."

Rickman laughed. "Hey, if Robert Downey Jr. playing Sherlock Holmes can do it, you can."

"The original private investigator." Zach tightened his grip on his cane.

"That's so."

"Any of your ex-military guys do this?" Zach flipped the card in his fingers. Just showed the name of the studio, phone, and an address in southwest Denver.

"Nope."

"Didn't think so."

Now Rickman sighed. "Get on with your life as it is now, Zach."

Zach turned and left.

He didn't go to the gym like he'd thought he would; instead he gave the number for Bartitsu for You a call and found an instructor who was willing to meet with him.

TWENTY-THREE

THE SPARRING WITH the tall skinny white guy with a mustache waxed into points and fuzzy sideburns didn't go as well as Zach would have liked. He couldn't take the man down and that was solely because the dude was awesome with a damn cane. At least he didn't go down himself and was sweating less in his shirt sleeves—ungartered—than the instructor.

Pretty much a draw.

Mr. Laverstock pulled a large white handkerchief from his trousers pocket and wiped his face. "We can work one-on-one as we have now, or I have a schedule of classes." He walked into the open doorway on the far end of the room and returned with a sheet of paper. Zach glanced at it and noticed it was the same as the one posted on the bulletin board. The class coming up in a half hour was called "Victorian Vixens."

"Our rate sheet is on the back." Laverstock looked Zach down and up. "You're good. Even good with that cane when you don't know much of what you're doing. Get some sturdier orthopedic shoes and braces for your left foot and ankle. These are the best folks." He handed the sheet to Zach along with a card. Then he patted his face again with the handkerchief. "Get a brace so you can move your foot better and get more aerobic exercise."

"Thanks for the time." Zach bit off the words.

"Welcome." Laverstock scooped up a water bottle from the floor and arced a stream of it into his mouth.

Zach left the building that looked like a failed restaurant, a small standalone place in the lot of a big mall.

A woman wearing a long skirt, a fitted jacket, and a huge hat got out of a sports car. He stared. She raised her brows and winked at him, giving him the once-over and a flirtatious smile.

"I'm early," she said, twirling her cane.

"I'm late," he responded.

She pouted, noted his cane and how he leaned on it, which had his mouth flattening, then walked past him, her skirt swishing. All right, he turned and looked.

And she twitched her ass at him.

He could only think of how Clare might look in the getup. Woman must have had one of those . . . bustles? . . . on. Now that he thought of it, Clare's ass looked good under a sundress, would look good augmented with that bustle thing, and, most especially, would be a fine sight bare.

Just that morning Mrs. Flinton and Mrs. Magee had commented on how he walked carefully, no doubt from "hammering the bad guys." Rickman had told him to get on with his life. The card Laverstock had pressed on Zach was in his jacket pocket; the woman—one from the Victorian Vixens class?—had coolly noted his cane and that he had to use it.

From the minute they'd met, Clare had treated him as if he . . . as if he didn't have a cane . . . like she'd have treated him if they'd met before he'd made the stupid mistake that had gotten him crippled.

Last night he'd told her of the painful loss of his brother and gotten understanding, tenderness, sweet sympathy.

A bird called. Zach tensed, slid his gaze around. A woodpecker, not a crow.

So far he hadn't seen any crows today, and no unfulfilled rhymes dangled. Not that he was thinking about that.

No, he was thinking about Clare. She had her problems, her vulnerabilities, too. He could easily call up her white and frantic face, her dull and blind-looking eyes, when they'd been in LoDo less than twenty-four hours ago.

Another vehicle, a minivan, drew up, and a lady in a white blouse and long skirt got out, pulling a cane she didn't need to walk with from behind her seat. One of those standard wooden deals with a curved top, instead of his straight-handled cane. She smiled at him and hurried into the dojo—not a dojo, a studio.

Greetings and laughter came from the building behind him. *Get a brace*, Laverstock had said.

Clare Cermak had braced Zach last night, was bracing for his spirits. He'd go see her. She'd do him fine.

Clare had worked on the kitchen, emptying drawers, pretty much just moving into boxes the plastic containers in which she kept everything. The remembrance of the lonely melancholy of the Native American pulled at her, along with Enzo's big dog eyes and huge expectations. So she nerved herself and returned to the ghost.

His passing took a very short time and was unnerving. He'd spoken oddly in her head with more images than language; she'd had to assure him that no one of his tribe remained for him to protect, that his horse was gone, too. Then he'd walked down the rise, sending a cold wind her way, and vanished.

Enzo had congratulated her, but with less enthusiasm than when she'd helped the little girl. By the time Clare got home, she'd recovered her warmth and eyed her house. Even with all the fans and cross-ventilation she could manage, it would remain hot. Not conducive to research.

Now that she knew she was home for the rest of the day, she changed into an old and shapeless faded blue cotton sundress—the coolest thing she had in her closet. She opened the place up and continued with the kitchen; most of that would have to move with her. Naturally her new kitchen was a gourmet one with about three times the amount of cabinet space Clare had here. Her low-cost dishes would fit in one of them. Though she'd been bequeathed one of Great-Aunt Sandra's sets, that fine china wasn't for every day. Not that she cared. Clare's mother got a set and so did Clare's sister-in-law.

The kitchen was done quickly. Clare left out only those dishes she might need over the next couple of nights—a single setting.

A couple of hours of work and Clare was wringing wet. Enzo kept her amused with comments, still strictly in his doggie state, running back and forth and *through* the box fans she'd set in the back and front doors. Apparently dodging the blades was great fun. The thought made Clare's head hurt.

She had canceled her appointments with Dr. Barclay. Unfortunately, he kept Saturday hours and his receptionist had put on the man himself, who expressed extreme concern, but Clare had been so relieved she'd acted like her pre-curse-gift self and had laughed, saying she'd come to terms with herself. On impulse, she'd offered to take him out for lunch. To her surprise, he'd accepted, and for the next day. They made a date downtown at one of the fancier restaurants. She could afford it now, and the meal might be less than he charged for a session, and worth it to get rid of him. Could she ever forget the misery she'd felt in his office enough to enjoy the attractive man's company?

No.

And with all his smoothly groomed, expensive looks, Barclay wasn't nearly as sexy as Zach Slade. The doctor's whole person didn't affect her as much as one intense look from Zach. How great that Zach believed in her . . . or was willing, at least, to listen. Just thinking of him made her hotter than ever.

She moved on to her next task, discarding the shelf paper and cleaning the cupboards, and forgot about Barclay.

Soon she'd have to take a break and a shower. She glanced at the desk holding her powerful laptop and a stack of books. The genealogy program whispered to her; so much more fun than packing and cleaning. Ignoring it, she grabbed a portable music player, set the playlist for rock, and stuck in the earbuds, determined to finish the living room. Already she had a stack of stuff that wouldn't be moving with her lined up against the far wall. The television monitor was only three years old, so she'd take it.

Zach's here! Enzo zoomed from the backyard through the kitchen, probably through the fan in the front door and Zach, too.

"Clare!"

The second time a man had shouted at her that day, though with all the fans and her earbuds in, she didn't blame him. She hurried to the living room and saw him on the other side of the screen door, staring down at Enzo, who hopped around and rubbed against him.

She'd gotten the idea that he could hear the dog, even without being in contact with her. But then Enzo wasn't just a ghost dog. He was also some sort of spirit that Clare didn't think too hard about. Especially when a handsome and sexy guy scowled at her under shaggy hair. She pulled out her earbuds and plucked her music player from her dress pocket, setting it on the coffee table. Then she moved the box fan from the door and turned it off, and unlocked the screen door.

"Clare," he said.

"Yes?" She backed up as he came in, darkly intense.

Two good paces in and he yanked her to him.

Wow, he was a solid wall of muscle and his strong arm went behind her back.

"Clare." His other hand went to her chin and she let him tip it back for a kiss.

His eyes held stormy secrets.

She rubbed her hands up and down the sleeves of his fine white linen dress shirt. He'd left whatever jacket he might have been wearing in his car. "Zach."

His mouth came down on hers and pressed once, his tongue probing along her lips for her to open to him.

She did. And closed her eyes, willowed against him—such a solid man. Tasted him as he rubbed his tongue against hers. Felt the tightening of her nipples in desire, and more, she felt his erection, as solid as the man. She'd been sweating while working, and now she dampened, all over and under and in between with the flush of arousal. She *ached* for him, for intimacy, for completion.

For release.

He'd been sweating, too, doing more than working inside and walking around outside. That should have turned her off. It didn't. His smell went straight through her and had her sex clenching with need.

Yes, he smelled right.

She pulled away, still leaning against him. "Zach. I'm all sweaty. I mean, I've been packing."

His gaze swept the room: the organized empty boxes against the wall, the half-filled ones just beyond the kitchen threshold. The arm around her back fell and his fingers touched her bare leg below the hem of her short dress, feathered along her skin. He grinned. "Nice." Leaning close again, he dipped his head near her shoulder, kissed her neck up to her ear with a touch of tongue, tasting her.

When he raised his head his cheeks had flushed, giving him a ruddier look, accenting that hint of Native American blood. Oh, yes, sexy!

He smoldered. She'd never had a look like that aimed at her. Her knees weakened; her whole body loosened. "You taste like woman. You smell like Clare."

She had to inhale deeply just to have enough control to take a tiny step away from him, blushing herself. His hand curved around her cheek, thumb caressing her. "Peachy, the pink under your golden skin." He bent and kissed her quickly. "Redder, fuller lips, just for me."

He shifted; his arm came around her again and he lifted her from her feet, took the couple of steps to the couch, and sank down with her, her on bottom, him on top. Though he'd done all the work, her heart thundered at being in a sexual position.

"Clare." He swept kisses along her neck and her mind began buzzing, doing a slow swoop of rationality sinking and rising in a sea of red desire.

Pushing the straps of her dress down and the bodice to her midriff, he flicked the front clasp of her bra open.

His hands on her bare breasts felt wonderful, so fabulous that she moved under him, aligning her body so she could rub against him in just the right spot, just the right way. Was that whimpering and panting hers? Oh . . . yes!

She slid her hands inside his pants. Smooth linen shirt under her palms, heavier trousers against the backs of her hands, then cotton boxers . . . male skin, lightly haired along his thighs, smoother on his butt . . . she began to slide her hands toward his front when he groaned, stopped her, rolled them over on the couch with her on top.

Good, she could breathe. She found the clasp of his waistband. His shaft was so hard and strong and long and thick and she needed that in her *now*.

"Wait. Wait." His fingers stopped hers.

"What?"

"Rubber."

Her mind went blank, then, "Oh. Protection."

He cracked a laugh. "In my wallet, bought them last night."

She bent down and kissed his mouth, swiping her tongue along his lips. When he opened his mouth she rubbed her tongue against his as she rubbed her lower body against his and stopped only when her mind was sinking into the world of blazing lust. She dug the word she'd wanted to say from her brain. "Optimist."

Another laugh. He lifted his head for a very brief kiss. "After last night, I knew we'd wind up in bed together. Realist."

"Bed? This is the couch."

"Great couch, you're gonna take it with you, aren't you?"

"Hadn't planned on that, but yes. And you're lying on your wallet."

He arched again, stroking her with his body in just the right place. While she gasped with pleasure, he tipped her in toward the back and shucked his pants and boxers, then took care of protection.

She'd wiggled out of her dress and underwear, only glancing at the front door before he rolled her back over and kissed her, hot open mouth to hot open mouth. When they broke for a ragged breath, he said, "You coulda kept the dress on."

She couldn't even answer as she poised over him, rubbed her sex back and forth along his. So extremely, sensually good. Again. Again. Pleasuring herself, glorying in feeling how he thickened under her, became more rigid.

His hands cupped under her bottom and his hands against her skin broke the minor trance of escalating passion . . . and added a new element all at once. Her eyes had closed and she'd breathed in the thick air and the scent of them . . . him and her, mingling. Now her gaze went to his strained face, his own pupils so dilated she could see only an edge of green.

"Clare. You're. Killing. Me," he panted.

More sweat beaded on his forehead, appeared as if it might run down his temple. She had to taste that, the essential Zach. So she leaned forward, nearly stopped as the tip of him touched exactly where she *needed*. She sucked in a breath and trailed her tongue across his forehead. Salt and Zach . . . the taste of plains instead of city . . . sage, something like piñon pine.

And he angled her and thrust up into her and she moaned as he fit so well.

Paused. Cloth on his chest instead of skin that she wanted to feel. She unbuttoned his shirt. Muscles, little hair. Nice.

"Sexy woman," he said.

TWENTY-FOUR

WHY WAS HE still talking? She began to move . . . rise until only the tip of him was in her, slowly, slowly slide back down. His jaw bunched, more color coming to his face, accenting the hue of his eyes. Beautiful man.

"Slow is good," he slurred.

Still talking. So she started a rhythm, watching his face, feeling him flex and throb and fill her.

They moved together, spiraling up to the pinnacle of teasing ecstasy with each surge of their bodies. Zach's eyes blurred . . . because of her own vision or his, she didn't know, but her palms on his chest got a little slippery and she dug into his chest hair and he grunted and his hips moved faster.

"Cla-are." Her name came broken on a jerky breath, like nothing she'd heard before, ever, and her body clenched tight and hot around him and he thrust and rapture shattered her into sparkling diamonds turning into rain, into mist, her spirit free and flying before coalescing back into her pulsating body and she felt him arch. His fingers clenched into her butt and she peaked again, quick and hard, and fell forward gasping.

"Clare," he murmured, his hands falling from her.

She found the fast pulse of his heartbeat in a thick vein in his neck and licked it and he shuddered. "Clare!"

Subsiding on his chest, stroking his muscles instead of digging into them, Clare sighed out, "Zach."

They lay there together, their hearts pounding and their breathing steadying into unison, taking long minutes for themselves. Clare's mind seemed to turn on first and she said, "Wow." Very hot, very sticky between them, and she didn't mind.

Zach grunted a laugh, rubbed her back, ran his fingers through her hair, lifting it away from her damp nape, and the quiet whoosh of the fan overhead impinged on her hearing as her body cooled.

Her lover lifted her chin so their gazes could meet; his eyes were sensual and a lazy smile curved his lips. He looked satisfied, knowing that he'd pleased her and had reached climax, too.

After a quick kiss on her lips, he rolled her to the back of the couch, and the change in angle told her she wasn't nearly as recovered from the fabulous sex as she'd thought, since her stare stayed fixed as she moved. She blinked and refocused just in time to see a taut backside turning into the small hallway that held her bathroom.

"I'm starving," Zach called. "Can you order something in? Something that will be ready after shower sex?"

Clare scrambled to her knees, shoving her hair out of the way, her brain flipping through cuisines. She so rarely ordered delivery, she had to think about it. "Pizza or Chinese?" she asked.

"Surprise me," Zach called as he turned on the shower.

She didn't have that big a water heater. Grabbing her phone from the table, she ordered Happy Family from the Chinese restaurant; it would arrive in half an hour.

Running to the bathroom, she stepped into the tub shower, her toes curling. Steam rose around her and even in the heat, the humidity felt blissful.

Zach was simply gorgeous. All right, he looked as if he'd lost some weight, but he still had excellent definition. Better than she. She bet she'd have to up her exercise program if she wanted to keep him as a lover, and she did.

In the damp, his hair appeared to wave more than she'd noticed; her fingers itched to touch it. It was longer, shaggier than she usually preferred. She liked his hair, and the looks of him, his slow smile that melted her.

She was very glad she'd added nonslip strips to the bottom of the tub.

What with another round in the shower, the arrival of good Chinese food that they both ate with chopsticks, and easy conversation, any problematic after-sex tension just evaporated. There had been only a couple of hitches in their post-coital glow—one when Clare asked Zach to move the puzzle box from the coffee table to the top of her one knickknack cabinet, and one when Enzo made a clever comment about how good they were together.

She and Zach had played footsie under the dining room table, so he seemed to hear, and occasionally respond, to the dog. He *didn't* seem to want to analyze the psychic stuff or talk it out. No doubt a man thing to just accept it without dealing with it, so she went along with him.

After dinner, he helped her tidy up, finish packing the living room and start on her small home office. As the sun set, they were rolling around in her bed, learning each other's bodies, though through distraction or Zach's avoidance, she didn't get a good look at his injury. Not that she cared much; the man was an attentive lover and there were other parts of him that proved more interesting and demanded more of her attention.

They finished up the last of the Chinese when dark fell, and he rose to go. She hadn't asked him to stay overnight, and he hadn't pressed to sleep with her. He had called Mrs. Flinton and Mrs. Magee earlier to let them know he wouldn't be back until after dark. He and Clare had spoken about their respective moves. His voice held affection for the ladies, and she thought it was a good fit for him and them, for the time being.

All the changes in her life had such sharp edges right now that she didn't want to hurt herself more than necessary . . . perhaps become more attached and dependent on Zach just because he'd come into her life at this time. All that could wait for later.

Not to mention the fact that he'd made his discontent with her current house evident with a couple of grunts. Neither of them believed this house would sell soon in the sluggish market, nor would it sell until the weather cooled down. The lack of air-conditioning this year was a real liability.

Clare would focus on her new house and her new gift, have this house professionally cleaned and take Arlene's advice about when to list the place with an eye to selling. In any event, she should get enough to pay the mortgage off and maybe a little more, which just plain satisfied her. She'd done fairly well.

But at the door, when Zach pulled her against him and despite all the sex they'd had, her nerves picked up an anticipatory buzz.

He kissed her. "I like you a lot, Clare."

"Ditto."

"Not over?"

Her heart gave a hard thump at the question. "No."

"Good." A short kiss. "Later."

"Later."

The cane added to his swagger.

Her energy seemed to drain out as she turned out the porch light after Zach drove off, then reluctantly stopped the fan and moved it away, closing and locking the door. Such a small starter house, but she'd been happy here. Her parents had been appalled. They'd come once, dismissed her house and Clare herself.

Two more days and she'd be gone.

Turning off all the lights, she shuffled through the heat and fell onto the clean sheets on the bed that she and Zach had made together. Her insistence on that and his male teasing made her smile. She knew Enzo had joined her since he radiated cool.

"Good night, Enzo." She reached out and petted his back, her fingers turning icy in an instant.

Good night, Clare. You are doing good. Mostly, he said.

She sniffed, but no ghosts, no nightmares, and no chills racked her body while she slept. Though she wasn't nearly as comfortable as when she'd been crowded on the couch with Zach the night before.

In the morning, Clare had a list and a tight schedule and concentrated on packing, ignoring the lure of research on the computer. The more she worked, the more she thought of questions about Jack Slade, Cold Springs Station, ghosts, mediums, and the rules of her gift.

She thought of Zach . . . tried to set aside the remembrance of his hands on her body, her hands running over his muscles, but the sex had been so incredible, and the man himself was enthralling. She should, of course, do that web search on him, but it really didn't matter who he was . . . *before*.

He was an intense man, and she believed that was nothing new to him. And that he'd told her about his brother, opened up a hurt that was so devastating she could still hear it in his voice, touched her. His story made her more protective of him and his feelings, though she wouldn't tell him that.

He had issues, but didn't everyone? And sharing emotions, intimacy, was *almost* as good as the sex. She felt he was negotiating rough waters like her.

Clare wasn't the person she'd been *before*, just a little over a week ago. She wasn't an accountant, had no job, had no intention of being a professional . . . medium? . . . she *hated* that word. She had no intention of becoming a professional Ghost Seer, or Apparition Mover, or Phantom Vanquisher, or *whatever*. She didn't need to work. All she needed to do was practice her gift enough to keep the madness and chill away.

That didn't sit well, to do the minimum and not her best. But she'd been pulled into these new circumstances kicking and screaming, against her will, and didn't want to do more than the minimum to get by right now. Later . . . when she'd become accustomed to her new situation, after she'd learned all she could, she'd probably feel different.

Her tablet alarm rang like tolling bells. Time to buy Dr. Barclay lunch and show him the improved Clare and get him out of her life.

* * *

Rickman had spoken with Mrs. Flinton about her case the day before and had finessed from the older lady that her father's family, who'd taken her in when she was a child, had also kept good records, ledger books that she'd stored in the attic. Zach's boss had approved using Clare as a financial consultant, and that morning Mrs. Flinton had handed Zach the three ledgers from the year in question; they smelled of dust and mothballs.

Ready to see Clare again, get her focused on something other than her new strange gift and the death of her aunt and everything else surrounding that, Zach texted her to meet near noon. She said she'd be having lunch at an uptown restaurant. Zach smiled. He'd figured Clare for being careful with her money, but now that she had a whole lot more to be careful with, she seemed to be eating out more often. He hoped she continued to eat, but she'd looked good the day before, had been energetic with sex, and sharing the Chinese food had been fun.

Zach had considered a messenger bag or a briefcase and gone with the case. Odds were he wouldn't be carrying anything of extreme importance and all he had to do with a briefcase was drop it if he got in danger, unlike a bag that could hamper him.

So he strode into the restaurant, waved off the hostess, and scanned the first room. Whomp! Emotional fist in the gut. Clare sat at a table with a professional, distinguished type of guy in a thousand-dollar suit. Wavy gray and white hair, well-kept hands, smooth hands, and a face women would like. Gym-muscular, trim, but he still had years and pounds and polish on Zach.

Didn't look like an accountant, possibly a lawyer, could be a medical doctor, definitely not a broken-down ex–deputy sheriff.

No dirty dishes showed, but a half glass of white wine stood before Clare and a tall tumbler of water with lemon before the guy.

The dude was flirting extremely discreetly, and the helluvit was that Zach couldn't read Clare well enough to know how she was taking that flirt. She wasn't flirting back, like she had with Zach when they'd met, but from the tilt of her head and her listening expression, she could be interested.

Possessiveness surged through him, along with a wave of protectiveness. Clare had been through a lot lately. He didn't want some guy twisting her around more than she was.

Zach's hand clenched the handle of his cane as the man brushed Clare's fingers when he reached for his water glass.

TWENTY-FIVE

SHIFTING A SHOULDER to release tension, the one without his holster, Zach began to move toward them . . . slower than he wanted because he had to proceed cautiously to take care with his foot drop. Since he was considering the bartitsu lessons, he might let the thought of a brace worm into his head.

Halfway across the room Clare glanced up and saw him. Her eyes seemed to light and Zach wanted, badly, to lengthen his stride but cursed instead within his head.

By the time he reached the table, the guy had become aware of him; his smile for Clare faded and he slanted his body to see Zach.

The man scanned Zach from top to toe, then met his eyes with a penetrating gaze and Zach's stomach clenched. He knew that look and now he knew that professional. Shrink. Psychiatrist, psychologist, life coach, counselor—though the guy must have an MD or a lot of other letters after his name to be able to afford the shirt, suit, tie, cuff links, watch, and shoes he wore.

Zach came up and put his briefcase down, lifting his hand to Clare's shoulder. "Hey, Clare. Good to see you. I have something you might be interested in," he said easily, smiling at the guy in the suit. "Zach Slade."

"Dr. Madison Barclay." The man inclined his head at Zach. Didn't offer his hand, so he wasn't so interested in Clare that he wanted Zach's free hand off Clare, and he didn't want to shake hands with Zach. Zach had dealt with all sorts of therapists and psychiatrists, both after his brother's murder and with regard to his mother's mental illness, as well as more recently after the shooting and his crippling. Some were worth the pain of sessions, some just wrongheaded, and some were scammers about as good as any other con men in the business.

"I was seeing Dr. Barclay recently," Clare said a little stiffly.

Barclay's eyes tightened when he heard her call him by his title.

"Isn't that unethical, hitting on a client?" Zach said.

"He's not my psychologist anymore," Clare said. She wiggled her shoulder and Zach reluctantly dropped his hand.

"Not so very long with me." The man smiled again at Clare. His teeth were too even and white. "But I know Clare well," he said with a pompous note in his voice. Since he hadn't reacted to Zach's surname, Clare must not have spilled about the ghost of Jack Slade.

Zach smiled slowly and just had to put his hand back on Clare's shoulder and squeeze. "There's knowing and knowing."

Barclay's jaw set.

"And speaking of that." Zach set the briefcase on the table, flicked the lock open, took out a ledger book and placed it near Clare, flipped it open. As he'd expected, her gaze became glued to the columns of figures.

"What's that?" asked the shrink.

"Antique financials in a case I'm working on. Expenses, I believe. I think Clare can track them for me, give me some insights."

She was running her fingers down the columns, reading the handwritten pages.

"Give her a project outside settling her great-aunt's estate and moving into her new house. Good for her, don't you think?"

This time Barclay's smile was chill and aimed at Zach. The shrink folded his pristine napkin and rose slowly, moving his chair back, and inclined his head to Zach. In a rich, mellow tone, he said, "You are obviously a very angry man." His gaze flicked to the cane, to Zach's orthopedic shoes, back up to his left knee. Okay, the man was sharp enough to spot the weakest point of Zach's body. Kudos.

Barclay continued, "If you wish to see me on a professional level, we can work through your issues with your disability."

Zach showed his own teeth. "Sure. Until then, you might want to consider that I'm armed and dangerous." He shifted and leaned on a chair enough that his jacket would gape to show his shoulder holster.

The psychologist retreated a step as surprise came to his eyes, and then his cheeks took on color.

"Clare." Barclay raised his voice. "Thank you for the lunch."

Clare jolted and looked up, her gaze sliding back and forth between them, her expression wary that she'd missed something—like a clash of males. She bit her lower lip and Zach wasn't the only one who focused on her mouth.

Standing, she offered her hand to the shrink. "And thank you for agreeing to have lunch with me, Madison. I enjoyed it." Her smile was simple and sincere and Zach saw the guy softening. Too damn bad.

"I'll see you later," he said, pressing her fingers.

"Outside your office, sure," she said, rushing her words slightly so that Zach hoped she didn't mean them. The doctor preened. Then, without another glance at Zach, the psychologist walked away with a smooth stride Zach watched and envied.

When he returned his attention to Clare, she'd sat again, was sipping her wine and reading the ledger entries as if they were riveting. Zach took Barclay's seat and scrutinized her. Why was he so very attracted to her? Yeah, she was sexy as damn all, lovely, repeatedly presented riddles, and had haunting eyes that continued to suck him in.

He leaned back, lifting his right heel in a move he'd practiced to look casual, and contemplated his feet in good cotton socks and ugly leather shoes, not cop shoes. His left foot, ankle, and tibia didn't look damaged.

And then he understood why Clare had slipped under his defenses and into his heart more than anyone else in a long, long time. It wasn't that Clare didn't know he was "disabled." It was that she made absolutely no fuss over the fact. Just a minor part of him being Zach Slade.

Even though he knew his injury wasn't minor. It had damn well ruined his life . . . all right, ruined his *career*. And, yeah, he sure as hell remained furious about that.

She'd accepted him just the way he was now. Didn't think about how he might have been *then*, when he was whole.

As far as he knew, she hadn't done a simple Internet search on him . . . and he did know enough that if he asked her now not to, it would pique her curiosity enough that she'd head straight for her computer.

She didn't have the driving curiosity that he did.

Eventually she'd see him as he had been; the pics were up there. Hell, pics of his shattered tibia and droopy foot were up there. Until he and she were more involved than a few nights of awesome sex, he'd like her *not* to be able to judge him against the man he once was. Right now he was too thin, his muscles shrunken, and he'd had little aerobic exercise.

For that he'd need even better shoes and a brace.

Finally, after she'd turned to the next page, he said, "So, you had lunch with the doctor. Is he any good as a psychologist?"

She looked up and grimaced. "He is supposed to be the best, but he wanted to discuss my childhood and I wanted to know if I was going crazy by seeing ghosts. He *is* expensive. I wished to end our association on a good note, so I took him to lunch." She pouted. "On Sunday. He ordered the most expensive item on the menu, too."

Zach chuckled. "And you, what, had soup?"

She shrugged. "I had a good meal." She waved a hand. "Something or other." She matched his gaze and repeated. "He always expected me to talk about my childhood. Not my favorite subject."

He got what she was saying. He never liked talking about

his childhood, not even the better times before Jim was killed. Two of a kind, there.

"Have you had lunch?" she asked.

"Nope."

"I'll look at this while you eat, but I've already paid my bill."

Zach laughed, shook his head. "Clare, you're a treasure."

She grinned. "I know."

But as he signaled the waitress and gave her his food and drink selection, he didn't like the shadow in the back of his mind that whispered that it mattered, a lot, that Clare had had lunch with some other guy. And to remember that she broke up with men at restaurants.

Clare took the ledger home and for once the sky had clouded over so she could sit in her dry backyard without experiencing ferocious heat. Along with the ledger, Zach had provided a list of the eleven items Mrs. Flinton recalled from her childhood home and wanted back. Attached to the list were drawings or photos of similar items, and Clare's eyebrows rose at the general six-figure amount that the furnishings would be worth now.

Rubbing her hands, then setting a notepad and pencil next to the book, she began studying the ledger.

She soon became accustomed to the overly fancy cursive writing and the standard expenditures . . . and began to see that some items were "sold" to a friend or relative of the guardians' family, unrelated to Mrs. Flinton by blood, only by marriage, for a nominal amount. Clare's mouth tightened. This had been just plain stealing.

With all her accountant senses alert, she scrutinized each entry.

Now and again, when her eyes hurt or she ran out of iced tea or lemonade, she went back in, eyed the packing that needed to be done, and did some physical work on her move. It was unlike her not to stick with a task until it got done, no matter the hours needed, but today she found that changing up the work was more efficient and helped her focus her attention on different items than Zach Slade. Honestly, the man and her budding relationship with him tended to dominate her thoughts more like she was a teenager than a mature, professional woman. She almost felt giddy when he was near. The surge of welcome, inner sexy heat helped her pack up her bedroom faster.

Unlike her office and living room, the bedroom had furniture she'd be giving away to a local charity: good, uninspired pieces except for the bed. In the back of her mind she acknowledged that she'd always expected to have antique furnishings that her parents kept in storage or from Aunt Sandra. That was a little creepy.

When she had to close the back door because the sun slanted in, she took *another* shower, donned another sundress, and moved the search inside. After a while, she had a list of names and called Mrs. Flinton.

"Hello, Clare, dear. How are you doing, and how is dear Enzo?"

Just that easily the zone she'd been in when focused on the ledgers shattered and she was flung back into the new odd land she inhabited. She cleared her throat and headed to the refrigerator for another glass of lemonade. "I'm fine, Mrs. Flinton." Clare poured more liquid into a tall glass. "Uh, everything went well, and I am, uh, adjusting to my new, uh, circumstances." Stop those "uhs"!

"I'm actually calling about your case. Did Zach tell you I'd be looking at your guardians' books?"

"Yes, I authorized you with Tony Rickman."

"Ah, good." Clare had forgotten Zach's new boss's name. "Um, yes. I've examined one of the ledgers and found a couple of names . . . leads . . . and I'd like your permission to check those names with an online genealogical program I'm, uh, using."

"Oh! That sounds wonderful! Now why have I never considered tracing my own gift?"

Once again, Clare's mind was wiped clean of figures and headed over into family trees. "Ah, I *did* want to ask if you have done research into your family and if you might have a family tree."

"I do, of course," the woman said. "Somewhere, and copies, too, I believe. But I've always considered living in the present and with an eye on the future the best balance for one with psychic talent, especially a ghost seer, don't you?"

Clare's palm went sweaty around her phone, her mouth dry. She looked with longing at the glass of lemonade, but she didn't want any sound of swigging to go over the phone, so unprofessional. "Absolutely, concentrate on the future," she agreed.

"And I've heard those computer programs are so clever!" Mrs. Flinton enthused. "Maybe we can get together some time . . ."

"Sounds excellent," Clare said. "But I truly wish to follow this thread while my discovery is fresh, though I do have thorough notes, of course."

"Naturally, Clare." Mrs. Flinton sounded disappointed. "But I'll let you go. I believe you will find my family tree on the major genealogical website under Flinton-Patterson-Wembly, and it's public." She spelled out the hyphenated names.

"Thank you," Clare said. "I should, ah, hand off this report to Zach today."

"Oh! Such progress. And you *must* come to tea again, soon."

"Soon," Clare promised. "Thank you, good-bye!" She clicked off, feeling sweaty again. Putting her phone down on the kitchen table—which she was giving away—she drank half the tumbler of lemonade.

Still hot, she took a paper towel, dampened it, and wiped her face and neck.

You did not say "hello" from me, Enzo accused, sitting next to her, pouting.

Clare jolted. "Sorry." This dichotomy of having her new life impinge on her old seemed to be discombobulating her brain.

She accessed the online genealogical program, found the names of the people who'd "bought" the furnishings of Mrs. Flinton's childhood home. Several of those lines had grayed-out "living offspring," but Clare could give the names of the parents, and grandparents, to Zach and he could do the rest. Meanwhile, she leaned back in her chair with a sense of contentment at a job well done.

She chuckled. Rather a new way of thinking of "forensic accounting."

That evening she sat on her front stoop. Most of her personal property was in boxes, ready to move.

Tomorrow she'd have a new view if she happened to want to sit outside on the front porch in the evening. Across a wide street she'd see the beautifully landscaped lawn and garden of a lovely house in the Spanish-influenced style. Not as beautiful as her new home, but nice.

And if she wanted to sit outside in the back, there was the bricked patio, the gazebo, or the lawn. With the twelve-foot-tall redbrick walls, she could make one corner of the yard a small secret garden. That might appeal.

She could have a pet. She slid her eyes toward Enzo, who lay, more transparent than ever, with his paws curled over his belly on the lawn going yellow from her lack of attention over the last week.

She'd like a cat.

A shiny black Mercedes pulled up in front of her house. The passenger door opened and a woman shot out toward Clare. "Ms. Cermak?"

Clare blinked. "Yes?"

Two seconds later the plump middle-aged *weeping* woman stood shaking in front of Clare, waving a photograph at her. "Please, please, Ms. Cermak, contact my Mary and tell me how she is."

"What?"

"I'm Jennifer Creedy. Our . . . my . . . our daughter Mary. She passed on last month. Please. I need to know—"

TWENTY-SIX

CLARE'S JAW DROPPED. This couldn't be happening. She looked around wildly, but who else could the woman be talking to?

"I heard you were a medium. I've tried everyone else, heard you were new to town."

Standing, Clare sidled away from the distraught woman.

"Please, please, I need to know," the woman pressed.

Know what? Her daughter was dead. From the glance Clare got from the picture, the child looked in poor health but happy. Why would her ghost hang around? Clare didn't know all the rules yet, but she was certain that her gift didn't deal with contemporary ghosts. "I can't help you," she said.

The soft thud of the other car door sounded and a man in an expensive dark suit, also middle-aged and portly, came up to them. He put his arm around the woman's waist. "Jennifer, you're babbling; lay it out for Ms. Cermak."

"Oh. Oh!" More tears, sobs, and wailing. Clare *felt* her eyes widen in horror.

"I can't help you." She tried to back away, but her heels hit the stoop step.

"Shh." Mrs. Creedy's husband squeezed her, helped her

lower herself to Clare's concrete stoop. "Just calm down a little." He pulled a large handkerchief from his pocket and handed it to her. "You said we'd take this slowly, and you jump out of the car when it's still nearly running."

"Oh, Bill!"

"I'll talk with Ms. Cermak, why don't I?"

Face muffled in the handkerchief, Mrs. Creedy said, "All right, Bill. Sorry."

He patted his wife's shoulder. "It's tough."

But his face hardened when he glanced up at Clare, jerked his chin to have her move with him a few feet away. He looked through the open door as he did so and his lip curled. "I don't approve of you people. You *leeches*. But my wife needs reassurance. So I'll give you a grand to tell her what she wants to know. Just do it, you fraud."

"I'm not!" Clare's voice rose. "I *don't* see ghosts."

Another black look. "You fucking lie."

Fisting her hands, she fought for control, jutted her own chin up, *willing* back tears and staring at Mr. Creedy with hot eyes. "I cannot help you. I cannot help your wife. And I don't need your money."

"Look, woman—" Creedy grabbed her arm.

"You'll want to let Clare go," Zach said in a softly dangerous voice.

Creedy stiffened, dropped his hand, and swung around.

Clare hadn't noticed Zach drive up.

Mr. Creedy flushed and raised his hands. "Fine, fine." He appraised Zach and dismissed him. That informed Clare the man wasn't as nearly as intelligent as he thought he was.

Enzo appeared, stared hard at the woman with those unfathomable misty eyeholes. The mantle of the *Other* was upon him. *Tell her it was time for the child to die.*

Clare gasped. *Are you crazy! That's . . . that's horrible. And trite!*

TELL HER. I can see what will comfort her. This will work for her.

Shivering with stress and the chill emanating from the dog, more to share comfort in this surreal experience than anything else, Clare sat down and put her arm around the sobbing woman's shoulders. "It was . . . it was time for your Mary to die."

The woman's head came up. "Really!"

God called her to partake in the joy of being with Him, Enzo said.

Clare would never believe such words if something happened to her child, never. She didn't have such faith.

But Mrs. Creedy's gaze had latched onto Clare. Being serious was not a stretch, nor was keeping her voice soft. "God . . . God called Mary to partake in the joy of being with Him," Clare said, and hoped she wasn't struck down for saying words she didn't believe, couldn't understand herself.

Mrs. Creedy's expression eased.

"You should talk to your minister about this."

"That's what Bill says." Mrs. Creedy turned to look at the men.

Zach stood with deceptive casualness; something about the way he held his stick showed Clare that he wouldn't hesitate to use it as a weapon.

She stood and urged the middle-aged woman to rise with her. "Well, your husband knows you the best, doesn't he?" She groped for more words of solace, *hated* this; it all made her feel fake. Terrible! "You have your husband, too. He is grieving, too."

Zach's face paled and his lips thinned. He'd be remembering his brother.

"Cleave to your husband, give and take comfort from him," Clare said thickly, hoping against hope those were the right words to say. She thought of the photo and how cheerful the little girl had looked, summoned up standard sympathetic sentiments. "She . . . was . . . *is* . . . joyful."

"Yes, yes she *is*!"

Clare straightened to her full height. "Go in peace and with peace in your hearts."

"Oh, yes! Thank you!"

"You're welcome." Clare had done nothing.

Mrs. Creedy turned and took a stumbling step to the car. Zach set his free hand under her elbow, helped her to the vehicle and opened the door. "Just you sit and rest, now," he said.

The guy reached into his jacket and came out with a wallet. Clare moved close to him. "Don't you give me anything. I don't want it, and I certainly don't deserve it."

His eyes narrowed and his head tilted.

"*Take care of her.* Show a little sensitivity. Don't bring her back, and don't give my name to anyone. I'm not in the medium business. Just go away." She flapped her hands. "Go. Now."

With a shake of his head, he stuck his wallet back into his pocket and went to the car.

They drove away. Clare sank to the stoop again and put her head in her hands. "No, I am absolutely *not* doing any darned consulting! That was horrible and I didn't know what to say and I couldn't help them anyway!"

"He's not grieving."

"What!" She lifted her head and glared at Zach.

"He didn't abuse his daughter, but he wasn't interested in her."

"How do you—cop instincts?"

"Yeah. I've seen plenty of loss and I've been on the inside of a family who lost a child. I don't think Creedy wanted the kid, and he won't miss her."

"That's awful."

Zach shrugged and lowered himself to sit beside her.

"How did they get your name?" he asked.

The question jolted Clare. "I . . . I don't know." She wrapped her arms around herself.

Zach put his own arm around her and drew her closer. "Cold?"

"Enzo . . ." Had she ever told Zach that Enzo wasn't *just* a ghost dog? She didn't think so, and this whole scene made her want to be as normal as possible. "Enzo said he knew what to say to Mrs. Creedy."

Zach grunted, then repeated, "How did they get your name as a medium?"

Clare winced. "I'm not a medium! I don't like that word."

"What do ya wanna call it?"

"Ghost . . . ghost seer, I guess. Would Mrs. Flinton have told them about me?"

"Doubtful. She must have gone through similar scenes."

Shuddering again, Clare said, "So despairing and desperate."

"Yeah. You've kept your life pretty level," Zach said.

She pivoted to face him, glare at him. "Have you forgotten all the crap I've been through lately?" Flinging out her arms, she said, "This wouldn't have happened to me without my *gift*." Tilting her chin, she said, "And maybe I like my life easy . . . as an adult. And as an adult I can *choose* an easy life." She inhaled deeply. "Yes, my former life disintegrated around me and I'll be rebuilding it. I'm dealing with the change. I'm handling it." She *was*. "But I prefer to craft it according to my own plans." That sounded good.

Enzo yipped. *You are doing good!*

"Thank you, Enzo." She met Zach's eyes. "But I won't be hanging out a shingle as a medium. Not like Great-Aunt Sandra did. And I certainly didn't get the word out—however the word of something like this spreads—that I was open for business. I don't want to be, or be seen as, some sort of fraud."

You are NOT a fraud! Enzo hopped around her. *Sandra wasn't either!*

"I want to take this slowly, what's wrong with that?" Clare demanded.

Respect showed in his eyes, a corner of his mouth lifted in a half smile. "Nothing. Word did get out, though. I wonder if they have your phone number, too."

Blood simply drained from her face. "I've had my cell off." She fumbled in the pocket of her skirt, glanced at it. "Fifty calls. *Fifty!*"

His smile became sardonic. "You're the new sensation."

"To heck with that!"

"Clare," Zach said reasonably, taking one of her hands. "Who could have known about you?"

"I don't know!" She jerked her hand away so she could rub her temples, then dropped her fingers and went back into the house. After Zach came in, she closed and locked the front door, then stomped to the backyard and the little concrete patio and picnic table.

"Who did you talk to about . . . your gift?" Zach asked, taking the seat opposite her.

Enzo barked. Zach looked in his direction, then away as if

uncomfortable. The man had been great with the Creedys, but Clare got the idea his patience with paranormal stuff was wearing thin.

So was hers, but this was her life, now.

She turned her mind to the problem. "Like I said, Mrs. Flinton, Bekka, you . . ."

"Not us," Zach replied.

"The only one I told about the ghosts was Dr. Barclay."

"I can't see that guy breaking client confidentiality."

Clare shrugged. "His assistant and receptionist might have heard something while I was coming and going, but I don't know . . . and I don't know whether they'd gossip about that or not.

"Pretty juicy gossip, seeing ghosts. And one or the other of them could be a believer . . . unlike Barclay."

Zach nodded, "Unlike Barclay."

Clare sighed. "Maybe they thought that me seeing ghosts wasn't illogical and a mental problem, but a . . . a real psychic gift." The admission still felt bitter in her mouth.

"Could be." Now Zach shook his head. "Useless talking to them, they wouldn't admit discussing a patient."

"No."

"Anyone else?" Zach asked.

"I didn't tell anyone else." She grimaced. "Maybe someone at the auction house—"

"I don't think so." Zach grinned. "You were acting a little strange, but so were other people."

"Oh."

"Want some lemonade?" He came around and kissed her.

"Yes, please."

"Right."

"Um," Clare said. "I can't think of anyone else, unless, of course, the ghosts told someone," she ended with forced humor.

Zach paused by the door, shook his head, and went inside.

"Yeah, I didn't think so, either," Clare muttered, petting Enzo, who closed his eyes and leaned against her.

When Zach came out again, he carried a beer and a glass of lemonade on a small tin tray in one strong hand. "Why don't we wind down." He shrugged one shoulder. "Eat in a while, and later . . ." He smiled slowly.

Her heart began to pick up beat. "Absolutely."

She was up before dawn, moving what furniture she could and arranging it and organizing her boxes for the local movers to take from this fifties neighborhood to the more charming twenties one across town.

Zach had opted to sleep at his own apartment after another bout of sex, and that was fine with her since she liked to supervise her own way.

If all went according to her plans, her property in this place would be moved in the morning—the real estate agents had been happy to give her the code to her new home as soon as her first cashier's check had cleared—Clare would attend the closing, and the huge truck bringing her share of Great-Aunt Sandra's antique furniture would show up at the new place in the afternoon.

Clare hurried to the door and opened it, then set up the box fan, trying to minimize the heat. This would not be pretty, with her and men sweating during physical labor. She hoped the movers actually showed up on time at seven thirty A.M. for all their sakes. She truly didn't think it would take very long if they were efficient, and they'd *promised* efficiency, the reason she'd chosen them, since they certainly weren't the cheapest company out there.

A small square newspaper lay on her stoop, the tiny neighborhood paper. She went out and scooped it up, and hurried into the kitchen to turn on the coffeemaker, one of the items she'd take in her car.

As she waited for the brew, she glanced at the paper, froze. *What is it?* asked Enzo, just appearing.

She just wanted to point to the headline, but figured even a supernaturally intelligent ghost dog couldn't read. So she forced her lips to say the words of the banner and first paragraph:

BREAKING NEWS! THE GHOST,
WAITING BRAVE, IS GONE!

Two evenings ago, for the first time since our little neighborhood was founded, a member of the local Paranormal Research Society phoned in that the Native American ghost who lingers on Purple Ridge has passed on to his just reward. Apparently, several people note his presence each day, particularly in the evening, and were surprised to find his shade missing Saturday at dusk.

They are right! He is gone, and your work was noted and appreciated, Enzo cheered.

"Great," Clare said, wiggling as a tingle slithered down her spine. Had someone associated with the local paper told the Creedys about her? She should have asked, but all she'd wanted was for them to go away.

The doorbell rang, followed by knocking on the metal screen door. Clare tossed the paper in the last open box, waiting for the coffeemaker, then hurried to the front and found a big, scowling man with grizzled gray hair. A moving truck stood at the curb. Yay, they were early!

She turned off the fan and moved it out of the way and against the wall, smiling. "You're early!"

"Boss said there wasn't any air-conditioning here."

"No, I'm sorry."

He grunted, scanning the living room, the hallway, the part of the kitchen in view. "Organized. Good job."

"Thank you."

The mover rolled his shoulders. "What're the big items?"

"The couch and a bed."

"Huh. Should get this done fast, then."

"I hope so."

He turned and called to two other men. "Let's rock and roll."

Clare got out of their way.

Enzo followed the guy, tried to rub his legs and the others. No one paid him any attention.

For once, all went like clockwork, and Clare's old home was closed up by midmorning, she was the proud owner of her new home by noon, and her great-aunt Sandra's items were moved in and her new house eminently livable by the end of the business day. Amazing.

She began to be aware of the tiny hairs on the nape of her neck . . . they seemed to mark the passing of time. Now and again during the day she'd found herself scanning for Jack Slade's ghost, dread ratcheting up her nerves. She rather wanted to see him, get on with this task and get it over with so she could concentrate on *learning* about her new circumstances. To no longer be rushed, not worry that she might do something wrong that would hurt Zach or Enzo, or *her*. Pressure might drive her totally over the bend . . . the edge of madness that she'd never noticed in herself but knew would always be there for the rest of her life.

The deadline to save Jack Slade was in three days . . . until when? Next year? Next century?

Next year would be so much better.

Jack is a tough and determined man, Enzo said, standing next to her on the sidewalk of her new home. *He is MOSTLY a sane ghost. They can devolve over time.*

Doggie Enzo didn't use words like *devolve*, so it must be the Other. Though her neck was beginning to ache, she kept staring down the street, not wanting to turn her head and look at Enzo.

The apparition of the gunman has been waiting for what you call a ghost seer, a ghost layer. If you fail him this year . . . he might not stay in control. And like the legend he was in his own time, both for good or ill, he could become a legendary problem, rippling and ripping the psychic planes.

Clare thought the older woman who lived across the street and one house up was peeking at her through the curtains. Clare believed she could see the glint of opera glasses. The yards in the neighborhood were large.

She would prefer to think about nosy neighbors, but sighed. "Ripping the psychic plane," she murmured, trying not to move her lips. She stretched as if finished with a big job, and pasted on a pleased smile as she turned to her front steps between the bricked columns that marked the opening of her front wall.

Since her back was turned to the woman, she said, "Ripping the psychic plane sounds bad."

TWENTY-SEVEN

RIPPING WILL CAUSE ALL people discomfort, and attract minor psychics who will try to lay the ghost and get eaten instead.

Her breath sucked in, hard and sharp. "That's an option? Being eaten by a ghost?"

Yes, but you are strong, stronger than even your great-aunt Sandra, so you should be able to handle a simple devolved ghost in time . . . but eating the spirits of others shatters them and the anomaly becomes bigger and more difficult to banish and—

"I get the idea. It's best to handle Jack Slade here and now." She opened the gate and went through, not bothering to lock it because though it was the original gate, several yards down the street was the cut for her driveway and that was open.

Yes, the specter of Jack Slade is eager to move on and helpful, but it remains a dangerous ghost. A good spirit for you to attract as your first major test.

"Great," Clare said. For sure, the sooner this was done, the better. Where was the gunfighter's phantom? Would she have to leave a trail for him to find her? Go back to her old house? She was *so done* with that place.

But she still wasn't convinced, deep down, that she wanted to see him again, or that she could do this.

A few minutes later Clare relaxed in her new home. One she could envision living in for the rest of her life. The last truck was gone, the heavy furniture set exactly where she wanted, and the boxes for each room stacked neatly against the walls. As she'd suspected, the items she'd received from Aunt Sandra's home looked perfect in her new house, especially the furnishings she'd chosen for the living room with the huge multipaned and roundly bowed window.

She stood there, since she disliked the specially made window seat pads the former owners had left. Looking out at the green and grassy front yard, the brick wall and iron gate, pleasure welled through her.

Her gaze was caught by a fluttering—a white and misty pulsing—at the window of the second floor of the Spanish-influenced house across the street.

Hand at her throat, she drew back in horror and spun to stare at Enzo, who lay on one section of the wide butterscotch leather couch her aunt had had in her consulting room . . . much as the live dog had done.

"I shouldn't be able to see any ghosts in this area . . . in this neighborhood . . . it was built too late for my time period, in the twenties!"

Enzo lifted his head, then loped over to the window, hopped onto the semicircular window seat, and stared out.

Clare found her hands in her hair, tugging, as she muttered. "There are rules, right? I need to understand the darn rules!"

There are always . . . anomalies, Enzo said. *But you are not experienced enough to handle THAT specter. Maybe in a few years. We should not discuss this, now.* He seemed to shiver, then ran back to the corner of the couch and curled into it.

"Great. Just great. The view from this window is *ruined* for me." She tromped back to the couch. Yes, she was being a drama queen! Sniffing, she rubbed her arms. She'd turned on the air-conditioning, hadn't she? Because August continued to be record breaking? Yes, she had, and now she wished she hadn't.

With a little more control she sank into the couch. She'd hated the wild drama of her parents, and as they continued their out-of-control emoting, she didn't spend much time with them, and she buttoned down her own tendencies to any great emotional reactions. But look what her gift had driven her to! She was changing and no longer recognizing herself. So she took a couple of those deep breaths that Enzo had coached her in when she'd had her meltdown a few days ago. Her cheeks heated as she thought of the mess she'd been in public.

"Anomalies," she said quietly to Enzo, repeating that word. Anomalies in accounting never meant anything good—usually hours of work backtracking to a mistake . . . or fraud.

We will not talk of her now.

So the ghost across the way was female. Clare shrugged and thought about making *two* home offices, one for the regular business of her life, and the second for all the wretched books and research and whatever that seeing ghosts would entail. Yes, that was a good idea. Different computer, desk, and setup . . . she wondered what color to paint that office . . . and maybe put it on the first floor instead of the second floor. Her real office would be next to her bedroom.

A couple of minutes passed before a chill no longer skidded along her skin. The contemplation of good, solid, *practical* ideas had helped with that. Another deep breath. She'd get through this, and without drama.

Enzo hopped down from the couch to walk over and sit about a pace away from her. He cocked his head and looked her up and down, his forehead wrinkling. *You have only helped SIMPLE ghosts pass on, spirits without much trauma.* Only one thump of his tail. The darkness of his eyes seemed to swirl.

Clare thought of the Native American. She figured he'd had plenty of trauma, she just hadn't comprehended it. She swallowed, matching gazes with the dog. "What do you mean?" Her voice went high and her skin goose-bumped. She scrambled futilely for something else to think about, but . . . knowing the rules was important.

His mental voice began to take on that hollow depth she dreaded.

You think your gift demands the little effort you've expended so far? That helping souls transition is easy?

"No, no, I don't think that at all," she snapped.

A low thrum, not quite a growl, sounded in the phantom dog's throat.

There is a special process for sending ghosts from this world to where they need to be.

All sorts of alarming ideas in that sentence made her brain hurt.

A process you must learn by doing.

She wet her lips. "A process I haven't done and that isn't easy," she stated.

The dog dipped his muzzle and radiated sternness.

After an uneven breath taken and released, she held up a hand at the spectral Lab. "Let me guess. If I don't learn to do this right, I'll . . ." What would be the worst? "Go crazy," she said. *"Crazier."*

Enzo whimpered.

Clare gulped, then couldn't fend off the emotional train wreck of the whole hideous week. Just when she'd thought she'd gotten better, accepted strange stuff that she never thought she'd believe in in a million years, the universe whacked her again. She burst into tears.

Flattening out on the couch, she let herself empty of tears, release all her anger and self-pity, sobbing, breath hitching, even letting a few wails out. When she thought of the loss of her great-aunt Sandra, she cried some more. She should have spent more time with her aunt that she'd loved, but Clare had wanted so much to be normal. Now she had regrets.

The door knocker banged, easily heard from where she lay. That had to be Zach. Naturally he'd show up when her face was red and blotchy, her eyes swollen.

Clare jackknifed up and yanked out tissues, took care of mopping up, though she wished she could take the time for a nice cold washcloth. Anyway, Zach was a manly man and probably didn't care for tears. If she didn't say anything about her crying jag, he probably wouldn't.

When she opened the door, he examined her. "You okay?"

"Yes, thank you."

He nodded.

She stepped back and let him into the entryway, saw him inhale the scent of well-cared-for wood and leather.

"Nice house. Really elegant."

His eyes were those of a cop, scanning everything, checking for exits, no doubt.

She shut the large door behind him and gestured for him to follow her. "You want something to eat and drink? I have coffee, tea, milk . . . and two sorts of pie."

He grinned and focused on her. "Pie? What kind of pie?"

"Blueberry with a crumb crust and—"

"Sold on the blueberry," he said.

"Me, too." But she walked slowly enough through the opening hall so he could check out the living room on the right and the door to the garage on the left before she turned toward the kitchen.

"Very elegant house. Know it cost you a bundle, looks worth it."

She cringed as she thought of the price, then straightened the line of her shoulders and lifted her chin. "I have the money," she said calmly, then glanced back at him and smiled. "I fell in love with the house."

"Plenty to fall in love with," he agreed.

Enzo loped up to them, straight through a wall. *Zach is here, Clare!* He wagged his whole body, the Other who used the ghost dog as a mouthpiece gone, leaving pure puppylike joy.

"Yes, Zach is here." She glanced down at the dog.

He barked.

Zach's hand clenched the handle of his cane, but he said courteously enough, "Hello, Enzo."

He is talking to ME! He sees ME!

Clare stepped into the big kitchen with new appliances. "I don't think Zach sees you, Enzo—"

"I don't," Zach said.

"But he hears you." She waved to the counter where an untouched blueberry pie stood on a platter under a glass dome. She'd bought several pies for the movers, some of whom had been female and all of whom had appreciated the food and drinks.

"There're some pizzas in the fridge."

"Pizzas? Plural?"

"Yes. And some good beers and lagers, too."

"You fed the movers."

"Yes." She could afford to be more generous now, to reward good work with more than sincere thanks. "I even gave both sets—the ones who moved me from my house, and the ones who showed up from Chicago with Great-Aunt Sandra's things—a bonus."

Zach stopped in front of her and patted her cheek. "Good going, Clare."

Then his eyes deepened, grew intent; his fingers lingered on her face. She reached up and put her hands around the back of his neck, stroked his nape, and he shivered, his eyes closed. Oh, yes, she'd discovered what he liked.

Slanting her head, she pressed her lips to his, ran her tongue along his lips, nibbled the lower one . . . and listened to his breath come short. He tasted of salt and nuts with a hint of coffee. Licks of hot desire flickered in her, spreading from her core, and she needed to feel all of him. Sliding her hands down his arms, she moved to stroke the sides of his torso, then curved her palms over his hips and guided him back to brace against the kitchen island. Then she pushed against him so she could *feel* him, the tensile strength of his muscles, hard. So, so, sexy.

She just dived in, letting his body cradle hers, appreciating the length of him. Again she took his mouth, found his lips open and realized her eyes had closed at the touch of him.

His tongue rubbed against hers and the taste of *Zach* exploded in her mouth and she went damp.

He held her tight and that felt so good! A person, a solid being, interacting with her. She hadn't had any but the most superficial of contacts with anyone other than him since the hugs from her co-workers when she'd left her job last week. Far too long, and she shouldn't, couldn't become dependent on him, but the man *did* feel good against her, vertically and horizontally.

His hands went to her butt, lifted her a bit and settled her against his arousal. Oh, yes, yes, yes!

Big hands, big erection. All hers, soon, but she had to

breathe. She drew back, mind spinning, blood pulsing with yearning.

He grinned, seemed to hold her easily, as she balanced with her hands clamped around his biceps. Those were nice and hard, too. The man had no give in him whatsoever . . . at least not physically; his mind seemed plenty flexible.

"What kind of bed do you have here?" he asked.

She cleared her throat. "The same bed. Great-Aunt Sandra gave me the sleigh bed from one of her guest rooms as a housewarming gift when I bought my own home."

He tousled her hair, pushed some strands behind her ear. "So I can't offer to break in a new bed for you."

"You haven't seen the master suite. It's wonderful." Her voice came out breathy. "On the second floor." She gave a little cough. "We have this tiny elevator . . ." He scowled.

". . . and wide stairs with a landing." She smiled. "Your choice."

His brows were still down. "Let's see those stairs, probably an awesome banister, right?" He gestured with his chin at the open door leading to the narrow secondary staircase off the kitchen. "Or we could go up that way."

She wiggled and he put her down. Keeping her eyes on his, she drew her hand down the center of him to his most interesting muscle, traced it, testing his hardness, his length and breadth and thickness. Eyes going dark, he hissed out a breath, caught her hand in his, leaned back, and demonstrated exactly how he liked her to caress him.

Her breasts felt heavy, knees a little weak, mouth dried as heat spread throughout her body in a pounding throb of need.

Then he shaped her breast, fingers circling her nipple, lightly squeezing until she panted with him, knew her eyes had dilated as his had.

"Come with me." She took his hand, heading back through the dining room to the hallway, and opened the tiny elevator door. He tugged at her fingers, and she smiled at him. "*My* elevator. I want to ride in *my* elevator in my new house." Her eyes gleamed. "I want to make out with my lover in *my* elevator in my house on the way to the bedroom."

Zach stared at her flushed face, couldn't say no to her as she pulled him into the tiniest elevator he'd ever seen. It actually had a metal gate she had to draw closed and lock. She punched the button, then crowded him into the corner, not more than a couple of steps, lifted one of her legs and wrapped it around him between him and the wall. As she rubbed against his hard dick, he forgot everything. His aching foot. His name.

All he knew was the need to take this woman now. Get inside her. Make her climax around him so he could shout in release. God, he needed the release.

The slow elevator stopped.

His woman moaned and arched her hips against him, sending fire through him. He plunked her down, hands slipping under the waist of her jeans, under her panties, gripping the softness of her ass. Soft everywhere, especially her thighs against his hips.

He trailed his fingers to her dampness—wet!—tested her, slipped a finger inside her, pressed.

She screamed with pleasure and fell and took him off balance, and shooting pain yanked him back to the here and now. He drew his hand from her and they fetched up against the side of the elevator as he put out his arm to brace them. His cane had fallen to the damn floor—a floor too small to hold a man of his size lengthwise, the only thing that had saved them.

Damn, damn, damn, damn, *damn!*

Laughing, *laughing*, she helped steady him and levered them up.

"Wow," she said. "You are one incredible man. We tried out the elevator instead of the bed." She frowned. "Wait, you didn't . . . ah . . . um." Swiftly she unlocked the gate, opened it, opened the regular door. Then she bent and handed him his cane and took his free hand. "Yeah, we gotta get to the bed ASAP." She bounced as she walked, dammit, not an athletic female, but a completely healthy one. He *hated* this, his non-flexing ankle, his weakness.

The heat of irritation and anger turned back into lust when she stood with him beside the bed.

TWENTY-EIGHT

SHE UNBUTTONED HIS shirt, opened it, smoothed her hands over his chest, flicking her nails over his nipples, had him swelling against his pants again. He welcomed the greedy passion, the lack of thinking that would come with surrender to sex.

Her hands went to his fly and he closed his eyes, tried to settle into a balanced stance that had once been second nature, had to grip his cane. Then he gripped it even harder as she unzipped his work trousers and slid them down his legs.

He stepped out, glad she always seemed focused on his dick instead of the hideous scars on his leg and ankle.

She stood, skimming her fingers up the inside of his thighs, and he flinched and his cock jerked at the anticipation of numbing pleasure. Her fingers came closer and closer to where he really wanted them, and she cupped him and he kept an aching groan behind his teeth and fought to keep from grabbing her. He'd give her a little control before he ripped it from her, letting the reins of his own self-command blow away in the hot wind.

The slightly dazed look in her eyes, the plumping of her lips, the flush in her cheeks, all gave him gut-deep satisfaction. She was in this thing with him, all the way, and as completely as he.

He'd stop thinking soon, but now he savored the thickening and heaviness of his dick. His own lust and the evidence of hers. Hell, even his cheekbones felt hot as she smoothed his pants with trembling hands, folded them over the back of a chair. Oh, yeah.

Bracing his leg against the bed, he propped his cane on the curved wooden footboard, slid his thumbs into his boxers and dropped them, nearly groaning with pleasure as his erection was freed.

She turned back and her gaze went straight to his cock and he swelled even more and gritted his teeth as she sauntered back toward him, eyes glittering. Standing no more than a foot from him, with her usual efficiency, she stripped, jeans and cotton panties dropped, showing the slight curve of her stomach, the pretty dark curls covering her sex, her long tanned legs. His breath caught, his turn to focus on her every movement as she pulled up her tee, folded it, paced back and put it on the seat of the chair holding his pants. His mouth dried as she unhooked her bra and let her beautiful full breasts spill from it, the tips rosy and nubby with passion.

When she bent down to pick up her jeans to fold them, too, Zach thought he'd whimper. His mind went blank and all there was, was the blood pounding inside him with need, need, need.

Walking back, she wore that half smile before sex that yanked at his heart as well as his balls. She touched him and that was it; he picked her up—hardly noticing the pang in his leg—and threw her to the middle of the queen-sized bed. White bedspread, golden Clare. Perfect.

"Zach," she said, and he didn't know if it was slurry because she said it that way or he heard it that way. She lifted her arms and his gaze went to her breasts and he had to taste them.

So he did. Touching her, he made sure she quivered, shuddered, slicked with sex, and yelled his name as she climaxed. She yanked at him, pulled him over her, not pleading, no, *demanding* he thrust into her. He did that, too, slid into wet heat that drove him mad and he pounded into her and the bite of her nails on his shoulders added to sweet, sweet desire, stoked him and he grabbed her hard and held her and their bodies arched and flexed in a hammering rhythm and he emptied into her, whispering her name as she yelled his.

Slowly the rushing of his heartbeat in his ears calmed. His chest didn't rise and fall so raggedly and the noise of his harsh breathing diminished. His muscles should work now, and he rolled and slipped from her and grunted at the loss.

Turning his head, he saw that her brown hair had tumbled around her face, no smoothness here, and she looked great. "Give me a coupla minutes," he said.

She laughed, teeth white in the fading light. Man, he wanted to study her, a golden goddess against the white, like he'd seen her moments before, like the image that would be burned in his memory forever. Her pupils had turned more golden-brown than green in the hazel of her eyes. Her lips were red, her cheeks pink under that tanned skin, peach.

Just absolutely beautiful.

Perfect.

As he was not. He'd never be whole again. No, he didn't like that thought and pushed it away.

They showered in an awesome glass deal that had six crossing streams. He got his hands all over her slippery, sexy body, and this time he didn't disgrace himself in a small enclosure.

Clare changed back into one of the sundresses she preferred, this one with a built-in bra that he approved of, and, to his disappointment, she slipped on cotton panties. White, sort of innocent. The more he thought about that, it drove him a little crazy. But despite her wild Gypsy side that she let loose in bed, Clare *was* innocent in most of the ways he wasn't. She believed the best of people, believed they'd try their hardest— with the exceptions of her parents. She lived by her rules, and as far as he could tell, she hadn't broken any of the major ones that were important to her.

He'd broken quite a few rules . . . but none that were important to him.

They didn't eat in the formal dining room, thank God.

That would have reminded him of his childhood before he'd lost Jim. The room was pretty enough, with a polished and gleaming dark wood table and a set of eight chairs with nice tapestry cushions. Instead, with a wide wave of her arm, she indicated the patterned brick patio and a couple of fancy outdoor lounge deals. They didn't look new, but they did appear originally expensive. Probably some of her great-aunt Sandra's furniture.

Since he believed Clare wanted to putter by herself in her own new kitchen, Zach went out to one of the two loungers with a nicely sized rectangular table set between them. He cranked the chair to a notch he preferred, then settled in, gritting his jaw at the continuing ache of his leg. He wasn't much use to carry stuff since he had only one free hand.

Clare walked out with a pizza box smelling of cheese and dough and pepperoni and his mouth watered. On top of it she balanced two plates, a couple of beers, and a bottle of lemonade. She arranged everything on the table, and when she lifted the lid of the box, he saw that she'd put at least three types of pizza inside to choose from. Very efficient, that was his lady.

He took a meat-lovers' slice and bit into it, not quite searing his tongue or the roof of his mouth. Fabulous.

"What did you do today?" Clare asked, opening her lemonade.

He grimaced.

"Oh. Do you not want to talk about your work?"

What he was doing was hardly work. "I looked into those names you gave me. Three turned out to be dead ends. Only one old guy was still alive and living in a state-run nursing home. He said he didn't recall anything about his father getting furniture from Mrs. Flinton's childhood family. I got the impression his family probably sold the furniture as soon as they'd received it. He was all about needing cash." Zach frowned, remembering the interview. "He pretended I was one of his nephews and tried to hit me up for money."

"Pretended?" Clare asked.

Zach leaned back in the lounge. "Yeah. He was sly, yeah, sly. He might have known what happened to the stuff. If this

was a violent case, I may have gone back and reinterviewed."
He shrugged. "Guy is soft, got the idea that he didn't work
much in his life, depended on others to take care of him."

Clare's mouth turned down before she said, "A sponger."

"A moocher," Zach said at the same time.

They smiled, but one of those shadows was in her eyes and
she thought it applied to him in some way. "I am not a moocher."

"Of course not," she replied absently in a matter-of-fact
tone. She glanced toward the house; the light was dying, the
sunset gone fast behind those high redbrick walls. A small
light in the kitchen beamed welcome and comfort. "I'm sorry
the leads I gave you didn't pan out."

He shrugged. "Not surprising, after all these years."

"Um, did you speak with Rickman about it?"

"Of course." Not that their meeting had been long. Rickman seemed much less intense than usual, almost offhand.
Zach thought it was a strategy of the man, whether to show
him the guy was really hands-off and trusted him, or waiting
for Zach to really commit to the company . . . or having decided to give him enough rope to hang himself and get him
out of there with no hard feelings by Mrs. Flinton.

When they were done, Clare tidied up the meal, came
back out, and, to his surprise, sat on his lap and leaned against
him.

Tenderness surged and he let it wisp through him like a
balm, soothing stuff he hadn't known hurt.

Head tucked under his chin, she said, "My first night in
my new home. I love it here."

He stroked her hair, her back, soaking in the quiet. The
heat didn't seem as bad since he knew a few steps would take
him into cool relief whenever he wanted. Studying the yard,
he thought the mature trees and the tall brick walls kept it
shady during the day. "Good choice and good job getting this
place. It suits you."

Her sigh was long. "Thanks. I'm glad you like it."

A few breaths of quiet. "Would you like to stay with me
here tonight?" she asked.

Always. The word came to his mind, shocked him silent.
Nope, he didn't fall that fast or easily. He didn't fall at all, and
he should pull back now. Instead he said, "Sure," stuffing the

notion of love in a back cupboard in his mind. Neither he nor Clare had mentioned love.

Both of them were enjoying the sex.

"I have a work bag in the car." His mouth kicked up. "With clean clothes." Women preferred that. He'd whistled when he'd thrown it in, like this time with Clare was sliding from a few nights' sex into an affair or something. Studying her, he acknowledged she was still damn compelling. If he looked at her too long, too closely, his dick stood right up. And if he unexpectedly caught a whiff of her—Clare or that exotic perfume she wore that revealed that true wild self of hers—he wanted to start a-nibblin' on her and get her under him, over him—get into her *fast*.

"Good," she murmured. "That's good."

So he held her as twilight deepened into night and crickets whirred their syncopated songs.

Enzo's rapid yips woke her. She jerked to sit and reached for Zach's hand. He stiffened beside her and though he didn't draw his fingers away, neither did he intertwine his with hers. Glancing down, she saw that his eyes were open and alert and revealed no emotion, which struck her as part of his cop manner. She couldn't tell whether he'd just awakened and did so fast and ready for anything, or whether he'd been awake thinking private thoughts.

Jack Slade is here! Enzo barked. *He's come at last!*

TWENTY-NINE

"GREAT," CLARE SAID as Zach grunted.

She watched as the apparition walked through the shut door of the master suite, into the conversation area, then to the end of the bed. He didn't look around or show that he was aware of the change in her surroundings. How much did a ghost know of those? The cowboy had known of the EZ Loan, but Clare understood that he'd been a ghost tied specifically to a location. Too many aspects she still didn't understand.

She was glad she wore a nightshirt; still, she wished she had on underwear.

The ghost appeared to be a little . . . worn, not as substantial. Clare stiffened. Had something happened to him? Or was it something in *her*, the warning that if she didn't "work" harder at her gift, she might go mad?

Good evening, ghost seer, the apparition said.

Zach's fingers tightened around her hand. She turned her head toward him. He nodded, mouth flattening.

"Hel . . . Hello, Jack."

I have found the exact location of the second ear I cut off Jules Beni. The ghost lapsed into silence for enough beats for

Clare's mind to wing to the puzzle box and its contents, in the house safe in the living room.

"Where is it?" she asked.

It is buried in an old depression that held a post of the corral behind the barn at Virginia Dale. There is no barn or corral now.

Jules Beni had been tied to a corral post.

Jack Slade's lips twisted. *And that hole is close to a post holding a large sign reporting lies about me.*

"What lies?"

That I robbed the stage. He grew more dense, the angles and shadows of him more defined. *Betrayed my employer. I might have been bad when drinking, but I was an honest man in my work!* His chest actually seemed to rise and fall with agitated breath. He turned his glittering eyes on Zach. *And I led no robbers in Montana, you who upheld the law, there.*

Zach sat, grimaced, lifted a hand. "I've never been in Virginia City, Montana. I worked south of there." He hesitated. "And I'm a law officer; I don't believe in the vigilante 'justice' that condemned you."

Jack Slade inclined his head. *Thank you.* He seemed to actually pace along the end of the bed, not drift. *I don't like people thinking I was so bad as to rob gold going to pay soldiers at Fort Laramie.*

Again the ghost looked at Zach. *Needed my reputation to keep order. That was the only thing that worked with the roughnecks under my direction, with outlaws and horse thieves like Beni, with the damn French ranchers and the Sioux. You know about rep.*

Zach grunted, but Clare saw him nod.

The ghost continued, *Then I got to liking my bad reputation too much.* He moved his hand in a smooth gesture. *Things happened. When drunk, I turned into a different person. And after Beni shot me*—his image rippled—*the pain never quit, and I drank more and I lost control.*

The apparition lifted pale hands, waved them. *But that is all past. We must hurry. The date of my wrongdoing is in three days. We must be ready—YOU must be ready to help me right the ill I caused. We should leave shortly, go to Virginia Dale, Colorado, then on to Cold Springs.*

She supposed that was more efficient, but she'd just gotten her own home and she'd been traveling a lot lately and didn't want to spend another night on the road. "They aren't in the same direction," she pointed out. "But they can both be day trips from here."

The ghost scowled.

"I don't ride horses," she said. "And our vehicles are very fast." She scraped her mind for other reasons. "I'd like to be rested and . . . and prepared. It will be a long day tomorrow, digging up . . . doing what needs to be done, and an even longer day"—she swallowed—"the day I help you . . . transition. Let me get some rest in my own bed in between times."

Pacing faster until he blurred, the specter said, *It comes near, my time; we cannot linger. I MUST go on. My Virginia waits for me. I can't bear to be trapped any longer!*

Sucking in a breath, Clare strove for more logic.

But Slade vanished.

She was cold, cold, trembling with it.

Zach drew her under the covers and gave her blessed warmth and mind-destroying release.

She rose at dawn after a restless sleep . . . even the two times she and Zach had made love hadn't released all the anxiety she had about digging up something on land that didn't belong to her.

She dressed in jeans and a thin long-sleeved cotton shirt in a pastel pattern and hiking boots. The jeans and boots would help with rough ground, cactus, any snakes. The shirt would keep her arms from burning at high altitude. She stuck a small blue bandana in her pocket and laid out a straw cowboy hat.

One last time, she studied the location of the former Overland Stage Virginia Dale Station on several different 3D world maps on her tablet, but they could only give her two dimensions for this out-of-the-way place.

What she *wanted* to do was call someone who belonged to the Virginia Dale Community Club to ensure that the gates would be open. If they were standard country gates they'd prevent cars but not people from going in. The place *was* on the historic register list, after all. She'd even found a site for people leaving small caches for others to find by GPS, so it was probably open to the public. Of course the building itself would be locked. The next event of the club wasn't until September.

She didn't recall ever driving up that way, off the interstate. Well, there was a first time for everything.

Enough of soothing paperwork. On one of her moving trips she'd dropped by a sporting goods store and purchased a sturdy camp shovel that she'd left in her car.

Now to prepare for the rest of the day. She began packing lunch in a small cooler: cold chicken strips, hard-boiled eggs, iced tea, and beer . . . just in case Zach wanted to come. She thought he might.

He clumped into the kitchen in his boxers. That she'd heard him told her he was still groggy.

"Coffee?" he grunted.

She'd put it on earlier, had gotten involved on the computer and hadn't even had a cup, so she poured for two.

Zach let the taste of premium coffee lie on his tongue, really good, and Clare looked equally good, though her appearance as Cowgirl, or maybe Hiking Girl or Mountain Girl, was a new side of her.

Seven A.M. and she seemed to be heading out. He blinked at her. He'd hoped to have more time to think about this whole business, especially since she'd kept waking him during the night with her tossing and turning. The sex had been amazing, though.

But the whole woo-woo thing had ruffled his nerves, begun to wear on him. He knew she hoped he was joining her. He had the time, both of them knew that, but he sure didn't think he had the desire.

She gulped her coffee, not treating the brew with the respect it deserved, and glanced at the kitchen clock. Yep, he'd noticed at least one clock in every room in this place, too. Didn't think some of the rooms had previously had them.

"I'd like to get on the road soon, before rush hour traffic."

Too late, but it would be easier once she passed downtown and headed north away from the influx into downtown Denver.

"Uh-huh," he said. He could stand here and drink coffee

with her, get some food from the fridge, or go back upstairs—
by way of the elevator, though that smacked of running away
from the decision. He didn't have trouble with decisions and
hadn't ever had trouble disengaging from a lover before . . .
before, when he was a different man.

He didn't want to hurt Clare's feelings. But he'd already
hesitated too long.

She paled. "Are you going to come to Virginia Dale with
me or not?"

He fumbled for an answer, let show his irritation at the
whole screwed-up mess that had been scraping his nerves for
days. Sending her a sharp look, he said, "Somehow follow a
ghost somewhere to illegally obtain a grisly piece of human
flesh?" Grisly to her, at least.

"Do you believe I can see ghosts, Zach?" She was steady:
posture, gaze, voice. And quiet, a little too quiet, tipping him
off that this was a vital question.

He would have liked to say, *I believe you believe you see
ghosts*, but that was too wishy-washy, more lie than truth.
And something that jerk Barclay might say. So his eyes met
hers and he said, "Yes. You can see ghosts."

"And you can see ghosts, too."

"No!"

"Don't give me that." Her expression was all impatience.
"You *saw* them! The cowboy outside the land office, Jack
Slade." Now her tone rose and Zach didn't like it. He used his
flat cop stare. It worked. She took a step back.

"I don't see ghosts." Flat voice to match flat stare.

Another step back. Her chin trembled.

He felt like he walked along a narrow shelf trail in the
mountains that might crumble under his feet at any moment.
Losing her, losing him, one of them falling beyond reach and
hope. So he amended, "I can see ghosts when I touch you.
This is about *you*, Clare, not about me."

She said, "There's been a congruency of lives intersecting
here: me, Mrs. Flinton, and you. All of us with a gift—"

"No, Clare." He repeated, "The gift is yours. I don't have
one. You're deluding yourself. You just want to have company
in . . . all of this." He waved.

Her face crumpled for an instant, then tightened. She

walked deliberately to the other side of the breakfast bar, flung stuff in her cooler, and zipped it shut. "All right then. Thank. You. For. Your. Former. Companionship. I won't be a burden on you or on anyone else, emotionally or in any other way. I won't inflict my ideas on you or anyone else. I won't *be* with anyone who cannot give me respect." She paused, swallowed. "And respect my gift."

An emotional blow right to the middle of his chest. She was dumping him! That wasn't what—

But she'd skittered around him and headed toward the big front door.

THIRTY

HE RECALLED THAT her car was parked on the street as if she'd wanted people to know the house wasn't empty anymore. "Wait just a damn minute," he said.

"Don't cuss at me!" He winced. His mother had been hard on him and Jim about bad language. One of the last things he'd promised his brother was to keep the cursing mild. He'd kept that promise.

Now he heard the sound of Clare's sucked-in breath. "Get your stuff and let yourself out." Her words were rushed. "I have to go. I have to beat traffic." She opened the big front door and zoomed out.

Following her, he stopped on the front porch, wincing as he noted a neighbor couple across the street staring at them. "Clare," he called.

She flung a look at him after she opened the car door and set the cooler in the back. Her voice quivered. "I'll finish examining the ledgers, and messenger them to . . . your company . . . with my notes as to where . . . your client's . . . property might have been dispersed to . . . for another point of your investigation . . . I'll send them on to . . . your address . . .

when I'm done." She obviously watched her phrasing because of the listening ears.

Her expression grimaced into a fake smile and she didn't meet his eyes.

He lingered in the deep archway of the door, though his white boxers and orthopedic shoes must be readily visible, and searched for something to say. Couldn't find it.

"Good-bye, Jackson Zachary Slade." One last hard and disappointed glance from her grazed across his eyes. Then her breasts rose with another deep breath; she glanced across the street at the neighbors and walked back to the foot of the porch, this time with a direct stare. "But, Zach, this argument isn't about psychic gifts, this is about change happening when you don't want it to, and accepting it and managing change." She turned on her heel, circled to the driver's side of her car, and opened the door.

"Are you going to let this 'gift' define you? Rule your life?" Zach managed. Screw any show he was giving the couple on the sidewalk across the street; he moved to look at her above the roof of her car.

She gazed at him. "My gift *is* my life now, Zach. Unlike you, I've accepted that I can't go back to what or who I was.

"You ran away from your previous life in Montana instead of dealing with your change of circumstances there. You never reference in the slightest your weakened leg. Well, you can run away from me, too. Good-bye." She got into the car, didn't even slam the door. It closed with a final thunk. A few seconds later she drove away.

Barking came from beyond Zach, passed him, caught up with the car, and then Zach heard a long doggie whine. Enzo was probably saying something to Zach; thankfully he couldn't understand it.

And they left and the bright day seemed harsher, the sun metallic in its color and radiation. Blue sky brassy. The sidewalks glaring white.

The moment stretched hot and still and breathless.

Instinctively, Zach tensed, waiting for the whir of wings, the caw of crows.

Nothing.

Because he *had* been on that steep and scary mountain shelf trail, an emotional spot. Now solid ground had crumbled under him and he was free-falling and all he could hear was the wind whistling by.

Ignoring the disapproving neighbor couple, he went back into the house and closed the door. He'd shower and change, then gather all of his stuff that might be here. Ready, once more, to leave another segment of his life behind.

Clare stopped a few blocks away and let the sobs of hurt and anger wring her dry. She knew there was no chance of Zach coming after her, which was a darn shame. After wiping away her tears and blowing her nose, she shook her head. It was exceedingly odd to think that she had adapted to the change in her life better than Zach, a man who was used to acting quickly in situations in flux.

She flushed again when she remembered seeing her new neighbors come out their door across the street like they were ready to take a morning walk. They'd gotten an eyeful and heard an earful. Not the kind of first impression she'd wanted to make in the block.

Well, *they* shouldn't judge whether she was weird. After all, they had a ghost in their attic.

Ghosts. Yes, dealing with ghosts was her life now. Anyway, she had a job to do for the apparition of Jack Slade. She straightened her shoulders.

Enzo whined beside her. *You wanted him to help you.* Big doggie eyes. *I'm sorry he won't.*

"Is that allowed, human help?"

Of course. We could take Mrs. Flinton!

"No."

She blew her nose one last time and started driving. "I can do this myself. I'm just a little unsure." She was more cowardly than she'd expected but wouldn't admit that aloud. Even if Enzo could hear her mentally, or peek into her heart, or whatever, she wouldn't admit her anxiety in words.

Here's Jack! Enzo enthused.

The specter stood, drifted, just beyond the front of the car. Swallowing the last of her tears, Clare put her hands on the wheel; the ghost came up to the driver's window that she'd rolled down. The morning hadn't been cool until he appeared.

Clare swallowed. "I need to be going. The sooner this is done, the better. So, uh, sit with Enzo—"

I am getting in the backseat for now! Enzo leapt through the passenger seat to sit behind her. Clare's slight hitting of the brakes and the little jolt didn't budge him. Jack Slade passed through the door, through *her*, which nearly had her screaming at the freezing cold, and folded himself in the seat, appearing uncomfortable. The man had managed five hundred miles of stage line, checked on every one of his stations, must have spent hours in a coach, but looked wary about the car. She just wished he'd disappear.

Proceed. He waved his hand.

"I'm not one of your drivers."

A small smile curved his mouth. *You are now. But I can be a gentleman.*

"I know that." Despite all his problems, she still believed he was more sinned against than sinner. He'd *been* the law, ensuring that the passengers of his division of the stage line, the drivers, his station people, and the mail were safe, and did that mostly by reputation. His death in Montana—vigilante law—had not been just.

He touched her hand with icy fingers and she shuddered. *You have a generous nature. I was a good manager but bad when drunk or bored.*

"All right," she said, then cleared her throat. "Traffic isn't too bad at this time of the morning, but we're going straight through the city, so please don't be distracting." She turned onto a main thoroughfare toward northern Colorado and Virginia Dale.

The little road trip would be interesting. Everyone said Slade had found a gem of a small valley for his headquarters. Again she wished she'd arranged for a guide, but that would entail waiting until the person left before digging around in the earth for an ear.

All right, she was a weenie about that, too. She'd hoped that Zach would handle the ear.

The ear is in a bottle, said Jack Slade. She suppressed a lurch and tightened her fingers on the wheel.

His mouth turned down.

"What?" Then her mind raced, pulling pieces together. "Oh, the station was once a store and later a community center that had dances." She could see it. Boys joking around, sneaking the ear out of the glass case during a crowded event, seeing if it could fit into the bottle . . . then, perhaps, wondering how to get the thing out and, if they broke the glass, whether it would be damaged.

She'd have to retrieve it. A ratty ear. Maybe nibbled at by shrews or mice or chipmunks or insects . . .

The ear is mostly intact. It remained dry.

"Oh." *Mostly* was a very inexact word.

A while back there was another ghost layer who did not help me.

"I'm helping!"

Yes, you are, and I thank you. His head swiveled as cars moved along both sides of them. *I will meet you there, at my former home. I know the way there and back better now, in this time.*

He vanished and she felt a warm flood of relief, until she wondered how he'd be when she was actually in an area he'd lived for a while.

Zach allowed himself some muttering. Damn it, he *had* been rebuilding his life. He'd gotten a job, hadn't he? Gotten an apartment.

He'd fallen into the job and apartment.

He'd been working on a case.

That he hadn't taken very seriously.

He hit his apartment at Mrs. Flinton's in a foul mood, only to have her knock politely on his door and smile sweetly at him even when he glared at her, guilt that he'd been taking her case easy chomping at him.

"Good morning, Zach!" she chirped, and set her walker too close to him, in his personal space. He knew the ploy but fell back anyway, especially when he smelled bacon and eggs and something wonderful from Mrs. Magee, who stood behind Mrs. Flinton.

"I think he's had an argument with Ms. Cermak," Bekka

said in her Minnesota accent. "He's back earlier from her place."

"And grouchy," Mrs. Flinton added as she followed him to the breakfast counter separating the Pullman kitchen from the living room. Zach took a barroom stool, nice and plush under his ass. Clare's breakfast bar had had those high, fancy wooden swivel chairs.

This was so much better. Really.

Mrs. Magee set down the covered dish. "Eat, then rinse off the dish and silverware, leave them in the sink, and I will collect them later." To his surprise, she kissed his cheek. "I like having you here," she ended gruffly, then left his apartment.

He looked at Mrs. Flinton. She smiled a too-innocent smile and waved wrinkled-papery-tissue hands. Aged hands. Unlike the callused, strong ones the ghost of Jack Slade had had. A man who'd died at thirty-three. Given his druthers, Zach would like to see his own hands old and wrinkled.

"Go ahead and eat, I know you want to," she said.

"Impolite when you aren't eating," Zach said, raising the cover and setting it aside, trying to discreetly sniff the thick-looking farm bacon and not drool.

"We've had breakfast and I'm full; do go ahead and eat, Zachary. But I will put on some tea, thank you." She went to the electric stove and turned the burner on under the kettle.

He didn't wait another second and dug into the cheesy scrambled eggs.

A couple of minutes later, he helped Mrs. Flinton onto a stool next to his. She sat with a straight back as she drank some tea she'd taken from his cupboard that smelled floral.

He sipped at the last of the coffee in his go-cup that he'd poured in Clare's kitchen and frowned.

"It will be all right, dear boy."

He grunted, then made himself answer in words. "Thank you, Mrs. Flinton."

"Even though you've been spending time with Clare—and I *do* want to see her new home, it sounds wonderful!—are you happy living here, Zach?"

Forcing himself to focus and ignore a little, niggling worry about Clare in the back of his mind, he met Mrs. Flinton's blue eyes and said. "Sure."

She smiled and patted him on the cheek. "Well, we didn't take much time to become accustomed to each other at all, did we? Just almost a week of little adjustments." Her pink-lipsticked mouth curved and her blue eyes twinkled at him. "I would very much like you to stay here with me and Bekka." Mrs. Flinton glanced over her shoulder at the open door leading to the hallway. "She likes you, too, as she showed. You should be honored; she isn't a demonstrative woman." Mrs. Flinton laughed. "You can always determine whether you're in her good graces by the food she gives you."

Zach had already noticed that. He was getting full and balanced meals, cupcakes for dessert, and good bottles of wine that he wouldn't mention to Mrs. Flinton. But that wasn't what had his gut tightening. "Nearly a week?" How could time go that fast? Over the past months, especially when he'd been in the hospital, in a wheelchair, on crutches, the seconds had crawled with near-eternal slowness.

"Yes, dear." Another pat on the cheek.

Almost a week. That meant at least a week since he'd visited his mother. His belly clenched harder. Acceptable that he didn't visit often when he didn't live close, but he was in Denver now and she was in Boulder.

He had to go see her soon. Dread seeped into him. He didn't tell himself it would be easy, get easier, as he had when younger.

"So, Zachary?" Mrs. Flinton asked. Her gaze had turned quizzical as if she understood he'd zoned out.

He took a stab at an answer. "I'd like to stay." To his surprise, that was the truth.

Her face cleared. He'd answered correctly. She mentioned a price that would get him a sleazy flop for eight hours.

"Daily?" he asked.

She slipped down into the cage of her walker and looked shocked. "Of course not, Zach! Monthly."

He shook his head. "Can't do that." Thinking of the ads he'd seen, he countered with a standard Denver rent, managing not to wince, though his salary if he stayed on with Rickman would cover it.

Mrs. Flinton crossed her arms. "That is far too costly, Zach."

"I can afford it."

"And I can afford to let you rent the apartment for what I feel is right for us both." She sniffed.

So he spent the next five minutes negotiating his rent *upward*, until they reached an agreement and she left his new place clunking down the hall with her walker. Then he closed the door behind her, slid onto the leather couch—nice and wide and long—and let his instinct rule to marshal his thoughts before he went on another round of interviews for Mrs. Flinton's case.

He'd have to visit his mother, soon. A fleeting thought that he might be able to take Clare slithered through his mind before he winced and recalled that they were done. Too damn bad because he could *see* Clare with his mom; they'd like each other, and bringing Clare along sure would ease the whole thing for him.

He rubbed his chest, hurting inside.

During the trip, Clare kept the windows up, the air-conditioning on. Enzo cheerfully remarked on the beauty of the country. He hadn't gotten out much when he was with Great-Aunt Sandra; people had come to *her*.

"Didn't she have any quests like this?"

The dog hesitated. *Not so much. You should read her journals.*

Clare wanted to bang her head against the wheel; of course she couldn't while driving down a two-lane highway at seventy-five miles an hour. "I'll get to them," she muttered. One she was reading was entertaining but had little helpful information.

Of course you will read them.

An idea occurred to her. "You might be able to tell me what journals I should start with."

The air in the car simply *changed*.

I might, said a hollow mind-voice from Enzo.

No, she was *not* looking over to the Other. "Never mind." She'd just passed the sign for Virginia Dale, the abandoned café and post office. Down the hill she saw a widening of the road and a brown marker. Checking the mirror—no one was

behind her—she slowed. Yes, the sign said POINT OF INTER-
EST. That had to be it.

Across the cattle gate the road was dirt and washboarded.
She took it slow, her palms dampening despite the cool air
coming from the Other-cum-dog. The directions, printed
out and copied to her phone, had said the drive would take
two hours and forty-five minutes. It lied. She was there in
two hours. She swallowed, not really appreciating the mountain view, the wide meadow, the rocky outcroppings. She
came to a fork and a yellow gate and stopped. Yes, this was
the place, onward. The road became a narrow passage. She
could see this road as the main stage line, pretty much a one-
car deal. Maybe she'd better get an SUV. She didn't like
SUVs.

She turned a corner and could see the station. Shock!

There was a house, a ranch, buildings, *whatever* just below
the station, on the other side of a barbed-wire fence.

Heart thumping, she crept along the road, hoping no one
saw her, would come greet her . . . anything. Why in tarnation
had she worn a floral shirt? She should have stuck to natural
beige or brown, should have *bought* a beige or brown shirt. At
least she had a straw cowboy hat.

At another open barrier, she read the sign. Of *course* it
said not to disturb or take anything, gave the penalty. It specifically mentioned *no digging*. She swallowed.

And right there, in the middle of the open space by the
large wooden sign, stood the ghost of Jack Slade. Yes, if anyone found her digging she could get in deep trouble. She'd say
she was looking for the GPS cache? Putting one down? Maybe
that would be all right.

But her mouth had dried.

There's Jack! Enzo yipped with the enthusiasm of a ghost
dog, not Other spirit.

"I see him." His standing by the sign that lied about him
just seemed too sad. Yet such things would be part of her life.

And she was accepting the change in her life, and doing it
darn better than Zach. She pulled up before another log house
that research had told her was built in 1909, and wished her
car were beige, too, instead of black. Even a white car would
be dirty with dust by now and less noticeable.

Zach wouldn't be letting the proximity of people shake him. He'd act as if what he was doing were all right and proper.

She was so not Zach Slade.

As she got out of the car, the heat struck her. Anyone with sense would be inside.

Enzo shot through the car and behind the building, nosing one of the outhouses.

Welcome to Virginia Dale. Jack Slade beamed. *Isn't it beautiful?*

It was, except for the ranch that looked scruffy, the ranch that hogged the stream that had had Slade building the station in the first place.

Did you really name it after your wife? Clare tried out a little mental telepathy to the phantom.

Yes, my beautiful and strong and fiery Virginia. She waits for me beyond the curtain, you know.

Clare didn't know, and didn't know whether *he* knew or sensed it or just hoped. She didn't ask.

He turned and stared at the plank building undergoing restoration. *Our life here was exciting and challenging.* He shook his head. *I did much better when given a tough job than when things ran smoothly. That was when I began to drink more, from the boredom and the pain.*

"Uh-huh." Now he wanted to be chatty; just great. With gritted teeth she walked down to the sign. "Just where is the bottle, and how far down is it?"

THIRTY-ONE

NOT FAR, ABOUT two feet. He hovered over an area behind the sign.

She was absolutely in the open with nowhere to hide. The
closest place would be a group of rocks, but they were behind
another barbed-wire fence. She circled a clump of prickly
pear cactus and looked at the spot the ghost indicated. At
least it was under grass and not one of the hard-packed dirt
trails.

I have been loosening the soil day and night, the ghost
said.

"You know the passing hours?" Clare asked.

*I am aware of the waning of the moon. It will be just after
the new moon and very dark at Cold Springs the day after
tomorrow.*

"When I'll have to put the ears back on Jules Beni? Is he a
ghost, too?" Her voice had risen and she shut her mouth.
She'd read somewhere that high voices carry farther, are easier to hear. She'd be making that trip alone except for ghosts,
too, and it was wise to do it at night, she guessed.

*If you don't follow through on this quest, it will be bad for
you,* Enzo said, with big, sad eyes.

All evidence said she'd go mad. Her lips felt numb. "What will I have to do?"

Jack Slade answered, *The scene when I walked up to Beni's body against the corral post and cut off his ears—my worst, deliberate act made in cool blood—repeats again and again throughout the day of my crime. You will see it, feel it, as I do, experience it with me. But this time when I see the holes where his ears were, we will put the ears back.*

"Oh, joy." She shifted feet. "I still don't know where Cold Springs is."

I can take you there. There will be no digging, like here.

"We should get on with that. You loosened the soil, you can do that? Affect the environment?"

This was my home, land I chose and named, even though I did not own it.

"Oh."

It was a job that took will and determination and concentration. A fleeting smile, and, yes, the apparition was denser here, more defined. *I was good at my job that took those qualities.*

"Extraordinary," Clare said.

Yes. I was also good with risk, when sober.

Enzo, who'd been sniffing around the old pump, galloped up faster than a live dog. *Clare is not a risk-taker.*

"No joke," Clare muttered. "Let's get this thing started. I want to be out of here. I'll go get the spade"—she wished she'd purchased some sort of sturdier shovel—"and some liquid." When the phantom began sinking into the ground, maybe loosening the soil, she turned hurriedly away so she couldn't see the strangeness, caught herself, and sauntered back up to the car, though her body had tightened with nerves. Quick movement caught the eye.

And she'd have to pray that no one else wanted to visit the station while she was about her business.

This was her life now. Doing things she didn't want at the beck and call of wretched ghosts.

Or going mad.

She got the camp shovel out of the back of the car along with all the liquid she had. She could always stop somewhere on the way home and buy more.

It is as soft as I can make it, Jack Slade said in her mind. He inclined his torso. *And I thank you for your help.*

"Yeah, yeah," she muttered.

She emptied her water and her iced tea, then poured the beer on the ground, ignoring Slade's wince.

With one last scan of the area and seeing no one in sight, she crouched down and levered up the dry grass and some soil, working at it slowly, carefully trying to spread fresh and damp earth along the ground near her instead of piling it. She fell into a rhythm and stopped when her body began to protest the activity. Standing, she walked toward the cool shade cast by the building and surveyed the land. Still no activity at the ranch; perhaps it was one of those deals that did most of its business at certain times during the year. The stream appeared cool and flowing and lovely.

She rolled her shoulders, wiped her face and neck and palms with her bandana, and headed back to her hole. Just a little longer, she hoped.

Grunting as she stooped again, she continued with her task, keeping an eye out for people on the ranch. It was down the hill, and some buildings might block her, but she felt far too vulnerable.

"The least you two can do is tell me if anyone is watching or coming."

Jack Slade shook his head. *Not fond of risk.*

"No." And here she was, talking aloud again, had been all morning, to no one anyone else could see.

You must take some risks, now and at Cold Springs. Jack Slade drifted a little, hesitant. *Cold Springs is on privately owned land.*

Cold Springs sounded wonderful right now, a nighttime trip, driving under a huge sky of rarely seen stars and maybe the Milky Way, which couldn't be seen in Denver . . . the pretty images ground to a halt. "Privately owned land. I'll have to trespass."

Yes, Slade said.

You can do it! I will be with you! I can keep watch! Enzo barked.

"You both *do* know that ranchers in Wyoming have guns?" Clare said.

Slade's nostrils widened as if he snorted.

"Yeah, yeah, I know you're the original badass gunman, Slade, but I've never even held one."

It is too bad that Zach won't be with you, Enzo said.

The springs are gone, along with the old station house. It is now very close to a farmed field.

"Yes, I'll miss Zach," Clare snapped, more hurt than she cared to admit even to herself. She dug deep with her spade. "Farmland, great. Even Wyoming farmers have guns."

Clink.

You've got it! Enzo bounced around her.

"I think so," Clare said, digging more carefully now, widening the hole around the angled bottle made of dark glass. Five minutes later she'd retrieved the thing. The bottle was dark green bordering on black and nine inches long. She brushed clinging dirt off it.

"I can't see through it!" she said, frustrated.

The ear is in there, Jack Slade said.

Enzo poked his face into the bottle. *Yes, it is there, a human ear, a little shriveled and almost whole.*

"Eww." She laid the bottle in the grass, took her blue bandana from her pocket, and wiped her face, then the object of her quest. Gently, she shook it, thought she felt a little shifting dirt. As far as she was concerned, the ear was good enough for now.

We did it! We did it! We did it!

"Yes," Clare said, tiredly.

She spent long minutes putting the dirt back in the hole, arranging the grass again, making the evidence of disturbance minimal.

When she returned to the car, all she wanted was a bath. She toyed with driving into Fort Collins and renting a room, but she ached to be in her new home with her belongings. That was the payoff for her gift to see ghosts, and it was almost sufficient.

Wrapping the bottle in paper towels, she maneuvered her car seat back and forth to wedge the bottle safely under the wonky seat, not wanting the filthy ear-holding object in her cooler. Desultorily she ate a couple of small chicken strips and an egg and wished she had a drink to go with her food.

"Leaving now," she muttered, knowing that both Jack Slade, who'd disappeared into the station where he'd lived, and Enzo, amusing himself by passing through the large jumble of rocks, could hear her.

Slade didn't appear, but when she passed the rocks on the way out of the gate, Enzo slipped inside the vehicle and sat upright in the passenger seat, and it didn't even faze her. He looked at her, his head wrinkling. *There are graves behind the rocks. Not many, but one of them was a baby.*

"What a wonderful thing to hear. Any ghosts?"

No, they are long gone.

"Fabulous."

Oddly enough, the Flinton case looked like it would break wide open, with the newer bunch of leads on the furniture and antique silver. Clare's examination of the books, particularly the receipts, showed whom many of the items had been sold to. And though they'd been lost for decades, Zach felt an urgency to find them, give Mrs. Flinton closure, at least.

But throughout the day he felt a persistent itch between his shoulder blades and thought about the argument he'd had with Clare.

When he was downtown working, he got hungry and avoided both restaurants he'd met Clare in . . . but he bought an e-copy of the main and massive biography of Jack Slade that Clare had a half dozen bookmarks in.

Interesting reading. The story drew him in, though he skimmed it since he knew the general details of Slade's life. He paid particular attention to Virginia Dale. There were no pictures of the place in the book, but he found some online.

As he closed his tablet and finished his drink, he tilted his chair back and considered what he'd read. Joseph Albert Slade's story was tough in so many ways. Yeah, he might have suffered from PTSD, but the guy sure hadn't handled himself.

A trickle of pride welled in Zach. He'd done better, all around. Might never be the success the original Jack Slade had been in his heyday as a division manager of the stagecoach and Pony Express, but Zach wouldn't be shooting up saloons, begging for forgiveness, and strung up by a vigilante committee either.

By early afternoon he wanted to call Clare. Not really to apologize. More like just to make sure the trip had gone okay.

And had she found the ear?

Yeah, sure, that was truly a burning question.

But they'd made a deal not to check up on each other . . . words that echoed hollowly in his mind from a couple of days before. So it would be pushy if he called, especially since though her words bugged him, maybe even really got under his skin and stuck like barbs in his brain, he didn't want to talk about it.

And that deal *was* Before. Before she dumped him. Before he left and accepted the dumping.

An hour later he'd found Mrs. Flinton's antiques, about three quarters of them along with the silver set. So he met with her and Rickman in Rickman's office.

They sat in a well-appointed conference room that looked out over the mountains. Only Zach glanced at the panoramic view of brown hills and gray peaks that held tiny streaks of snow on their faces—the weather had been hotter than usual up there, too, though not as bad as in Denver.

"Zach?" rumbled Rickman, obviously wanting backup for a quietly sobbing Mrs. Flinton. "Why don't you go over it again?"

He'd given one report, and he didn't think Mrs. Flinton could hear him well over her "happy tears," but he limped over to the conference table and the pics Rickman had printed from Zach's phone.

"Clare found notations in one of the ledgers that seven pieces, including the silver set, were sold to a family friend. And those stayed together for a couple of generations. I found them in a garage. Sorry the photos aren't great."

Mrs. Flinton swallowed and lifted tear-blurred eyes to him. "They look like they've been cared for."

"In general, yes, but the lady I talked to said they'd been her mother's and grandmother's and those ladies had used them." He cleared his throat. "The Arvada neighborhood is upper middle class, and the woman didn't seem to know what the items were worth."

Rickman rubbed his new buzz cut. "The sale looks to Clare like it was legal?"

"Yes, sir."

After blowing her nose in a fancy handkerchief, Mrs. Flinton lifted her chin and said, "I want them back."

"I think a check would make the current owner very happy. Neither she nor her children want the furniture, but keeping it together might mean something to them." Like her great-aunt Sandra's had meant to Clare and her brother. All still in the family.

Sitting up straight, Mrs. Flinton nodded. "And they'd know where the pieces were and that they'd be cherished." She blinked. "Do you think she'd welcome an appraiser?"

"If you paid for it," Zach said.

"You think she might shop around for another buyer if we sent an appraiser?" Rickman asked.

Zach leaned on the table, glanced at the grainy photos. "She's a nice lady. I don't think so. They've just been sitting in one side of her triple garage for a couple of years. I'm sure she'll run it by her family, though, her husband and her three girls, but I anticipate they'd sell. I was up front about the whole deal, seemed a case to be that way."

Mrs. Flinton took out her smart phone from her bag, scrolled through her contacts. "I have an appraiser I trust. You can contact him and the lady and set up the appointment?"

"Sure, we can," Rickman said. "You don't want to be there with the appraiser?"

"No."

"I think we can get this done in the next couple of days," Zach said.

"That's lovely." Mrs. Flinton pushed back her chair. Zach helped her and steadied her while Rickman got her walker. But she held out her hand to Zach. "Thank you, Zach. I'm so pleased."

"Good job," Rickman said gruffly.

Zach shrugged.

"And give my thanks to Clare, too," Mrs. Flinton said. Canny old lady, she knew something was up between him and Clare, but he wasn't about to confirm that.

"We can give her a finder's fee, standard rate," Rickman said, moving to the door to open it."

"I don't think she'll want that," Zach said. "She doesn't need the money."

"A laborer is worthy of her hire," Mrs. Flinton said. Zach thought that was from the Bible. "You can tell her that. She's a sensible girl."

Yeah, she was, even with her new "gift."

The drive home seemed endless, traffic heavier and slower, the light brighter even against her sunglasses, Enzo either chirpily offering comments, noting ghosts in buildings as she drove through towns, or a little too quiet.

By the time she pulled into her driveway, a headache raged between her temples and she yearned for the cool dimness of the house and a tepid bath with fragrant herbs and soothing music. She fumbled for the garage door opener, but it didn't seem to work.

Crap! So hot and weary and not nearly as pleased at a task well done as she would have been after a good audit. This ghost bit was tiring and strained her mind and imagination . . . not to mention her sore body, especially her hands. Working with figures was so much more personally rewarding.

She turned off the ignition and sat a moment. She'd only have a couple of minutes before the heat in the car became insufferable. No, she wouldn't deal with the darn bottle and its contents right now—whatever shape the thing might be in. She'd leave bottle and all tucked under her seat. It was safe enough under her seat since she had problems moving the darn thing back and forth.

Getting out of the car and walking to the narrow side house door nearly hidden by ivy, she was barely able to think, her neck was so tight and her head ached so much.

Clare, watch—

Something hit her head and pain exploded, taking her into hot darkness with it.

THIRTY-TWO

BY LATE IN the afternoon, Zach had made some decisions on a personal front. He'd leased a truck and ordered a hooked cane recommended by the bartitsu guy. He'd signed up for some private lessons in the mixed martial art.

He missed Clare. He'd liked knowing she'd be there for him with sweet serenity when he'd finished his day. And though he hadn't liked her words, he'd liked her fire, the passion he knew she locked down. Liked that he could bring that out in her, that she felt passionately about him.

And he had to acknowledge the bottom line. The bottom line was that he had made a mistake and paid a tough price for it and his life had damn well changed.

Clare's life had changed because she'd been born into the wrong family. Nothing she could have done about that . . . except, from what he'd overheard in conversations between her and Enzo and seen in her notes, read in the journals of Sandra Cermak he'd peeked into . . . Clare had a choice of dying or accepting her gift, going mad or accepting her gift.

Not a choice he'd have to make.

* * *

Hearing a noise, which turned out to be her own whimpering groan, roused Clare. Her whole body felt stiff and she thought she lay on a cot.

What was going on?

She'd heard Enzo yell mentally, and then her head had gone from miserable ache to magnificent piercing pain. She touched it: a huge bump and—yikes!—tender.

She sat up groggily, hot and sweaty, her mind muddled. Her stomach roiled, but she squeezed her eyes shut and forced it to calm by sheer will. More sweat leaked from her pores at the effort, and the drying of it cooled her slightly but felt like it left a film over her skin.

Where was Enzo? He could keep her cool.

Or the apparition of Jack Slade.

They weren't here right now; she'd sense them even with her lashes shut.

Rubbing crust from her eyes, then just plain rubbing her eyes, she opened them to see the small back bedroom in her old house that she'd used as an office. Enough time had passed that twilight shrouded the room. Again her stomach tightened and did the roll thing and she had to concentrate on not vomiting.

Increment by increment, she set her feet under her and rose and wobbled the few paces to the door and tried the knob. It was locked. She swung around too fast and had to lean a shoulder against the wall. Then she stumbled to check the two vertical windows and blinked. The rectangles of light showed bright in the darkening room and she could see that the cranks to open the windows had been removed.

Crap! She'd been kidnapped and was locked in a room of an empty house.

A house everyone knew she wouldn't visit.

She breathed slowly through her nose, examined the room. She'd done a quick surface cleaning but the service she'd hired for the deep cleaning wouldn't be coming for days; they'd been backed up. Arlene, the agent who'd be handling the sale, wouldn't be checking on it for a week or so, and wouldn't be checking on Clare for a couple of days. Arlene had dropped by to see how the move was going and left five gorgeous bouquets for individual rooms along with effusive thanks.

Clare's mouth dried, and she tasted bile and swallowed the burn back down. Her breathing turned fast and ragged. Weakening knees had her staggering back to the cot, sitting again and rubbing her head—her temples, touching the bump, owie!—and pushing her fingers through her hair. She tugged, trying to clear more fogginess from her mind.

Think!

Panting, she worked through who would miss her and how soon. Zach. No, they'd broken up. Wait, wait. She'd told him that she'd finish the ledgers and messenger them to Rickman.

Her mouth turned down. She hadn't told Zach how close to done she had been with the records; he might expect them in two to three days.

She sucked in a shaky breath. Time to effing figure out what was going on. Again she swallowed hard, wished for some water to rinse out her mouth, and stood.

The door opened.

She rushed forward, met outstretched arms that shoved her to the floor, and her mind began to whirl again. Oww! A couple of seconds passed before she croaked, "Who . . . who?"

A snort, and simply the sound of it clued her in.

"Ted Mather!"

"That's right." He stood at the threshold of her room with shadows clinging to him, but unlike the ghosts she'd been communicating with lately, Ted was all too dreadfully solid. "Get back on the cot."

"But . . . but *why*?"

A sound of disbelief. "You *are* slow, aren't you." His head tilted. "Though I s'pose the hit on your head didn't help. Sorry about that," he said cheerfully.

Clare rose painfully and sat on the cot. She eased her fingers through her hair, ran into some clumped blood near her wound. Ick.

"Why?" she repeated.

"Because you can talk to ghosts, probably can talk to the ghost of Jack Slade, and he knows where the gold is from the robbery he masterminded," Ted said, as if *that* were reasonable.

She stared at him, *feeling* her pupils dilate even more than needed in the twilight. How could the research assistant have possibly guessed? Did he have some sort of psychic gift, too?

Clare grasped for rational thought. "That's an interesting theory," she said. "But Jack Slade died in Virginia City, Montana. He didn't even spend much time in Denver."

Ted shrugged and didn't come any closer. "You began acting odd at the library. I followed you once to an upscale shrink's office, heard something about 'ghosts,' and then you added books on being psychic and mediumistic to your reading pile."

She glared at him, outraged. "You followed me!"

He nodded, then waved a casual hand. "Then there was that whole business outside the library during lunch. You were obviously interacting with someone or some*thing*."

Suppressing a wince, Clare stared at him. "It was you," she accused. "You spread the word that I was a medium."

"Just wanted to see what would happen. It was interesting, especially when you got rid of that Native American ghost. I was watching then, too. So I knew you were the real deal."

"Believing in ghosts is crazy."

"'There are more things in heaven and earth, Horatio, than are dreamt of in your philosophy,'" Ted quoted. "I guess you proved that to me." He rubbed his hands and smiled, and Clare knew the man wasn't quite sane. "Now, let's get down to business. You tell me where the missing gold shipment is."

"There is no missing gold shipment."

Ted tsked. "Now that is wrong. The robbery occurred, that's a fact."

"When?"

"Eighteen hundred and sixty-three."

Clare gritted her teeth. "When?"

"Dunno. I found an entry in the library for gold receipts, but by that time I knew you were my best and fastest lead."

"Jack Slade did not mastermind the robbery."

Ted pursed his lips. "Everything online says he did."

"Don't you know that you can't believe everything you read on the Internet? What of your own studies?"

He jerked a shrug. Even in the gloom, she could see his lip curl. "It was taking too long. Summer doesn't last forever, you know, especially at higher elevations when you want to dig something up. You know about digging up treasure, don't you, Clare?"

This time her stomach seemed to swoop inside her. She blocked the image of an "almost whole" ear. "I didn't dig up a chest."

"No, it didn't look like that," Ted agreed.

He'd been there, watching! And she hadn't even sensed him. Hadn't seen a car. Neither of the ghosts had informed her of that. Geez, she'd been so clueless. And worried about the wrong people observing her.

His smile widened, showing the edges of his teeth now. "I'd prefer you to talk to your friendly ghost sooner rather than later so we can get on with this."

"You've got to be kidding." She moved her tongue across her teeth to get a little moisture going in her mouth. "What are you going to do to me?"

"Oh, I'll let you go when you tell me what I want to know. I don't think you'll be able to hold out very long. This house is hot and I'm not going to let you have any food, and not much water. You're not a woman accustomed to that, are you?"

She just stared, could feel her throat dry as he spoke.

"So why don't you tell me about the gold?" he persisted.

"I don't know anything about that gold."

He tilted his head in the opposite direction. "You know, I believe you. After all, with your new inheritance you don't need money, do you? You inherited upward of twenty million, didn't you?"

He'd been researching *her*! Fury helped drive the fear away.

Ted jutted his chin. "Just talk to Slade for me, why don't you?"

"It doesn't work that way," Clare said.

"Oh, I believe you can 'call' him or 'summon' him or whatever"—another casual gesture—"whenever you want. After all, your great-aunt Sandra Cermak boasted that in an interview or two I've read."

Geez.

She blinked rapidly, sorting through arguments. "I'll be missed."

A ripe chuckle. "I don't think so. I saw that touching farewell to your ex-lover; that was a break for me. Your new house's security hasn't been breached, though I did disable the garage door. All will look fine, there. And I drove you here in your own car."

"My neighbors here will—"

"Accept that you came back for some reason . . . and if we can't reach an agreement in a couple of hours, I'll move it, leave you alone here in the dark."

That really didn't matter to her much, but she managed a flinch as if it would.

"I'll let you stew all night." He wrinkled his nose. "I'm sure the room won't be very pleasant when I come back in the morning, and it will be harder to sell a house when someone's urinated and defecated in a room, won't it? All lose-lose options for you, Clare."

She might vomit first.

"Perhaps I should offer some incentive."

He stepped back and locked the door, but returned in under a minute.

Under his arm appeared to be a plastic bottle of water; his right hand leveled a gun at her.

Sweat popped from her and she bit her lower lip to focus on that instead of her churning belly.

ENZO, she shrieked in her mind. The phantom dog did not answer. *Great.* He'd been pretty nearly inseparable from her and now he wasn't here. Where the heck was he?

She stared at Ted, tasting bile again, acid searing her throat. He didn't look scary, really. Unless you looked at his eyes . . . or his smile . . . or the gun he was holding. Her throbbing head indicated he would use violence to get what he wanted.

"So, what do you think? Ready to talk?" He offered the water.

She *yearned* for it. But, blinking, she saw that the cap had been broken and the bottle opened. No telling what filthy drug he might have put in there. Or could it be a fake-out and he expected her to notice that it had been opened and have qualms.

She realized she didn't know enough about the jerk.

She could hold out for a little bit, until her aches subsided, her head felt less muzzy.

"I think I'll refuse your so-generous offer."

Color flushed his face reddish. The heat couldn't be good for him. As for her, she knew she had a sweat stain along the spine of her shirt. "Fine!" He kicked the door shut hard. The tongue of the lock didn't catch, and it bounced. Clare could have told him it would.

Scowling, he shut the door and locked it. This time she heard additional sounds, as if he'd added another lock on the outside of the door!

This was her house, had been *her* home, and she knew all its quirks. She went to the high window that didn't close all the way, leaving a tiny gap she had to block during the winter.

Ted had managed to shut it, but she'd bet anything that even without the crank handle, she could open it. She set her hands against the window and tried to slide it open. It budged a tiny bit. She hissed a frustrated sigh. Maybe in several hours she could get the thing open. She didn't think she had that amount of time, despite what Ted said. He was an impatient man, wanting, like so many people did, instant gratification . . . like quick access to mythical 1863 gold.

Now that Ted had mentioned it, she needed water. It had been a "trip day," so she hadn't drunk a lot. It had also been hot and she'd done minor physical labor. She was probably dehydrated.

She hadn't eaten much either, and the way acid pitched in her stomach, she was glad of that. Soon, though, her bladder would be bothering her. She'd stopped once on the way back at a gas station to refuel the car to full and to pee, but that had been hours ago.

Enzo! she called again, and waited futilely for an answer.

She was right; Ted returned only a few minutes later with only the gun.

"A gunshot will be noticed in this neighborhood." The area was solidly middle class.

His pursing lips made his mouth tiny. She'd never noticed his mouth was smaller than average, though when his grin showed his teeth all the way to his incisors, his mouth looked huge.

"You're right." He pouted. "I'll have to work with a knife first, I suppose."

THIRTY-THREE

HE TURNED AND left, not even closing the door, but Clare was busy holding her hands over her mouth swallowing and swallowing again. She should just upchuck and get it over with, instead of fighting to be mannerly, civilized, decent. Belatedly she lumbered to the door, found it blocked by Ted.

Again he shoved her back and she landed on her rump and winced, and then her eyes went to the gleam of a knife in his hand.

"I should maybe start with a knife. I have handcuffs and ropes and stuff, too, but I wanted to be nice about this."

Her heart thumped hard, her pulse in her temples drowning out everything else.

Around sunset, after a workout and shower and dinner, Zach got so twitchy that he couldn't stay in.

The bartitsu studio was having a class that he'd been invited to observe and he decided to do that, dressed in old jeans that had plenty of give and a T-shirt.

As he exited his apartment, his scalp tingled and his hair

rose. He heard a caw and instinctively his shoulders hunched. Didn't matter that he couldn't see the damn crows, he knew they sat on a power cable above and behind him. He could almost imagine the number of them . . . No. No, he couldn't. So he'd have to turn around and look.

He let his shoulders sink, gripped the handle of his cane, and pivoted around.

Seven. Just like a few days before. *Seven for a secret not to be told.* Hell, he was in the business of secrets, ferreting them out. Shouldn't he have expected this more often?

Then two more crows joined their friends. Fear skewered Zach. Nine. *Nine for hell.*

The last time he'd seen nine had been when he'd gone to help Clare and had noticed the bank robbery. Clare's secret, the bank robber's secret, whichever had pulled him had been . . . dire, hellish.

Not just run-of-the-mill secrets like who bought Mrs. Flinton's antiques.

And he knew deep down in the marrow of his bones, in the ache around the damn titanium, that trouble had found Clare. Again.

If he went to her, he'd be admitting her insights were right, wouldn't he? That he really had to accept the changes in his life, move past the denial part of the stages of loss that the shrink he'd talked to had laid out.

He'd passed right through the bargaining, not his kind of deal, and hard to bargain when you usually figured you'd lose, especially when you couldn't control your own damn foot. Not hard to show the anger part, but he'd faked the acceptance, hadn't truly gotten out of the denial phase. Deny, deny, deny. Change his venue so he could continue to deny.

Usually he didn't let his mind play tricks on him, but he had now. He wasn't *ready* to accept that his previous career was over, that his life had changed.

Crap. Where had his balls gone? Emotional courage. He'd always thought of himself as strong in every way, but he was nothing but an emotional coward.

Disgust at himself rolled tsunami-like through him, threatening to overwhelm. He could just go under. Prove himself weak, a lot weaker than his father. The thought of that man flashed anger that buoyed Zach. Like always, he wouldn't ever be less than the General.

As far as Zach was concerned, the guy knew nothing about emotions. So Zach hurt, in his ankle and his mind and his heart. He damn well *grieved* for the life he had lost.

He stomped to his new vehicle, lifting his knee high so there was no chance of dragging his foot.

Yeah, he'd been avoiding the gut knowledge that Nothing Would Ever Be the Same. Because he sure didn't want to wack out like Clare had.

She was better now . . . and his father, who'd stuck his always-vestigial emotions into the deep freeze when Jim had died . . . Zach didn't want to be anything like General Slade. Better to hurt and suffer and . . . be a whole man. So he wouldn't lie to himself anymore. He might not be able to admit, aloud and in words, that he hurt, but that was different.

Time to find out what danger threatened Clare.

He opened the door and stepped up into the truck, bumped his ankle and sweated and swore as his vision went white with pain. Then he set his jaw and went on, hit the ignition, exited from the drive, and turned onto the street. He glanced up at the line of crows. They were gone. He kept on swearing as he drove to Clare's new place.

She wasn't at home, the security was on, and there was no sign of her car. As far as Zach knew, she could have decided to keep on going to Cold Springs.

Wait, wait, she hadn't taken the puzzle box with the other ear. He was certain of that. He'd left after her, and the box had been on the fireplace mantel in the living room. He'd noticed because it was the only object on the mantel.

He looked at his watch: after seven. Naturally he'd checked out the trip time, and she should have been back midafternoon at the latest, even with the worst traffic streaming into Denver.

A cop hunch about trouble skittered along his spine. He'd just have to find her.

Clare moved to the cot, sat with her feet together and her hands in her lap.

"Such a good, quiet girl you look," Ted crooned. "Ready to reconsider?" he asked.

Through stiff lips she said, "What will you do to me if I do tell you whatever you want to know?"

"Let you go . . . if it's soon. You don't want to make me *too* mad."

As far as she was concerned, he already was mad in the crazy sort of way.

"Let me go? That's it?"

He chuckled. "You wouldn't go to the police about this."

"Yes, I would," she shot back before she could think better of it.

Shaking his head, he said, "You'd sound crazy . . . some guy kidnaps you because he wants you to talk to ghosts?"

She swallowed. "I'm not the crazy one."

His lips tightened and his hand holding the gun quivered a little bit. "Maybe not. But you're getting a rep as a medium. The cops don't care for frauds."

"I'm not a fraud!" She jumped to her feet and the knife jerked as he followed her movement. She wrapped her arms around herself.

He waved the knife again and she couldn't prevent a shudder. His smile widened to the crazy grin she distrusted. His creaky cackle of a laugh rasped her ears and her nerves. "Tsk, tsk, Ms. Cermak." He shook his head. "Such a liar you are, about being a psychic medium, about being able to summon ghosts and talking to them, about everything!" He sliced air with the knife. "About not knowing of the gold robbery. Especially the gold robbery."

Nothing she could say would make a dent in Ted's obsession; she was doomed.

"I—"

A timer dinged. "Ah, my pizza is done," Ted said.

Clare stared. "You used the *oven* in the house?"

"Yes, the heat is incredible; I thought it might add incentive." With a glance around the bare room, he said, "This bedroom sure holds on to the heat, doesn't it? But I think I'll have some food and a nice cold drink now." Smacking his lips, he shut and locked the door.

Instants later the smell of hot cheesy dough and pepperoni

seeped through the cracks in the bedroom, making her mouth water, though she still felt queasy.

Clare got to work on trying to inch the window open; it moved about a sixteenth of an inch a shove. She'd become more and more aware of her bladder until she shifted from foot to foot. This bedroom shared a wall with the bathroom; so close and too far!

The cot had wooden legs. She could lift it and break the window glass, then set the cot down and try to climb out through a narrow window jagged with glass. But she believed it would take more than one jolt and neighbors wouldn't notice the noise. Ted would hear it and run in with his knife and his gun and rope or chains or whatever else he might want to use on her.

So she grunted and pushed and pushed and . . .

A chain rattled. How could he eat so fast? Would he torture her with food and drink?

Yes, he would. He stood in the doorway, with the gun, snarfing down pizza and making yummy noises, all the while watching her.

If she'd had any outrage left she'd have spit at him.

Think and think again!

Her car was out front. He'd said so. All she had to do is get out, run away. She might be able to do it. Outrun a bullet? Her inner critic laughed and laughed. But Ted wanted something from her; he wouldn't shoot to kill, would he? Any shot in this neighborhood would be heard and reported. She could run faster than he. She was younger and probably fitter. She hadn't ever seen him move at more than a walk. And she didn't know what kind of shot he was. Was it worth the risk?

Yes, said Enzo, materializing next to her. He sat and offered a paw as if to shake.

Where have you been!

With Jack Slade. There are problems, he is devolving.

I have effing problems, too!

Enzo cocked his head. *Yes, you should leave. We should leave.*

Can you help? Distract him somehow?

The Lab barked loudly, circling the room at a run. Ted showed no sign that he saw or heard the dog.

Maybe if I talk to you . . .

I don't think that would be good, Clare.

She huffed a breath.

Enzo went up and sniffed Ted. *He doesn't smell sane, Clare.*

And Enzo knew sane and insane, she reminded herself.

I can't affect him. He believes in ghosts in his broken mind, but not in his gut. It's the gut and instincts we can work with only.

Clare slid a glance at Ted. "You know, I dug up something. I didn't have time to fully examine it." A lure, a temptation . . .

He bit.

"What was it? I couldn't see." He sounded petulant.

She wet her lips. "A bottle."

"A bottle?" His eyes narrowed as if he couldn't decide whether that information was interesting.

"I couldn't tell whether there was anything in it." She widened her eyes, jerking a little as if she regretted her words, and shook her head. "No, nothing more than a bottle."

"It didn't look like a strongbox . . . but all reports said the strongbox was broken and the gold gone."

"I'm sure the bottle came *later*. Nothing to see. Really." She smiled too brightly, wondering if the simple reverse psychology she was using would actually work. She didn't think it would on a non-obsessive normal person, but Ted wasn't normal.

"Maybe I should go see," he said.

"Oh. All right." Just as she knew this house, she knew her car. The bottle was jammed under the seat and the seat didn't move easily . . . a little back and forth manipulation of both automatic and manual levers would be necessary to retrieve it. She was *sure* getting the bottle out would frustrate Ted. Perhaps he'd want her to do it. Let her out to do it.

He pivoted in the doorway and she thought of jumping him since he held the gun loosely, but then he took another step into the hall and she'd missed her chance. Zach wouldn't have. Zach wouldn't have gotten kidnapped in the first place. Stop thinking of Zach and concentrate on *herself*.

The door slammed shut and the knob lock clicked.

Next time she had to be prepared. It would be so good if he'd let her pee.

Meanwhile her stomach pinched and the lingering smell of pizza didn't sit so well with her.

His footsteps stomped back and he flung the door open, scowling, now holding the gun with some purpose. "I can't get the damn bottle from under the seat." Gesturing with the gun, he took a few steps back.

Clare scuttled forward, past the threshold, and all she could think of was getting out, forget the bathroom for now.

Near-suffocating heat wrapped around her, but *fresh* air came from the open front door, along with the last smudge of twilight before real night. That would make shooting harder, right?

I have a plan, she sent to Enzo.

THIRTY-FOUR

YES, YES, YES!

At the right minute, I'm going to run for it. And pray that she didn't end up as a ghost herself. No, she wouldn't. She had few regrets . . . even Zach . . . she'd said what had to be said. She put all thoughts but her plan aside.

If you—or the Other—can give me any help, please do so.

Enzo didn't answer that comment.

Ted motioned her to the door with the gun, looking all too serious. She magnified a cringe. The hole of the barrel of the gun seemed gigantic, as if it could swallow her. As if it would shoot a cannonball to shatter her into a thousand bloody bits. She opened the front door and went into the front yard and sent her gaze up and down the street for anyone, any hope, to no avail.

The driver's-side door of her car remained open. She glanced back at Ted; he was walking toward her. A key was in the ignition—so the automatic seat control would move. Could she possibly drive away? Maybe . . . then the gun touched her back, like nothing she'd ever felt, but unmistakable against her spine. Perhaps she could bend, kick him, or something . . . but she wasn't a very physical woman.

"You try to sit in the seat and I'll shoot you," Ted said.

"You need me."

He shrugged. "Maybe. But there are other mediums. I just hadn't thought of that angle."

"Or you could actually do research," Clare said bitterly.

He backed out of hitting and kicking range.

She bent down. She kept a tidy car, not a loose pen or even a paper clip to throw. Only the spade, and if she tried to heave it at Ted and hurt him, she just knew she'd fail. *Forget acting impulsively and stick with the plan.* A little toggle here, a touch there, and the seat rose. As it tilted forward, she yanked out the paper-towel-wrapped bottle with a grunt, got a good grip on the neck.

"You have it?" Ted asked.

She hesitated an instant, then answered, "Yes."

"Bring it out."

She did, straightening and slamming the car door. That sound wasn't as loud and didn't travel as far as she liked, wouldn't upset the neighbors . . . should she have turned on the radio, blasted music? She'd have been blasted herself.

Ted stood a few feet away, gun aimed at her middle; she forced her gaze away from the hole in the barrel.

I know what you're going to do, Clare. It will work! Enzo cheered.

This time she hoped he had preternatural knowledge, or precognition, and it wasn't simply empty encouragement.

"Hold the bottle up so I can see it," Ted commanded.

He should have turned on the porch light. No hint of any contents was visible.

She hefted it in her hands, frowned and put it to her ear, then shook it a little. "Huh."

"What is it?" Ted insisted with the ring of desperation in his voice.

Clare studied it. "There might be something in here," she whispered. She flung it at him and he squealed like a young girl, hopping back as the thing shattered at his feet.

She grinned, with teeth. "There's an ear."

He screeched, high and clear, and she took off running. She could make it a few blocks to a local bar and safety.

Then she heard the shot, saw chips of concrete fly from the sidewalk no more than a pace ahead of her.

"I'll shoot again!" Ted threatened.

"Take the ear," Clare yelled, feeling reckless, running harder. "It's worth something, I bet." But her body began to stress how physically hard the day had been. Her wind was poor.

He shot again, and she tripped, turned her ankle, and went down.

"Clare!" Zach shouted.

Zach. Her ankle sent spears of red-hot pain, her head throbbed, the world wavered around her. She mewled.

Rapid footsteps, a whoosh, thunk, and yell of pain—from Ted—and then Zach was there.

Clare threw up, just missing his shoes.

Zach had taken Ted's gun and hit him, but the guy had a hard head because while Zach helped Clare, Ted escaped.

She cleaned herself up in the bathroom as he called the police, which was unnecessary since everyone on the block had, and now popped out of their doors and milled around the dark street punctuated by porch lights and headlights from the police cruisers. When an ambulance came, Zach strong-armed her into going to the hospital. At that time, Enzo winked out. He said that the ambulance smelled of too many dying and dead and he couldn't keep himself together, which clued Clare in that he wouldn't be visiting her in the hospital, either. She hoped her insurance would take care of this, it was so expensive.

She also fretted about the bottle glass, the ear, and most of all, the spade with dirt in the back of her car. What would the police say? Would they confiscate the ear? *Then* what would she do, especially since Jack Slade's ghost was devolving? Would they arrest her for going to a historic place and . . . defacing it? Stealing from it?

Her blood pressure was high and she said it was from the stress of being shot. They hydrated her with a tube in her hand, wrapped her ankle, checked out her head, and gave her a little something, she didn't know what, that settled her stomach immediately. It turned out that she had a sprained ankle and a mild concussion and she should rest.

Then Zach and the cops were allowed in. He looked comfortable and happy in cop company. She sent a speaking look to Zach and when he didn't say anything, she tugged at one of her earlobes. He shook his head.

Relief surged through her in waves as she realized no one was going to charge her with anything. No trip to Virginia Dale, old bottle glass, or dirty spade was mentioned.

Someone in the neighborhood had been in their side yard watering when Ted fired the first shot. So there was an eyewitness to his attempted murder. Clare had to sip from her water at that. The witness had also seen Zach and Ted's scuffle—Zach's word, though he frowned heavily and Clare sensed that he was wishing he'd hit Ted harder, put him down and out. She reached and took his hand, held it, and said simply, "I'm glad you stayed with me."

The police had found the knife, ropes, and a pair of handcuffs that Zach smirked at, so she thought they must have come from a sex shop.

She told them everything she knew about Ted, letting her confusion show with regard to the man and his madness, repeating again and again that treasure hunting was foolish. The fact that she still sat straight and looked like an accountant—she visualized herself wearing a sober suit and treating the policemen like her most straightlaced client—and had *been* an accountant, only quitting her job a week before because she'd come into an inheritance, helped a great deal.

So did Zach. He didn't mention anything regarding "seeing ghosts" or his own "hunches." The police recalled him from a few days before, and he had an easy manner with them, adapting to their rhythm.

They let her ramble until she got to the kidnapping, then asked for more details.

And then they told her he'd gotten clean away. She stared at the cop in charge for a long minute as shock rolled through her. "Got away?"

"He's not using his own vehicle," Zach said. "And he gave notice to his professor that he was quitting his job immediately this A.M." Zach squeezed her fingers. "We'll find him, and until then, I'll stay close."

She drank a mouthful of water, she was so dry. A few seconds later she straightened her spine and shoulders. "All right." She tried a smile; it didn't feel too shaky. "After all, we've beaten him so far, haven't we? He missed me both times he shot at me."

Zach said gently, "You tripped, Clare."

Again her mouth dried. A shudder rippled through her. "Oh." After clearing her throat, she said, "Can I leave now?"

Apparently a doctor was in the other curtained-off space. He strode in and took out the tube in her hand. "We'll release you. Watch that ankle and take care of yourself." He shot Zach a look. "You help her take care of herself."

"I will," Zach said.

She looked at the policeman who'd introduced himself, but his name escaped her. "Thank you," she said.

"Just doing my job," he said, smiling, and wrinkles showed around his mouth and eyes. "I hope not to see you again, Ms. Cermak."

"Well," she said, "not in the line of duty, though if you're friends with Zach, it may be another story." She smiled and concentrated on getting off the exam table.

"Thanks for your cooperation," the policeman said. "Zach, later."

"Sure, Phil," Zach said as the guy left.

Clare let her shoulders droop and put on the clothes she'd throw away as soon as she got home. "Thank you for coming for me, Zach." She looked him in the eyes. "I don't know how you found me."

"It wasn't too hard. You weren't at home and I had a hunch. . . . Anyway, the only two people I could think of who were associated with you now were Barclay and Mather. Barclay was clear. I looked into Mather's whereabouts, learned he'd quit precipitously, and his car was found on your block. Your new block. Yours was missing. Just used logic after that." He shrugged and took her hands. His mouth turned down. "I know we have to talk about—stuff. But not here, okay? Meanwhile, get used to the fact that I'll be with you."

He pressed her hands, his eyes going darker. "And you were right about . . . other things."

The comment made her flush, hold tight to his hands, too.

He didn't show any stress at her hard grip. "You're a hero. You saved me."

"You saved yourself."

"But I fell, and sprained my ankle. I might not have made it, been able to follow my plan."

One side of his mouth quirked up. "You'd have thought of something."

She sighed. "I suppose so. Can we really get out of here?"

"I'll take you home."

"And stay with me?" She hadn't told him last night, but her bedroom had a low, masculine-looking dresser that she'd hoped would prompt him to leave more things at her place. She felt a little wary about mentioning it now, but perhaps soon.

"I'll stay." He remained stern-jawed until they reached the parking lot and a big black pickup truck.

He opened the door.

"This is yours?"

"Yeah. Leased it today. A patrolman will bring your car around to your new place when the cops are done with it. Might even be there before you get there."

She shivered but didn't want to mention her fears aloud.

He opened the door and helped her up. She stopped an instinctive comment about having such a vehicle with his hurt leg.

"Black's not great in the summer heat," she said instead, closing the door and pulling her seat belt on. The truck smelled new, too.

He grunted. "It's good for nighttime, for, say, driving to a scene to trespass."

There was that.

"It gleams," she pointed out, then said, "Oh."

He slanted her a grin. "Yeah, it won't by the time we traverse a few dirt roads to Cold Springs."

"It's pretty big."

"Tell me, Clare, you think a big black truck will stand out in Wyoming farm and ranch country?"

"Well, no. No, I don't."

"Didn't think so."

She waited until he was out of the parking lot to say, "Where's the ear?"

"Jack Slade's ear?"

"That's the one."

"We didn't find it."

"It was in the bottle that was shattered on my old drive-way."

"*In* the bottle?"

"I got the idea teenaged boys goofed around at some point in the past and stuffed the ear in a bottle." She sniffed.

He kept his face bland. "Ah." Then he said, "Did you see the ear?"

"Yes, but just for an instant. It made Ted scream and I took off. We'd better go back and find it." How could she help Jack Slade move on with only one of Jules Beni's ears? How would that affect the ghost, the procedure, the rules . . . *her*?

THIRTY-FIVE

ZACH SAID, "I don't think *we* should do that. I think you should take a hot bath in that big spa tub of yours."

She looked down at herself, flinching at the coating of sweat she felt, the dirt, and sniffed. She didn't smell too bad, she didn't think, but a bath sounded heavenly.

"You don't smell like anything except your own sweet self," Zach said, as if he'd read her mind.

Yet duty called. "I need to find the ear before we go to Cold Springs. The thing was sort of withered and leathery and brown; maybe it fell on my dried grass or something. Perhaps Ted kicked it during your scuffle. Or you did, or—"

I hid it from the sight of everyone! I've been keeping it safe until you could get it! All the people are gone now! Enzo yipped as he materialized on the front seat between Zach and her. He leaned into her and licked her cheek. *You did fine. You did great.* His cold tongue actually felt good.

"Thank you," she said.

"Enzo's here," Zach said in a resigned tone.

"Yes. Enzo said he, uh, masked the ear from everyone's vision."

You talk right about stuff, Clare. You are learning how things work. Enzo approved.

Zach pulled into the drive of her new home. "Can Enzo point me to the ear?"

It is easy to see if I let it!

"He says it's pretty visible."

"All right." Zach exited his side and weariness spun through Clare's body and she slumped. The door opened and Zach released her seat belt and lifted her from the truck. Beneath her closed lashes, tears welled. Such a strong man, this man, in every way. So he ducked an issue or two. Which man didn't? Which person didn't?

On her feet, she leaned against him as he leaned against the truck and wrapped her arms around him, moved her head so she could hear the thump of his heart. It sounded a little fast to her.

"I'm so glad you came for me."

"You said that before."

She arched away to look him in the eyes, but their lower bodies still pressed together and she felt him harden. And she wanted him atop her, in her. She slid her fingers into his hair at the nape of his neck. "I like your hair. I like you, Zach." She didn't have to stretch far to find his mouth, and the taste of him jolted through her. She hadn't even known she'd missed his taste . . . they'd only been apart for less than a day . . . but she'd thought they were over. Steeping herself in him and kissing him was so very necessary right now. An ethical man as well as a strong man. She nibbled on his bottom lip, swept her tongue across his mouth. His arms came around her and he angled his head, took control of the kiss, his hand going to her butt and pulling her closer.

Just plain wonderful after all she'd endured that day.

His hands trailed up her sides to her shoulders and he lifted his head, breaking the kiss. "You go soak."

"My ankle's wrapped."

"I can rewrap it. I have to go get the ear," he murmured, close to her own ear, giving it a tiny nip.

At that she drew back. "Ick." Hefting a sigh, she nagged, "We need to go to Cold Springs for Jack Slade."

Enzo barked. *We need the ear!*

"We can go to Cold Springs for Jack Slade tomorrow evening, leave after rush hour."

She tensed. "Maybe we should leave tomorrow morning instead, stay over."

"We'll see." He kissed her hard and briefly. "Go in. I'll be right back and we can discuss it then."

"And other things."

He winced, manlike. "I said you were right, didn't I? Isn't that enough?"

"I suppose, for now."

"For now," he agreed. He gave her another quick kiss. "I'll be right back, but since Mather is still out there and you now have mucho bucks to contribute to police charities—"

"Which I will!" she added stoutly.

"—there will be a couple of police cars driving by at intervals until we—they—catch the guy." He glanced at his watch. "The first patrol check should be any minute, and a cop should be dropping your car off shortly, too. Now open the door, go upstairs, and don't drown in the tub before I get back."

She entered the security code and used her keys on the two locks, then looked up at him. "Do you think two locks are enough?"

"The security's good, not great. I'll look at it more *later*."

"Okay." She kissed him now. "Be safe and come back soon."

But as he was closing the door behind her, he heard, "I'm not packed. I need to pack food and drink for the trip, and some clothes in case we decide to stay over . . ."

He checked the locks and the keypad and drew in a shaky breath of his own, letting a little of his control crumble. Fuck, he'd been scared for her! It had taken all his willpower to act cool in front of the other cops, to not wrap his hand around her wrist and keep her with him at all times. He knew they'd seen his strain, but, hey, no man was completely cool when someone threatened his woman. And, for now, Clare was his woman. He wasn't nearly finished with her . . . out of bed or in it. Not that he could see where this thing with her was going. Hell, he couldn't visualize past tomorrow and the trip to Cold Springs.

And he'd better get his ass in gear, even though his jeans pulled tight across his groin and his semi-erection as he hauled himself into the truck. He scrutinized the block, but it was darker than the neighborhood Clare had lived in before, with large lots set back from the street, and more discreet porch lights. He saw nothing.

Pulling his door shut, he hit the ignition and drove across town to Clare's old neighborhood, preparing to hunt for a dead ear. Much as she might not like to admit it, Clare needed that ear to get on with her life, so he'd fetch it for her. Feeling really stupid, he cleared his throat and said, "Enzo, are you here?" A riot of loud barking came from his right.

"Okay, okay, I hear you." He paused. "And don't tell Clare I said that . . . or Mrs. Flinton, either." Who knew where a ghost dog could go, how fast, and who it might talk to?

A cold nudge on his neck had him nearly jumping from his seat. "I guess that might be you."

The cold spot slid a couple of inches. He'd been slimed.

"Keep your damn nose to yourself," he said, then heard a doggie bark-chuckle.

"Yeah, yeah, I'm not Clare, I don't have to be nice to you." He thought a very chilly breeze ran over his crotch. "Cut that out!"

Another yip, this one definitely amused.

Zach had a one-sided conversation all the way to Clare's old place, and hoped he didn't sound too crazy. He didn't *feel* crazy. He didn't even feel too awkward like Clare obviously did.

He parked on the street. This one appeared quiet, too. The neighbors had all either gone to someone's house to talk, or retired to their own homes. Either way it looked like he had a good opening for a little contamination of a crime scene—if the lab folks hadn't already done their job, which he thought they might have.

"It's going to be in and out, mutt. Let's get this over with ASAP and back to Clare." A spot between his shoulders tingled. He stopped but heard no whir of wings, no caws. Too dark to see crows unless they were pushily evident.

Sliding from the truck, his foot didn't work properly and he jarred it, bit off a curse at the pain. Maybe he'd go back to a damn car, or the standard Colorado vehicle, an SUV. He didn't like SUVs, too prissy. He shut the door quietly and limped as lightly as he could up the driveway. And there, like a small, irregular oil spot, was the ear.

A flurry of barking and cold slipping *through* his legs. "I see it, already." He bent down and scooped the ear up, stuck it in his pocket.

Like the first Jack Slade, Joseph Albert Slade, this Jackson Zachary Slade carried an ear in his pocket. Zach smiled, slid his gaze around in another quick exam of the neighborhood, and returned to his truck. He pushed the speed limit all the way back to Clare.

And found her in the kitchen, cooking. The food and her damp hair and pearly skin smelled perfect when he put his arms around her and kissed her. But he made sure he frowned when she looked up at him. "You didn't rest."

"Not just yet." Her body stiffened. "I just want to—"

"Clare, it's been a hard day. You need some downtime. I put the ear with the other in the box."

"Thanks. I'm still a little jittery." She turned in his arms and hugged him tightly.

He closed his eyes at the feel of her, soft. Exhaustion hovered in a red tide at the back of his eyes. He didn't dare keep them closed. "We're going up, now."

"We're?"

"Yeah, *we're*. And no tempting me, woman. Sleep . . . first."

Clare chuckled and, needing that flavor of him again, kissed him. "We'll see." She linked arms with him, but as she walked with him, her jitters diminished; just having him here helped.

They'd no sooner gotten to the bedroom, disrobed, and settled under a sheet when the ghost of Jack Slade came screaming through the bedroom windows. "It has to be tonight!" The phantom streaked through the master suite, all white and raggedy, not at all human.

She sensed even Zach heard something . . . a whistling of the wind in the night. She moved closer and put her hand on his lightly haired thigh.

"What?!" she and Zach demanded together.

This is the day, this is the day. I intended to follow you back to Denver, but was jerked back and trapped the rest of the long day in Wyoming. Reliving the horror of my old actions.

"I can't see you!" Clare shouted, unnerved by the flying thing.

It—he—coalesced into an extremely transparent human.

"You said September first," Clare panted.

I was wrong, it is today . . . we have only a few hours left . . . just enough time for you to do this . . .

"We can't possibly get there before midnight," Zach said flatly.

No, no, no, no, noooooo. The ghost disintegrated to a skeleton, then a white and tattered specter. *I shall go maaadddd.*

For a guilty instant, Clare felt a niggle of relief. Maybe he'd vanish and go mad somewhere else and she wouldn't have to deal with another ghost until she was more experienced.

"Small plane, helicopter," Zach said.

Clare flinched at the expense of it all. "How do we arrange—"

"Gotta bring Rickman in on this. He has men," Zach said roughly. "And guys who are proficient in black ops, who won't talk."

She set her jaw, not ready to agree to exposing herself any further, still hoping to be a little honest about the whole darn thing.

Wait! said Enzo. The telepathic word compressed the air in the room . . . made it vibrate . . . since the ghost dog housed the Other in his body. *The witching hour is four* A.M. *. . . . That is a good time for spirits to transition. We have no later than dawn, which is a little after six* A.M. *now. If we get there before dawn, he can move on.*

Everything in Clare tensed again. "Did you hear that?" she asked Zach.

He scowled, "Unfortunately, yes. But at least it gives us the option of driving."

"That's good." Clare sucked in a huge breath, releasing it in little choppy pants. "Let's do this, then."

THIRTY-SIX

"NOPE. YOU NEED to nap."

The human specter solidified. *You will be there?* The hope in Jack Slade's voice, a man's voice again, made Clare blink fast. "Yes."

Zach heard another bark, then watched as the dog—whom he hadn't seen, only heard—became visible and went over to lean against the phantom of Jack Slade. The guy was nearly concrete now. Zach could only see vague lines of one of the bureaus behind him.

After rubbing Enzo, the gunman inclined his head at Clare, stuck out his chin at Zach, and faded away. Clare sighed. If Zach let her go, he figured that she would pace restlessly. He hadn't noted the habit much at her former house, but this house was big enough for her to get a long run going.

You need to nap. The big dog leapt onto the end of the bed.

Zach took her fingers from his thigh, squeezed, and trailed his own up her bare arm. "Yeah, let's nap."

You need to nap, too. Enzo stared at Zach.

Clare bit her lip. When her voice came, it quivered. "I know I need to nap." She put a hand over her stomach. "This is going to be it, the big deal."

The big deal, Enzo barked.

Dropping a kiss on her head, Zach said, "You can do it."

She leaned against him, then drew away a bit, eyes fixed on something he couldn't see—visualizing the future? The apparition of Jack Slade again? Some other demanding specter?

"I *will* do it." Her hands fisted. Finally she shuddered and let out a deep breath, and sank back on the thick layered pillows she liked. Her gaze met his. "I'm even more wound up than I was." She reached out and stroked his chest, dragging her nail gently over his nipples, spiking his arousal. "I think a good release would help us sleep."

He totally agreed. Zach had had enough of lying in bed alone. He thought he heard caws outside the window and his shoulders tensed. No. This was happening far too often . . . since Montana. Maybe since before then. Since his mistake. Nothing he would analyze now, especially not when Clare came closer and said, "We really need to break in my new bedroom more." She whirled her hand. "Fill it full of good energy."

He noted the strain in her eyes. She was a woman completely unused to violence and had been swept into a violent plot. He dealt with violence every day, lived within its confines, and so had the police who'd questioned her, and the counselor who'd stood by her.

She needed this time, this sex, with him more than he realized.

He'd wanted to make love to her tenderly, but nerves fizzed in him, too. He took her chin in one hand and locked gazes with her, while his other hand stroked down her body, found a hard nipple on her plump breast, felt the curve of her hip. He shifted until she was on her back and he on his side. His fingers feathered to the apex of her thighs and she opened for him . . . was damp and his cock thickened, his blood pulsed heavily.

Then she touched his erection, rolling a condom over him that he hadn't even known she'd had. She curled her fingers around him and he brushed away her hand. "I don't have much control." Keeping his breath steady was impossible. He moved over her, slid into her. Perfect.

Her hips arched and his breath caught as he slipped deeper

inside her. Need threatened. Soon. Soon. Soon he'd let the reins go.

"Fast and hard would do me," she said.

Lust simply blew his mind away. He plunged inside her, keeping his eyes open and staring at hers, linked together.

Dimly he heard her cry out and she tightened around him, and he let himself go.

Two hours later he opened his eyes, saw that the alarm would sound in a couple of minutes. He'd thrown the incredibly soft sheet off himself, the air-conditioning turned up just enough to make the house a good temp. Gazing down at Clare, who had the sheet up to her neck, Zach thought that she might always have a problem with cold.

She should move to a warmer climate. And that notion made his heart twinge and his dick twitch. But her great-aunt Sandra had lived in Chicago, so Clare should be able to manage Denver.

Besides, she *loved* this house. Zach was just beginning to let liking for this house sneak under his guard. He'd lived a lot of places when he was growing up, tended to stay no longer than five years at one job since he'd started working as a cop. Had never had a home.

Clare had moved around, too, but he figured this place was definitely home for her.

She woke slowly, blinked up at him, and smiled. Then she sat up and stretched and kissed him. As she glanced out the window, he saw when knowledge and dread came to her eyes at what it was finally time for her to do.

Then she looked over at him and Zach understood with a sickening jolt that his bad knee, the hideous red scars, his foot a little floppy and unable to flex, were bare to her sight. He froze. She shifted toward him. The view of her naked breasts swaying distracted him, fuzzed his mind until she sat cross-legged, another fine view, and stroked his scars with her fingertips.

"Oh, Zach, how much pain this caused you."

He just couldn't move away; he was immobile under those light touches.

"And how it hurt you," she crooned.

"It destroyed my life."

Sighing, she continued to caress, meeting his eyes with a sad smile. "What a pair we are." She tapped her temple. "My 'gift' wounded me, ruined my life. It just happened on the inside and doesn't show as much on the outside."

"You're stronger for it," he said. "Wiser."

Even in the dim light he saw her roll her eyes.

He went on, "This . . . gift . . . you received *didn't* ruin you. It enriched you. . . ." He let more truth out into the world, words he needed to say aloud. "And my injury didn't wreck my life, just my career. I was stupid and I paid."

Clare angled her chin, but her lips still curved in that half smile. "And I spent my life ignoring what Great-Aunt Sandra might have taught me, rebelling against the craziness of my parents and her 'weirdness.' I could have accepted earlier, could have learned, could have been prepared."

"We are a pair," he said.

Her gaze was straight as she continued to pet him. "This finished your career, but it's made you stronger, Zach." A breath that lifted her full breasts. "I'm glad I met you now."

"Yes."

Enzo barked, breaking the moment. *Time to go.*

Clare leapt off the bed. "I need a brief shower. I'll be ready in under fifteen minutes." She gestured to a curvy love seat where Zach now saw she'd laid out her clothes: new jeans, a silk blouse and light leather jacket, buffed hiking boots. Incredible.

"I can't go face that situation without looking my best!" She hurried to the master bath.

"I'll get the ears," Zach said, and grinned at her expected squeal.

But when he swung his legs from the bed to the floor, he saw that the scars weren't as red as before, and his left foot dropping and brushing the plush oriental carpet as he walked felt sensual, almost acceptable.

Clare made good on her word, and she and Zach and Enzo were out of the house in under fifteen minutes, along with the cooler full of snacks, drinks, and chicken strips, and her overnight bag containing her tablet and some clothes.

When Zach put her bag in the compartment behind the truck seats, Clare noticed he had the duffel he usually carried there, the one that had come and gone at her place. The one she'd insisted he take with him that morning—so very long ago! And so very much change happening to her so very fast. She wasn't the same woman as she'd been even that morning.

But they'd cleared the air, for now, between them.

She'd offered to share driving time with Zach, but he turned her down and gripped the wheel a little harder. Since she had a brother who insisted on driving instead of letting her help, she settled back in her seat, only a little disgruntled. That was a minor battle for another day, though she noticed Zach drove a consistent seven miles over the speed limit.

Enzo curled up near her, but she didn't pet him. From what she understood her role would be, she'd be interacting deeply with Jack Slade, freezing and in color. Why hadn't she realized that the shawls Great-Aunt Sandra draped herself in weren't only for show?

Before they'd left the Denver suburbs behind, Enzo had dissipated into nothingness. She was sad to see the dog go but dreaded discussions with the Other.

Talk with Zach was infrequent and casual. She sensed that he'd dropped into that long-distance driver's concentration that didn't allow for much of anything else, and she knew if she opened her mouth she might simply babble her fears for the entire trip. So she stiffened her spine and kept him stocked on drink and food.

They paused only once at a rest stop to stretch. Since the stop was relatively close to Torrington and Cold Springs, she *did* stretch and limber up, anticipating the hike off the road to the area of the defunct station.

Just south of Torrington a grayish oblong patch coalesced out of the darkness, slowly becoming defined as the ghost who'd haunted her since she'd returned to Denver.

He floated several yards ahead of the car. Clare tensed.

"Jack Slade?" Zach asked.

"Yes."

He picked up her hand and put it on his thigh. "Better if I can see him through you."

"Thank you," she said quietly, spreading her fingers, feeling the taut denim over muscle. She wouldn't push Zach on whatever psychic powers he might have. From the conversation she remembered between him and Mrs. Flinton, the older lady, so much more experienced than Clare, believed that Zach had some sort of gift.

They continued driving, following the specter, and then it zoomed away, and back.

We're close! the ghost said, hovering in front of the truck in a manner that made Clare's stomach lurch.

"Can you hear me, Jack?" Zach asked.

The phantom's face solidified more, and Clare swallowed. *Tell the driver I can hear him.*

"Yes, he can hear you," she relayed. Her nerves began to twang in anticipation of what she'd have to do.

"Stick to the roads," Zach said. From the sound of it, he spoke between clenched teeth. "And don't make us go through any damned barbed wire."

The ghost frowned, appearing more raggedy: no feet, his legs ending in filmy white streamers. Clare sensed that he had a pinpoint focus: to get through this night, one way or another. She gulped.

I will lead you to the best place, he finally said in her mind. *I will trace the modern roads.* He vanished.

Clare's doom came closer.

THIRTY-SEVEN

THEY WOUND THROUGH the narrow streets of a shabby trailer park. Now and again off to the left or right were short gravel drives that went nowhere, where there'd once been access to fields that now only showed thrusting grass in faint dirt ruts.

Zach cursed mildly but continually as he wove through the lanes that were more country than town.

There is a sharp turn, here, follow me! Jack Slade said, indicating the bend, then flickering out. Due to his excitement or some other paranormal phenomenon that she didn't know about?

"I saw him," Zach said, and Clare realized she'd left her fingers on his leg, but they'd traveled up more toward the crease in his thigh. He didn't seem to mind, though she was sure he noticed. A trickle of easy contentment mixed with the excitement churning through her blood. She was so, so lucky to have him with her.

No matter what happened in her life, she needed to remember and cherish this moment. No matter what happened with her and Zach . . . and she hoped they were only on the beginning of their journey together . . . she had to remember what he was doing for her tonight. Not leaving her alone to face her first major ghost laying . . . transitioning . . . passing on into the light . . . heading through the door to the next world or whatever came after death. She'd had little religion or personal spiritual philosophy but figured she'd be developing one soon. Her mouth twisted; she'd have to, it would be a necessity, wouldn't it?

A bump jolted her from the thoughts she'd wrapped around her like an insulating blanket.

"Damn washboard road."

They proceeded slowly, but it wasn't more than five minutes before the ghost appeared again.

"There! There he is, and more distinct than I've ever seen him!" Clare said.

"Yeah, yeah. I see him pretty damn good, too." A slight pause. "Well, crap."

"What?"

"Look ahead and a little up."

She sucked in a breath. "A ridge. Full of houses. Some of them with porch lights on."

"Damn it! All of the huge state of Wyoming with farms and ranches of thousands of acres and the damn site is near a damn suburb of Torrington."

"The trailer park isn't that far behind us, either," Clare said.

"I know it." Zach turned into dirt ruts that his headlights illuminated. They also caught the shine of white letters on a sign: Posted. No Trespassing. Keep Out.

"Well, darn," Clare said. She was breathing fast. "At least there's a draw . . . a tangle of bushes and cottonwoods, and it looks like we'll be below another ridge, maybe hidden a little?" She kept her voice quiet but couldn't stop the anxious rise in tone.

"Not good enough," Zach said grimly, killing the lights. He jutted his chin. "Did you see the irrigated field? I betcha anything the damn station will be in the middle of that wheat."

"Oh, dear."

He opened the door and she did the same and hopped out, landing on dry grass that crackled under her feet. A mass of crickets went quiet.

"Let's head on along the bottom of the ridge," Zach murmured. He rubbed the back of his neck. "At least there's no moon. It's a new moon tonight. And let's do this fast. Ted's around. I just feel it."

Clare smiled at him and his heart squeezed. He'd do a lot for that smile. "I know I can trust you."

She will not be aware of the normal world, Enzo said in a fussy tone.

All Zach's muscles tensed; he had to pry his teeth open to say, "What?"

Patting him on the arm, Clare turned on a small flashlight she must have pulled from her pocket. She outlined the continuing dirt rut between the ridge and the wheat field, heading toward a glowing blur a couple of yards away. The thing winked out when she raised her hand from his arm. "I trust you." She stopped a moment, her face pale but her big eyes wide. "Time to confab with the notorious Jack Slade and send him to his . . . on."

"To his just reward?" Zach asked dryly.

Clare shivered a little and he wondered if she felt the cold of ghosts. Zach himself felt warm, though the sky began to rapidly cloud over, blocking even the starlight on this night of the dark of the moon.

"I hope there is a great deal of mercy," Clare murmured.

Zach would second that. "I'll follow close." He clicked on his Maglite.

She nodded, said nothing about him being crippled, as usual. She trusted him as backup and he trusted her. She'd do her job to the very best of her ability. And she'd be a good partner, take charge of the situation and spare him what she could.

Some partner he was. He should have asked one of the special forces guys to help them . . . help Clare. He wanted her safe, and he couldn't protect her the way he could have a few months ago.

The going was rough. He had to watch every step, and each step hurt. He should've gotten a goddamned brace. Clare was at least three yards ahead of him.

"Hey, Jack," she said softly.

From one step to the next, as if she crossed some invisible

boundary, the night sliced in two. Instead of the subtle tones of night, the blasting uber-rich color of a hot August day hit her eyes. Instead of fragrant scents of grass and crops and land drifting to her nostrils, horrible odors assaulted her nose—horse poop, blood, and death.

The man slumping on the post before her had voided himself. A pool of dark red liquid surrounded by buzzing flies marked the packed dirt at his feet; two holes on the opposite sides of his head were red, horrific.

She screamed but heard nothing . . . except Jack Slade as he stepped before her, still in his shades of black and white, worry lines dug into his face. He wasn't the only man there, but the two other cowboys, both vivid in life as Jules Beni was in death, stood with disgruntled expressions, waving at the body and seeming to yell at Jack. Clare couldn't hear them.

Jack angled to follow her gaze. "They aren't really present, just part of my torment, the continuing loop. I just told them that they wouldn't be getting the larger reward for Jules Beni, since he wasn't alive." Jack sounded as if he spoke, words forming in air, not mind-to-mind.

The apparition turned fully around to survey the scene with her. His hands rose and dropped in a futile motion. "You know I went to Fort Laramie and told the commanding officer I'd be hunting Beni. He gave me his blessing, such as it was. I'd boasted I'd cut Jules's damn ears off and wear them, and I had to do it."

A deeper timbre entered his voice along with an edge. Jack rubbed his chest over a couple of the bullets left in him. "I'd been avoiding Jules as long as I could." Jack's lips curled. "Scared then of getting shot and more hurt, like I'm scared now I won't pass on." He didn't look at Clare. "I had to cut off his ears, to keep my reputation, and once I saw him dead, I wanted to. So I did." He shook his head, sighed, glanced sideways at her. "All right, maybe I was a little wrong about the first part. I didn't have to cut off his ears." Jack rubbed his own. "I knew no matter what happened that day, people would say I was the one who killed Beni; my rep woulda been fine without the ears."

Clare nodded. "They said you tied him to a pole and shot bits of him for hours." Instinctively, she looked at the dead man again. He'd lived to be significantly older than Jack Slade, and she couldn't tell how many times he'd been shot because his shirt was so stained she couldn't separate the fresh blood from anything else . . . but she didn't think he'd had a six-shooter emptied into him like Jack had.

"I didn't torture him or kill him," Jack Slade said simply.

Enzo appeared. *Why are you still here, Clare? The cold is killing you and you haven't even merged with Jack yet?* The ghost dog asked telepathically.

"I had to tell her my story," Jack said.

Enzo snorted, glaring at Clare. *You don't have to listen to their stories. You can't afford to.*

She moved cold lips, answering aloud. "I think I do. To understand my . . . my place in this . . ." So *hard* to lift a hand and gesture, her fingers a tiny flick instead of a wide movement. Alarm flared in her mind and sent a spurt of warmth through her.

Jack sighed and it was more hollow and otherworldly than his words had been.

"Do you have the ears?"

They were in her jeans pocket. She nodded. Her lips turned down. Time to get on with the whole weird business.

Take my hand. Slade's voice was back to ghostly thought echoing in her mind.

She knew what that meant; when she initiated contact with the ghosts, the cold was so much worse. Freezing enough to stop a heart. She stared and stared at his hand. For once Enzo didn't prod. Zach wasn't near, but he wouldn't attempt to stop her from doing her job. He understood. She wished she did.

"Just what are you all doing on my land at two in the morning, messing around with my crop?" snapped a weathered older man in a cowboy hat, holding a shotgun.

Zach didn't answer, more focused on a blurry movement in the brush to his right, the crack of the breaking of dry branches. If he pulled his gun, the farmer might shoot him.

"Well?" the guy demanded.

The tiniest glint on a gun barrel in the draw. Zach leapt forward into the big farmer, knocked him aside, fell himself.

Ted rushed from deep shadows. The bastard had another gun. "You can't make Jack Slade move on before he tells me about the gold." He shot but missed Zach since he was already rolling away.

"What the hell!" shouted the farmer.

"I'll get *her*, slow her down." Mather panted, pivoted, and aimed at Clare.

Zach reached for his gun, shot.

So did the farmer.

Take. My. Hand, Jack Slade said.

She was too tense, too wired, all her muscles tight, her nerves quivering through her body, but Clare reached out, grasped the ghostly hand. And it seemed he moved *into* her, slowing her motions, stopping her heart in truth for one terrible second before she, they, took up a stance before the ever-running, looping scene. He settled in her, not as a man, but as a hard ball of ice in her torso.

And she was blazing color, too, seeing the events take place, *feeling* what Jack did, his continual agony of the bullets and buckshot still inside him, his fury at Jules Beni.

She strode up to the corpse and a knife was in her hand, and then she watched as she deftly *cut* the ears off with a couple of slices. "He's dead right enough," Jack said, the only words she'd actually heard, though the cowboys had come and their mouths had moved and arms waved in a heated discussion with Jack. He poked a hole in one of the ears and threaded his pocket watch chain through it, the ear now a bloody fob. Then he stuck the other in a pocket. Her gorge rose and she stumbled a couple of yards back.

Got the ears? the phantom asked. *It's time.*

It's time, Clare! Enzo chimed in.

She wanted to rub her arms, but her hands were bloody and one held a knife and the cold numbed her fingers. She could *feel* her energy draining as she swayed.

THE EARS! both Jack Slade and Enzo shouted.

The gunfighter's image rose in her mind, his determined expression let her know he wouldn't let her give up. He'd haunt her for sure, as a mad specter, if she didn't do this for him, she just knew it. His face began to fade to a skull, then gained substance again . . . repeated the cycle.

Reaching into her jeans pocket, she fumbled to find the opening. She should be able to see her breath, she was so cold . . . dangerously cold.

Clare, Clare, hurry, hurry, hurry. You have to do this fast! Enzo whined and jumped around her. When he lit on her feet, she could swear she could feel his weight.

Better get it done, Slade said. *Or we'll both die . . . or go mad.*

Her focus narrowed to one thought, too late to think the whole thing was weird and crazy and unreal. She managed to thrust her fingers into her pocket and touched the earlobes. They felt warm and plump and throbbing.

THIRTY-EIGHT

ZACH GRABBED HIS cane, levered up to his good foot, went over to where Mather shrieked and thrashed. Zach scooped up his gun, then hit the kidnapper's jaw harder than he had the night before, and Mather lay still. Zach took the handcuffs he'd had attached to his belt and restrained the perp.

"Godamighty," said the farmer, slower getting to his feet. "What's going on?"

"He's a kidnapper," Zach said.

"He's a crazy."

"That, too."

"And who might you be, Mr. Colorado License Plates?" He examined Zach top to toe. "What are you doing here? And what the hell is she doing?" The farmer turned and stared at Clare. She seemed to be sleepwalking, her fingers curved around what Zach knew was a pair of ears. Zach tensed in case he'd have to hold back the man if he went after Clare.

"Getting rid of the ghost of Jules Beni?" Zach offered.

Scratching the beard stubble on his chin, the farmer's gaze slid toward Zach. "Is that so?"

* * *

She smelled death and lurched forward to the remains of Jules Beni with the holes on each side of his head. No longer dry and leathery, the ears pulsed in her hands, seeming all too real. Hauling in a breath, teetering, her mind fogging with cold, Clare aligned the ears against the corpse's head.

It vanished . . . and the whole scene drained of color, tinted browns, like shades of sepia.

Jack Slade pulled from her and it hurt, hurt, hurt, ice slicing her guts. She wobbled where she stood.

Mather groaned. Zach looked at the farmer. "I appreciate the help in getting this one."

"He after your lady?"

At hearing Clare called "his lady," the adrenaline zooming along in Zach's bloodstream went straight to his groin. "Yeah. He's also on the run from the Denver cops."

The farmer shook his head. "Well, he'll spend some time here, I reckon. Trespassing, attempted murder. Though I s'pose the sheriff will be glad enough to hand him over to your Denver boys."

"No doubt."

"Now why don't you finally give me your name?"

"Zach Slade, ex–deputy sheriff out of Montana, current private investigator from Denver." He offered his hand. "I don't have a card."

"I don't want one." A grunt. "Slade, huh?"

"No relation to Jack."

"Didn't think so." The man tipped his cowboy hat up, scrutinizing Zach. "You look a little familiar, though. You got family around here?"

Zach pulled a face. "No, the family home is in Boulder, Colorado."

A crack of laughter came from the farmer. He slapped Zach on the back with his free palm. "Not a place I'd feel comf'ble in." Now he held out his hand. "I'm Mike Gurey."

Taking his tough-skinned hand, Zach shook it briefly, a firm grip from both of them.

"Boulder is better left to the university and New Age crowd. How did you know we were here?" Zach asked, trying to keep the man's attention on himself. Clare stood in a trancelike state.

The guy hesitated; his wide flannel-covered shoulders shifted. "Just had a feelin'."

"Uh-huh," Zach said. He moved wrong and his left foot dragged on the ground. Heat rushed under the skin of his neck and cheeks.

Gurey glanced at Zach's ankle. "Foot drop, eh? You need more than a lift in your shoe. You need a brace, son," the man said, not unkindly.

"I've figured that out," Zach said.

A wind whipped in from nowhere, shrieking through the still night. The farmer flinched. "I think I'll head off my neighbors and meet the sheriff on the road."

Zach wished he could go, too. "I guess I'd better stay here."

Gurey clapped him on the shoulder as he gave a last glance to Clare, who was gesturing widely, then wrapped her arms around herself and trembled.

"I'll be glad when the weirdness is out of this part of my land," the farmer said, and added, "She's one in a million."

"Yeah." And Zach was damn glad that the man strode away without saying more or giving advice.

He hurried as fast as he could to Clare. He'd be faster and steadier with a brace.

The ghost of Jack Slade stared at Clare, and for the first time the dark lines worn of worry, of drink, had vanished from his face, and undimmed joy shone in his eyes. "Thank you for helping me." He inclined his torso slightly. "And thank you for being willing to help those, like me, who are trapped. Hello, Jackson Zachary Slade." He smiled beyond her, then she felt Zach's strong arm around her waist.

Jack Slade angled his head at Zach. "Those who keep the law are not only the lawmen, you know. Those who find justice for others don't always wear a badge."

Zach jolted beside Clare.

Still smiling, the apparition said, "I am whole enough to pass through." Then the ghost's head cocked. "Virginia?" He *laughed*. "I hear you, Virginia, don't scold me for being late, I'm coming!" With a wide grin he dissolved into a shaft of golden light that blinded her.

Euphoria washed through her, just like the golden light. She sighed and tension released. She *had* deeply affected at least one "person" with her gift, *had* helped. She had a new talent that she could use, and a challenge in learning how.

She wouldn't be a failure, wouldn't go mad, wouldn't die.

When her eyes adjusted again, it was night and she heard distant sobbing. She froze. "Do you hear that?"

"It's Mather."

She looked at Zach; he seemed more relaxed, too. Well, the woo-woo part of the evening was most likely over. "Ted?" she asked.

"Yeah. He tried to attack you, but between me and the farm owner, we restrained him."

"The farm owner," she breathed.

Zach's arm tightened. He brought her close. "You're cold."

"Yes."

YAY CLARE! Enzo yelled, zooming around her in circles, leaving streaks of silvery drool in the air, leaping now and then and licking her hands.

"Yay, Clare!" Zach said, and laughed, then laughed some more as she moved from his grasp and twirled around him, mixing in a few Gypsy steps that Aunt Sandra had taught her, flinging her arms up, her head back and wanting, want-ing, *wanting* bracelets and necklace and a headband that jingled with coins.

She was free.

Whole in a way she hadn't been, ever.

Only some of that was due to her accepting her gift, though she felt *right* about that. Most of her happiness was the sheer pleasure of being with Zach. A man who might deny his own sensitivities, but that was all right. Didn't she know how hard it was to accept the weirdness in your own life? If the consequences hadn't been so dire and fatal, she wouldn't have accepted them herself.

Zach would come to acceptance of his own gift, or not.

She'd watch for those little odd moments of his but wouldn't say anything. *His* choice. She wouldn't push. Yet.

But it had been a long, long time since she'd felt so happy, happy enough to be dancing as twilight smudged into dawn.

Zach watched Clare dance. For sure he'd have to get her one of those Gypsy outfits, unless she had one tucked away he hadn't seen.

His smile straightened as in the distance he saw the flashing lights of a police vehicle, heard the static of the radio. His jaw clenched. That part of his life was *over*.

"Come on, the authorities"—not him, not ever again—"are here. We have some explaining to do. Don't mention the ghost."

She sniffed and took his free hand, linking fingers with him. "As if I would."

The time with the sheriff of Goshen County and the Torrington police—Clare wasn't sure who had jurisdiction, but they were both there—went a whole lot faster than her earlier questioning. The farm owner backed Zach up as to the murderous assault by Ted Mather on Gurey, Zach, and Clare. She'd been oblivious. Would that always be the case? She hoped not.

Once the police in Denver got on the conference call, everything went even faster, until they were on the road again, Zach still driving, after breakfast.

Again the trip passed without any great revelations on either of their parts, and they made excellent time.

At the sight of the two small carriage lights on each side of her front door welcoming her home, an upsurge of pure warmth banished the last of the cold of the crazy adventure from her bones. She *was* home, this was home, where she was supposed to be. She understood now that she'd recognized the house.

As she'd recognized Zach, but she'd let that knowledge curl in the back of her head and her heart for now, a cherished secret.

He got out of the car, alternating leaning on his cane and raising his left knee high, higher than a usual gait, higher than *he* usually walked, since he tried to deny his disability as much as he could. He had to be even more weary than she.

When he opened the door of the truck, she slid down smoothly and into his arms. They held each other close and she realized she'd been wrong. Her house hadn't vanquished the cold, not by itself. Zach had, and more, now he actively provided heat . . . body to body.

She would need that in the future, wouldn't she?

She'd certainly need Zach, for more than just sex, or companionship, but because of that recognition he was the right man for her. She'd find a way to keep him.

They walked to the door holding hands.

He used the keypad and she the key; once inside, he disarmed the security. Waiting in the hallway was Enzo.

You did really, really good, Clare! We are proud of you!

"We?" asked Zach.

"Don't ask."

"Okay."

Clare, you did GOOD! Enzo shouted, and tilted his head at her, obviously wanting some acknowledgment.

She wet her lips. "Thank you, Enzo . . . it . . . felt satisfying to help Jack . . . move on." That was the truth. She might have a strange vocation now, but she was making a difference, and that was vital for her. She'd just never figured on doing it this way.

Enzo looked at her with a doggie frown. *You aren't going to make me leave, are you? I want to stay!*

"No," she said. "You don't have to leave." She smiled at the transparent Lab. "Looks like I have a ghost dog sidekick."

Enzo yipped and his butt wiggled in pleasure. Zach grunted, turning his head to look at her. "How about a lover? I don't want to leave, either."

Lifting her hand to stroke his cheek, she said, "I'd like that," she said.

"Let's go to bed." His smile quirked as he bent down and brushed her forehead with a kiss, then glanced at Enzo. "Beat it, dog."

With a last bark, Enzo ran through the walls toward the backyard. They took the elevator up, with Zach leaning on her a bit. She liked that. She'd leaned enough on him, too.

They could lean on each other.

When they entered the bedroom, Zach propped his cane on a chair, took off his jacket and let it fall onto the chair, and began to unbutton his shirt, then just stopped. "What's that?"

"What?" she asked.

"That thing on top of that inlaid bureau. It wasn't there when we left."

"Oh. That gleam of gold on top of *your* dresser?"

Zach's gaze cut to her. "My dresser?"

"It's empty, for you if you want it." At his hesitation her shoulders began to rise with tension.

"Sounds good," he said, casually, and limped over to the bureau. She joined him.

"Huh."

With him she looked down at a gold coin, a pretty woman's face on the front.

Zach fingered it. "'Twenty D', dollars. Twenty-dollar gold piece, nice." Then he put it back. His gaze met hers before they both stared at the antique pocket watch, surely gold, though the chain looked more like brass, with stains along it. Zach lifted the watch and turned it over, reading the inscription aloud. "Joseph Albert Slade." Zach glanced at her. "Probably worth a pretty penny."

"Put the gold piece and the watch in your dresser, Zach, and come to bed," Clare said. For once in her life, she let her clothes drop where she stood.

"I think I'll do that," Zach said, holding out his hand. She took it and he raised her fingers to his lips and kissed them, then smiled at her with tenderness in his eyes. "To the future and us."

She danced back a step or two and touched a kiss to his lips. "To the future and us."

Author's Note and Acknowledgments

This is a work of fiction and I am a romantic, so I have placed the absolute best light on the historical figure of Joseph Albert (Jack) Slade, his character, and actions and the events of his life.

Some small discrepancies: I could not discover the exact date of the death of Jules Beni (aka Jules Reni), so I chose August 30, which falls in the general time period.

I completely made up both the puzzle box (which was one that would have existed at the time) and the bottle (circa 1880s) and their locations.

The coin Zach found on the dresser is an 1861 Double Eagle, Coronet Paquet reverse. There are three in existence and they are valued at about four-point-four million dollars (and the story of why there are three includes the Pony Express and the San Francisco Mint). How Clare and Zach are going to explain where the twenty-dollar gold piece came from will be a challenge.

I did visit Virginia Dale (though in May), which is available for tours and is being rehabbed; many thanks to Sylvia Garofalo for the tour and all her information.

Please, if you want to support the efforts to restore this building, the last original stage station in Colorado, the last station of the Overland Stage, on its original site, you can contribute here: Virginia Dale Community Club, 844 CR 43F,

Virginia Dale, CO 80536, or by PayPal online here: virginia
dalecommunityclub.org/howyoucanhelp.htm.

About Cold Springs . . . I believe there were at least three
places of that name; this is the one in southeastern Wyoming,
near Torrington. A couple of original sources called it "Cold
Spring" or "Spring Ranch."

It took me weeks and help from librarians in Colorado and
Wyoming and many e-mails to find the exact location of Cold
Springs Station. I was helped by a fellow writer friend (thanks
Liz Roadifer!) and the Wyoming Library Roundup, which
happened to be published at just the right time and led us to
wyomingplaces.org.

As to the place itself, I went close to Cold Springs Station,
the location of which is on private property. The building and
the corral no longer exist. The owner of that farm in *Ghost
Seer* is completely fictional.

Many, many thanks to Calvin and Isabel Hoy, who welcomed me to Tea Kettle Ranch Bed and Breakfast outside
Torrington, Wyoming, a wonderful and serene place to write
and see storms and meteor showers: teakettleranch.com.
Thank you also for the maxim: Stay overnight at Cold Springs
and you'll be back.

Photos of these places are online on my Pinterest page:
pinterest.com/robindowens.

As I write this, I am in the midst of revamping my mor-
ibund website, robindowens.com, but you can catch me
mostly on my blog: robindowens.blogspot.com, and if you
want interaction, I'm frequently on Facebook: facebook.com/
robin.d.owens.73.

Thank you to Dan Rottenberg for his definitive work, *The
Death of a Gunfighter: The Quest for Jack Slade, the West's
Most Elusive Legend*, and his help regarding the robbery
question and the Cold Spring/Cold Springs issue through
e-mail. Mr. Rottenberg has an excellent website on Jack Slade
here: deathofagunfighter.com.

Also thanks to Roy Paul O'Dell and Kenneth Jessen for
their biography *An Ear in His Pocket: The Life of Jack Slade*.

Richard Francis Burton and Mark Twain/Samuel Clemens
are beyond mortal thanks, but their works were interesting if
not very helpful. Burton went off on a rant about a "Bloomer"

woman at Horseshoe Creek Station instead of describing Slade. Twain's account was entertaining though mostly a tall tale. . . . Twain wrote his brother nearly ten years later asking what Orion Clemens recalled of Slade on their trip west since Twain wanted to put Slade in *Roughing It.* Then Twain went with his own description instead of Orion's memory.

Thanks to Kevin Pharris for *The Haunted Heart of Denver*, a fun book that helped me with Clare's traumatic episode and will be of use in the future.

More thanks to the librarians at the Denver Public Library, and those of the History Colorado Center.

And thanks to Dr. D. P. Lyle for his expert opinion that the objects of Clare's quest would still survive and for helping me with Zach's disability.

Thank you, as always, to my critique groups and beta readers, especially Paula Gill for her medical help.

Finally, there are reports that Jack Slade's ghost just may be where he died—in Virginia City, Montana.

As for what is coming up for Clare and Zach . . . have you ever heard the tale of the amorous miner whose bones appeared in various beds, J. Dawson Hidgepath, and the town of Buckskin Joe?

TURN THE PAGE FOR A PREVIEW OF THE NEXT
BOOK IN ROBIN D. OWENS'S GHOST SEER SERIES

GHOST LAYER

COMING SOON FROM BERKLEY SENSATION!

ZACH SLADE'S NEW cane had been delivered when he was gone, a better weapon. The hook handle could snag and yank a leg. Though, of course, it wasn't large enough to fit around his new lover, Clare, and bring her to him for a kiss . . . or more.

The box the cane had come in leaned against the gray rough-cut stone of the mansion where he rented the house-keeper's suite. Sticking both old and new canes as well as the box under his left arm, he unlocked the side doors to the great house. Since he'd been shot below the knee, which severed a nerve, and his left ankle and foot didn't flex, he lifted his knee high to simply walk into his apartment.

Yeah, he was disabled. Had foot drop. His career as an active peace officer, his most recent job as a deputy sheriff, was over at thirty-four.

Instead of wallowing in anger, move on to damned acceptance. He wouldn't slip back into denial again. He'd finally gotten beyond that. Maybe.

He let the heavy security door slam behind him. Cool air flowed over him from his apartment, and he realized how sticky he was from the long two-day drive from Montana. At least his clothes fit better. He'd finally packed on some more muscle after his weight loss due to the shooting.

Zach tossed the box and his old cane on the empty surface of the long coffee table in front of the big brown leather couch in the living room. Then he slashed the new wooden cane through the air in some fighting moves. He was learning bartitsu, the Victorian mixed martial art that featured cane fighting.

There'd been no bartitsu studio in Montana, where he'd testified against the parole of a serial killer he'd put away a year and a half ago.

He held the cane in both hands, tested it . . . yeah, he could snap it if he wanted; his upper body strength had increased, what with being on crutches for three months.

The peace of his apartment wrapped around him. It had come furnished for a man, except for the small twenty-inch TV screen. Big, long couch he could sleep—or make love— on. A couple of deep chairs, the sturdy coffee table, and a thick old rug with faded colors that must have been expensive at one time.

A floral scent teased his nose and he saw a colorful bouquet of fresh flowers on the dark granite counter of the breakfast bar separating the Pullman kitchen from his living space. He didn't need flowers in his apartment, but guessed both the old ladies—the housekeeper, Mrs. Magee, and the wealthy owner of the mansion, Mrs. Flinton—thought he did.

He'd pushed the drive because he'd wanted to see Clare, even though those weeks had been the weirdest in his life. More weird than when he'd gotten shot a few months ago. That had just been stupid and devastating.

Right now all he wanted to do was sluice off the travel grime and rest a little so he'd be in prime shape for Clare.

After a quick rap on the door between his apartment and the rest of the mansion, Zach's elderly landlady, Mrs. Flinton, opened the door and glided through it with her walker. She'd taken him under her wing when he'd arrived in Denver a couple of weeks ago, insisted on renting him this place at a nominal fee.

"Zach, it's so good you're back," Mrs. Flinton said.

He grunted, then realized he wasn't among his former cop colleagues anymore and had to actually respond. "Good to see you, too. Good to be back in Denver." And the helluvit was, that was the truth. He'd left the scene of his ex-job and the shooting in low-populated Plainsview City, Cottonwood County, Montana and traded it for big-city Denver, and remained okay.

Mrs. Flinton stopped close and tilted her creased cheek as if for a kiss. So he gave her a peck. She smelled better than the flower bouquet, her perfume fresh and perky. "Have you called Clare yet?" she asked.

He leaned against the back of the couch. "Not yet. I just got in ten minutes ago." And the time with Clare had been so intense that week . . . then he'd been called back to Montana, and now . . . he just didn't know.

Scowling at him, Mrs. Flinton poked his chest with a manicured, pale pink fingernail. "Did you two talk while you were gone?"

"We texted some," he mumbled. Then he rubbed the back of his neck. His hair had grown longer than he'd ever kept it as a deputy sheriff. But his neck, and his fingers, and the whole rest of his body recalled intimately Clare's fiddling with that hair, how she liked it shaggy.

"The week with Clare before I left was pretty extreme," Zach told the older woman. Yeah, extreme with events, and incredible sex, too . . . and startling intimacy. A whole week had passed since the end of her first case and he still hadn't forgotten much of anything.

His body yearned for Clare.

Mrs. Flinton tsked and shook her head. "You're doing the rubber band thing."

"Wha?"

"Coming close together, then drawing back."

"It's not only me!"

She sniffed. "Clare needs support during these first weeks of learning her new ghost layer gift, as I know from my own experience."

"She's got that damn ghost dog, Enzo, to help her," Zach said.

Another finger poke and a steely gaze. "That's not the same."

His phone buzzed, and he welcomed it, paused when he saw Clare was calling. Mrs. Flinton noticed, too. Suppressing a sigh, that his first call with Clare after he'd returned to town would be overheard, he answered, "Zach, here."

"Hi, Zach," she sounded like the former accountant she was, cool and professional. Her voice still zinged down all the nerves in his body.

"I just received a call from your boss, Tony Rickman. . . ." Zach lost the rest of the sentence at the pang that he was now working as a private investigator for money instead of in the public sector to serve and protect.

Mrs. Flinton elbowed him, bringing his attention back to the call.

"Sorry, missed that, say again?" Zach asked.

"Zach, do you know why Rickman would like to meet with me?"

That made him blink. "No. He didn't say anything to me about that. When did he ask you?" Zach's thumb skimmed over his phone, hovered on the icon for video calling. Wasn't ready to push it and see Clare's face if she was on visual, get slammed with more mixed feelings.

"Rickman called not more than ten minutes ago and wants me there within the hour." Her words were crisp.

"Meet her there," Mrs. Flinton said.

"I'm sorry?" Clare asked. "I didn't hear that."

Now Zach rubbed his forehead. "I just got back from Montana. If you want, I can meet you there at the top of the hour."

"Oh."

"You didn't tell her when you were coming home?" asked Mrs. Flinton.

"Zach?" Clare asked.

"No, Mrs. Flinton," Zach said loudly. "I didn't tell either of you when I'd be in. Wasn't sure of the drive myself. Get over it."

Mrs. Flinton pouted, then angled closer to Zach's phone. "Hello, Clare, you and dear ghostly Enzo-pup need to come over for tea again."

"Oh." Just one small word and Clare sounded confused, wary. Just like Zach. He smiled.

"Do you want me to meet you at Rickman's?" Zach asked.

A small pause. "All right. I've never met the man and can't understand what he wants. I only did that little accounting job for him." Clare sighed. "The ghosts have been bothering me more lately, especially downtown, I'll call the car service."

"That sounds excellent, dears," Mrs. Flinton said.

"Gotta clean up. Later," Zach said, bending a stern look at Mrs. Flinton. She just smiled and sashayed out of his apartment. He understood why the housekeeper, Mrs. Magee, preferred to live in the carriage house. At the moment, a little space between him and the mansion would be welcome.

Zach rubbed his neck again, limped over to close the door behind his landlady—he only had his orthopedic shoes on for driving, not his light brace for his left ankle and leg to prevent the foot drop—and headed to his bathroom.

A few minutes later when he left his apartment and his ass complained at hitting the seat of his truck again after driving for so long, he just grumbled under his breath. Then he looked up and saw crows sitting on a power line, half a dozen of them, quiet in the heat. His jaw clenched. He hadn't seen any of the damned birds in Montana, but here they were.

As always the Counting Crows rhyme his maternal grandmother had taught him ran through his mind.

Six.

Six for gold.

He ignored their beady eyes as he exited the circular drive.

Clare Cermak changed clothes just because she'd be seeing Zach. She didn't care what Rickman—whom she'd never met—or anyone else at his business thought of her . . . except Zach, her newish lover.

They'd gotten so close when she'd thought she was going crazy. It turned out that along with her Great Aunt Sandra's fortune, Clare had inherited the family "gift" for seeing ghosts and helping them move on to . . . wherever. She still had a shaky grasp on that, particularly since she preferred rationality in her life. Her now exploded past life as an accountant.

Hello, Clare! We are going OUT? Enzo, the ghost Labrador dog, sent mentally. He'd materialized from nothing to sit panting at her feet, gray-white shadows and shades.

"Yes. Zach's boss, Tony Rickman, wants to see us for some reason."

We are seeing Zach? Enzo hopped to his feet and his whole body wiggled front to back.

"Yes, apparently he's back from Montana." She frowned, not knowing exactly how she felt about that. She'd missed him outrageously in bed. No, scratch that thought, she missed him outrageously, period, darn it. She wanted him . . . and she'd forever be grateful that he'd helped her during the time she'd had to deal with her first major ghost. Did that make her dependent on Zach? She didn't think so. They had a lot in common and he was just plain fabulous in bed. . . .

CLARE!

She thought back to what Enzo had asked. "Yes, we are seeing Zach." Grudgingly, she added, "You can come with me." Not that forbidding Enzo would make any difference. He materialized and vanished as he pleased.

I would like to see a new place with new people and maybe some ghosts?

"A highrise downtown." All right, she admitted she was curious about Zach's place of employment. Frowning, she glanced at the old map of Denver she'd hung on the wall of the tiny bedroom she'd designated as her "ghost laying" office in her new home. "There might have been buildings there in the late eighteen hundreds," she said to Enzo.

The dog itself—himself—had told her that the human mind could only comprehend ghosts from slices of history. From her experimentation this last week, she'd determined that her period was from 1850 to 1900. She seemed to specialize in Old West phantoms.

A toot in the driveway announced that the car service she now had on retainer had arrived. She couldn't drive in heavily ghost-populated areas anymore, it was too dangerous when apparitions rose before her or pressed around the car, or invaded it.

She locked up, greeted the driver, and sat in the back of the Mercedes, heart pounding at seeing her lover again.

Zach arrived at Rickman Security and Investigations before Clare, shoved through the heavy glass doors—wouldn't surprise him if they were bulletproof—and into the lobby area. The walls were pale gray, the reception station dark gray stone with a glossy black top, and black computer and phone accessories.

He nodded to the receptionist before heading straight to his boss's door. Zach stood with his hand on the lever until the electronic lock buzzed to let him into his boss's office, decorated in gray and cream.

Two men watched him with military assessment as he entered. The craggy-looking man in his late forties with a buzz cut and salt-and-pepper hair wearing an engraved wedding band was his boss, Tony Rickman, who sat behind his dark wooden desk.

The guy standing near the desk, six-foot-six, two hundred seventy five pounds, pale white or blond hair in another buzz cut, light brown eyes, had "ex-special-ops" written all over his body and attitude. He wore expensive black trousers with knife-edge creases, dull but not scuffed shoes, a black silk shirt, and a lightweight black jacket.

"Hello, Zach," Rickman said.

Zach nodded and spent effort to keep his walk as smooth as possible, even with his cane and brace, as he headed for the far left of the four gray leather client chairs. "Hello, Tony."

"Clare Cermak called you?"

"That's right."

"Obviously, you're back from Montana." A note in Rickman's voice told Zach the man had expected Zach to check in.

"Just arrived a half hour ago." He sat and stretched his leaned legs out, propped his cane against the chair.

"Make yourself at home," Rickman said.

Zach smiled. "Thanks, I will."

"I don't believe you've met another of my operatives, Harry Rossi. Harry, this is Zach Slade." Rickman gestured to the guy, who scrutinized Zach and his threat level. Zach stood, studying Rossi with his flat cop stare. Wouldn't surprise him in the least if the guy had broken into a few places. Something—shadows—in the man's eyes showed he'd had to kill. Zach figured that showed in his own eyes.

After a few seconds, the big man smiled and took a few steps toward Zach, half the distance between them. Zach came the other half and offered his right hand that he kept free for his sidearm under his own jacket. Both of them were carrying and Rickman probably had a weapon in easy reach.

"Good to meet you," Zach said.

"Likewise," said Rossi. A quick, hard grip and then they retreated at the same time.

"Rossi works mostly as a bodyguard," Tony said.

Zach nodded. "Looks good for that."

Rossi gave a quick grin, ostentatiously adjusted his shirt cuffs.

Returning to his chair, Zach said, "I don't think Clare needs a bodyguard . . . yet."

With a bland smile, Rossi said, "Not with you around."

"Looks like we need Clare," Tony said.

"Is that so?" asked Zach.

A quick double buzz came from the door lock as the receptionist opened it.

Clare walked in and Zach had the novel experience of having his heart jump in his chest. Damn she looked good.

Rickman stood and so did Zach, automatically moving toward her. Just a step or two and he scented the exotic fragrance she wore that reminded him of more than kisses. He fought to control a hard-on. Did the damn multiplication table.

Still, she looked good, better than he'd last seen her the morning he'd crawled out of her bed and headed to Montana. Better than he'd ever seen her.

She'd come into her own, was done with the worry over closing out her great Aunt's estate, moving into her own home, and dealing with a gunfighter ghost. The yellow sundress she wore accented her golden skin and hazel eyes. Her brown hair with red tints was rich and glossy. He thought he made a noise in his throat.

She smiled like she was glad to see him and all his irritation at the wearying day vanished.

"Hi, Clare." Moving quickly, he took her hand, kissed her cheek. Oh, man, that perfume and her natural scent did a number on him. He didn't want to be with her here, with two other guys in the room. He wanted to be in her bed, or have her in his.

She brushed a kiss on his lips and relief flooded him. They were still on the same page, goddam good.

"Hi, Zach."

He didn't put his arm around her as he turned to face the men, but kept his body intimately close. "Clare, the guy behind the desk is the head of Rickman Security and Investigations, Tony Rickman. Beside him is Harry Rossi, another of Rickman's men." Zach had no clue how much she observed. As far as he knew she wouldn't recognize a military man by his stance, his movement, his attitude. Wouldn't know when a guy was armed. She'd once said she didn't watch crime shows, so she was learning about police officers from him.

"How do you do," she said politely.

Rossi nodded and stood at ease. Rickman came from behind the desk and offered his hand. Clare donned her professional-woman manner, gripped it and shook.

"Please, have a seat," Rickman said. "Would you like some tea?"

She gave him a cool stare. "You've been talking about me with Mrs. Flinton? She's the one who offers me tea."

Rickman's gaze cut to Zach. The guy wanted back up. Zach decided to test his luck, put his hand around her upper arm and gave the lightest of tugs toward the chairs, stepped toward them himself. She slid her glance to him, and followed, answering Rickman's question. "No tea, thank you. Coffee would be good."

"Fine." Rickman returned to his desk and pressed the intercom. "Coffee, cream and sugar for Ms. Cermak."

Zach took the last chair left, after Clare sat down. He wished it were closer.

"You asked for this meeting?" Clare said.

Rickman lowered into his executive chair, but kept his manner casual. "Thank you for your work on the accounting edgers in Mrs. Flinton's case. She has spoken highly of you," he said.

Clare inclined her head.

"We have a problem we'd like you to help us with," Tony Rickman said.

Clare stilled beside Zach, wet her lips. "As a forensic accountant?"

A long, thumping pause.

"I'm afraid not. As a ghost layer," Rickman said.

Clare flinched. Her fingers tightened on a small purse she'd moved from her shoulder to her lap. "I'm not in that business."

"Can you please hear me out? We have a problem," Rickman repeated. "Or rather, one of our clients has a problem." He gestured to Rossi, who treated Clare to a smile that showed male appreciation and twinkling eyes. Zach revised his first good impression of the man.

"I'm the bodyguard to Dennis Laurentine," he said.

"The billionaire," Rickman said.

Clare blinked. "Dennis Laurentine? No. He's not. As of last month Forbes's website listed his net worth as being valued at approximately nine-hundred-sixteen million. That makes him a multimillionaire, but not quite a billionaire."

Rickman looked disconcerted. Rossi's smile widened.

"Never argue with an accountant about money," Zach said, lounging even more in his seat.

Clare sighed. "Well, Mr. Laurentine is very wealthy, and a client my former firm would have loved to have—would love to have. What does that have to do with me?"

"Why don't you, ah, tell the story, Rossi," Rickman said.

"Sure." He moved to the front of Rickman's desk, leaned against it, his gaze focused on Clare. "Mr. Laurentine has a ghost problem on his ranch in South Park." The ends of his mouth lifted in a half smile. "Or, to be accurate, a bone problem. A dead guy is leaving his bones around."